VICTORIA WALTERS

# MURDER AT THE VILLAGE CHURCH

hera

First published in the United Kingdom in 2023 by

Hera Books
Unit 9 (Canelo), 5th Floor
Cargo Works, 1–2 Hatfields
London SE1 9PG
United Kingdom

A CIP catalogue record for this book is available from the British Library.

Print ISBN 978 1 80436 037 8
Ebook ISBN 978 1 80436 926 5

Look for more great books at www.herabooks.com

Printed and bound in Great Britain by Clays Ltd, Elcograf S.p.A.

# Murder at the Village Church

Victoria Walters is a full-time author living in Surrey. Victoria writes the bestselling women's fiction series GLENDALE HALL, and the cosy crime series THE DEDLEY END MYSTERIES. She has been chosen for WHSmith Fresh Talent and shortlisted for two RNA awards. Victoria was also picked as an Amazon Rising Star.

Follow Victoria on social media here:

Instagram: vickyjwalters
Facebook: Victoria Walters author
YouTube: Victoria Walters
Twitter: Vicky_Walters

# Also by Victoria Walters

## The Glendale Hall series (in reading order)

*Coming Home to Glendale Hall*
*New Beginnings at Glendale Hall*
*Hopeful Hearts at Glendale Hall*
*Always and Forever at Glendale Hall*
*Dreams Come True at Glendale Hall*

## The Dedley End Mysteries

*Murder at the House on the Hill*
*Murder at the Summer Fete*
*Murder at the Village Church*

## Standalone novels

*Summer at the Kindness Café*
*The Second Love of my Life*

*To my mum for always being my first reader*

# Chapter One

Rain blurred Nancy Hunter's view of the High Street as she looked out of the Dedley Endings Bookshop. 'Have you seen the weather?' she asked her grandmother, looking over her shoulder at Jane Hunter, who was behind the till organising customer orders.

Jane followed Nancy's gaze and sighed. 'Maybe I should call off the meeting,' she mused. Jane was the head of Dedley End's Events Committee and they were due to meet once the bookshop was closed for the day on the village green. 'I really hope it cheers up for Saturday,' she said, worriedly. The village's first-ever pumpkin patch was due to open at the weekend.

Nancy's beagle, Charlie, was curled up on the shop's window seat, his favourite spot. She gave him a pat before walking back towards the till. Nancy paused on the way to rearrange the table of Halloween-inspired reads, which had got messy during the after-school rush. The Dedley Endings Bookshop only sold books in the crime genre – thrillers, detective stories, cosy series and true crime – and it had recently become even more popular with people in the village and tourists staying in the Cotswolds thanks to her and Jane's real-life sleuthing.

'It will,' Nancy said to her grandmother. 'The pumpkin patch was such a good idea of yours. We'd always lacked an event between the summer fete and lighting the Christmas tree. And we've always enjoyed theming the shop for Halloween so now the village can join in.' Nancy had a passion for crime stories thanks to her father, George, who fostered her love of the books from a very young age. Even though he was no longer with them, she knew he would have heartily approved of Dedley End celebrating spooky season. 'I just wish we didn't have quite so much on our plates right now.' She looked up and shared a significant look with her grandmother.

'It's good to keep busy,' Jane replied cheerfully. She always said keeping busy was the best tonic in life. 'And we can't do anything about your mother for the time being so, while we wait, we can throw ourselves into making this event one of our best.' She looked outside. 'There now, the rain has stopped. We'd better get ready to close and head over to the green.'

Nancy nodded and continued to tidy the shop, trying not to think about her mother – but it was impossible. Ever since the summer, Samantha Hunter had been on Nancy's mind more than she had for years. Samantha had left Dedley End when Nancy was six. For twenty-one years, there had been no news of her and Nancy had resigned herself to never knowing why her mother ran away. She had not even known if she was alive. And with her father having passed away four years after Samantha left, Nancy had accepted that her grandmother was her only family. That was until they found out that her mother had been spotted at a Christmas party in Norfolk. Now all Nancy could think about was solving the biggest mystery of her life. But they were waiting for the person who owned the house Samantha had been seen at to come home after a long holiday before they could investigate the sighting. And Nancy was getting impatient.

mystery for them to solve but then she remembered her focus needed to be on her mother at the moment.

'Just come and see,' he replied.

Intrigued, Nancy promised they'd find him as soon as the meeting was over and then she had to hang up because Gloria, the vicar's wife, was asking where Nancy wanted the stall selling books to be positioned on the green.

## Chapter Two

After the pumpkin-patch meeting finished and everything was set for the weekend, Nancy, Jane and Charlie walked towards their cottage, taking a detour to find out what Jonathan wanted to show them. He met them at the top of the road next to theirs, not far from Dedley End High Street.

'About time,' he greeted them impatiently as Charlie bounced up and down at his feet letting out a bark of excitement. 'Hello, boy,' he said, patting the beagle. Then he smiled at Nancy and Jane. 'I heard Craig, the estate agent, talking in the pub the other night about how everyone was going to be shocked about a new resident in the village. So I asked Roy from Roy's Removals to give me a nod when someone moves in – and he did today,' he said, his eyes twinkling. 'Come and see,' he said, beckoning them to follow him.

Jonathan was two years older than Nancy, at twenty-nine, but was two inches smaller than her, something that she had often teased him about while they were growing up although he then got his own back by starting her 'Nancy the vampire' nickname at school. Jonathan had messy dark hair and dark eyes, and was as usual dressed in a scruffy pair of jeans and a cosy jumper with a coat thrown over it.

'I can't believe you're still wearing that coat,' Jane tutted at him as they followed him down the road. 'You've had it for years.'

'It's a classic,' he protested. He looked at Nancy. 'I wore this when we went to Alton Towers, do you remember?'

Nancy grinned. Jonathan would never care about clothes but, somehow, he pulled off the scruffy look. 'Gran is right then, you need a new coat... we were eighteen when we went to Alton Towers.'

'I stopped growing then,' he replied with a shrug. 'Unlike *some* people.'

She rolled her eyes. They had been friends since childhood and were always teasing each other. 'Anyway, why should we be so fussed about someone moving to the village? I know most of us have lived here all our lives but it's not that unusual, is it?' she asked Jonathan as they walked down the road.

'They finally sold Rose Cottage,' Jonathan said, nodding ahead. They saw the removal van and men carrying out furniture from it. The gate to the house was open, as was the front door. And standing around, making no attempt to hide their curiosity, were about ten villagers. 'And the new owner is famous. Or should I say infamous,' he added, enjoying himself as Nancy and Jane looked at him in surprise.

'Infamous for what?' Nancy asked, wondering if she should be worried now.

'It's Sebastian Holmes,' Jonathan said with a flourish as they paused across the road from Rose Cottage.

'Who?' Nancy asked at the same time as her grandmother gasped out loud. 'What?' she asked Jane nervously.

'Why would he move here?' Jane asked in shock.

'Exactly,' Jonathan said. 'Why indeed?'

'Who's Sebastian Holmes?' Nancy repeated.

'Only one of the country's most notorious criminals,' Jonathan said darkly. 'He just got out of prison. He served a thirty-year sentence. He was a member, a very important member, of *The Club*,' he added.

*The Club* Nancy *had* heard of. She sucked in an uneasy breath. The notorious gang had been the subject of more than a dozen true crime books, with the police having failed to destroy their criminal network even decades after the gang had sprung up in London.

Nancy was just about to ask why Holmes had been in prison for thirty years when a man stepped out of the front door of the cottage holding something. Suddenly, Charlie let out a bark and pulled on the lead. 'What are you doing?' she asked in surprise. He was usually so well behaved. But he had set off in a mad dash across the road leaving Nancy no choice but to follow. 'Nancy!' Jane cried as Nancy was yanked past her and Jonathan.

Nancy pulled the lead, trying to slow Charlie down and calling his name, but he wasn't put off and headed straight for the cottage. Charlie didn't stop until he was just inside the open gate, the man at the door having walked forward watching their approach, looking amused.

Charlie barked and sat down suddenly, almost tripping Nancy up. She skidded to a halt. 'Charlie, what is the matter with you?' she asked the beagle who was looking at her as if nothing had happened. 'You almost pulled my arm off. Where is the fire?'

The tall, thin man smiled. 'That might be my fault,' he said in a deep voice with an East London accent. He showed her the paper plate in his hands. 'I'm having a sausage sandwich. Moving is hungry work. May I?' he asked her. She nodded, glancing over her shoulder. Jane was waving frantically to her to get away and Jonathan was watching them with concern.

Nancy turned back to the man. 'You're moving in?' she asked him.

'That's right. I'm Sebastian Holmes,' he said. He looked unremarkable, nothing like a criminal mastermind but, by the lines of his face, his grey hair and frail frame, she could see the years in prison had taken their toll. She watched as he offered Charlie a piece of sausage and her dog took it eagerly. Charlie was usually a good judge of character so she was taken aback he was so willing to be fed by Mr Holmes.

'Everything okay?' Jonathan asked, now behind her with Jane, both looking on in astonishment at the former gang member feeding Nancy's dog.

'He's a good boy,' Sebastian said, patting Charlie. He looked at Nancy, who had been watching in stunned silence.

She cleared her throat. 'I'm Nancy. Nancy Hunter. This is Charlie. My friend Jonathan. And this is my grand-mother Jane,' Nancy said, gesturing behind her.

'It's a pleasure. A real pleasure. And do call me Seb. Please.' He looked Nancy right in the eye as he held out a hand. There was a kindness in his smile that put Nancy at ease as she shook his hand.

'I work for the *Cotswold Star*, if you ever want to tell your story...' Jonathan began.

'I'm here for a fresh start,' Seb interrupted him, firmly. He glanced at Nancy. 'It was nice to meet you though. I'd better get on, I don't want the removal men to smash my TV now, do I?'

'Welcome to Dedley End,' Nancy found herself saying. She felt Jonathan and her gran look at her in surprise, but

Seb dropped her a wink and nodded at the others. Then he looked behind them and he frowned at the people watching him, before he turned quickly and strode off inside the pretty Cotswold stone cottage that didn't appear to suit the man at all.

'Well, that's a turn-up for the books, eh?' Mr Peabody walked up to the gate then as they watched Seb walk through his new front door and close it firmly. 'We'll have our work cut out there,' he added. Mr Peabody had lived in Dedley End for all his life – like Nancy, Jane and Jonathan – and had been a police officer until his retirement twenty or so years ago. He still kept up with the local force and Nancy had often seen him having a drink with DCI Brown and his deputy, DC Pang.

'Let's hope not,' Jane replied. 'We've had enough crime in our village thank you very much.' Nancy and Jonathan exchanged an amused glance though because they knew she had thrown herself into helping them solve murders in the village. She likely would be happy to have another one to investigate.

'Did you know of Holmes's gang when you were on the force?' Jonathan asked Mr Peabody.

He shook his head. 'That was all dealt with in London. Dedley End has never had any trouble with gangs or organised crime, thank God, and I hope it stays that way. I know the gang have a sort of romantic mythos surrounding them thanks to the way they started out – targeting the rich and supposedly helping the poor – but they are criminals. No sugar coating that fact, if you ask me.' He lifted his hand and ticked off their crimes on his fingers. 'Armed robbery, drug dealing, blackmail, kidnapping, murder, they've done it all.'

'Why has he come to Dedley End?' Jane asked again.

'It's not a typical place for a former gang member to settle, is it?' Jonathan agreed. 'Out of anywhere in the UK, he chooses our village.'

Nancy looked at him. Even last year, she would have said that nothing ever happened in their peaceful, safe village but the past few months had seen murder change all that. Now they had a career criminal in their midst. Perhaps Seb Holmes had been drawn to their corner of the Cotswolds because it had been talked about in the press so much lately.

'Well, if he gets up to anything untoward, I know you three will find out about it, eh?' Mr Peabody chuckled heartily. Talking of infamous people, Nancy, Jane and Jonathan had become that in the village themselves after bringing two killers to justice. 'Anyway, I'll let you all get on, I think I'll head to the pub for a pint.'

They waved as Mr Peabody strode away.

Charlie let out a little whine. 'Oh, yes, sorry, boy. We can't stand here all night, you'll want your dinner. I'm getting hungry too. Coming with us, Jonathan?' Nancy asked him.

'Definitely with this news to digest,' he agreed. They set off for Jane and Nancy's cottage around the corner.

'I remember when Sebastian Holmes was arrested,' Jane said as they walked. 'It was huge news after he had evaded the police for so many years.'

'I don't remember his story,' Nancy said. 'I know of the gang, of course, but not what happened to him.'

'He was fairly high up in the organisation and had been up to all sorts for years, but he was finally arrested during an armed robbery – they were trying to steal jewellery from a shop in Hatton Garden when the police turned up mid-raid,' Jonathan told her. 'There were rumours one of the gang had grassed on them, but no one ever found out who.'

'They threw the book at him, didn't they?' Jane asked.

Jonathan nodded. 'They pinned a lot of unsolved crimes on him although they didn't have a whole lot of evidence, but they'd failed to catch the gang for so long they had to be seen to be doing something to stop them. Holmes got thirty years in total.'

They reached Jane and Nancy's cottage. It was dark outside but the cottage was lit up in welcome. Nancy let them in and took Charlie off his lead. She closed the door behind them, grateful to be in the warmth after a long day. They shed their coats and shoes, and all went into the kitchen to get some food.

'I worry that our village is becoming a little bit unlucky,' Jane said as she put the kettle on while Nancy fed Charlie and Jonathan opened the fridge. He was at home in the cottage after spending so much time there through the years. 'Last Christmas, poor Lucy Roth was murdered, then we had the murders this summer, and now a member of a crime gang has moved to our village. I suppose they do say bad things come in threes.' She shuddered at the thought.

'But he's been in prison for a long time, hopefully the past is behind him now,' Nancy tried to reassure her.

'They do say he turned over a new leaf in prison. Denounced his criminal past and promised to go straight, that's why he got parole,' Jonathan agreed as he pulled out last night's left-over stew. 'And how dangerous could he even be now? I mean, he's your age, Mrs H… I mean, not that that's old…' Jonathan said, suddenly backtracking.

Jane sighed. 'I'd stop talking now if I were you.'

Nancy smiled at the two of them. They did always lighten the mood. 'Hopefully he just wants a peaceful retirement in our lovely village. Charlie certainly seemed to warm to him and he's usually a good judge of character,' she said as she slid his bowl of food to him. 'Does the gang still operate, do you think?'

'Oh definitely,' Jonathan said. 'But it's different now. They were almost local celebrities in East London when they started out, but now they are more under the radar. Had to be with modern technology, more ways the police could track them down. The rumours are that they use bribery to corrupt people in high places to help them make money and, of course, evade justice. The leader of *The Club* has never been found, even after all these years.'

'Hmm, well, it's nothing to do with us, is it?' Jane asked. The three of them looked at one another, the hint of a mystery an undeniable draw.

'We need to concentrate on finding my mother,' Nancy said, although she couldn't deny she was curious about the gang and how they had evaded justice for so long.

'You're right, love,' Jane said.

'Oh.' Jonathan slapped a hand against his forehead. 'With all the news, I forgot to tell you,' he said. 'Will Roth messaged me to say that Hugh Windsor is back from his trip and he's going to set up a time we can go to his house.'

Goosebumps appeared on Nancy's arms. 'Oh, that's such good news,' she said, relieved that they would finally be able to go to where her mother had been last seen.

'You might not think that when I tell you the next bit,' Jonathan said, looking reluctant to. 'Will said Hugh wants him and Richard to come with us.'

Nancy leaned against the kitchen counter with a sigh. That definitely wasn't good news.

# Chapter Three

'You're going to wear the carpet out,' Penelope said on Thursday morning as Nancy paced back and forth in the bookshop. Pen worked there part-time and was also a childhood friend of Nancy and Jonathan. 'Mrs H will kill you.'

Nancy paused, knowing her grandmother wouldn't be happy if she made a hole in the carpet. 'I can't help it, I'm so nervous about today,' she admitted.

Pen leaned on the till counter, her blonde hair falling across her face. 'It's only natural. I mean, not only are you going to be in the house your mum was in for the first time in years but you've got to put up with Tricky Dicky and a Roth as well,' she said, her eyes wide.

Nancy sighed. 'Only I would end up driving to Norfolk with my ex-boyfriend who had me followed and a member of the family from hell,' she agreed. She had a chequered history with the Roth family although she had liked Will when they had first met. 'Thank goodness Gran and Jonathan will be there.'

'And you need to ignore Will and Richard and focus on your mother. I mean, this is the first lead you've had since she left Dedley End, I really hope you can find her.'

'Thanks, Pen,' Nancy said, gratefully. 'I just need to know what happened to her even if she doesn't want to see me. I think I was lying to myself for a long time that

I didn't want to ever see her after she walked out...' She trailed off as it was still hard to say the words out loud that her mother had abandoned her. 'But once Richard told me that Hugh Windsor had seen her, I knew I couldn't just leave it. I suppose I hate to see a mystery unsolved.'

Nancy glanced at the picture of her father that hung on the wall of the bookshop. She had long been unsure about how her father had died in a car crash but now knew a drunk driver had forced him off the road and the Roths had covered it all up. The only way she could bear to take this trip with Will was because he hadn't known about it. He had been lied to by his family as well but that was where the similarities ended. He still had both his parents around. Nancy was relieved that she knew what had happened to her father although it didn't stop her missing him every day. She really hoped she'd find the same relief if she could track down Samantha Hunter. But that remained to be seen.

'You'll solve this one, Nancy, I know you will,' Pen said then with certainty.

'I hope so. All I've ever had to go on is my mother leaving a note saying that she couldn't cope with family life. I was too young to ask my dad much and now I can't. Her being seen at this party is the first we've heard of her since she left Dedley End.' She wished she knew what her mother had been doing all this time.

'I wonder if she's still in Norfolk,' Pen said.

'I just hope we find some clue to where she is,' Nancy said.

The bookshop door jingled and Nancy turned to see Jonathan and her grandmother walk in. 'Are you ready, love? Will is due any minute to pick us up,' Jane said.

'I think so,' Nancy said, pulling on her coat.

'Whatever happens it doesn't change all the support you have here,' her grandmother told her gently. 'If we find Samantha or not, you have a family already.'

Nancy nodded. 'I know.' She smiled at them all, already feeling better to have them by her side. She looked again at her father's picture and knew that he was with her in her heart as well. She had no idea if her mother would want to see her again but, if she didn't, Nancy knew her grandmother was right – she wasn't alone. A car beeped outside and Nancy exhaled. 'Okay then, let's go.'

'Good luck. Let me know how it goes. And don't worry about the shop,' Pen called as Nancy, Jane and Jonathan filed out with a wave to her. Outside, a sleek black car was waiting and they climbed into the back as Will Roth and Richard Bank were in the front.

'Right then,' Will said once they were settled. He gave them an awkward smile then turned around to face the front. 'Let's go to Norfolk, shall we?'

Richard glanced back and smiled at Nancy, but she looked away out of the window. The drive from the Cotswolds to Norfolk was strained; no one really had the energy for small talk and Nancy felt everyone's relief when the outline of Hugh Windsor's vast Norfolk estate finally appeared ahead.

'Here it is,' Will said, breaking the silence. He peered through the windscreen wipers as the grand house emerged from the rain in front of them. 'Let's hope Hugh can help,' he added, glancing at Nancy in the rearview mirror. He spoke with a cut-glass accent, and had floppy hair and a charm that made it hard not to like him but Nancy had learned not to trust any member of the Roth family.

Nancy looked out at Hugh Windsor's house. She had been itching to see it after Richard told her Hugh had seen her mother at a party he'd thrown there the Christmas before last. Hugh had been away all summer in his house in the south of France so this was the first time they could come to his estate. The sprawling mansion was even more grand than Roth Lodge and Nancy had been intimidated when she had walked in there for the first time. But from first-hand experience, she knew that having money didn't make you better than anyone. Her friends had more integrity in their little fingers than the Roths had, so she wasn't as nervous about meeting Hugh Windsor. She needed information from him, his money didn't matter. But she did wonder if her mother had been nervous when she walked in for the party here or if Samantha Hunter now ran in these kinds of circles all the time.

Will drove up the gravel driveway and parked in front of the stone fountain.

Nancy took a deep breath as she climbed out of the car. Jonathan held the door open for her. 'Are you okay?' he checked in a low voice as he shut the door once she was out. She nodded but didn't actually trust herself to speak. She followed Will and Richard up to the house and smoothed her brown skirt and cream jumper nervously. She pulled at the beret on her head and tapped her boots on the floor until her grandmother raised an eyebrow at her and she made herself stop. She had so much rest-less energy running through her body and was eager to get inside. She knew her mother wasn't still here, but somehow being in the same space as she had been for the first time in twenty-one years felt monumental.

A man dressed all in black opened the door. He was tall and lean; a lot younger than the Roths' butler who

Nancy had met a few times. She caught a glimpse of a tattoo twisting up his arm underneath his jacket, which surprised her.

'Welcome. I'm Gary, Hugh Windsor's butler. Please come through.' He led them through the vast hallway into an elegant drawing room, where they were told to take a seat and drinks would be fetched along with the man of the house.

Jonathan whistled as he looked around. 'Even bigger than Roth Lodge,' he commented to Will.

Will nodded. 'And much older too. I remember coming here when I was little and playing hide-and-seek. My mother couldn't find me for two hours.' He smiled for a moment then it faded from his face. Will had returned to his grand family home in Dedley End, Roth Lodge, to build an accountancy business with Richard but the rest of his family were still in exile from the village after the scandal of the murder at the house on the hill. Nancy hadn't wanted to see the Roth family ever again, but fate seemed to keep throwing her into their path.

'That painting of London looks like an original,' Richard said, breaking the awkward silence. Richard and Nancy had been a couple at university, and briefly reunited last Christmas. She still found the Dane handsome and appreciated the fact he was always well turned-out in his suits – plus he was one of the few people she knew who was taller than her. Unfortunately, his personality was nowhere near as appealing as his appearance. Nancy sighed. Not only did she have to deal with Will Roth being back in her village but Richard had moved into Roth Lodge too. She couldn't help but wonder at her luck sometimes. But by putting up with them both today she just might find a breadcrumb about her mother she could follow.

Will nodded. 'It is.'

'I wonder why he has a painting of London,' Jane said as they all looked at the landscape.

'It's to remind me of where I came from.' In swept the lord of the manor. Hugh Windsor was larger than life – tall and portly with a red complexion. Gary the butler followed with tea in dainty china on a tray. 'Ah, my dear Will, and Bank… it's good to see you again.' He shook their hands heartily. Nancy was sure she saw Richard wince a little at Hugh's vice-like grip. They had met at Richard's leaving do before he set up a company with Will. It was there that Hugh had told him that he'd seen her mother. Hugh turned to the other three. 'Welcome to the old gaff.'

Will introduced the three of them to Hugh. Once they were all seated with cups of tea in their hands, Nancy leaned forward to get down to business.

'I would love to know what happened at your Christmas party, and how my mother came to be there. I think Will explained that I haven't seen her since I was six years old and no one had any idea what had become of her until she turned up here,' she said, gesturing around them.

Hugh took a moment to respond, seeming to relish having their full attention. 'Well, we throw an annual Christmas party here. We invite everyone from the nearby village and all my family come and our friends too, and we have a big knees-up. I recognised one of the locals – Pete, he runs the local garage. Anyway, I was struck by the woman he was standing with. She was very beautiful. I can see the resemblance.' He winked at Nancy who tried not to recoil in disgust. 'I asked to be introduced to her, and Pete said her name was Sally and they'd been drinking at the local pub when he'd invited her to come along as his plus-one at the last minute. She was dressed up though. My wife commented on her dress. And then I recognised her. It was when she smiled at my wife. I thought, "What a lovely smile, I've seen it before." So, I said, "Haven't we met?" She looked startled when I asked her that. And then it came to me.' Hugh let out a roar, which made them all jump. 'I said, "You're Samantha Hunter, we met in Dedley End, you ran the bookshop there." I pride myself on never forgetting a pretty face you know.' He waited for their response.

'I'm sure they never forget you either,' Nancy replied, cringing at herself but she sensed flattery was the only language this man understood.

'Indeed, indeed.' Hugh beamed at her. She saw Jonathan splutter into his cup of tea out of the corner of her eye and she bit her lip to not laugh. 'Here's the thing though. As soon as I said her name, her whole face changed. She looked... well, horrified. She stumbled back into a waiter and dropped her glass of wine. It shattered everywhere. My wife was soaked in wine. Chaos! The staff rushed over and everyone was in uproar and I don't know...' He frowned. 'I lost track of Samantha. When everything was cleared up, I asked the staff to look for her, but she had disappeared. Ran out, it seemed like. I mean, it was bad form to smash a glass but no need for that. I said to my wife about how strange it was but then I had a brandy and forgot all about it until I went to that company do in London and I chatted to Will and Bank.' Hugh nodded at Will and Richard. 'When they said they were moving to Dedley End, I remembered what happened.'

'When I spoke to you on the phone,' Will said, 'you said you'd speak to the man Samantha came to the party with – this Pete?'

Hugh nodded. 'I did, lad, I did. Well, I got my butler to do it. I don't go into the village myself, of course. Anyway, Pete said she had approached him in the pub wearing that dress and had started to ask about my party.' Hugh straightened importantly in the armchair. 'She had said she'd always wanted to come. So, he had invited her. I think he thought he was in luck, if you know what I mean.' He chuckled, shaking his head. Nancy looked at Jonathan, unsure how she was expected to respond to that.

'And Pete never saw her again?' Will asked, saving Nancy.

'He says no,' Hugh confirmed.

Nancy sighed. Her mother had wanted an invite to Hugh's party. But then had fled once she had been recognised. She hadn't wanted to be seen. So, had Samantha forgotten she had met Hugh or had taken the risk because she was so desperate to attend the party? Nancy had no idea what reason her mother would have had to want to be there. Surely it hadn't been just to enjoy the free bubbly. 'Do you have a guest list by any chance?' she asked Hugh. 'I'd love to know who else was at your party.'

'My wife keeps them so we know who not to invite the next year if they drink too much or are boring,' Hugh said with a chuckle. 'I'll have my butler print it off for you.' Then he clapped his hands. 'Now we have got that over with – who's up for a game of snooker?'

# Chapter Four

While Jonathan was dragged off by Hugh, with Will and Richard following, Nancy and Jane were shown by the butler into a small morning room. 'This is where Mrs Windsor spends most of her time,' Gary explained.

'Where is the lady of the house?' Jane asked.

He looked a little bit uncomfortable. 'Well, when Mr Windsor is here for his country pursuits, she stays in London. She won't come back until Christmas usually. She doesn't really like the country life.'

Nancy and Jane glanced at one another. Nancy was sure they both wondered if it was her husband she didn't like rather than the country.

'Anyway,' the butler said. 'Here we are. I've printed out the party guest list.' He showed them the printed paper on Mrs Windsor's desk. 'Let me know if you have any questions. I'll be clearing away the tea things.'

'Thank you,' Jane said, smiling at him. They watched him leave. 'Well, what did you have in mind when you asked to see this, love?'

Nancy leaned over the guest list. 'I suppose I'm confused why my mother came to this party. All this time, no word of her at all but then she shows up at a party thrown by someone she has met in Dedley End. Why? Okay, she might have forgotten that she met him but he recognised her immediately. Let's face it, he's not someone you wouldn't remember.' Nancy couldn't remember much about Samantha Hunter. Most of how she pictured her mother came from photographs. She didn't know her mother, but it felt hard to believe you'd completely forget meeting someone as larger than life as Hugh Windsor. 'If we assume she did know of Hugh, why would she want to come to his party in the first place? She's spent all this time away from Dedley End, we've heard nothing of her for all these years, but then she suddenly lets her guard slip just to attend a fancy party?'

Jane shook her head. 'I know it's been years but I don't think Samantha would be that keen to go to a party. She never seemed interested in the high life to me. And the fact that she used a fake name to attend must mean she wanted to keep the fact she was here a secret. Hugh told us that the man she came with thought her name was Sally.'

'And when Hugh recognised her, she ran away, so she clearly had wanted to be here incognito,' Nancy mused.

'You think she ran away because she was worried we'd find out?' Jane asked her, gently.

'Maybe.' It hurt Nancy to think her mother was that desperate to stop them knowing where she was. Nancy ran her finger down the guest list. 'But then again, if she is so desperate that we never find her, why come to this party in the first place and risk Hugh recognising her?'

Jane nodded. 'If she really doesn't want us to ever find her it was a strange thing to do, even using a fake name like she did. Hugh still knew she was Samantha. So, she clearly doesn't look much different despite all the years that have passed by.'

'Unless she *wanted* him to recognise her? So we would know she was here? It was to give us a message?' Nancy hated to hear the hopeful tone in her own voice.

'But how would she know we'd ever find out? We'd never met Hugh before. It was just chance that he got talking to Richard and Will about Dedley End.'

Nancy sighed and went back to the list. Her gran was right. Samantha had panicked when Hugh mentioned Dedley End and taken off in a hurry. She clearly hadn't been happy that Hugh had known who she was. 'None of it makes any sense to me.'

'Maybe there was a particular reason she had to be here,' Jane suggested. 'It was worth the risk to her?'

Nancy looked up at her grandmother. 'But what could have been the reason?'

'I wish I knew. But it feels significant after all this time of not hearing any news of her. And when you take in her reaction when Hugh recognised her...'

'What do you mean?'

'He said she fled in panic. Even if you don't want to come home because you gave up being a wife and mother, and don't ever want to come back, it still seems an extreme reaction. She could have asked Hugh not to tell anyone in Dedley End she had been there.'

'It does sound almost like she had been scared that he recognised her.'

'She can't be scared of us,' Jane retorted.

'No, but she might be scared of someone else,' Nancy said.

'Anything jumping out on the list?'

'There are a lot of important people on here,' Nancy said as she spotted familiar public-life figures on it, such as politicians, army ranks, even the Met commissioner, plus a couple of celebrities, but she wasn't sure that meant anything other than Hugh Windsor was a wealthy man mixing in the highest social circles.

'That MP,' Jane said as she pulled out her reading glasses from her handbag and perched them on her nose. She pointed to 'Sir Basil Walker'. 'I recognise his name.'

'Me too. Didn't he have to resign after some sort of scandal came to light last year?'

Jane stood back up and took her glasses off. 'Yes, there was something about him awarding a government contract to a company that wasn't all it seemed. There was a strong whiff of corruption.'

'Do you need air freshener?' Jonathan poked his head around the door. 'I heard something about a strong whiff.'

Nancy rolled her eyes. 'We found an MP on the list who had to resign as he was corrupt.' She showed Jonathan.

He nodded. 'Yes. Walker awarded a government contract to a building company.' He frowned, thinking. 'It was to build a new bridge and they got millions, even a billion, but the project never got off the ground. It turned out it was a shell company and the Government lost all the money. Walker was found to have known all along the company wouldn't build the bridge.'

'That's right, I remember it now,' Nancy said. 'Someone sent in a recording of Walker bragging about having taken a cut of the money, right?'

'An anonymous tip-off,' Jonathan confirmed. 'He was sacked and they launched an investigation, the police were called in, but not much has been reported since. Walker must have been able to quash it somehow.'

'Where is he now?' Jane asked.

'I heard he'd moved abroad,' Jonathan replied.

Nancy stared at Sir Basil Walker's name on Hugh's guest list. 'Do you know when this all happened?'

Jonathan pulled out his phone and did a quick online search. Then his eyes widened as he looked up at Nancy and Jane. 'It says the recording of Walker confessing was received the day after this party. It was delivered to the Speaker of the House of Commons, someone the sender must have known would act on it.'

Nancy stared at him. 'The day after Hugh's party?'

Jonathan looked at her. 'The day after. What are you thinking?'

'Well, if someone wanted a confession then drawing one out at a party when that person is relaxed, likely drunk, and not on their guard would be a good way to do it,' Nancy said. 'But it could just be a coincidence, right?'

'I don't typically believe in coincidences,' Jane said.

'It does seem that the party could be linked to Sir Basil Walker's downfall,' Jonathan said.

'But how would it relate to my mother though?' Nancy asked them.

'I don't know but I told you, there has to be a significant reason for your mother to have been here that night,' Jane said, firmly.

The door opened behind them, making them jump. 'Lunch is ready,' Gary said, eyeing them a little suspiciously.

'Okay, thank you,' Nancy said. She quickly snapped a photo of the guest list on her phone before following Jane and Jonathan out of the room, her mind whirring with just what happened at Hugh Windsor's party.

Nancy, Jane and Jonathan left Hugh's estate in the afternoon with Will and Richard and, as they drove out of the gates, Richard glanced at Nancy over his shoulder from the passenger seat. 'You were very quiet during lunch,' he said.

Nancy was surprised he had noticed but she nodded. 'I've been thinking about my mother. I suppose I thought maybe being where she was last seen might make me finally understand something about her, but she's still just as big of a mystery as ever.'

'Maybe there's a reason for that,' Richard suggested. They all looked at him. 'I'm just wondering if she wants to be a mystery, you know? That she used that fake name and ran off when Hugh recognised her because she really doesn't want you to look for her.'

'Well, we know that she walked out without telling anyone where she was going and hasn't been in touch since,' Jane said shortly. 'But now that we know she's alive and in the country, we can't ignore that. Nancy needs to know what happened to her.'

'But maybe it's not in Nancy's best interest to look for her. Maybe she'll get hurt if she does,' Richard said.

'What do you mean?' Nancy asked him, wondering if he knew something she didn't.

'If you find her and she, well, doesn't want to know you,' he mumbled, uncomfortably.

Nancy had, of course, wondered the same thing herself. She thought back to the painful day of her father's funeral. She had been ten and her mother had been gone for four years. She had been devastated to lose her father too. She felt like an orphan and clung to her grandmother, worried she might leave her too. But there was a little bit of hope that day too. She kept an eye out. She watched. She waited. But the day passed and her mother didn't turn up. If she couldn't be bothered to see Nancy at her father's funeral, Nancy had decided that she wasn't interested in her mother any longer. 'I decided long ago to leave my mother alone. To accept that she left and didn't want to come back or be found,' Nancy said, hoping her voice sounded steady. She didn't want to get upset in front of Richard or Will. 'But I've never stopped wondering where she is or what she's doing or really why she left in the first place. And I thought it was impossible I'd ever find out, but when you said she had been seen at Hugh's party, it was my first clue in over twenty years, and I couldn't ignore it. I can't ignore it,' she said with feeling. Nancy had always thought of the worst possible reason her mother had gone. Her gran had told her that Samantha had left her husband a note saying she couldn't cope with family life. Nancy had taken that to mean she hadn't been able to cope with her. She had decided her mother hadn't loved her enough to stay. So, she was prepared that Samantha might not be happy to see her. Might not even want to talk to her. But at least she would know for sure why she left and never came back. Even if it was hard. Even if it did hurt. Even if her mother rejected her once again.

'I just don't understand why you'd want to put yourself through that,' Richard continued.

Nancy opened her mouth to reply but Jonathan beat her to it. 'Nancy needs to know what happened to her,' he said, crossly. 'It's Nancy's decision and we should support that.'

'I'm only trying to look out for Nancy,' Richard replied, throwing Jonathan an angry look.

'You don't need to look out for her, she has friends to do that,' Jonathan snapped back.

'Actually, I can look after myself,' Nancy replied, coolly, annoyed at both of them.

'Of course, you can, love,' Jane agreed. She glared at Richard, who turned around to look out of the window. Jonathan pulled out his phone. Will reached out and turned on the radio, and they drove the rest of the way back to Dedley End in silence.

## Chapter Five

Will dropped Nancy, Jane and Jonathan off at Nancy and Jane's pretty Cotswold stone cottage. Then he and Richard drove home to Roth Lodge.

'Well, I'm glad that's over,' Jonathan said as the three of them stood on the pavement watching Will's car drive away.

'We should check on Penelope at the bookshop,' Jane said.

'Let's bring Charlie. He needs a walk and it's dry, thankfully,' Nancy suggested.

'I'll come too,' Jonathan said. 'I was looking into Sir Basil on the way home. We need to talk about that now we're away from Tricky Dicky and Will.'

Nancy went inside and put her beagle on his lead. Then the three of them set off in the direction of the Dedley End High Street with Charlie wagging his tail happily.

'So, what did you find out about Sir Basil on the trip home?' Nancy asked Jonathan, breathing in the autumn air and glad to be out of Will's stuffy car.

'So, after the anonymous tip-off was received, they set up a group of MPs to investigate. Sir Basil hastily resigned, and it was all brushed under the carpet and the contract awarded elsewhere. He then left the country. There were rumours this wasn't the first time Walker had done something to feather his own interests while he was MP, but he always managed to get away with it until the phone recording of him bragging about the money he'd made on the bridge-building contract was sent in.'

'Do you think someone could have recorded him bragging at Hugh's party?' Jane asked.

'It would be a good place to do it like Nancy said,' Jonathan replied. 'Someone could have talked to him at the party and recorded their conversation. The fact the recording was sent to the Speaker the day after the party means it's possible, right?'

'Shall I ask what we are all thinking – could that person have been Samantha?' Jane asked.

Nancy stared at her. 'I know we believe there must have been a significant reason for my mother to have been at that party but that's a pretty big leap, Gran. What would have made her want to bring Sir Basil Walker down? How would she have known he was corrupt and why would it have even mattered to her?'

Her grandmother sighed. 'You're right. She never seemed interested in politics when she lived here. It's not like she ever ran in Sir Basil Walker's circles.'

'Or worked in them,' Nancy added. Samantha had been working in the village pub, the White Swan, when she had met Nancy's father. And then she had helped him run their bookshop. 'Why would she suddenly have become a whistle-blower?'

'Although, until a murder happened on our doorstep, us three had never even thought about trying to get justice ourselves,' Jonathan observed.

'So, something happened to make Samantha want to bring Sir Basil down?' Nancy asked. 'But what?'

No one had an answer to that, so they walked to the bookshop in thoughtful silence.

Nancy opened the door. Penelope was at the counter serving a family and she waved cheerfully at them. Nancy let Charlie off his lead so the dog could jump up onto the window seat. She turned to Jane and Jonathan. 'I think we need to speak to DCI Brown.' Nancy had a thorny relationship with the local police after getting involved in two of their murder investigations but, in the end, the detective inspector had asked Nancy to come to him if they were ever inclined to investigate crime in the village again as he'd rather they did it together than anyone get hurt. 'I know we wanted to keep it quiet that we're looking into my mother so she didn't find out and get spooked but I think we need help at this point. He might be able to tell us more about what happened after my mother left.' She looked up at her father's picture on the bookshop wall. 'Dad said the police opened a missing person's file on her, right? So, DCI Brown could tell us if they ever found out anything about where she went.'

Her gran nodded. 'It's worth a try. Your father went alone to the police station. He didn't want me to come. He was so upset. He said the police opened a file, but didn't seem keen to investigate much because Samantha had left a note. George found out she had got on a train to London the day she left and that's all we ever knew.'

'Did you keep the note?' Jonathan asked.

Nancy looked at him. She had never asked that question. Her pulse sped up at the thought of seeing her mother's words in black and white saying she had to leave her husband and daughter. She didn't think she could bear to read it.

Jane shook her head. 'George said the police wanted to keep it in her file just in case. I didn't see it myself.'

Nancy wondered if that was strange or not. 'Maybe DCI Brown will let us see it then. At least we can find out what's in the file on her. Let's go and see him in the morning.' The other two agreed and Nancy, as usual, felt much better now they had a plan of what to do next. 'Right, we'd better get to work. Are you going to the newspaper office?' she asked Jonathan, who nodded. 'Let's head to Woodley first thing then.'

'I'll put the kettle on,' Jane said, walking into the back office.

'It's the sort of thing you would do though,' Jonathan said to Nancy once they were alone.

'What do you mean?'

'Your mother… if she was involved in bringing Sir Basil down. Look at what you've already done. You brought Lucy Roth's killer to justice and forced the Roths to leave the village with their reputation in tatters. Then you showed the world that a bestselling author wasn't the man they thought he was… This Sir Basil sounds like he is cut from exactly the same cloth as all of them.'

Nancy knew he was right. 'But even if my mother was at Hugh's party for that reason, it still doesn't help us find out why she left or why she has stayed away, or where she is now.'

'No,' Jonathan agreed. 'But it suggests there is more to her story than a woman not being able to cope with family life, doesn't it?'

Nancy couldn't help but hope he was right.

# Chapter Six

That evening, Nancy and Jane sat at their small pine table in the kitchen, eating spaghetti bolognaise with Charlie asleep in his bed in the corner. Their cottage was a cosy sanctuary after their long day.

'I know that Richard was poking his nose in earlier,' Jane said as she sipped her favourite tipple of gin and tonic. 'But I do agree with him in that I don't want to see you hurt again by your mother. I'll never forget the look on your face as a little girl when your dad told you Samantha wasn't coming back.'

Nancy knew her grandmother wanted to protect her, she always felt the same way towards her. They were each other's only family. 'I know, Gran, but I think I need closure. I need to really understand why I never heard from her after that day. Perhaps I was so eager to help solve Lucy Roth's murder and the murder on the village green because I have lived with an unsolved mystery all my life. I don't want anyone else to have to live with not knowing the truth. And now there's a chance I might finally uncover the real reason she left Dedley End, I can't walk away even if it might not be the truth I want to hear, can I?'

Jane nodded. 'I know what you mean. When we found out who caused your father's car crash, I felt an immense sense of relief. Obviously, it didn't bring him back and

I've had to accept that my son is gone, but I had always wondered what happened and knowing did bring me peace and closure. I know it did for you too. You deserve the same for your mother. You know I'll be here every step of the way. Whatever happens, you'll always have me.'

Nancy had kept her emotions at bay for most of the day but she felt her eyes well up at that. 'And you'll always have me,' she promised her grandmother, fiercely. Charlie let out a whimper. 'And you, Charlie boy, we're a family, the three of us.'

'And I suppose Jonathan too,' Jane said as she carried on eating.

Nancy smiled. Jane liked to give Jonathan a hard time but she was very fond of him. And Nancy agreed. She thought of him as family too. She hid the sudden blush on her cheeks by quickly having some of her drink.

–

First thing on Friday morning, Jonathan drove over from his flat above the local convenience store, to pick up Nancy and Jane and drive them to Woodley's police station. It covered the surrounding villages in the Cotswolds. DCI Brown lived in Dedley End, having moved there five years ago, so the three knew him better than most of the other local officers. After being involved in his murder investigation, they now shared a mutual respect.

They drove through the High Street and up the hill past Roth Lodge and out on to the winding road that led to the next town to Dedley End. Nancy always felt a shiver run down her spine whenever she was in a car on this road – it was where her father's car crash had happened when she had been just ten years old. It was the same reason she had never learned to drive. Jane glanced over her shoulder from the passenger seat to give Nancy a reassuring smile as they drove down the road. Once they reached Woodley, Nancy could relax again and her thoughts turned from her father's crash to her mother.

Jonathan parked opposite the police station and the three walked in and asked for DCI Brown at the desk.

'What are you three up to now?' DCI Brown asked as he strode out from the back. He had a twinkle in his eyes though. His younger constable, Pang, followed him but his eyes were narrowed. 'Pang, go and take down Mrs Smith's statement about her break-in and then meet me at Rose Cottage,' he said.

'But you might need me here,' Pang protested.

'I need you out there more,' DCI Brown replied, firmly.

Pang nodded and walked out, glancing back at Nancy before he left. She offered him a smile but he didn't return it. She knew he disapproved of their sleuthing and the fact they had kept DCI Brown out of their investigations. However, the inspector himself had come to a truce with them about it so she wasn't sure why he regarded them so suspiciously.

'Come through,' Brown said to them, leading them into a small room with a table and four chairs around it. 'To what do I owe this pleasure then?' he asked, folding his arms across his chest as they sat down.

'Are you meeting with Sebastian Holmes?' Jonathan asked before Nancy could respond.

'I hope you're not fishing around him,' DCI Brown said, giving them a stern look. 'He's a dangerous man and we'll be keeping a close eye on him. We're just going to pop by and introduce ourselves so he knows that. I don't want any trouble in the village. We've had a peaceful few months since the summer fete and I'd like to keep it that way.'

'We're not here about Seb,' Nancy said, quickly giving Jonathan a look. DCI Brown raised an eyebrow at her familiar use of the criminal's name, so Nancy continued hastily. 'We're here about my mother. I think you know she left Dedley End when I was six and we haven't heard from her since, but we recently discovered she is alive and I've decided to try to find her.' Nancy took a breath. 'I know this isn't your usual case or anything but we trust you, so I hope you don't mind us coming to you for help.'

He was surprised but pleased, Nancy noted. There were more lines on his face than when she first met him and some grey peppering his fair hair, likely due to the hectic past few months. She knew he was a fair man – he had acknowledged their help in his murder investigations, after all. Even though she didn't always trust he would get justice in every case, she believed he always tried to do so. 'How can I help?' he asked.

'Well, my father said that when my mother left, he came to the police station to ask what could be done to find her. He said a missing person's report was filed, although the police said they couldn't do much as she had left a note to say she wanted to leave.'

Jane took up the story. 'George said the police kept the note for the file so we were wondering if we could see it in case there is anything in it that might shed light on where she went the day she left.'

'Hmm, okay. Let me look. Everything is on our electronic systems now.' He asked them for Samantha's full name, date of birth and the date she went missing and then left to investigate, leaving the three of them to wait nervously.

# Chapter Seven

DCI Brown came back a while later, his white shirt sleeves rolled up. He walked into the room with a frown on his face. 'We have nothing on file relating to your mother.'

'No missing person's file?' Nancy said, confused.

'No... but you said she left a note. When an adult who isn't vulnerable does that, we don't tend to file a missing person's report,' DCI Brown explained. 'I can't find any record of a discussion with your father. And we didn't keep a note.'

'But why would George tell me that you did?' Jane asked, confused.

'He definitely said that?' DCI Brown asked.

'Well, yes, he came here the day after Samantha had gone when it was clear the note wasn't a joke... He said the police opened a missing person's file but advised him that, because she left of her own free will, they couldn't really investigate. But he definitely said they kept her note just in case. Why would he lie about that?'

'Because he didn't want you to see it?' Jonathan suggested. 'Or...'

'Or...' Nancy repeated when he trailed off.

'Or there was never a note.'

Nancy and Jane exchanged a look. Why would Nancy's father make that up?

'What did he say she wrote in the note?' DCI Brown asked Jane.

'That she couldn't cope with family life,' Jane replied.

'And that's the last you heard of her?'

'George said she'd been seen getting on a train to London,' Jane replied to DCI Brown. 'That's all we ever knew. George said there was nothing he could do. I suppose...' Jane paused, unsure.

'What?' Nancy prompted.

'I suppose George was upset and did talk about trying to find her but he didn't do much to find her, now that I really think about it. But I thought it was because he was brokenhearted and wanted to focus on looking after Nancy, you know?'

'Perhaps there was more to her disappearance,' DCI Brown suggested. When they all looked at him in confusion, he sighed. 'Perhaps there was trouble in their marriage, more than you knew, Mrs Hunter, or maybe... well, perhaps Samantha was unhappy or—' he broke off to clear his throat. 'She was even scared.'

'George would never have hurt anybody,' Jane cut in, furiously. 'My son was a good man. A good husband and father!'

'He was always so gentle,' Nancy agreed. She was trying to remain logical but the idea of her father driving Samantha away with his temper was ludicrous. 'No, it can't be his fault in that way. But, were they unhappy, Gran?'

'They fell in love at first sight, I always said. She had just moved here from London and served him in the pub and that was it. They were a perfect fit. You know, like some people just are?'

Jonathan glanced at Nancy then at DCI Brown. 'I take it she has no criminal record. We need to ask,' he added when Jane gave him an incredulous look.

'No, I checked,' DCI Brown replied. 'Maybe she went back to London to family, to friends there?'

'She had no family, she always said,' Jane replied. 'She didn't keep in touch with anyone that we knew of. I'm sorry I can't be more help.'

'How was she the days before she left?' Nancy asked. 'Did you get the sense she was unhappy?'

'Not unhappy as such but, now I think about did, she did change. She was always calm… but she became almost paranoid. She added more locks to the bookshop and they put in CCTV. She started staying at home more. I thought she was unwell but… I don't know, maybe she was planning to leave and was upset about Nancy? Wanted to make sure she'd be safe if she left?' Jane asked.

'Or maybe she *was* scared,' Jonathan said.

Nancy looked at him. Twice they had talked about her mother being scared of someone. First when she left Hugh's party in a panic after he recognised her and now in explaining her behaviour before she left the village. 'Maybe she wasn't running away to someone but away from someone,' Nancy said. 'Maybe it was my father or me or both of us like she said in her note, but maybe it wasn't.'

'Do you know much about her life before coming to Dedley End?' DCI Brown asked.

'Not really, no, she was quite private about her past,' Jane said.

'We can look through her things at the cottage again although she didn't leave much,' Nancy said, not feeling hopeful they would find anything to help. 'And we can look through Dad's desk as well. In case he did keep her note.' Although Nancy was starting to think that this note was fictional. But she had no idea why her father would have made it up.

'Let me know what you find. I can do a bit more digging as well,' DCI Brown said.

'Maybe keep it quiet though, as much as you can. I don't want my mother to know we're looking for her in case she runs again,' Nancy said. 'She might go abroad this time.' She left out the other reason – that she was worried if her mum had been scared of someone then they might find out. Even though Samantha Hunter had abandoned her, she was still her mother. She couldn't help the urge to protect her family.

DCI Brown nodded. 'Keep in touch.'

–

Jonathan came back to the bookshop with them so they could open up for the day, going into the back office with Nancy, who offered to make them all hot drinks, and then he pulled out his laptop from his bag. 'I thought I could dig through the newspaper archives to see if your mother's disappearance was reported on at all.'

'Great idea,' Nancy said as she made tea for her and Jane, and coffee for Jonathan. Penelope had the day off so it was just them working in the shop today and she had lots of customer orders to sort through and the shop needed a good tidy, but it would be hard to concentrate after what they found out from DCI Brown. 'I still don't understand why Dad lied to my gran about the police making a report and keeping my mother's note. Or why he might have lied about there being a note at all. Or maybe he destroyed the note because it would upset me too much to read it one day?' Nancy sighed. She could believe that her dad had done that to protect her, but she was unsure why he hadn't told his own mother the truth. It was strange to think of her father hiding anything. Nancy had such fond memories of him. Her mother was a hazy memory to her, but her dad and his love of reading and passion for their bookshop stuck firm in her mind. She could picture his happy smile even now. Had he really hidden things from her and Jane? It didn't fit with his character at all.

'If, and it's still a big if, he knew more than he told you and Mrs H he must have had a good reason for it,' Jonathan said, confidently. 'You and your grandmother – I mean, don't tell her this – are the most loyal people I know and he was your family.'

Nancy turned around to smile at him. 'Well, that means a lot. Thank you, Jonathan.'

He looked up from the laptop and met her gaze. He held it for a moment and Nancy felt that everything would be okay as long as she had him by her side. He cleared his throat and she looked away. 'I'm going to ring Tony,' Jonathan said then. He called the editor at the *Cotswold Star*. 'I'm trying to find something in the archives but nothing is coming up. Do you remember anything about it?' he asked his boss. 'Samantha Hunter. She left Dedley End twenty-one years ago, she ran the bookshop here with George Hunter... Yep, Nancy's parents. We thought she was reported missing by George Hunter but there's nothing on record at the police station. And I can't find anything that was written about it in the paper. Hmmm... really? You did? Why? That seems so strange. You didn't think to...? No, I know, I know. I understand... Okay, thanks, Tony. I'll see later.' Jonathan hung up as Nancy brought over their drinks. 'No wonder I can't find any articles,' he said as she passed him his coffee. 'Tony worked for the paper then as a reporter and when he heard people in the village talking about her going missing, he went to his editor about it, who told him there was no story and to not write about it. He said it was a domestic dispute, no local interest despite your parents being well known and people being so shocked that Samantha suddenly left the village.'

'Could we talk to the old editor?'

'I'll get in touch with Roger and see if he'll speak to us,' Jonathan said. 'See if he can shed any more light about the day she left. And why he didn't report on it. I need to get into work but I'll let you know when I hear back from Roger.'

'Thank you. I'd better go out and help Gran. It's time to open up.'

## Chapter Eight

After a busy day in the bookshop, Jane and Nancy had to make sure everything was in place on the village green for the opening of the pumpkin patch the following day, so they didn't have a chance to look through any of Samantha's belongings or George's paperwork. Jonathan had managed to get in touch with Roger, the former local paper editor. He had invited them on Sunday after church to talk about Nancy's mother, so that was something.

Saturday dawned dry with watery autumn sunshine. Nancy helped Penelope get the bookshop stall ready as the pumpkin patch came to life around them. They were both dressed up for the occasion – Nancy was in a 1940s dress with pin curls and red lipstick; Penelope wore a Catwoman costume. Pen had been friends with Jonathan and Nancy since school, and she had a little girl called Kitty. Her husband was in the army and was away a lot but he had a week's leave coming up. She couldn't stop smiling.

'I'm hoping I can look through everything at the cottage after we finish here,' Nancy said to Pen. 'In case there is something Gran and I missed over the years. It's so weird to not even know if my mother left a note when she left now or not.'

'Why would your father have made that up? To protect you?'

'Maybe. All I know is he didn't try to find my mother. He seems to have just let her go,' Nancy said.

'Perhaps because you were better off without her?' Pen suggested gently.

Nancy looked at her as they arranged crime books on the table to sell. 'Richard said something similar, that maybe I'm setting myself up to get hurt by looking for her. And I know that he could be right... but the more I find out about my mother, the more I don't understand her at all. I just can't leave it, Pen.'

Her friend nodded. 'I get it. You love to know how a story ends. You used to read the back page of books first when we were younger. And your mother has always been there, this mysterious figure, a part of your past that you don't really know. You lost your dear father. It makes complete sense to want to know your mother. None of us want to see you upset, that's all. I never want to agree with your dick of an ex,' she said, making them both smile. 'But I think that's what he meant.'

Nancy nodded. 'I know, thank you. It means a lot to have you all support me. I can handle it though, Pen. I promise. I just hope I get to find out the truth. We're a bit stuck at the moment.'

'There, the stall looks great,' Pen said, stepping back to admire their handiwork. 'It's time,' she added, looking over to where Rev. Williams, dressed as a scarecrow, was welcoming villagers in.

'It has all come together,' Nancy said, looking around pleased at all the pumpkins piled up, the hay maze, and the stalls selling wares and food. There was a smell of toffee apples in the air. Everyone was dressed to make the atmosphere a mixture of fun and spooky.

'Oh, look who it is,' Pen said. Nancy followed her gaze, and saw Richard and Will walking past. They weren't wearing costumes and stuck out on the village green. 'Apparently, they go to the pub for a drink every Saturday night now. So much for keeping away from the village.'

'They're hoping locals will become clients,' Nancy said. 'They don't want to only focus on their London contacts, they want to do accounts of people round here, build up a reputation in the Cotswolds. I feel like it's Will trying to make up for his family keeping away from everyone for as long as they did.' For years, the Roths hadn't had anything to do with the village they lived just outside of until they opened up their house for Will's sister's engagement party at Christmas. And that had ended with a murder. Will seemed determined to restore his family's standing in the village but Nancy wasn't sure that would ever be possible.

'It'll take more than that,' Pen remarked. She looked at Nancy. 'And how do you feel about Richard now? Spending the day with him when you went to see Hugh Windsor can't have been easy…'

'It wasn't, but he knows that there is nothing between us now. And Jonathan would likely kill him if he thought otherwise.' Nancy chuckled a little.

'We all would. But Jonathan definitely bears a grudge. I can't blame him. Richard is a dick.' They both giggled, unable to help themselves. 'Well, I'm glad he's firmly in your past.'

'Hopefully, I won't have to spend any more time with either Richard or Will Roth,' Nancy said. 'Anyway, when does Ollie arrive?' Nancy asked about Pen's husband.

'On Tuesday. Kitty is so excited, she keeps making him cards,' Penelope replied. 'I can't wait to see him and for a whole week. It's been ages since we had that much time together as a family. You're such a gem for letting me take some time off of work while he's here.'

'Don't be silly, you know I wouldn't take you away from your family time. We'll manage just fine.'

'I can't wait for him to come home,' Pen said. 'Oh, here's the Morris family.' They had their first customers then, a family they knew well from the bookshop, who bought a couple of books. Nancy noticed after they left that people were staring over at the drinks stall. She wondered what had caught their attention.

'Have you seen him?' Ruth Stoke, dressed as Anne Boleyn, came over to them.

'Who?' Pen asked her.

'Sebastian Holmes is here. Can you believe it?'

Nancy looked at where Ruth was pointing and saw Seb sipping on a pumpkin spiced latte as he looked at one of the pumpkin displays. He too wasn't in costume, but that was probably for the best as people were blatantly staring and looking nervous. Nancy could only imagine the stir it would have caused if he had dressed for Halloween as well. It was a strange sight to see him wandering among the wholesome fun of the pumpkin patch. But Nancy wanted to give him the benefit of the doubt and hoped he was here to turn over a new leaf.

'Oh my, he's coming over,' Ruth said as Seb seemed to notice them looking and began heading their way. 'I'm off to find my son.' She walked off, throwing Seb a disapproving look over her shoulder.

'Hello, Nancy, I believe you and your grandmother are behind all of this?' Seb said to her as he reached the stall, lifting his paper cup in greeting.

She smiled. 'That's right. It's our first pumpkin patch so we're hoping for a good turnout.'

'No Charlie today?' he asked.

'Charlie tried to make off with his sausage sandwich,' she explained to Pen, who looked stunned at her conversation with Sebastian Holmes. 'Jonathan has Charlie, they'll be here soon. Anyway, this is Penelope, she works in the bookshop with us.'

'Hello,' Pen said, her eyes wide.

'It's a pleasure.' Seb looked at the books in front of him. 'Nancy, I recently read a Poirot novel. Is there anything similar that's more modern?'

'I don't have anything here but I can give you some recommendations,' Nancy said, always happy to help a reader. 'We have a really good cosy crime table at the moment, if you want to come by the bookshop?'

Seb nodded. 'I will. I've heard a lot about your bookshop. I've been looking forward to taking a look around.'

'Oh, have you?' Nancy knew the bookshop was more well known now that she and Jane had got involved in crime solving – Jonathan had written about it in his newspaper and some of the nationals had been at the summer fete to report on bestselling author Thomas Green's fall from grace. Still, she was surprised someone who had been in a London prison would have heard about it.

'Someone I know is… a big fan, let's just say.'

'Oh, who?' Pen asked him, curiously.

At that moment, a family came over to look at the books, although the parents clocked Sebastian and eyed him nervously. Nancy saw him step back and watch them a little sadly and she couldn't help but wonder if he had anyone in his life who was pleased to have him out of prison. She hoped so. She stepped out from the table. 'Please do come by the shop,' she said to him.

Seb pulled out a packet of cigarettes and a book of matches. He saw Nancy's face. 'I know, but some days these were the only thing that got me through.' He opened the matches – hot pink. Not what Nancy would have expected him to buy – and struck one. 'I will come by the bookshop, thank you, Nancy. Not everyone has given me a warm welcome, but you have.'

'I'm sorry,' she began.

Seb shook his head. 'I understand it, Nancy. It'll take a long time for people to see I've changed, but I'm going to try to show you all. I actually went to the vicarage yesterday to speak to the vicar and his wife.'

'You did?' Nancy was surprised to hear that.

'I wanted their support to attend church services. I used to go in prison and it gave me a lot of peace. Rev. Williams said I would be very welcome.'

'He's a good man,' Nancy said. She had grown up with the vicar and his wife being close friends to her and her grandmother, and she thought very highly of both of them. 'I'm glad you'll be coming to church,' she said, warmly.

'Well, I want to make this my home.'

'Why did you choose to come to Dedley End?' she couldn't help but ask. 'It's very different to London.'

'It is.' He looked at her right in the eye. 'I made a promise to someone that I'd come here once I was released.' He nodded across the green. 'That's Will Roth, isn't it?' At her raised eyebrow, he shrugged. 'I keep up with the news, heard a lot about his family.'

'The rest of the family haven't been back to the village since Christmas,' she said. 'Will moved here this summer though with his business partner.'

'Nancy's dick of an ex-boyfriend,' Pen added. She saw Nancy's face. 'Oh, sorry,' she mumbled.

'We all have people in the past we'd rather forget,' Seb said. 'So, Marcus Roth isn't in Dedley End?'

'No, but the rumour is he's planning to come and stay soon,' Pen said.

Nancy nodded. 'I've heard the rumours too. I knew they'd never stay away for good and now that Will is making a name for himself in the village, maybe Marcus thinks they can all start over.'

'None of us will forget what happened at Christmas,' Pen said. She saw Seb raise an eyebrow. 'If you heard about the Roths, you'll know there was a murder at their house,' she said.

'I heard about that and that you were involved in the investigation, Nancy,' Seb said. 'Which I believe hasn't been your only murder case.'

'No, but I'm sure that's all over now,' Nancy said.

'Nothing used to happen in our village. But it's back to being safe and sound now,' Pen said.

Seb glanced at her and Nancy was sure that he looked unconvinced. 'So, you won't be asking Will Roth to do the bookshop accounts then, Nancy?'

She shook her head. 'I only work with people I trust,' she replied.

'We'll stay away from them,' Pen agreed. 'And if Marcus does come back, he will be shunned, so hopefully he won't be here for long,' Penelope added.

'Well, I'll never set foot in the house on the hill again, at least I can promise that,' Nancy said.

Sebastian kept his eyes on Will and Richard for a moment. 'That sounds very sensible to me. Right, I'll let you get on, Nancy.' He nodded at her and then strode off.

She watched him go. She wasn't sure how someone who had been part of a gang should act, but she didn't think Sebastian was at all what she would have expected.

When they were alone again, Pen leaned in. 'I still can't believe Sebastian has moved here. I heard he was really high up in that gang and that maybe he still is.'

'He says he's changed,' Nancy said.

'Hmm, well, let's hope so. But I wonder if someone like that really can change.' Pen turned to greet some more customers and Nancy watched Sebastian walking across the green. She thought about what he had said about promising someone to come to Dedley End. She couldn't help but be intrigued about who that was and why they would want him to move to her village. There was a story there. And then there was his interest in the Roth family. A family who she knew to be toxic. She just hoped it wasn't anything to worry about because she needed things to stay peaceful in the village while she tried to find her mother.

Nancy heard a joyful bark, and saw Charlie and Jonathan walking into the pumpkin patch. She burst out laughing. Jonathan was dressed in a Dracula costume and he'd put a bat outfit on Charlie. 'You two get my vote to win the costume contest,' she said, reaching down to greet her happy-looking beagle.

Jonathan grinned. 'The prize is a free meal at that new fancy restaurant in Woodley. I told Charlie if we win, I'd have to take you instead but promised we'd get him his own special dinner.'

Nancy met his gaze and smiled. 'It's a deal.'

# Chapter Nine

After a long day at the pumpkin patch, Nancy was glad to retreat to their cottage. Penelope's daughter had come by with her grandparents and Pen had left for a family meal with them so Nancy, Jane, Jonathan and Charlie had walked back from the village green to their cottage as evening swept over Dedley End. Jonathan and Charlie had indeed won the costume competition, the bookshop stall had sold well, which pleased Nancy, and Jane was delighted everyone had enjoyed their first autumn celebration. They were all in good spirits, albeit tired, from the day. They couldn't rest for the evening though as Nancy wanted to go through everything she had left from her parents in case they could find something that shed light on her mother's disappearance.

'I heard Sebastian Holmes caused quite a stir turning up today,' Jane said when Nancy came downstairs after having a quick shower and changing out of her costume. Jane had also shed her costume – she'd dressed as a witch – and was making sausages and mash. Jonathan had taken off his cloak and fangs, and wiped off his face paint; Charlie was no longer a bat and had curled up for a much-needed nap in the corner of the kitchen.

'And Will Roth and Tricky Dicky acting like part of the village,' Jonathan added. He lifted the boxes Nancy had brought down from the loft and from her father's desk in the living room onto the kitchen table to start sorting through. Nancy had looked through most of it before, but there might have been something she had missed and she hadn't been trying to find her mother then, so she hoped something might jump out at them.

'I found those two as well,' Jane said, nodding at another two boxes. 'They were at the back of my wardrobe and I have no idea what's in them.'

Nancy looked at the boxes. 'This is everything apart from my mother's wedding dress and the clothes she left,' she said, sitting down. 'And everything of Dad's that isn't related to the shop as that's in the office there. Not much at all.'

'This will help give us energy for the task.' Jane carried over steaming-hot plates full of comforting food. Jonathan had poured Jane and Nancy their favourite tipple – gin and tonic – and had a beer for himself. 'I never found anything that gave a hint to where Samantha had gone apart from her being seen heading to London. She didn't have much related to her family or her past before she came to Dedley End.'

'Which is odd, isn't it?' Nancy said, opening one of the boxes her gran had found as she ate. 'It's like she came to Dedley End to start over.'

'She didn't like to talk about the past, only that she had been born and raised in London but got tired of city life,' Jane said. 'Wanted to move to the countryside and said she had no family and no ties to keep her there. She was a little bit sad when she mentioned it, but it wasn't often. She focused on the present or the future. She and George had such big plans.' Jane sighed. 'Perhaps I should have pushed her to open up more but she and George were so happy. They fell in love so quickly and settled down that it felt like there was no point. She slotted into our family like she'd always been here.'

'Why did she abandon it all then?' Nancy wondered aloud. She pulled out a couple of photo albums from the box.

'Perhaps her past caught up with her,' Jonathan said. 'Whatever she didn't want to talk about in London, you know?'

'There are so few photographs belonging to Samantha,' Jane said as she picked up one of the photo albums Nancy had put on the table. 'A few of her as a baby with her parents and this one of when she was in London and working in a pub there.' Jane showed them. 'She was Samantha Smith back then.' Jane pointed out Nancy's grandfather and grandmother on her mother's side. 'Samantha's parents died before she came to Dedley End,' she said. 'She didn't want to talk about it and I understood that. I don't even know their names. I told her she looked like her father. I can see him in you too, Nancy,' she added.

Nancy nodded, sad that she'd never known her other grandparents.

'Such few mementos from her past. What about any official documents? Her passport, birth certificate?' Jonathan asked.

'We assumed she took them with her,' Jane replied.

'So, we can't find her family from that. She didn't mention anyone that she might have looked up in London if she did go back there when she left?' Nancy asked, hopefully.

Jane shook her head. 'I'm sorry. I wish I could help more, love.'

'It's not your fault,' Nancy reassured her grandmother. She finished her dinner then opened another box. 'Oh, this is books. Must be Dad's,' she said, picking them up.

Jane looked over. 'Oh, no, they're true crime books. George only read fiction, you know that. Those were your mother's. I kept them in case you might want to read them one day. I had forgotten about them being in the back of the wardrobe.'

Nancy looked up in surprise. 'I didn't know she was into true crime?'

'That's why they decided to only stock crime books. George loved his detective fiction and Samantha loved all the memoirs and biographies, it was a shared passion of theirs. I think it's what drew them together.'

'Oh.' Nancy liked the fact that her love of books came from both of her parents. She turned one of the books over. '*How The Club Corrupted the Government: The True Story of the Gang's Political Power*,' she read the title aloud. 'It's all about how the gang are rumoured to be bribing politicians for influence and power and, of course, money.' She opened up the book and gasped. On the inside page was a list of names in pencil. 'Sir Basil Walker is on this list,' she said, showing it to the others.

'That's your mother's writing,' Jane said, putting her reading glasses on to see. 'So neat, I was always jealous. Who else is on the list?'

Nancy read them out and Jonathan Googled each one. Four had been accused of corruption and had ended up resigning or being sacked from government jobs, and one had been killed in a robbery at his home. The other two were retired. 'There's one name left.' Nancy gasped when she recognised it. 'The current foreign secretary?'

'That's worrying,' Jonathan said, which was putting it mildly, Nancy thought. 'So, why did your mother make this list? Are they all in the book?'

Nancy flicked through it. 'A few are, others not. She must have thought they were all being paid by *The Club*.' Nancy gasped. 'Oh. So, does this mean she was at Hugh Windsor's party to find evidence that Sir Basil Walker was corrupt?' Nancy had gone back and forth about that idea since they realised the recording of Walker confessing was sent in the day after that party, but here was proof that her mother had been looking into the gang and the people working for them. 'I can hardly believe it.'

'Your mother is a whistle-blower?' Jane said in awe.

'She had this list before she left the village. She was looking into *The Club* all those years ago. But why? Unless she knew them when she lived in London?' Jonathan asked. 'What if your mother has been trying to bring the gang down ever since she left Dedley End?'

They took that in for a moment. Nancy dropped the book onto the table and looked at her grandmother and Jonathan. 'Does that mean that she might have known Sebastian Holmes? That he might know of her?'

'Oh, my goodness,' Jane said. 'Should we be worried about him being here in the village then?'

'We need to find out if he does know your mother,' Jonathan said. 'But very, very carefully. He says he's turned over a new leaf but he could still be part of the gang. He could be trying to stop Samantha. He might have come here because he thinks you know where she is, Nancy.'

'I don't know. There was something about him...' She trailed off wondering if she was being silly in thinking that Seb could be trusted. 'He said he did know of us, the bookshop and our murder investigations, and he knew of

58

the Roths, too. He mentioned promising someone that he would come to Dedley End too,' Nancy remembered. Had he come to keep an eye on them all? Was he friend or foe? 'How do we find out if he knows my mother?'

'We're due to talk to the old editor, Roger, on Sunday. We can ask him if he wrote about *The Club* back when he worked at the *Cotswold Star*, if he ever found any link between Samantha and the gang, and go from there,' Jonathan said. He looked at Nancy. 'We will get to the bottom of this, Nancy.'

She nodded. 'I just can't believe my mother might have been investigating that gang. I mean, how did it even start? When she left us or before? Was it the reason she ran away?' Nancy stared at her mother's handwriting in frustration. She hated not being able to connect the dots yet.

# Chapter Ten

Roger Morgan lived in Woodley, just around the corner from the newspaper office he worked in for forty years before he reluctantly retired and became a keen gardener, he explained to Nancy and Jonathan when they went to his house after church. They sat with mugs of tea in his small living room as Roger reminisced about his days as editor of the *Cotswold Star*. 'It was different back when I started with no online edition or the internet for research. I had to be out there in the villages digging for the news myself. I got to know everyone really well. I went to the news. It didn't come to me.'

'We get a lot of people contacting us now,' Jonathan admitted. 'People are eager to share their stories.'

'It's how the world is now with social media. Everyone thinks their life is important enough to share. And, let's face it, that's not always the case.' He chuckled. 'But back then, I had to prise stories out of people. I thrived on breaking stories. It was in my blood. Still is, but I have to content myself with just reading the news now and not writing it. And there has been a lot to read around here lately.'

Jonathan nodded. 'I used to worry about there not being enough going on locally to really sink my teeth into but not lately.'

'You've broken a lot of big stories,' Roger said with some envy in his voice.

'Nancy has become a bit of an amateur sleuth so I've stuck by her side,' Jonathan said with a smile at her.

'We've investigated it all together,' she said, shaking her head.

Roger nodded. 'I've read all about it. Bookshop owner turned detective. What's given you the bug, Nancy?' he asked her, with open interest.

'It's all been rather accidental… The wrong place at the wrong time, really. But maybe it's because I've always loved mysteries, and mysteries have always been part of my life. In the books I sell in the shop, but in my own life too. I know what it's like to not know what's happened to the people closest to you and I don't want that to happen to others.'

'And people tell her and her grandmother things they'd never reveal to the police,' Jonathan added. 'They've read all the crime stories written pretty much, but they also read people well. Even our DCI Brown has had to admit he couldn't have solved the murders in our village without them.'

'Now you've turned your sleuthing to your own mystery?' Roger asked. 'You're here to ask about your mother.'

Nancy nodded. 'I didn't think I needed to know why she left, but I do. Now that we know she is alive. I just want to put the puzzle pieces together and then I can finally move on.'

'The problem is digging into the past inevitably leads to finding things out you might have been better off not knowing.'

Nancy raised an eyebrow. 'Is there something I shouldn't know about my mother?'

Roger sipped his tea and took a moment before replying. 'When Jonathan asked to meet to talk about your mother, I almost said no. I was good friends with your father. George and I used to have a pint together regularly. As he ran the bookshop, sometimes he could give me a good tip-off from something he heard in the shop that led to a story. I often talked about the shop in the paper too – we helped each other out. We got on. We had a laugh.'

'I didn't know,' Nancy said, in surprise.

'I don't come to Dedley End much anymore,' Roger said. 'I have meant to come by the bookshop and see you but I suppose I felt like it might have been too hard knowing your father wasn't there. I was with George when he met Samantha.'

Nancy and Jonathan exchanged a look. Nancy hadn't expected Roger to reveal that. She leaned forward. 'What was she like? What was their meeting like?' She had been too young to ask her father much about Samantha – he had always seemed so sad if she ever asked about her – and she certainly hadn't thought to ask him how they met or his first impression of Samantha.

'Your mother arrived in Dedley End and took a job at the White Swan. She was young... well, we all were, about twenty-one I believe. And she was stunning. Not just pretty but she caught your attention. She had these bright, sharp eyes. And she was funny too. Everyone fell under her spell but George was a goner that night. The sparks between them were obvious to everyone. Love at first sight. I never believed in it but I swear I saw it that night.'

Nancy sucked in a breath. It wasn't easy to hear about her parents' happy beginning. There were many people in Dedley End who had known Samantha but there had always been a reluctance on their parts to talk about her for fear of inflicting further pain on Nancy. And she had been afraid to ask in case she was hurt further. Because what did she want to hear about the mother who had left? Would anything make that better? She had felt it was better not to know too much. Her grandmother had been the only one she could talk about it with but she had known Samantha as her son's wife. Roger was their friend. It was different. And he'd been there when they met. Roger knew it all. 'How did they go from that to my mother walking out?' she asked. It was a question that she'd been asking her whole life. She remembered her mother's laugh and her parents kissing in the kitchen, and Roger saying that they really did love one another fitted with Nancy's early memories. Memories that she'd blocked because of what happened to them next. But if they really had been that in love, Nancy found it even harder to understand why Samantha had left George and Nancy.

Roger sighed. 'I asked myself that question a lot. They always seemed a strong couple to me. When I met my wife, who's sadly passed now, the four of us would meet up for drinks. We had some really good times together. And when they had you, Nancy, they were over the moon. We came to see you just after you were born. Samantha was so in love with you. George doted on you both. I could see how happy they both were.'

Nancy was glad there had been that kind of happiness. She believed Roger. He spoke in that honest, no-nonsense way that Jonathan did. The news reporter in them both, perhaps. She trusted what he was telling her. 'What went wrong do you think?'

'My wife and I had to go and spend time with my mother when she became ill. I was given time off. We went down to Cornwall. When we came back, George came to tell us Samantha had left. He said she had left a note saying she couldn't cope with family life. I didn't understand. She had seemed so content. I asked him if he had tried to find her but he said the police wouldn't help as she'd left of her own free will, and he felt that if she wanted to go, he shouldn't try to drag her back. But he was devastated. I had never seen a man so broken.'

'It's all so confusing. My father told my gran that the police kept my mother's note but they have nothing on file. They didn't set up a missing person's file because she had decided to go and wasn't vulnerable or anything. I don't understand why my dad didn't try to find her. Or what happened to my mother's note. Did he destroy it or did it not exist in the first place?'

Roger frowned. 'George was always a straight-up guy. He wasn't a liar. Unless...' He looked thoughtful. They waited. 'You and Samantha were his life, his priority over everything. The bookshop meant a lot to him but you two were his world. I can imagine him doing anything to protect you both. Perhaps her note was too upsetting so he destroyed it so you wouldn't have to read it.'

Nancy gave a slow nod. She supposed that could be the case. 'Why wasn't her disappearance written about in the newspaper?'

'George asked, no, he begged me not to write anything about Samantha leaving in the paper. He said the local gossip was bad enough. He didn't want it in the paper for your sake. He was desperate for you to not be hurt any more so I agreed. He was my friend. And I felt the same way as the police – that there was no need for a campaign to bring her back, she had decided to leave. I agreed that there was no need to report on it. People run away all the time.'

Jonathan frowned. 'But as you say, Samantha went from a happy mother to saying she couldn't cope with family life, if we believe what George said was in her note. Did that sit right with you?'

Again, Roger thought about his reply before answering Jonathan. 'Honestly, no. But George was adamant that things hadn't been right between them for a while, they had just hidden it well, and he was broken up by it but he had to let her go. And even though not knowing where she was drove him crazy, he would sometimes admit to me, he didn't want to do anything about it. Said he didn't want her to cause you any more pain, Nancy.'

Nancy was uncertain what to think. On one hand, she understood her father had had a broken heart and had wanted to focus on his daughter, but some of his actions didn't quite make sense to her. And this note of her mother's was mysterious. Did it exist? What happened to it? Why had her father not tried harder to find Samantha? 'One more question,' she said then. 'Did you ever report on the organised criminal gang known as *The Club*?'

Roger was surprised. 'No, not personally although I knew about them and had friends at the nationals who really tried to find out who the gang were, how and where they operated and the people they had in their pockets. But they remain a mystery as far as I know. No one ever found out who was in charge. We never reported on them in Dedley End, although there were rumours their reach spread far from London and still does.'

'Samantha doesn't seem to have spoken much about her past apart from coming from London. Did you ever get a sense she was hiding something from her time back then?' Jonathan asked him.

'You are really testing my memory. I don't think so but we were young and carefree. We had fun. We didn't have too many deep conversations, you know? I suppose though now you ask, I didn't know much about her past or family or anything. But you don't think she had anything to do with *The Club*, do you? They have done some horrific things. I mean, that armed robbery with Sebastian Holmes is just one example; they were rumoured to have killed two members of a rival gang before that but it's not just all in the past. Last year, a banker killed himself and the police believed they had been blackmailing him, so either they pushed him over the edge figuratively, or killed him themselves and made it look like suicide.'

Nancy swallowed hard. The more she read and heard about *The Club*, the more unlikely it seemed her mother would have had any links to them. Yet she couldn't ignore the fact she had been at Hugh's party and Sir Basil Walker's dodgy dealings had been revealed the following day. Then there was that memoir in her mother's belongings and the list she had written of people *The Club* had in their pockets. 'She never mentioned them then?' Roger shook his head. 'As you know, Sebastian Holmes has moved to Dedley End. She never mentioned him, did she?'

'No. I can't see how your mother could have been involved with anything like that, and you should both stay away from Holmes. He might say he's left all those days behind him, but he was an influential member before he went to prison. You don't just walk out of all that easily.'

Nancy felt a cold shiver run down her spine at Roger's stark warning. She hoped she wasn't being naïve to not be more afraid of the former gang member who had moved to their village.

'Thank you for telling us what happened,' Jonathan said then as Nancy fell quiet, her mind whirring. 'We're a bit stumped where to go from here, to be honest.'

'You said you'd been to the police? But have you been to the police from that time? DCI Brown wasn't even in Dedley End when Samantha went missing,' Roger said.

Jonathan turned to Nancy. 'But we know who was.'

# Chapter Eleven

Jonathan and Nancy collected Jane from the cottage and the three of them headed to the White Swan for their traditional Sunday lunch, although they were later than usual after their meeting with Roger. Penelope and her daughter, Kitty, often joined them but they were getting ready for Pen's husband to come home so just the three sat at their usual table today. The pub was popular all year round, especially for its famous roast dinners.

After they had filled Jane in on what Roger had told them, she looked at Nancy with concern. 'After dear George's funeral, you stopped wanting to really talk about your mother. You stopped hoping she'd come back I think, so you didn't want to hear about the happy times. So, I kept quiet.' Jane reached out to squeeze Nancy's hand. 'I'm sorry if that made you think you didn't ever have a happy family life because that's very much not true. Your parents not only loved you but they loved each other. And George was devastated when Samantha left, as were you. I couldn't explain it then and I can't now. She did change as I told you, but it was a shock when I found out she had left. Maybe George didn't do as much to find her as we might have expected but he was hurt, you know? When someone leaves you, you can't help but blame yourself as much, if not more, as them.'

'It must have been so hard for him,' Nancy agreed. 'But why did he lie about the police and the note?' She looked over at the table where Mr Peabody sat. 'Roger's right – we need to speak to Mr Peabody and see if Dad went to him back then.'

'You go alone, love,' her grandmother said. 'We'll order for you.' As Nancy got up, she saw Jane lean in towards Jonathan. 'I'm worried about her,' Nancy heard Jane say as she went over to see Mr Peabody. She knew this quest to find her mother wasn't easy on any of them, but she didn't want her gran to worry about her. Yes, it was hard to talk about Samantha, but it was also the only way to get to the truth and, now she had started to try to unravel the mystery of her family, she couldn't stop. She felt like she was on the edge of finding out what happened. She just had to keep her nerve.

'Can I join you for a minute?'

Mr Peabody looked up from his pint and smiled at her. 'Of course. Nancy, you're always a sight for sore eyes. I just saw DCI Brown and that young Pang. They kindly bought me this.'

Nancy smiled. She knew that Mr Peabody sometimes had a drink with the officers, they respected their retired colleague and so did she. 'I haven't really spoken about it in the village but I need to tell you because I need your help,' she said as she sat down with him. He leaned forward, intrigued. 'I'm trying to find my mother.'

Mr Peabody's eyes widened. 'Well, I must say I have always wondered if you might try. Especially now you've proven yourself to be rather adept at solving mysteries. Do you have anything to go on though?' he asked, eagerly.

'Well, I never knew if she was even alive but someone saw her the Christmas before last in Norfolk. So, now I know that she's out there somewhere.'

'And you feel now is the time to find out why she left?'

'And why she never came back,' Nancy said.

'Well, I wish you all the best, you know that, Nancy. I'm glad for you that she's alive and out there.' He wrapped his hands around his pint glass. 'And I know you, you can handle finding out the truth about why she walked out on you. How can I help?'

'I know it's a long time ago but you were on the force back then. When she left, when she walked out, what did my dad do? Did he come and see you about it? Did he report her missing? I mean, did he ask you to help him try to find her?'

'It was a long time ago, you'll have to forgive me if my memory lets me down at all,' Mr Peabody said. 'The first I heard about it was here in this pub. Everyone was talking about your mother walking out. As you can imagine, lots of rumours were flying around. George hid away for a week or so, Jane opened the shop and we didn't see him in here. When we did, he just said she'd gone and that was it. Put a brave face, stiff upper lip, on it all. I admired him for that. I did ask him one night why he hadn't come to the station but he said she wasn't missing, she'd run away. He told me she'd left a note saying she couldn't cope, that she had to go. So, there was nothing untoward, Samantha made the choice to leave. And I suppose your father made a choice not to try to get her back.'

'So, he didn't come to the station at all? He didn't try to report her missing?' Nancy asked, her voice rising.

'No, definitely not.'

'He told Gran that he did,' she said, slumping back in the chair, more confused at her father's actions than ever.

'Maybe it's because that's what she needed to hear. No one knows what really goes on in a marriage, not even your nearest and dearest.' Mr Peabody lowered his voice. 'If it would help, I could tell you that most of the rumours flying around were that Samantha had left with someone. That she ran off with another man. I think most people kept quiet about that in front of your dad and your grandmother, but that's what we all believed.'

It was the first time Nancy had heard that. Her mind raced. 'Did anyone have any idea who she ran off with?'

'Someone from her past, someone from London, and rumour was she got on a train to London when she left.' Nancy nodded, that seemed to be fact now. 'As I say though, it was all gossip. I never saw her with another man but it did sound like the most likely reason to me when I heard it.'

Nancy thought about that. It did make more sense than her mother just abandoning her life for no reason. If she had met someone, or someone from her past had come back for her, maybe that had been compelling enough to pull her away from her husband. But her daughter as well? Nancy found herself wondering again, even though she tried hard not to, why she hadn't been enough of a reason for her mother to stay in Dedley End. Or if Samantha felt she had to follow her heart and run off with another man – why hadn't she taken Nancy with her when she left? But if it had been due to a man then he didn't appear to be with her now. She had been at Hugh's party alone. And how did running off with a man tally with her whistle-blowing on Sir Basil Walker or her writing that list of people in the book about *The Club*?

71

Nancy thanked Mr Peabody for telling her what he knew and returned to the others. 'Mr Peabody says Dad didn't even come to the police station at all. Said my dad believed Samantha had run away, there was nothing to investigate and he didn't want to try to get her back. And the rumour around the village that no one had the heart to say to Dad or to you,' Nancy said looking at her gran, 'was that my mother ran off with another man.'

Jane opened her mouth then closed it. 'Well, I suppose that could be true but honestly, love, I never saw her even flirt with another man once she was with your father.' Jane leaned back in her chair. 'I wonder if I ever really knew your mother at all.'

'Maybe not, maybe she made sure no one really knew her,' Nancy said. 'It's all so confusing. Everything we find out about my mother seems to contradict something else. Everything we know about my mother changes with each person we talk to.'

'Oh, I wish I had pushed George more at the time to open up to me,' her grandmother said. 'But I suppose I hadn't wanted to upset him more either. I stopped mentioning Samantha and focused on helping him raise you. And I was angry with Samantha, I can't pretend otherwise. I decided that maybe it was best not to talk about her after all the heartbreak she had caused. I accepted George just wanted to move on with his life and I tried to help him do that.'

'You were such a support to us,' Nancy told her. 'I know I couldn't have made it through losing my dad without you.' Her voice broke a little.

Jane dabbed at her eyes. They both took a moment to recover.

Jonathan looked away for a moment then he turned back. 'Do we think Samantha did run off with someone? After what Roger said about your parents' relationship, it doesn't sit right with me.'

'No and it doesn't help us understand any link between my mother and *The Club*. Unless the man she ran off with got her involved in all of that somehow?' It was a possibility, Nancy thought. 'If she did leave Dad for another man, then was he with her the day she left? Did they get the train to London together?'

'We could try to find that out,' Jonathan said. 'Maybe the train guard there remembers something from that day. It's still old Bill, isn't it?'

'It's worth a try,' Jane said, smiling at him for thinking of that. She turned to Nancy. 'Let's go there after the shop closes tomorrow and talk to him.'

Nancy agreed, glad they could try that. She looked out of the window and saw Sebastian Holmes walking past the pub. He glanced over and their eyes met. He nodded at her before carrying on. 'I wish we could talk to him about it all,' she admitted. Then they would know if he did know anything about her mother.

'It's too risky,' Jonathan said. 'If there is any connection between Samantha and that gang, they can't find out we're trying to find her, can they?'

'You think Seb is still in touch with them?' Nancy asked him.

'I think better safe than sorry.'

'Okay, you're right. Let's talk to Bill next then,' Nancy said, but she knew they would have to talk to Sebastian Holmes at some point, whether they liked the idea or not.

## Chapter Twelve

Nancy and Jane walked out of their cottage bright and early on Monday morning with Charlie on his lead on their way to open up the bookshop. There was a threat of rain in the air, the clouds above them a murky grey, so they set off at a brisk pace hoping to get to the Dedley Endings Bookshop before a shower started.

'Just the pair I was hoping to see,' a voice called out as they walked along the road. Seb Holmes quickly stepped through the gate of Rose Cottage as if he had been waiting for them to pass by. He clicked the gate shut behind him and tipped his fedora at them.

Nancy and Jane looked at one another, instantly on alert. 'Why was that?' Nancy replied as nonchalantly as she could manage. She watched in surprise as Charlie rushed up to him and wagged his tail.

'He really does like you,' Jane said, equally taken aback. 'You don't have meat in your pockets, do you?'

'No, but I do have this.' He held out a dog treat. 'Is that okay?' They agreed and he gave it to Charlie who wolfed it down. 'I was planning to come and see your bookshop. Can I walk with you? I assume you're heading in that direction.'

Nancy and Jane looked at one another again. Nancy knew they couldn't refuse without him wondering why they were suddenly less polite and perhaps they could glean something from him. 'Of course. We're just heading to open up,' she said. Seb fell into step with them, Charlie walking happily in between him and Nancy.

After a moment's silence, Jane looked at Seb. 'Are you all settled into the cottage now?'

'I have unpacked my last box so that's a relief. I didn't realise I had so much junk in my old flat. I've thrown a lot of it out. It felt good to have a declutter. I am enjoying the garden already. It's been a long time since I was able to be out in one. And I enjoyed the pumpkin patch and attending service at church yesterday – there is a lot going on in the village.'

Jane nodded. 'We like to come together as a community as much as we can. We are very close knit here,' she said, an edge to her tone.

'I can see that,' Seb said. 'The vicar and his wife have been especially kind to me.'

'Ah, Gloria is such a wonderful woman,' Jane said. 'Ever since she and the reverend moved into the village from Jamaica, we became firm friends.'

'I hope I get to know you both too,' he continued, smiling warmly at them. Nancy tried to see anything insincere in his face or hear it in his voice but she couldn't. He seemed genuine but she wasn't sure whether to trust her gut on that. 'Your bookshop seems as much the heart of the village as the church,' he added as they reached the High Street and they looked ahead to the shop. 'It's always been in your family?'

'My son, George, opened it and, after he sadly passed, I took over. Now Nancy is in charge,' Jane replied as Nancy unlocked the shop and let them all in. Jane nodded at George's picture hanging up on the wall. 'I can't believe he's been gone for seventeen years but he watches over us every day. This place was his pride and joy, along with Nancy, of course.'

Seb looked around. 'I can see why.'

Nancy turned the sign on the door to 'open' and watched Seb walk around the bookshop. 'My mother has been out of my life for even longer,' she said, waiting for his reaction.

He took a moment before turning around to face her. 'Oh?'

'She walked out on us when I was six. I haven't seen her since then.'

'I'm very sorry to hear that,' he said, looking her straight in the eye.

'Do you have family, Mr Holmes?' Nancy asked as Charlie jumped up on the window seat to watch as the shops opened up, and people walked past on their way to work and school.

'I told you – it's Seb. No, my dear. I burned bridges with my family a long time ago. *The Club* became my family. Well, I thought they were family. But once I went to prison, I realised how foolish I had been. Not one of them came to see me. I was angry for a long time, I don't mind telling you, but I've made peace with it all. No one made me do the things I did; all I can do is try to make up for it as much as I can.'

Nancy wanted to believe him, but she knew she should be careful. 'Are you in touch with anyone in the gang still?'

'No,' he said, firmly. 'I'm doing all I can to try to earn God's forgiveness for everything I did before I went to prison.'

'That is an admirable thing to do,' Jane told him.

'I don't know about that. It's the least I can do. I did some terrible things, Mrs Hunter. But I am sorry for it all.' He found a table of books. 'Oh, look at these lovely editions.'

Nancy wasn't sure what to make of this man at all. 'I wonder… how does one make amends? To earn forgiveness?' she asked him, curiously.

He looked up from the book. 'Everything I can,' he repeated.

Frustrated, Nancy tried a different tack. 'Actually, I've been reading a book about *The Club*. I found it in my mother's things,' she said. Jane, who had gone behind the till counter, stifled a gasp at Nancy mentioning that, but Nancy kept her eyes on Sebastian.

He looked at her as if he was also trying to figure her out. 'Oh, is it a good read?'

'It's interesting. The author claims that the gang corrupted a lot of high-profile people – blackmailing them into doing things that gained the gang money or influence or power.'

Seb nodded. 'The author is correct. They are still very much doing that.'

'They mention someone called Sir Basil Walker. Did you know of him?' she asked.

'I heard about the scandal he was involved with. I'm glad he was stopped. I knew of him when I was in the gang. He was part of it all for a long time.' Seb looked at them both. 'The gang are still very dangerous. It's fine to read about them but if you were thinking of doing any of your sleuthing into them, I would very much advise against it,' he said, seriously.

'How did you hear about our investigating?' Nancy asked.

'I read the papers every day in prison. You were headline news. And I know that you are both extremely…

capable. But *The Club* are different. For fifty years, they have weaved a web that has caught a lot of people. They are always out there. Watching...' He trailed off. 'What I'm saying is, don't get on their radar. That's somewhere you really don't want to be.'

'It's all so cloak and dagger,' Nancy said. 'How would I even know if I was on their radar? I don't know who's part of it, who is in charge, I don't know anything,' she said. The idea of this shadowy gang watching in the shadows was a scary thought but if her mother was involved, she could very well already be on their radar and she needed to know what she was up against.

Sebastian nodded. 'They rarely show themselves to their victims. They find out something about you, something you would do anything not to be found out and they use it and you to get what they want. They write threatening letters, showing you what they have on you, telling you what they'll do if you don't do what they want. I don't even know who is in charge, Nancy. Only a handful of people know that. We just called them *The Governor.*'

Nancy saw her gran looked as worried as she did. Somehow a nameless, faceless, villain was scarier than the murderers she had met in the past year. 'You didn't even know who they were?'

'That's how they've evaded justice all this time,' Sebastian confirmed. 'I don't mean to frighten you but just be aware that some of us have tried for years to find out who they are and stop them, and...' He looked annoyed with himself at what he had just said.

Nancy sprang forward and put a hand on his arm. 'You're trying to bring *The Club* down?'

Sebastian looked at her, then at Jane then back at Nancy, and nodded once. 'I can't just retire and let *The Club* carry on destroying lives,' he said then, his voice quiet and fierce. '*The Club* have corrupted a lot of people. They are powerful and dangerous. If anyone gets in their way, they get rid of them one way or another. Part of making amends for the part I played in it all is to try to find out who and where *The Governor* is. I can't retire in peace without trying to put an end to it all.'

Jane stepped out from behind the till and sank into the armchair they kept there. 'Oh my.'

'I hope I haven't worried you, Mrs Hunter,' he said, quickly.

'It takes more than that to scare us,' Nancy said, firmly. 'But you should be careful. If they are watching you, I mean. They might realise what you're trying to do.' Nancy felt goosebumps travel down her arm at the thought.

'You don't need to worry about me, Nancy,' he said. 'But don't make me worry about you. I know what you have done in the past, with those murder investigations, but the gang are in a different league. This isn't something either of you should get involved with. I need you to promise me that.'

'Are you doing this alone? Or is there someone else, others, trying to bring the gang down too?' Nancy asked, thinking about her mother. Seb stared at her uncertainly. Then the door behind them jingled merrily and in came a family on the way to school. 'Oh, good morning,' Nancy greeted, forcing on a smile, wishing she had been able to have longer to talk to Seb.

'Could you help us please, Mrs Hunter?' the mother called over. Jane jumped up to help and Nancy turned back to Seb but he was walking towards the door. 'Wait, Seb!' she called, rushing towards him.

Seb glanced back as he opened the bookshop door. 'Take care of yourself, Nancy.' He turned before she could respond and walked out of the door, closing it behind him. Nancy watched him go and wrapped her arms around herself, suddenly feeling cold to her very bones.

# Chapter Thirteen

After they closed the bookshop for the day, Jane and Nancy were picked up by Jonathan, who drove the three of them to the train station that stood on the edge of Dedley End.

Jonathan whistled as he drove after listening to Nancy and Jane recount their conversation with Sebastian Holmes. 'He's got balls, I'll give him that.'

'Jonathan!' Jane reprimanded him.

Jonathan grinned in the rearview mirror at Nancy, who was in the back of the car before giving Jane an apologetic look in the passenger seat. 'Sorry, Mrs H. But to be trying to bring that gang down, trying to find the leader, that's serious stuff.'

'I think he feels it's his duty as he was part of it. Like he needs to make amends for all he did when he was one of them, you know? To be forgiven,' Nancy mused.

They let that sink in. 'You know, it's interesting he told you both all that,' Jonathan said as they continued on the way to Dedley End's tiny train station. 'I mean, you just met and he said himself the gang could be watching. They are dangerous people, but he isn't concerned about revealing his plans to you?'

'I suppose because he knows all about our previous murder investigations,' Jane said. 'He knows he can trust us?'

'He also wanted to warn us not to get involved ourselves,' Nancy added. She frowned. 'There is something about that man… I almost told him what we'd found out about my mother. Instead, I tried to get him to say if he was trying to bring the gang down on his own or not. Hoping that maybe he'd admit he had help but…' She trailed off, frustrated.

'He made a hasty exit from the bookshop when you asked that,' Jane said, turning around to look at her granddaughter.

Nancy nodded. He definitely hadn't wanted to hang around after that. 'You know what I can't stop thinking about?' The other two waited. 'The fact that Seb Holmes wants to bring the gang down but has moved here. Surely it would be a lot easier to do what he wants to do in London where the gang started, where he lived and where he knows people. But no, he's moved to Dedley End.'

Jonathan met her eyes in the mirror again. 'You think that's deliberate?'

Jane looked shocked. 'You can't think there's anyone in the gang here, can you?'

'There must be a reason he's chosen to come to our village. And I don't buy it's just because it's a pretty place to retire,' Nancy said. 'Something doesn't add up about it all.'

'Well, we'd better keep our wits about us if there is something going on here,' Jane said worriedly.

'We will, Mrs H. Here we are,' Jonathan said, as he turned into the station and parked in the small car park that overlooked the platform. It was a small village station with white benches and pretty flowers hanging in baskets along the platform. The line ran in and out of London, and onwards to other villages in the Cotswolds. They left the car and walked up to the platform where there was a small ticket office run by a man affectionately known as Old Bill. He had worked for the train company pretty much his whole life and refused to even consider retirement. No one was sure quite how old he was but no one could remember a time when he hadn't run the station.

'Ah, Mrs Hunter, lovely to see you,' Old Bill said when they approached his booth. 'And young Nancy and Jonathan. Oh…' He rubbed his hands in delight. 'Are you three solving one of your mysteries?'

Nancy couldn't help but smile at his enthusiasm, despite the situation. 'Well, we're trying to.'

'I'm happy to help in any way. Reading about you solving murders has made this old man very happy. It's not often old Dedley End gets talked about, is it? Hang on…' He got up slowly off his chair and let himself out of the office. 'Better than talking through plastic. Let's go out on the platform. There isn't a train for half an hour so it'll be peaceful.' They followed him to one of the white benches where he sat down. Jane sat beside him and the other two stood in front of the bench, their backs facing the train tracks.

'We've come to ask about my mother,' Nancy began when he was seated and looking at her expectantly. 'You know she left the village when I was a child.'

Old Bill nodded and pushed his curly grey hair out of his clear eyes. 'Aye, Nancy, it was hard for your father and you both, we all knew that. A real shame. You were such a lovely family.'

'Were you working that day? The day she left?' Jonathan asked him, glancing at Nancy and Jane as if to check they were okay. Nancy gave him a little smile. It was hard to think of herself as being part of that family, as both her parents were long gone, but she knew she had to push through the pain to find out the truth.

'Of course,' he replied proudly. 'When your father came to see me afterwards, I told him that I'd seen her. She came right to my booth, as you just did, and bought a ticket to London. One way. Said she didn't know when she would be coming back and told me to have a good day. She got on the train when it arrived and that was the last I saw of her.'

'She was alone then? No one got on the train with her?' Nancy asked, putting her hands into the pockets of her tweed coat as a cool breeze wrapped around them on the platform.

Old Bill hesitated. 'No one got on the train with her.'

Nancy saw his hesitation. 'Was there someone with her though? Did someone drop her off?' She wondered if it was the man people thought her mother had been having an affair with.

'Someone dropped her off,' Old Bill confirmed.

'Not my father?' Nancy checked.

'No. They stood waiting at the gate to the platform there,' Old Bill said, pointing. 'Watched her get on the train and then they realised I could see them and waved me over and begged me not to tell anyone. And when George came to check she had got on the train okay he didn't ask about anyone else being here so I didn't say anything. No one else has asked about Samantha Hunter until you three now.'

'Hang on, George came to check she had got on the train?' Jonathan checked, frowning. Nancy understood why he was confused; the wording didn't make sense. Surely her father had come to find out where Samantha had gone?

But Old Bill nodded. 'He knew she had planned to go to London. He wanted to check she had got on the train. And actually, I think he also wanted to make sure no one had got on the train with her. I told him she was the only one who had got on at this station. It was after peak time, you know?'

Nancy stared at him. It was all making less and less sense to her. Her father's actions seemed strange. Not like a man devastated his wife had left him. Yes, he'd been upset – his old newspaper editor friend had confirmed that – but he hadn't gone to the police, hadn't tried hard to track her down. And the apparent note she left had not been seen by anyone else. And now it seemed like he had known Samantha had planned to go to London. So, maybe they'd had a row. Maybe he'd even told her to go. But that didn't feel like something her father would have done. Nancy wondered if she'd known either of her parents at all. 'Okay, but hang on, who was the person who dropped her off if it wasn't my father?'

'I suppose after all these years, and the fact is you...' Old Bill trailed off, unsure.

'I need to know what happened to her,' Nancy told him, urgently. 'I need to know why she left us. Please, Old Bill.'

'It's okay,' Jane reassured him. 'My son would understand. It's time now. Nancy needs to know.'

Old Bill nodded. 'Aye. I can see that. I always wondered if you would ask me one day. I hope I'm forgiven for this.' He looked up at the sky then back at Nancy. 'It was the vicar. Rev. Williams dropped your mother off here that day. And he told me not to tell anyone.'

Jane stuttered. 'The vicar?'

Nancy looked at Jonathan, who was as stunned as she was. 'Are you sure?'

'I'm sure,' old Bill insisted. 'He told me she'd asked him to bring her here and not to say anything to anyone. He told me it was for the best. I'm sure those were his words. And he's the vicar, of course I believed him, trusted him. I kept my word. I would have told George but, honestly, he seemed... relieved that Samantha had got on that train. I didn't understand it but I thought it wasn't my business, you know? What goes on in a marriage. Was I right to tell you?'

'Yes,' Jane said. 'Thank you. We needed to know. I don't understand it but we will. The vicar, he's a good man. A good friend to us. Right, Nancy?' After knowing the vicar and his wife for forty years since they arrived in Dedley End, Jane suddenly seemed uncertain and Nancy felt the same way. She couldn't understand why the vicar had never told them about this.

'There has to be a reasonable explanation,' Jonathan said. Even he sounded shaky though.

'I hope he'll understand me telling you,' Old Bill said. 'I didn't know you were looking for your mother, otherwise I would have gone to him and asked him. I'm not much of a church man myself but I respect the post, you know?'

'It's okay,' Nancy managed to say. 'I've only just started to try to find my mother. I can't thank you enough for telling me all this.'

'I'd better go back in, the next train is due,' Old Bill said, standing stiffly. They thanked him again and he wished them well, walking back to the ticket office.

'Now what do we do?' Jane asked Jonathan and Nancy.

'We have to go and see Rev. Williams,' Nancy said. She really didn't know how she was going to accuse a vicar of if not lying exactly, then concealing the truth and lying by omission for most of her life. However, if she had learned anything these past months since she witnessed the murder at Roth Lodge, she knew that people – even those you admired and respected the most – could hide all sorts of secrets.

## Chapter Fourteen

It was dinner time when Nancy, Jane and Jonathan walked up to the vicarage with the smell of garlic floating out through the closed front door. Next to the vicarage, the village church stood proudly in the fading light, its spire rising up into the sky.

'Hello, you three.' Gloria opened the vicarage door with a surprised smile. 'I was just saying to Lloyd that I'd made enough food to feed half the congregation. Please say you're hungry?'

'That would be lovely,' Jane said, cheerfully. 'Thank you, Gloria. Come on, you two.' She beckoned to Nancy and Jonathan who followed her inside. As they took off their shoes, Jane hissed. 'It's better to do it when he's relaxed and enjoying his wife's food.'

Jonathan sniggered and turned it into a cough when Gloria turned back to look at them. Nancy nudged him and they followed Jane and Gloria through to the dining room. Nancy had eaten at the vicarage a lot through the years but this felt so strange. She wasn't sure where to even begin the conversation with the vicar. She paused in the doorway as Rev. Williams got up when he saw them walk in to greet them warmly. He looked the same as he always did. Was acting like he always did. But Nancy wasn't sure whether to trust anything anymore.

Gloria rushed around to set extra places at the table and asked Jonathan to pour everyone a glass of wine, which he did looking as nervous as Nancy felt. Just how was she going to question the vicar's integrity?

'I'm glad I always make too much food now,' Gloria said, when they had all sat down. She carried in a large dish of shepherd's pie and added it to the bowls of vegetables and a gravy boat already on the table. 'Such a lovely surprise to have you join us.'

Nancy felt even more uncomfortable as the vicar said grace before they all tucked in and she had no idea how to even raise the subject of her mother. She picked at the delicious shepherd's pie and green vegetables for a minute before looking across the table at Jonathan in desperation.

He saw her silent plea for help and cleared his throat. 'So, there was actually a reason for our visit this evening,' he said. 'We have been trying to find out as much as we can about Nancy's mother.'

Gloria looked up with interest. 'You've been trying to find Samantha?'

Nancy nodded. 'Yes, ever since I was told that she'd been seen at a party. It made me realise I need to know what happened to her.' She looked at the vicar who still seemed to be concentrating on his food. 'Why she left, why she's never been in contact since, and why people have been lying to me about the day she left.' That made him look up.

'What do you mean?' Gloria asked.

'We've been talking to people about that day,' Jane told her. 'And things aren't making sense. I always thought my dear George had done all he could to find Samantha but that seems not to have been the case. He never went to the police. And the note he said Samantha left seems to have disappeared, or never existed, we don't know. Now we know George went to the train station not to try to follow her but to make sure she had got on the train to London. And he told his friend who was the editor of the *Cotswold Star* not to write about her disappearance. He didn't do anything to try to get her to come home. And I don't understand it.'

'What we also don't understand...' Nancy picked up, her heart pounding inside her chest at the thought of confronting such a dear family friend, looking at the vicar who was staring back at her, eyes wide, '...is why the person who dropped my mother off at the train station has never told us about it. Old Bill at the station saw them and they actually told him not to tell us or anyone. So, we never knew. We've been trying to find my mother and there's been someone we thought we knew so well who could have told us exactly what happened the day she left Dedley End. Because they helped her do it.'

Gloria turned slowly to her husband and they looked at one another. 'Oh, Nancy,' she said with a sigh.

'You mean you knew about it?' Jane asked her friend incredulously. 'You knew your husband dropped Samantha at the train station?'

Gloria nodded once.

Nancy turned to the vicar. 'Why did you keep this from us? What happened that day? Why did you take my mum there? Why did she run away?' She was aware her voice broke at the end of her sentence and she hastily took a long gulp of her wine.

Rev. Williams put his knife and fork down. 'Nancy, Jane, Jonathan, you must know that I would never want to keep anything from you or hurt you in any way. What I did was the opposite – I did it to protect you.'

'Protect me from what? Because my mum leaving with no explanation hurt a lot!' Nancy cried.

'No, not to protect you from emotional pain, but physically protect you from people that might have meant you harm. Who certainly meant your mother harm.'

Nancy looked at the vicar reeling. 'Who meant her harm?'

'Your mother came to see me the day she left. In a real panic. She said she had to leave Dedley End and she was devastated. She was crying and didn't know what to do. She had no idea how she could bear leaving you, but she knew she had to. For your own good. So you would be safe. So that all of you would be safe. And she didn't want anyone to know that George knew she had to go. So, she asked me to take her to the station. Told me George would tell everyone that she had written a note about not coping with family life. And she was going to get on a train to London while George was at work and you, Nancy, were at school. She had to make it look like she was running away, like she was a bad mother, that she didn't love her family anymore but it broke her heart to do it.' Rev. Williams sighed. 'It broke her heart. I saw it. I did as she asked and took her to the station and I told Gloria about it later. George only talked to me about it once. He stayed after church one Sunday and said that he had managed to get word that she was okay and they were both so grateful she'd been able to get away safely. And he had begged me, as she had done, not to tell anyone about it.'

'Did you ask them who my mother was running away from?' Nancy asked, although things were beginning to fit together in her mind.

'I did but both of them said it would only put me in danger to tell me any more than they had. I believed them though when they said this was to protect you. Samantha, before she got out of my car and got on to the train, she turned to me and made me swear to God and on my life that I would look out for you, Nancy, and if anyone came to the village asking about her, to tell you what had happened and encourage you to leave. That's never happened but the past few months, I've been nervous – what with you two investigating murders and all sorts – but nothing about your mother was ever said. Until today. So, I'm telling you everything she told me. I promised, Nancy, Jane. I swore to both Samantha and George… I couldn't break that but now that you know, I hope you can make sense of it. Because for years, I haven't been able to.'

'She left me because she was trying to protect me?'

Gloria nodded. 'She loved you, Nancy. There was no pretending about that.'

'But why did she leave?' Jane asked, her eyes full of tears. 'Why didn't they come to me? Tell me what was going on.'

'It was all done to protect you both,' the vicar replied. 'I have always believed that.'

Nancy knew he was telling the truth but it was hard to believe it herself after feeling for years like her mother ran away because she didn't love her.

'I'm sorry I've kept this from you both for so long,' the vicar said to Jane and Nancy. 'I've wrestled with it many times, but I promised George and Samantha.'

'What about when my father died?' Nancy asked. 'Did my mother know and why did she decide to keep away even then?'

'I promise I haven't heard from her all these years,' the vicar replied. 'But as it was nothing to do with Samantha leaving, I didn't think your poor father's passing changed anything. I don't know if I was right or wrong not to tell you then.' He looked anguished. Nancy knew he really did care about her and Jane, and she understood why he had stuck to his promise even if it was hard to hear about now.

Nancy looked at Jane and Jonathan. 'So, my mother was scared. She ran away from Dedley End from someone. To protect us from them.' Jonathan gave a small nod and Jane looked worried. Nancy knew they were thinking as she was. This had to be something to do with *The Club*. Who else would Samantha have feared like that? After finding the memoir about them in her belongings with a list of people she believed were involved with the gang, and the way she appeared to have targeted Sir Basil Walker at that party, it was no great stretch to think Samantha might have fled Dedley End because of *The Club*. Nancy knew she might still be on the run from them even now.

There was some relief mixed in with the confusion and fear – Nancy now knew that her mother had left believing she was protecting Nancy, not that she didn't love her daughter. Nancy still didn't fully understand why, or why she had never returned, but it helped a little bit what the vicar had told her. She just wished she knew where her mother was so she could find out the rest of her story.

## Chapter Fifteen

It was pouring with rain the following morning but Nancy hadn't been able to sleep so she got up and braved the elements to take Charlie for a walk before work. With the hood of her coat up, and her boots on, Nancy, with Charlie trotting eagerly ahead, walked out of the cottage. The morning light remained dim but they could find their way around their village even if they were blindfolded, so it didn't bother them.

Nancy couldn't stop thinking about all she had found out yesterday. After they had left the vicarage, Nancy hadn't really wanted to talk about it anymore. Jonathan had gone home and she and her grandmother had gone to bed, but she had tossed and turned all night. She replayed the day her mother left over and over in her mind but couldn't put the pieces of it all together. She knew now that her mother had left for reasons other than not wanting to be with her daughter and it was something she needed to process after wondering for most of her life whether her mother had even loved her.

Now it was possible Samantha had left *because* she loved her. Even if that did help a little bit, Nancy still longed to talk to her mother – to hear that from her own lips. And even though they had met murderers – and helped catch them – Nancy admitted she was scared to know her mother had lived in such fear that she had left her husband

and child. She didn't think it was a big leap to link her mother to *The Club* now and not only did one of their supposedly former members live in the same village, he had warned Nancy off investigating them. But how could she leave it alone when the trail to find her mother was leading her right to their door?

Nancy didn't plan it but she found her feet were moving in the direction of Rose Cottage. When Charlie realised, he sped up no doubt happily wondering what treat might await him there. She knew the smart thing to do would be to stay away from Sebastian Holmes and yet she couldn't shake the feeling that he was on her side. Jonathan and her grandmother would be furious with her if they knew she was talking to him alone but although they supported her and understood to a point, this was about *her* mother. It felt like it was her quest and there was someone just around the corner that knew more than he was letting on. She was certain of it.

Nancy, lost in thought, was startled when Seb himself opened his gate and stepped out in front of them. 'Oh.'

'Nancy! And Charlie!' Seb's eyes lit up. 'Out for an early walk?'

'Uh, yes, yes we are,' she said, hanging back as Charlie wagged his tail eagerly. 'We usually go to the village green before the bookshop. How about you?'

'I need a few bits of food in so I'm walking to the High Street. Shall we walk together?'

Nancy hoped that she wasn't doing something stupid by agreeing to that. They turned and set off towards the village together. The rain had turned to drizzle so she pushed her hood down, needing as much air in her lungs as possible. She hesitated about how to ask Sebastian if he did know her mother, so she decided to try to lead him there indirectly. 'Can I ask you something?' Seb indicted for her to go ahead. 'Do you think you really can find out who's running your former gang? I've been trying to find someone but I feel like I'm at a dead end. I'm wondering if I ever will. That maybe if you try hard enough, some people can still make sure they are never found.'

'I suppose it depends on what the reason is. I know *The Governor* is hiding because there are a lot of people out there who would want them dead, people they have hurt or used or blackmailed. Why do you think the person you're looking for is hiding where they are?' he asked, looking across at her. She watched him carefully. His eyes were kind and his expression was curious. She wondered if he'd guessed who she was looking for or not.

'I thought it was because they didn't like their life but now I think it was to protect the people they loved.'

They reached the village green then so Nancy let Charlie off his lead and the beagle tore off across the grass joyfully. 'If they were trying to protect you, don't you risk them and yourself if you keep looking for them?' Seb suggested then. 'Maybe you should trust that if it was safe to do, they would find you.'

Nancy turned sharply. 'That's hard when I haven't heard from them for most of my life.'

Seb pulled out a cigarette and used his hot-pink book of matches to light it as he had done when they'd been on the green for the pumpkin patch. 'I'm just thinking if they left Dedley End to protect you then coming back here would make all those years pointless, wouldn't it?'

'I suppose so, if that threat still exists. I keep thinking about who they might have been running away from. It could be something like your former gang?' she asked, slyly glancing at him to see if his face gave anything away.

'Then you definitely should leave well alone, Nancy,' he replied calmly.

Nancy was frustrated. They were talking in riddles. 'If they are something to fear that much, shouldn't you also stay away from them?' she demanded.

'Yes,' he agreed. 'But I have spent thirty years in prison helplessly watching them from behind bars continuing to do whatever the hell they want to and, now I'm free, I can't do that anymore.'

Nancy watched Charlie bark at a pigeon, wistfully thinking she could be that carefree. She sighed – she wasn't getting anywhere with Seb but then she had a thought. A frightening one. 'Seb, if you've been planning in prison to go after the gang, to try to find their leader and bring them down, why did you come to Dedley End to do it? Do you think…' She hardly dared say the words. 'That the gang are here?'

Seb looked at her. He took a long time to respond to her as if he was weighing up what to tell her very carefully. Nancy waited, her whole body tense, barely breathing in case she missed his reply. 'I don't know,' he said, finally. 'Some things don't make sense… some things point to London and others point… here.'

'Oh my God,' she said, shakily. Then she had another thought. 'You said you promised someone you'd come here. Was it because they thought the gang was here? Was it to protect us?' She said the word 'us' but she was thinking the word 'me'.

'Nancy, you are brighter than I even knew you would be.' Seb sighed then. 'I'm here to do some digging, but also to look out for you all.' He gave her a significant look. She opened her mouth, but he continued to talk. 'You might even know this a little bit after your own

97

murder investigations, but sometimes when you become fixated on justice and revenge, it's very hard to think about anything else. They can become an obsession. Your heart is in the right place but it ends up changing you. If you're prepared to do whatever it takes to bring someone down, you can't live a normal life. It becomes your life.' He touched her shoulder. 'The same can be said for this quest of yours, Nancy. Don't let it become your life. Don't let it ruin your life. Your mother wouldn't want that, Nancy. That I do know. I have to go. I'll see you soon.' He tipped his hat and strode off back towards the High Street.

Nancy exhaled and turned to watch Charlie sniffing a flower. She thought about what Seb had said. Her mother was fixated on something. On her quest. So, they were right. Samantha was on the trail of *The Club*, trying to bring them down. Ticking off the people that were helping them, such as Sir Basil Walker, and perhaps trying to get close to the gang and finally discover their leader. The mysterious *Governor*. And it had consumed her for all the years she had been gone from Nancy's life. And she hadn't returned because her quest was still on-going. The gang were still out there. Should Nancy leave her mother to it then? But what if Nancy was able to help her, what if they could end it together?

Then Nancy spun around. She looked but she couldn't see Seb anywhere. She let out a frustrated noise. 'Charlie, come on, we need to find him,' she called to her dog, her pulse racing. Because she had just realised something.

She hadn't told Seb she was trying to find her mother. But he had mentioned her first. He had known she was looking for her mother. So, he must know Samantha Hunter. What Nancy still didn't know though was how her mother had been caught up with the gang in the first place or how she knew Seb Holmes.

Nancy needed Seb to tell her everything now. She clipped the lead on Charlie and hurried in the direction he had gone.

–

Nancy walked into the bookshop with a sigh. 'I can't find Seb Holmes anywhere,' she declared to Penelope and her grandmother who had just opened up, and Jonathan who had brought hot drinks for them all. She had phoned them as she ran around the village and they'd told her to meet them at the shop. 'I tried all the shops, I went to his cottage but he wasn't there so I left Charlie at home and came here. I need to find him!'

'Tell us exactly what he said, love,' Jane said, trying to calm her down. 'You shouldn't have spoken to him on your own.'

'I know but I had to find out if he knew anything about my mother. And he does! Rev. Williams told us she ran from Dedley End because she was scared so with everything we've found out, and Seb knowing her, it must have been *The Club* she was running from,' Nancy said, shaking her head.

'Hang on, what's the vicar got to do with all this?' Pen asked, looking confused.

Jonathan filled her in on what Rev. Williams had told them about the day Samantha left the village as Nancy took her cup of tea and sank into the bookshop armchair. Her head was pounding. After not sleeping and her conversation with Seb then running around trying to find him, she felt rotten.

'Wow, Samantha was on the run. All this time,' Pen said, taking it in. 'But why do you think it's because of that gang?'

Nancy took another sip of tea and was fortified enough to answer her friend. She told Pen everything they had found out so far about her mother. 'So, I asked Seb about it all. I told him I was looking for someone but didn't say who. He admitted he was here because he thought there was a link to his former gang here and to keep an eye on us. And then he mentioned my mother! Said she was consumed by revenge and I shouldn't let the same thing happen to me. I didn't tell him I was looking for my mother so he must know her. If they are both trying to bring *The Club* down then maybe they are doing it together. Maybe she asked him to come here.'

'It's not a giant stretch at this point,' Jonathan said. 'We believe your mother grew up in London, as did Seb, and when she left here, she fled there. Perhaps she knew him in the past or went to see him in prison as she knew he was in the gang. To see if he had any information maybe?'

Nancy nodded slowly. 'It could have happened. I still don't understand why the gang would have been after my mother or why she's now trying to bring them down. She left Dedley End saying she needed to protect my father and me, but how did she end up having to do that?' The questions seemed to just get bigger.

'I can't believe Samantha had anything to do with that gang,' Jane said. 'It's so strange. She was so... normal. I mean, she worked in the pub then with George in the shop – what could she have done to get on the gang's radar?'

'Although we know better than anyone that no one really is normal,' Jonathan said. 'If Seb is working with

Samantha, he can get in touch with her, tell her Nancy is looking for her, he can tell us where she is.'

'Only if he wants to. And he keeps warning me to stay out of it all,' Nancy said. 'I'm not sure he will tell us what we want to know. Maybe my mother has told him not to.'

'Oh, Nancy,' Pen said with sympathy. 'But if she has told him that, it's not because she doesn't want to see you, she's trying to protect you.'

Nancy smiled at her friend although she wondered if both things could be true. Her mother did want to protect her but also had no interest in seeing her again. 'Seb could be telling her right now that I'm looking for her, that I know they are linked. It might make her go further underground. I shouldn't have said anything to him.'

'No, look, we've found out so much more because you did,' Jonathan reassured her. 'We were just guessing but now we know that somehow this all ties into *The Club*. We need to make Seb tell us everything now.'

'Let's try ringing the cottage. He could be in there hiding from you,' Jonathan said. 'I'll find it online.'

When Jonathan had found the number through the online phone book, Nancy went into the office to ring Rose Cottage and her heart soared when Seb answered the phone. 'Seb, it's Nancy, I've been trying to find you. I have to talk to you!'

'Nancy,' he said, his voice low and urgent. 'I've been up the hill to look at Roth Lodge and a huge car pulled up. He's back, Nancy. Marcus Roth is back.'

She was momentarily distracted. 'He is? Oh, God... wait, why were you looking at Roth Lodge?'

'I can't tell you any more, I'm sorry,' he said.

'No, you can't just casually drop my mother into our conversation like that! I didn't tell you I was looking for my mother.'

There was a silence. 'I'm sure you did.'

'Don't treat me like an idiot. I didn't. But you knew I was looking for her. And you're here for a reason. You can't leave me in the dark. Do you know my mother? Do you know where she is? Are you working together to bring down—'

'Okay, okay, yes, I know your mother. Yes, I am here in Dedley End for a reason. And I am trying to find *The Governor*. I think I might have found them.'

'You have?' Nancy felt a shiver run down her spine.

'I think you do need to know what we've found out. But I want to protect you, Nancy. Your mother does too.'

'The best way to protect me is to give me all the information so I don't need to go looking for myself,' she told him.

There was a short silence. 'I knew you would need to know it all.'

'I can't stop, Seb. If you don't tell me, I'll keep on digging, you know I will.'

Seb sighed. 'You really are your mother's daughter. Okay, Nancy. But we can't talk about it over the phone. Come to my cottage this evening. You can bring your grandmother and your boyfriend but don't tell anyone else. We have to be really careful who we trust. Dedley End isn't safe. Come straight from the bookshop. Six p.m. I'll see you tonight.' And then before Nancy could say anything else, Seb hung up.

## Chapter Sixteen

Nancy had never been more relieved than she was when she turned the bookshop signed to 'closed' and shut the door. 'That was the longest day,' she said to Penelope and her grandmother. They hadn't been able to concentrate on anything in the shop with thoughts of meeting Seb that evening filling their minds. Nancy had told Jane, Pen and Jonathan everything Seb had said although she had left out the part where he had assumed Jonathan was her boyfriend. No one needed to know that. Jonathan had had to go to the newspaper office to work, so he had left the other three to man the bookshop and speculate about what Seb might be about to tell them.

'I wish I could be there with you tonight,' Penelope said. 'I need to go and pick up Kitty from after-school club but ring me when you're home tonight, and tell me everything!' she pleaded with them as she put on her coat and picked up her handbag.

Nancy promised she would. 'I don't know quite how to feel knowing I might finally be getting some answers about my mother. From a former gang member.'

'Maybe there's a reason you've been drawn to crime for all these years,' Pen suggested. 'Just look after yourselves, won't you?' she checked.

'We'll be fine,' Jane said. 'Jonathan will be there.'

'I think Nancy can handle herself better than he can,' Pen said making them laugh a little bit despite their jitters. 'Okay, don't forget to ring me, otherwise I will worry all night.' She left the shop and Nancy turned to her grandmother.

'We'd better start walking over, it's getting close to six. Jonathan said he'd drive and meet us there.' She slipped on her tweed coat. 'You don't think we should call DCI Brown, do you?' He had made Nancy promise to go to him if she ever needed his help and not run off investigating alone. But this wasn't a murder case, this was about her mother's disappearance.

'Seb told you not to say anything to anyone, didn't he? That we needed to be careful who we trust.'

'He did. And we both feel like we can trust Seb,' Nancy said. 'I felt that way when we met him and the fact that he seems to be here to help us, that he knows my mother, we will do as he says but if we need to, we get DCI Brown's help, yes?'

'I agree, love,' Jane said. 'Seb has not done anything to make us doubt him. He wants the same thing we do – to stop *The Club*. But we should keep our wits about us.' Nancy agreed – they needed to be careful.

They locked up and left the bookshop, stepping out into the High Street. The sun had already set as they walked to Rose Cottage. Nancy and Jane normally would have paused to talk to regular customers and friends who they passed, but tonight they were both uneasy out and about in the village. Seb had told them Dedley End wasn't safe and they needed to find out what he knew. They walked quickly to avoid getting stopped by anyone. Nancy looked around them as they walked in case anyone was watching them and Jane kept glancing behind to ensure no one was following. They were both relieved the walk to Seb's cottage was a short one.

'I wish I knew what Seb was going to tell us,' Nancy said in a low voice once they were on a quiet road. Lampposts guided their path dimly. Above, the sky was murky and dark, no sign of the stars or moon this evening. The village felt eerily calm. Nancy would be relieved when they were safely inside Seb's cottage. 'You don't think Mum did anything bad, do you?' Nancy asked her grandmother nervously. 'And that's why she had to leave the village?'

'If she did then we'll deal with it,' Jane said. 'Try not to worry, love.'

Nancy saw the tip of Roth Lodge as they turned into Seb's road. She didn't want to tell Jane until later about Seb saying Marcus Roth was back in the village. They had enough on their plates right now. But it was another worry to add to the ever-growing list. She spotted Jonathan's car then. He'd parked at the end of the road and jumped out of the car when he saw them. Nancy was glad he was there to support them. If she and Gran were too shocked by what Seb might have to tell them, hopefully he would step in to ask the questions they needed to.

'Are you both okay?' Jonathan asked as he walked up them. 'I thought I'd park away from Seb's house in case anyone is watching,' he said, quietly.

'Good idea,' Nancy said. 'I'll feel a lot better once we get there.' They walked down the road together and up to Seb's gate and looked at the cottage.

Nancy hesitated. 'I'm about to find out what I've always wanted to know about my mother.'

'It's bound to feel scary but it'll be okay,' her gran said.

'Whatever Seb tells us, we'll work it out,' Jonathan promised her. He looked behind them. 'Let's just get in there.'

Nancy nodded. Taking a breath, she pushed on the gate and led the way up to Seb's front door. She rang the doorbell and they waited. She peered through the frosted glass. 'I can't see many lights on.'

'It's dead-on six, like he said,' Jonathan said when Seb didn't answer. He reached out to knock but the cottage remained sealed shut and silent.

'Shall we go around the back?' Jane asked. 'Oh. There's Mrs Smith.' She waved to the one of their neighbours who was walking past carrying a shopping bag.

'Are you all looking for Mr Holmes?' Mrs Smith called out. She lived in the cottage opposite his. 'I passed him on my way home. He was walking to the church. Said the vicar needed to see him in there urgently.'

'When was that?' Nancy asked her.

'Oh, only about half an hour ago, I think.' They thanked her and she went into her cottage.

'Why didn't he tell us if he'd gone to the church?' Jonathan asked.

'If he's helping the vicar then maybe we just wait and he'll be along soon,' Jane said.

Nancy bit her lip as she looked at the closed cottage door. This had been an important meeting. She felt even more uneasy than she had before. 'This doesn't feel right. I think we should go to the church and find out what's going on.' She was grateful that even if Jane and Jonathan thought she was overreacting, they still agreed.

They hurried back to where Jonathan had parked and he drove them to the village church.

Jonathan pulled up outside the vicarage and they saw Gloria and the vicar in their front garden talking to Mr Peabody. 'The vicar is out here but where is Seb?' he asked as he parked the car.

'Did we miss him?' Jane asked. 'Maybe he's already walking back home. It's dark, we may have not seen him.'

'Let's ask the vicar,' Nancy said.

They all jumped out of the car and joined the vicar, his wife and Mr Peabody at the vicarage gate.

'What are you doing here?' Mr Peabody asked, looking surprised to see them.

'Have you seen Seb Holmes?' Nancy ignored his question to ask her own as they reached the other three. 'Was he just here?'

'No, not today,' Gloria said. 'Why?'

'His neighbour said he came to the church – he told her you had asked to see him urgently,' Nancy said to Rev. Williams.

The vicar shook his head. 'No, I haven't spoken to him since Sunday service. The church is locked for the day,' he said, gesturing to it.

'Perhaps he's at the pub. Why not check there?' Mr Peabody suggested.

Nancy hesitated. She didn't understand why Seb wasn't at his cottage. Or the fact the vicar hadn't seen him today. She had a bad feeling about all of it. 'Can we please just check the church first? It would put my mind at rest just to make sure Seb isn't in there.'

'How could he have got in a locked church?' the vicar asked her. He saw Nancy's worried face then nodded. 'But, of course, Nancy, if you want us to check then we can.'

'Perhaps Holmes is a magician as well as a criminal,' Mr Peabody said with a chuckle.

'Please,' Nancy repeated urgently.

The vicar pulled out his keys. 'If you think we should. Come on.'

'We'll all go,' Mr Peabody suggested.

Nancy started to walk towards the church, the others following her, when she saw a car pull up.

'What's going on?' Richard Bank got out with Will Roth. They both started to walk over to them.

'What are you doing here?' Jonathan asked them suspiciously.

'We were coming to see you,' Will said. 'We need to talk to you.'

'Not now,' Nancy said, impatiently, taking off again towards the church.

'Nancy thinks Seb Holmes is in the church but it's locked,' Mr Peabody said, in confusion, as they all trailed after Nancy.

'How could he be in a locked church?' Richard asked.

'Something is wrong,' Nancy insisted.

'Let's just check to make sure,' Jonathan said.

'It can't do any harm,' Jane added. Nancy was glad of their support when the others clearly thought it was a crazy idea.

'Right-oh,' Rev. Williams said walking up to the locked church door with them all behind him, Nancy right by his shoulder, her unease building with every second that passed.

A noise broke through the nervous silence. It was muddled by the church door but it was like a faint crack of thunder. Then there was a second crack. They all stopped stunned.

'That sounded like…' Jonathan began.

'Gunshots!' Nancy cried.

'Oh my goodness,' Gloria said.

'It can't be,' Mr Peabody said in shock.

'Quick, open the door,' Jonathan urged the vicar but Rev. Williams' hands trembled as he tried to get the key in the lock. Jonathan took it from him and opened the church. He walked in followed by Nancy, her grandmother, the vicar and Gloria, Mr Peabody, Richard and Will.

They all stopped suddenly again just inside the church door and looked on in horror as they saw a body in the aisle lying face down on the hard floor, blood seeping out from their back.

# Chapter Seventeen

'Oh no!' Nancy cried, her voice echoing in the silent church when she realised that the body lying in front of them down the aisle was Sebastian Holmes. Her stomach dropped like she had gone over a hill on a roller coaster. Seb groaned. He wasn't dead! Nancy's legs felt like lead but she forced them to move forward.

'Someone call an ambulance!' Jane cried, the first to speak as Nancy went to Seb.

'And the police,' Jonathan added.

'I'll do it,' Will Roth replied, pulling out his phone.

'Who could have done this?' Gloria said, clutching her husband, who looked as shocked as she did.

'And, where are they?' Nancy said, looking around wildly, wondering where the shooter was.

'Nancy, he's still alive,' Mr Peabody called out urgently pointing towards Seb. She turned back and crouched down beside Seb, who was groaning face down on the cold stone floor. Blood pooled out towards the pew and Nancy tried not to look at it. 'We're getting help,' she said to him. He groaned again and turned his head towards her. She saw the agony on his face. 'Don't try to move. Who did this, Seb?' she leaned in closer to ask him.

Seb gave a slight shake of his head. Nancy supposed that as he'd been shot in the back, he didn't even know who had tried to kill him. She looked at his pale skin and the blood on his shirt – she wasn't sure if he was going to make it.

'The police and ambulance are on the way,' Will called out to them then.

'I don't understand who could have done this. The church was locked. Where are they?' Jane said, frantically.

'Did they get past us somehow? Shall I look outside?' Jonathan asked.

'Maybe we should wait for the police,' Mr Peabody suggested, sounding worried.

'Can't hurt to check,' Jonathan told him.

'I'll go with you,' Richard said.

Nancy turned to see Jonathan hesitate like he was about to protest but, given the gravity of the situation, he just nodded and Nancy's ex-boyfriend and best friend walked out of the church together. The others stayed behind Nancy and Seb in the aisle.

Seb touched Nancy's arm drawing her attention back to him. He nodded once with his head towards the pocket of his jeans, and then widened his eyes. He did the movement twice before Nancy realised he wanted her to look in there. She glanced at the others behind her. Will was talking to Mr Peabody who was telling him what he would do if he was still a police officer; Gloria was crying as the vicar held her; her grandmother was watching the church door. Nancy quickly reached into Seb's pocket. In there were his hot-pink book of matches. She pulled them out not understanding why he would want them. Surely, he didn't want to smoke right now? She held them out but he nodded at her. She held them by her pocket and he smiled weakly. She pocketed them, with no idea why he wanted her to have his matches so badly.

'We couldn't see anyone,' Jonathan said, slightly breath-less as he and Richard came back through the open church door behind them. 'There's no one else here.'

'No sign of a gun either,' Richard added, lifting his arms up in bafflement.

'What if they're still here?' Nancy asked, suddenly wondering if the shooter could be with them in the church. Gloria gasped in horror. The vicar held her close.

'You'd better check,' Mr Peabody said, pointing towards the altar.

'Stay here,' Jonathan said to Gloria, the vicar, Mr Peabody, Will and Jane who were still at the end of the aisle, a couple of metres away from Nancy and Seb close to the church door. He and Richard went by Nancy and Seb and walked towards the altar, turning to where the choir sat on a Sunday.

Nancy looked back at Seb and saw that his eyes had closed. 'Seb? Seb?' She reached for him but his chest heaved with one last ragged breath and then he fell silent, and went completely still. Goosebumps travelled down the whole of her body. Nancy reached out to take his wrist to check his pulse even though she knew the worst had happened. 'He's dead,' she said, her voice echoing around the church.

'Oh no!' Jane rushed towards them, followed by Will, the vicar and Gloria with Mr Peabody behind them. Nancy sat back on her heels and shook her head.

'I can't believe it,' Nancy said as they all looked down at the now lifeless body in front of them. The vicar began to say a prayer as Nancy stood up slowly, shocked that Seb had been gunned down in their church. Who could have done such a wicked thing?

'I heard the call on the radio,' a voice broke through, the sound of footsteps following. They turned around from Seb's body to see DC Pang hurrying up the aisle towards them. 'What's happened? Is everyone okay?'

'Sebastian Holmes has been shot,' Rev. Williams told him, gravely.

'Shot?' DC Pang looked past them at Seb on the floor. 'No one said that,' he said, horrified.

'I said he'd been attacked,' Will said. 'I'm sorry, I didn't think to say...' He trailed off. 'He's dead,' he added, dropping his head down.

'Did you see who did it? Did you find a gun? Step aside,' Pang barked to Mr Peabody, putting a hand on his shoulder. The older man moved to let the officer through.

Mr Peabody shook his head. 'The door was locked. We heard two gunshots and we rushed in but we were too late. Whoever did it must have gone.'

'Is anyone else hurt?'

'No, no,' the vicar told him as Pang walked up to the body. 'We're just shocked.'

They parted to let him through. He crouched down next to the body and checked Seb's pulse. He nodded. 'He's dead.'

'There's no one here,' Jonathan said as he and Richard came back from looking around the altar. 'Oh no,' he said, realising Seb had gone.

'We couldn't find the... killer,' Richard added. 'It's like they vanished into thin air.'

'A locked-room mystery,' Nancy said, quietly.

Her grandmother looked at her. 'What do we do?' she asked in a low voice.

DC Pang narrowed his eyes. 'You let the police deal with this,' he said coldly as he stood up again. He pulled out his radio but footsteps behind them made everyone look at the door again. 'I was just calling in,' he said as DCI Brown marched into the church then, accompanied by five uniformed officers.

Brown looked over. 'You're here already, Pang?'

'I was in the village just doing a walkaround before I drove back to the station to end my shift, when I heard the dispatch saying Holmes had been attacked, so I ran straight here. I was too late though. He's dead, Sir.' He gestured to Seb's still body on the floor. 'Sebastian Holmes has been shot.'

'God. Oh, sorry,' DCI Brown said, throwing the vicar an apologetic look. 'Do we need to call for armed back-up?' he barked, holding out an arm to stop any more officers from entering the church.

'Whoever did it appears to be long gone and there is no sign of the gun,' Pang replied.

'We need to search everywhere. Why are you all just standing there?' he asked his officers and began issuing directions to them all. Pang gestured to Nancy and the others to move away from the body to let the police through.

'We're safe,' Gloria said with relief to her husband.

Nancy looked back at Seb's lifeless body and thought Gloria had never been more wrong.

–

It felt like the vicarage had turned into a mobile police station. Everyone who had been in the church when Seb was found was interviewed by DCI Brown and DC Pang, while the church was filled with officers examining the crime scene and collecting evidence.

'Do you have any idea why Mr Holmes was in the church tonight?' DCI Brown asked Nancy as they sat in the vicarage living room. Gloria was making cups of tea for everyone with Jane, both glad of something to do, while the others were spoken to in turn alone by the police officers. They would need to make official statements at the station but DCI Brown wanted to find out all he could while it was fresh in their minds, he said. Like everyone else, he admitted he was baffled as to how the murder had been committed inside a locked church with no one seeing the murderer leave or anyone finding the murder weapon.

There was a knock and the door opened. 'Mr Peabody is due to take some medication – can he go home?' an officer asked.

'He can come in tomorrow to make his official statement. Pang, you'd better take him home, he was looking a bit peaky after we spoke to him,' DCI Brown said.

'But shouldn't I…?' Pang looked at Nancy significantly.

'We're almost done here anyway. Off you go,' the inspector told him, firmly. DC Pang got up and left Nancy and him alone.

'Quickly,' DCI Brown said, suddenly. 'Tell me anything you haven't told us,' he ordered her.

Nancy didn't miss a beat. 'Seb Holmes asked to meet us at his cottage to talk to us. When we got there, a neighbour said he'd been asked by the vicar to go to the church. I felt… uneasy. Why had he rushed off there instead of seeing us? So, we came here to find him and, well, you know the rest.'

'Why did he want to speak to you at his cottage?'

She leaned forward and lowered her voice. 'He knows my mother. He has been looking into his former gang, *The Club*, trying to stop them. And he thought he might have found their leader. *The Governor*. He was going to tell me everything.'

DCI Brown raised an eyebrow. 'How would Sebastian Holmes know your mother?'

'I don't know. He let it slip that he knew her, and then I made him promise to tell me everything tonight. I found some things in her belongings about *The Club* and Rev. Williams told me my mother left the village all those years ago because she was scared and wanted to protect my family. That's made me wonder if she was running from Seb's former gang. But Seb was going to tell me how it was all linked and now he's gone… what if I never find out?' Nancy shook her head. She was frustrated, upset and felt guilty too because it felt like this was her fault. 'What if me trying to find my mother has led to Seb getting killed?'

'I have no idea how your mother could be caught up in all this but we'll find out the truth.' He leaned forward. 'And we need to find Seb's killer. We are looking for evidence, but there isn't a lot to find. With no murder weapon, we have nothing to go on. Do you have any idea who did this?'

'Not yet, no,' Nancy said. 'But we need to find out how they got out of the church. Locked-room mysteries are all about the how. Once you work out how then you'll find out who did it. We'll help in any way we can,' Nancy promised him.

'You know I can't condone that. Officially.' DCI Brown stood up. 'I'll look into your mother again and see if I can find anything that explains her connection to Holmes or *The Club*.'

Nancy stood up too. 'Be careful. Seb said I shouldn't trust anyone. The gang have corrupted a lot of influential people,' she said, thinking about Sir Basil Walker and the others on Samantha's list in the memoir about *The Club*. People in high places. People they needed to be careful about. 'And there was a reason Seb was here in Dedley End and a reason he's been killed here.'

## Chapter Eighteen

Will Roth was waiting outside the vicarage when Nancy, Jane and Jonathan were finally allowed to leave by the police. It was late now, and Dedley End was calm and quiet, quite at odds with what had happened earlier. Nancy shivered when she looked at the church beside them. She didn't think she'd ever forget seeing the life fade out of Seb like she had. She would never get used to seeing dead bodies but they seemed to be following her around. She was worried that this wouldn't be the last one she saw either.

'Can I talk to you?' Will asked. He saw her face fall. 'Just quickly,' Will added, glancing back at his car. Nancy saw Richard was already inside it waiting for him. 'The reason we came to find you earlier was I wanted to tell you that my grandfather has come to stay for a bit and I didn't want you to be surprised if you saw him or someone else told you. I thought I should warn you first.'

'Actually, Seb already did,' Nancy said. She felt weary and didn't want to think about the Roth family on top of everything else. 'I don't know what to say. You know how we feel about him.'

'He won't be here for long,' Will said. 'I'm sorry. And if I can help any more with your mother, just let me know.'

'Does Marcus know Nancy is looking for her mother?' Jonathan asked.

Will looked surprised but nodded. 'Yes, I told him. He knows we went to see Hugh Windsor – they are old friends, after all. Right, then. I'll see you.' He gave a weak wave before turning and striding off towards his car. Nancy saw Richard watching them and she couldn't believe that after having to put up with them both being in her village, now Marcus Roth was back – the man who had hidden what really happened to her father for years.

'Why did you ask that?' Jane said to Jonathan when it was just the three of them again.

'I don't trust them,' Jonathan said, simply. 'We didn't want everyone knowing we're looking for Nancy's mother in case she found out and ran or hid from us even more. We didn't think about the alternative – that someone else might find out, someone who Samantha might have been running and hiding from all along.'

Nancy nodded. As usual, Jonathan was on the same wavelength as her. '*The Governor?* Seb thought he had found them. There is no way it's a coincidence that Seb died the same night he was going to tell us everything he knew.'

'But how would anyone have known Seb was going to talk to us?' Jane asked. 'We didn't tell anyone and I can't believe Seb would. I mean, he used to be part of *The Club*. Why would he let something slip like that?'

'He wouldn't,' Nancy agreed. 'It doesn't make sense.'

'But you still think he was killed to stop him speaking to us?' Jonathan asked.

She looked at the police officers outside the church watching them. 'Let's not talk about this here. Let's go home.'

The other two agreed and Jonathan drove them back to the cottage where they went into the kitchen. Nancy let Charlie outside, then fed him while Jane heated up leftover lasagne for them and Jonathan mixed them all a gin and tonic. Nancy made a quick salad and cut up some crusty bread. Then they sat down at the kitchen table. When Charlie had finished eating, the beagle came to sit by Nancy. She was grateful for his comforting presence.

'I can't believe we've had another murder in our village. It's starting to feel more than bad luck, I have to say,' Jane broke the silence after she took a long gulp of her drink and ate a mouthful of lasagne. 'Poor Gloria and Lloyd, they looked so shaken by it all. I can't believe someone killed Seb in a church!'

'They certainly can't be worried about what God thinks of them,' Jonathan said, dryly.

'And Seb had found God and was trying so hard to gain forgiveness too.' Jane shook her head. She looked at her granddaughter. 'Are you all right, love?'

'No,' Nancy admitted. 'I can't help but feel this is my fault for begging Seb to tell me about my mother and what he'd found out about his former gang.' She sighed. 'I told DCI Brown we were meant to meet him. He's going to look for any connection between Seb and my mother. So maybe he can help us. There's something I need to tell you though. Well, show you.' Nancy pulled out the book of matches that she had retrieved from Seb's pocket. 'Seb wanted me to have these. He made that very clear. But why? I know I shouldn't have taken what might be evidence but it was his dying wish.' She laid the hot-pink book on the table and opened it, expecting something inside. But there were only matches. 'He always used it to light his cigarettes. Why would he want me to have it?'

'Is there anything written on it?' Jane asked.

Nancy checked. 'It's just a normal book of matches,' she said, confused.

'Not quite,' Jonathan replied. 'It's very distinctive. Not to be stereotypical but I wouldn't have expected Seb to reach for bright-pink matches unless there was a particular reason.'

'Like what?' Nancy asked him. She frowned. 'I feel like when I first saw them in his hand, I did feel a slight flicker of recognition. But now nothing.'

'Let's do a quick Google.' Jonathan had a quick look online for 'hot pink' and 'bright pink' matchbooks but, apart from a couple of ones for sale online that weren't the same as the one on the table, nothing came up.

Nancy sighed. 'I don't think, unless we find something out about them, that it matters I took them from the crime scene, does it?'

'Seb wanted you to have them. It might just be for sentimental reasons,' Jonathan said.

'True. Maybe I'll tell DCI Brown when I next see him about them.'

'So, what do we do now?' Jane asked her grand-daughter.

'I said to DCI Brown that with a locked-room mystery, you need to find out how the murder was committed and then you'll find out who did it. I think we need to focus on that,' Nancy said. 'The church was locked, that much we know. I assume we agree that anyone could have copied the vicar's keys to use?'

Jonathan nodded. 'Easily done. He's always leaving them around. I found them once in the bookshop, remember?' Jane and Nancy murmured in agreement. 'And then it would be easy to lure Seb there. Everyone knew he was attending our church and that Rev. Williams had welcomed him.'

'The killer must have phoned him at the cottage and pretended to be the vicar.' Nancy sipped her drink. She wasn't eating much even though her gran's lasagne was delicious. Her appetite had failed her. 'Begged for his help. Maybe Seb thought he might be in danger. He must have thought it was an emergency to run off when he knew we were on our way.'

'Whoever it was must have been hiding near the entrance and then when Seb walked in, they shot him from behind,' Jonathan said.

'When I asked him who had done it, he didn't seem to know. I don't think he even saw them,' Nancy said. She couldn't believe someone could kill without even showing their face. 'Why lock the church behind them though?'

'To stop Seb from getting out?' Jonathan suggested.

Nancy shivered a little. 'You're right. He must have walked in, looking for the vicar, then the killer locked the door and shot him from behind.'

'Unless they locked the door from the outside after they shot Seb, then ran?' Jonathan asked.

'We would have seen them,' Nancy reminded him. 'We were right outside when we heard the shots. No, they locked the door either before or after they shot Seb and then escaped somehow without us seeing. But I'm at a loss as to how… We need to go back in the daylight and look around again, see if there's a way out we missed. I don't suppose the police will like that though.'

'We could go and see Gloria and the vicar,' Jane said. 'They'll need our support and we could do some sleuthing while we're there.'

Nancy had to smile at her grandmother's readiness to sneak around. She felt better that they knew what to do next. She couldn't just sit around feeling guilty about Seb. She agreed with Jane. 'It's the best plan we have right now.'

# Chapter Nineteen

A new day dawned and, before they all had to go to work, Nancy, Jane and Jonathan walked over to the vicarage carrying breakfast they had picked up from the cafe on the way. There was a cool wind this morning and the leaves from the trees fell gently like orange and gold snowflakes as they made their way to the vicarage. The church stood quietly. It looked the same as it always did but Nancy wasn't sure it would ever feel the same now. There was a uniformed officer outside the door who watched as they walked through the gate and up the path to knock on the vicarage door.

'Oh, it's you, thank goodness, I don't think I can bear to talk to another police officer for a while,' Gloria said as she opened the door in her dressing gown. 'We couldn't really sleep so we're not up and ready, I'm afraid.'

'We bought breakfast,' Jane said. 'We didn't like to think of you both alone this morning. But we can leave…'

'No, no! We'd like the company. And we couldn't manage dinner last night.' Gloria ushered them into the living room where the vicar was sipping tea in his dressing gown. It was a little disconcerting to see the usually well-turned-out vicar in that, and she was sorry to see the dark circles under his eyes and the nervous way his leg moved in his armchair. She had seen four bodies now and they all haunted her, so she understood more than he could know.

'They bought us breakfast,' Gloria said, smiling at her husband.

Jonathan handed around pastries to everyone, and takeaway teas to Jane and Nancy while he sipped his coffee. 'We can't imagine how you're feeling today. Has there been any news?'

Rev. Williams shook his head. 'No. The church is still taped off so we don't know when we're able to get back in. We are due at the police station to make our official statements this morning. I just don't understand why Sebastian thought he was coming to see me in the church.'

'Someone must have pretended to be you to get him there,' Nancy said. 'We'd really like to look around the church before we open the bookshop,' she added, deciding it was best to be honest.

'Oh, thank goodness,' Gloria said. They looked at her in surprise. 'I said to Lloyd this morning, didn't I darling, that I hoped you three would be looking into this. I respect DCI Brown, of course I do, but we all know that the last murder in our village wouldn't have been solved without you. And the thought of someone coming into our church and doing that...' She shuddered.

Rev. Williams nodded solemnly. 'I agree. Please help all you can. I left my sermon notes in there yesterday if you need a reason to go in,' he said. 'I really thought Sebastian was trying to turn his life around, I don't understand why someone has done this, I really don't.'

'We think Seb was trying to make amends for his past, that he wanted to bring down his former gang,' Jonathan said. 'The gang he was in is dangerous and powerful...

any one of them could have come here to kill him. And they're probably experts at hiding crimes too.'

'If anyone can find out who did this, it's you,' Gloria said with complete confidence. 'I'm scared to even go back into the church. What if whoever did it comes back?'

'I think they did what they came to do,' Jane said, reassuringly. 'They went to great lengths not to be seen, they wouldn't risk coming back. I think they're long gone from the village.'

Nancy wasn't quite so sure but she didn't say so – she could see the vicar and his wife had been shaken up a lot by what happened, and knew it would take a long time for them to feel comfortable in the village again. She just hoped if they could find the murderer, it would help. But this felt like their toughest investigation yet. 'Let's take a look around,' she said to her gran and Jonathan.

'Try not to worry,' Jane said as she stood up. 'We'll let you know if we find out anything. And please do the same.'

'Be careful,' Gloria pleaded.

–

The police officer on the door regarded them with slight suspicion but let them into the church when they said they needed the vicar's sermon notes and he was too nervous to come in. The aisle was still taped off but thankfully the body was no longer there. Seb had been taken to rest. Nancy hoped he could now do so in peace. A couple of officers were making notes while sitting on a pew but, other than that, the church was empty and it appeared the police were finishing things up in there. The officer told them to walk along the side furthest from the crime scene to pick up the vicar's notes and then he went back to his spot by the door.

Nancy led the way down the side of the pews looking, with a shiver, at the aisle where Seb had died. She paused and looked around, the others doing the same. The aisle led the way up to the altar with the lectern just in front of it. A font stood on the other side. Off to one side of the altar was where the choir sat and the organ stood. The other side led to a small room that they used for Sunday school.

'There is only one door in and out,' Nancy murmured, confirming what she knew about their small old local church. She looked at the stained-glass windows, watery sunshine shining through – clearly there were no windows the murderer could have opened and climbed through. 'So, how could the killer have got out once they killed Seb?' The church door had been locked with them all outside of it. It didn't make sense. She looked at the other two. 'Unless the shots we heard weren't the ones that killed Seb... I'm sure I read a book once where a gun was rigged on a timer to go off so the killer could get away and...' She broke off at Jonathan's incredulous look. 'No, you're right. I never understood how that was really possible unless you were an engineer or something. Locked-room mysteries can be so elaborate though, can't they?'

'They can,' her gran agreed. 'But this is real life. This murder can't have been committed by a magician. It was done by an ordinary person like us, so we should be able to work out how they did it, shouldn't we?'

Nancy sighed in frustration, knowing her gran was right. 'Okay, could they have hidden somewhere?' she wondered. She turned around, looked behind her and let out a small gasp.

'What have you seen?' Jane asked.

Nancy glanced at the police officers, who didn't seem to be paying attention to them, and walked back to a small enclave to the side of the door. There was a statue standing there with a stained-glass window behind it. 'I wonder...' Nancy walked behind the statue and crouched down. 'Can you see me?'

'You're so tall of course we can,' Jonathan said with a snigger.

'What about if you face the aisle, would you have noticed me as you walked in?'

Jonathan stepped back as far as he could without walking down the aisle. The two officers were looking at them now. 'I don't think I would have noticed you, no,' he said after a moment.

'I thought you were collecting notes for the vicar?' one of the officers called out.

'Oh, yes, we forgot where he said they'd be.' Jane hurried up to the lectern to collect them as Nancy slipped back out from behind the statue and looked at the door.

'What are you thinking?' Jonathan asked her.

'The murderer could have hidden behind there until we walked in and then ducked down behind the pews and slipped out of the door,' Nancy said. They had obviously been so focused on Seb that she didn't think they would have noticed anyone crouched behind the statue.

'But hang on, there wouldn't have been time for them to just disappear. I went outside with Dick, didn't I? We would have seen someone walking out of the door.'

Nancy gave him a withering look for using his nick-name for Richard in church. Her gran returned with the vicar's notes so they reluctantly left, waving at the policeman on the door and hoping they didn't look like they'd been doing something they shouldn't. They paused outside the church. 'Let's do the walk you did,' Nancy suggested.

Jonathan led them around the church. It was small so it didn't take them very long. There was nowhere around the church that anyone could have hidden – no trees or bushes. Behind the church was the cemetery and in front was the vicarage leading to the High Street.

'Maybe when you walked around the back of the church, they ran out of the front door,' Jane suggested. 'It was dark so maybe you missed them running away or they left in a car that was waiting for them.'

'They would have had to run really fast. It didn't take long to look back there. I'm sure we would have seen or heard something if they had come out while we were out here,' Jonathan insisted.

'If that's what happened then they would have been seen on either the main road or High Street CCTV?' Nancy asked. 'We'll see what DCI Brown says about that. But seems pointless to go to the trouble of locking the church and then be picked up on CCTV, doesn't it?' The other two nodded, at a loss like she was. Nancy saw the officer at the door staring at them. 'Let's drop these notes into the vicarage and go to the bookshop, we're drawing too much attention here.'

'I need to get to work anyway,' Jonathan said. 'Brown asked me to hold off from breaking the news until this morning so he can get a statement ready. I need to get my news alert out and write up a piece about Seb's murder before anyone gets wind of it on the nationals. I wish we had more to report though.' He looked at Nancy and Jane.

'You know that everyone will be waiting for us to crack this case like we've done before.'

'They might be in for a long wait,' Nancy said, feeling even more confused than when they had gone into the church.

# Chapter Twenty

After they closed the bookshop for the day, Nancy and Jane went to the police station in Woodley to make their statements with DC Pang, and DCI Brown came to see them when they had finished. 'I heard you were in the church this morning,' DCI Brown said, eyebrow raised.

'Rev. Williams needed his sermon notes,' Jane said, quickly.

'And he needed you to get them? Hmmm. So, what do you think?' he perched on the desk and looked at them as DC Pang sorted through the paperwork. 'You must have had a look round while you were there.'

'We noticed the statue by the door. And we wondered if the killer hid there and managed to slip out behind us while we were looking at Seb,' Nancy said, thinking there was no point in pretending they hadn't looked around.

DCI Brown nodded. 'I thought of that.'

'We didn't see them leave though,' Nancy said. 'I don't understand how.'

'We also don't know where they went after the church,' DCI Brown told them. 'We've been going through CCTV all night. No other cars were picked up in the High Street or the main road around the time of the murder that don't belong to all of you we know were at the scene. And officers spoke to a group of kids that they spotted in the High Street and they claim they didn't see anyone on foot who perhaps the cameras missed in the darkness. The village was really quiet. So, we are stumped at how the killer made a getaway from the church.'

'How is that possible?' Nancy wondered. The killer couldn't have just vanished into the night. 'And no sign of the gun?'

'No trace.' DCI Brown sighed. 'Right, Pang, we need to sort through everything we took from Mr Holmes's cottage – his laptop, phone, diary, and hope there is something that will point to who his killer is.'

'Right, you are,' DC Pang said, standing up. He glanced at them. 'Thank you for your statements. We'll be in touch if we need anything else.'

'I understand why you went into the church but whoever killed Mr Holmes is a very dangerous person and I don't want to be worrying about you two,' DCI Brown added to them. He glanced at the table then back at them. 'Leave it to us now, okay?'

Nancy nodded. 'We will,' she said, watching the two officers leave. She looked at where DCI Brown had glanced and saw a key on the table. She scooped it up. 'Let's go, Gran, quickly.' She hurried out, Jane mumbling behind her about her short legs, and was relieved when they were out of the police station.

'Where was the fire?' her grandmother asked breathlessly as she joined her.

'DCI Brown left these keys on the table. On purpose. Come on before anyone realises.' Nancy pulled out her phone as she started walking away from the police station. 'Jonathan, I know you're at work but you need to meet us now.'

–

Half an hour later, they walked up to Rose Cottage. Nancy held her breath as she tried the key she had taken from the police station and then exhaled as it opened the lock of Seb's front door.

Jonathan whistled. 'I can't believe he gave you Seb's keys.'

'There must be a reason he wants us to see inside. He clearly didn't want to say anything at the station though,' Nancy said, leading the way into Seb's cottage. The other two followed and closed the door behind them. 'They've taken all of Seb's electronic equipment and his diary so I have no idea what we can even find but DCI Brown clearly thinks there is something here that might help.'

'He really is open to us investigating, isn't he?' Jonathan asked in wonder. 'I never thought I'd see the day to be honest.'

'It's a big turnaround,' Nancy agreed. 'But maybe he agrees that the connection between Seb and my mother might be important. We just need to find out what their connection is. Okay, shall we all take a room and see if anything catches our eye?'

'I'll go upstairs,' Jane offered.

'I'll do the kitchen and dining open-plan bit,' Jonathan said, looking ahead.

'I'll take the living room then.' Nancy walked into the front room and paused for a moment. Seb hadn't had long to make this cottage his home. It smelled of his cigarettes though and of the lavender that stood in a vase on the windowsill. He had decorated it simply with furniture that looked second-hand but he had made it cosy and comfortable. She thought it was such a shame that he hadn't been able to enjoy it for long after all those years in prison. Why couldn't he have been allowed to live out his last years in peace?

Nancy went in and made her way to the bookcase behind the armchair. She spotted the book that Seb had bought from her bookshop on the table next to the armchair, along with his reading glasses and used ashtray and empty bottle of beer. She went over to the bookcase and had a look. There were a lot of classic crime books on there, some autobiographies and the Bible in pride of place. Then she saw what looked like a scrapbook or photo album. She pulled it out and leaned against the arm of the armchair to flick through it. There were a lot of newspaper cuttings. As she looked at them, she realised they all related to *The Club*: convictions; crimes that had never been solved; people who were in the list her mother had written in the front of the memoir about the gang; and cuttings about the day Seb was arrested during the jewellery robbery. There were photos too. Some of Seb when he was young with his family, then when he was older with his friends. Nancy wondered if any had been in *The Club* with him.

She turned the page and there was a familiar face staring back at her.

Nancy almost dropped the album in shock. 'Gran! Jonathan!' she yelled, standing up and looking at it stunned. 'Oh my God…' she said. Suddenly the connection between Seb and her mother made a lot more sense. They rushed in. 'Look.' She held up the photo so Jonathan and her gran could see. Her hand was shaking. 'Isn't that my grandfather with Seb?'

Jane stepped forward to look. 'Yes, he's younger there than the photos we have of him with Samantha when she was a baby, but that's him.'

'So, my grandfather knew Seb. What if they were in *The Club* together?'

'Do you know what happened to him? Is he still alive?' Jonathan asked Jane.

'Samantha said her parents had both died before she came to Dedley End. She didn't like to talk about it, which I understood. I don't think I ever knew the full story of what happened to them. I don't even know their names. I'm sorry, I should have tried to find out more,' Jane said, looking at Nancy worriedly.

'She wouldn't have wanted to tell you. I mean, how do you admit that your father was in a notorious gang.' Nancy took a breath. This was all too much to take in. 'I can't believe it but if he was friends with Seb back then, it makes sense to believe they were in the gang together. My grandfather was a criminal.'

'That's how Seb knew your mother. Now we know,' Jonathan said.

Nancy nodded. 'This is what DCI Brown was hoping I'd find. The connection between Seb and my mother. But now we have it, what do we do? Oh...' She looked at the other two in horror. 'What if my mother was in the gang too? Could that mean that she...' She trailed off, composing herself before asking the question she really didn't want to ask. 'We thought my mother and Seb might be working together to bring the gang down. But my mother might still be in the gang? What if she had something to do with Seb's murder?'

# Chapter Twenty-One

'Okay, we need more information,' Jonathan said as they sank into chairs in the cosy living room of Nancy and Jane's cottage. They watched him pace in front of them as they sat on the sofa. Charlie the beagle was curled up in front of the log fire, which they had lit as it was a chilly autumn evening. 'Just who was your grandfather, Nancy? Was he part of *The Club* with Seb and, if so, what happened to him? And how does this all link with your mother running away and what we've found out about her since?' He stopped pacing to look at them. 'Could she be involved in Seb's death?'

They had left Seb's cottage taking with them the photo of Nancy's grandfather with Seb, calling DCI Brown on the way home, who said he'd see them there when he left the station for the day. Nancy's mind was reeling from the revelations of the past twenty-four hours and her grandmother had been stunned into silence, which was no mean feat. Jonathan was trying to piece all of the puzzle together.

'Let's look up the gang and Seb's associates at that time, see if we can find any mention of your grandfather,' Jonathan said. He sat down and pulled his laptop out of his bag.

'And my mother,' Nancy added. 'What if they were all in the gang together? We thought my mum was protecting me this whole time, but what if she was just hiding her part in their network? I was just getting my head around the idea that for some reason she was trying to bring the gang down, like Seb was, but now I need to consider that maybe she's working for them. And could have been part of Seb's murder.' Nancy shook her head. She couldn't grasp the idea of her mother being a killer.

'Or she had left the gang and feared they would come after her,' Jane said. 'She didn't want them to find you, love, so she ran from Dedley End. Lloyd was adamant Samantha left the village to protect you. It has to be from *The Club*.'

Nancy smiled at her grandmother looking for the best angle on it all.

'Then it's more likely that one of the gang killed Seb, not your mother,' Jonathan added. 'They knew that they were trying to find out the leader and killed Seb to stop him from revealing who that is.'

Nancy definitely preferred the idea of her mother being on the run from the gang, rather than her killing Seb for them, but she knew they didn't really have any facts, just speculation at the moment. 'The problem with the idea of the gang being responsible for Seb's death is the locked church. How did they manage it?'

'Let's go through that night again,' Jane suggested.

'We went to see Seb and his neighbour said he'd gone to the church to help Rev. Williams but we know that's not true,' Nancy said, telling herself to focus on the facts. 'We sensed something was wrong about that as he'd arranged to meet us so we went to the vicarage. The vicar confirmed he hadn't seen Seb and the church was locked. He was outside with Gloria talking to Mr Peabody when we arrived.'

'So, we said we needed to see inside the church,' Jonathan picked up. 'And then Will Roth and Richard pulled up in Will's car wanting to talk to you, Nancy. Which we now know was to tell us Marcus Roth is back in the village.'

Nancy looked at him. 'Just in time for the murder,' she said. 'It could mean the Roths are up to their old tricks.'

'Let's just focus on what we know,' Jonathan said. 'We heard two gunshots so we ran over. The door was locked and we didn't see anyone outside so we have to assume the killer was still with Seb at this point. The vicar unlocked the church door and we all went in – us three, Mr Peabody, Rev. Williams and Gloria, and old Dickie and Will.'

'And when I saw Seb, I rushed forward to check on him. You were all behind me. Gran – what did you see while I was talking to Seb?'

Jane frowned but managed to rouse herself to answer. 'We were at the end of the aisle close to the door... Will called the police and ambulance. Gloria was upset so Lloyd was comforting his wife. Mr Peabody was close to them with Richard and then you stepped forward, Jonathan.'

He nodded. 'I suggested I look around and Richard joined me. So, we went outside but we didn't see anyone, then we came back and walked past you all to look around the altar, choir area and the Sunday school bit but, again, no sign of anyone or the gun.'

'And then Seb sadly passed away and, as we checked on him, DC Pang walked in. He'd heard on the police radio about Will's call and ran over to the church from the High Street. He checked and confirmed Seb was dead, and you and Richard joined us, so we were all together,' Nancy continued.

'Then DCI Brown and more police officers arrived. None of the police knew Seb had been shot. I don't think Will said on his 999 call, otherwise he would have brought armed officers,' Jonathan added.

'Will can't have been thinking clearly,' Jane said.

'Unless he didn't want them to bring armed officers,' Jonathan suggested. 'Maybe we need to ask him about that. And where his grandfather was that night.'

'DCI Brown says CCTV didn't pick up anyone fleeing the church and the kids out in the village saw nothing either. So, there was no sign of the killer leaving the church,' Nancy said. 'I keep coming back to that statue. They could have been hiding behind it and slipped out in a small window of opportunity as we were so focused on Seb, but why weren't they spotted leaving on CCTV then? Or by any of the police officers who all turned up not long afterwards?' Nancy frowned. It felt like it was impossible. 'Was it some magic trick?'

'Or they never left the church,' Jonathan suggested.

'What do you mean?' Jane asked.

'It was someone who was in the church with us,' Jonathan said. 'Someone with us that night killed Seb. And stayed with us the whole time. I don't know how they did it but how could it be anyone else?'

Nancy shivered at that thought. 'But who out of the people with us would have wanted Seb dead?'

'We should talk to everyone,' Jane said. 'See if we missed anything or one of them gives the game away.'

'But what was their motive? It can't be Gloria or the vicar and we know it wasn't one of us three. So, who is the most likely?' Nancy asked. 'We need to go to Roth Lodge, don't we?' she asked, her heart sinking at the very idea of having to go back to that house and deal with that family once again. She watched Jonathan's face. 'Have you found something online?'

He looked up from his laptop. 'I have.'

'What is it?' she asked nervously.

Jonathan turned the laptop around and Nancy and Jane leaned forward to see it. 'Look in this article about *The Club*,' he said, pointing out an old newspaper article. It showed a group of men in a London pub. 'Police believe the gang frequent the establishment and reportedly run illegal gambling there. The local community so far have refused to co-operate in the police operation. The pub has seen a reversal of its fortunes. It was almost closed last year but is now one of the most popular spots in East London. Locals claim the gang have saved it, which could explain the reluctance to aid the police.' Jonathan pointed to the photograph. 'That's Seb and your grandfather with the two other men.'

Nancy looked at the name with the photo. 'James Marlow.' She looked at her gran then at Jonathan. 'Marlow? But my mother's maiden name was Smith.'

'Unless it wasn't,' Jonathan said.

Before Nancy or Jane could respond, a knock at the door startled them. 'I'll go,' Nancy said, assuming it was DCI Brown. She beckoned him inside and led him through to the living room.

'You found something, I take it?' DCI Brown asked as Nancy handed him Seb's keys back.

'Yes.' Nancy picked up the photograph. 'That's my grandfather with Seb.'

'And we just found this,' Jonathan said, showing Brown the old newspaper article. 'It looks pretty certain that Nancy's grandfather, James Marlow, was part of *The Club* with Seb.'

DCI Brown whistled. 'Well done for finding that. Letting you go into Mr Holmes's cottage was very unorthodox but we found a bug in his house. Someone had been listening to his phone calls. So, I think whoever it was heard him inviting you to the cottage to tell you everything he knew so they lured him to the church to make sure he couldn't speak to you.'

Nancy paled. She hated the idea that wanting to tell her what he knew had got Seb killed. 'Seb was determined to bring his former gang down. They must have realised that. And he indicated on the phone that he'd found out who *The Governor* was. He was going to tell us all he knew about the gang, and their leader... There's no way *The Club* would have wanted him to do that.' She sighed. 'I wish he could have just told me everything.'

'What we don't understand though is if the gang did kill Seb to stop him speaking to us how they did it,' Jonathan said. 'We can't work out how someone got into that church and out again without any of us seeing them, so was it someone who was in there with us that night – someone we know?'

'But that would mean someone that night had links to *The Club* too,' DCI Brown said. His face turned hard. 'Is someone in this village working for the gang?'

Nancy felt sick at the very thought. 'Seb came to Dedley End for a reason. I think he wanted to keep an eye on me, we knew he knew my mother somehow and now it seems he was friends with my grandfather. Seb was here on a mission to bring *The Club* down. So, I think we need to accept that someone here knows something about all of this at the very least.'

'Maybe that's why the killer locked the church,' Jonathan said. 'They know us. They know the other murders that have happened in the village and wanted to make sure this was one we couldn't solve.'

Nancy stared at him. 'The killer is playing a game with us?'

'They won't win,' the inspector declared. 'If there is someone here behind all of this, we'll find out who. That gang have been a rot on society for fifty years. It's time they were rooted out.'

Nancy had a thought. 'Inspector, my grandfather's surname is different to what my mother told us... Maybe she changed her name or hid it because of the shame of him being in the gang. Is there a way to find out who she really was?'

'I'll look into it at the station, see if I can find out what happened to James Marlow and his family. And I'm going to speak to a friend at the Met. They've dealt with *The Club* more than I have. They might be able to help. But listen, if there is someone in the village linked to all this, we all need to be careful,' DCI Brown said.

Jane nodded. 'We will be.'

He looked at them all and Nancy could tell he wasn't fully convinced about that. 'Okay. Leave this with me then.'

Nancy showed him out of the cottage then locked the front door behind him, more nervous than she had realised. She knew there was a possibility that Seb's killer might still be in their village. Whoever it was could be out there watching them, enjoying the fact they didn't have any clue who had committed the murder or how.

She didn't like that thought one little bit.

## Chapter Twenty-Two

Nancy woke up when it was still dark. She could hear the rain coming down outside as she sat up in her lace nightdress. She yawned. The night had been restless after the revelations of the day before. She had spent most of her life surrounded by crime in a fictional sense – working in a crime bookshop and reading all the thrillers, detective novels and cosy crime she could lay her hands on and then at Christmas, real life crime had crept into her life when she attended the party at Roth Lodge where Lucy Roth was killed.

But now it appeared that crime went back to her very roots. Her grandfather had been part of *The Club* with Seb. Nancy had no idea how that related to her mother's disappearance. All she did know was that the one man who knew how it all connected had been murdered in the village church before he could tell her. If she could find his killer maybe she would finally understand what had happened to her mother, but part of her wasn't so sure. If someone was willing to kill to prevent the truth from coming out, would she ever really find out?

Nancy climbed out of bed and pulled on her dressing gown and slippers before heading downstairs. She peeped in the living room to see Jonathan, draped in a blanket, fast asleep on the sofa. He had said he'd better not drive after the drinks they'd had once DCI Brown had left, and

Nancy had felt better knowing he was downstairs all night. A few times in the night she had felt an urge to come down to see him but she had resisted. Now she watched him sleeping and felt a peace settle over her – before she felt rather creepy and hurried into the kitchen where Charlie was curled up on his bed. Her grandmother strongly disapproved of the beagle coming upstairs although Nancy did sometimes sneak him up there, so he usually slept in the kitchen near the warmth of the Aga. He got up when Nancy came in and rushed over, tail wagging. She crouched down to greet him. 'Good morning, boy. I hope you slept better than I did.' Nancy let him out in the garden and switched on the kettle. She wasn't up to much in the mornings before a large cup of tea and after her poor sleep, she might very well need two cups.

'Are you all right?' Jonathan appeared in the doorway yawning, running a hand through his tousled hair. 'It's early.'

'Sorry, did I wake you? I couldn't sleep,' Nancy said as she pulled out another cup from the cupboard. 'Want a coffee?'

'Always. No, it's fine, I was tossing and turning myself,' Jonathan said. Charlie ran in to see him so he shut the back door and sat down, patting the dog. 'Were you thinking about yesterday?'

She nodded. 'Poor Seb is dead. And we're no closer to finding my mother and I'm worried we never will get to the bottom of all of this. The one person who could have helped explain it all has gone.' Nancy brought over a cup of coffee for Jonathan and tea for herself and joined him at the table. She bit her lip. 'I feel really unsettled. This just all feels so personal, like we aren't safe here anymore and I've never felt like that before in Dedley End. What if Seb's killer is still in the village? What if they live here? What if they are watching us?'

Jonathan frowned. 'Are you thinking we should stop? I don't like the idea of a murderer getting away with what they've done to Seb and I know you don't. But I hate the thought of you being in danger. Mrs H too. If you think we should back off then maybe that would be for the best.'

Nancy sighed. 'I don't want to. But this feels different to our other investigations. I can't explain it. I guess I feel jittery.'

'Well, that's understandable. You just found out your grandfather was in a gang. And that Seb's cottage was bugged. Someone was watching him, listening to him and they heard he was going to tell you something. But look, that doesn't mean you're in danger specifically. They didn't want Seb to tell anyone about what he knew about the gang, not just you. This all could just be about *The Club* and nothing to do with your mother.'

'But if she left Dedley End because of the gang, it could all be about both.'

He nodded. 'If only Seb had told you everything when he first arrived,' he said, frustrated.

'Maybe my mother asked him not to but then he realised I was looking for her and he'd found out something, I know he had. He thought I needed to know. Or maybe he was going to warn me off.' Nancy sighed. It was so frustrating that she'd never know what Seb had been going to tell her. 'It's awful, isn't it? All those years in prison and then when he finally gets out… he's murdered. This gang, if they are responsible, and I don't see who else is behind it, are terrible people, Jonathan. I'm scared. But I also can't bear to think of them getting away with this, you know?'

'Me neither. But I suppose we have to decide if the risk is worth the chance to get justice.'

Nancy looked at him. She knew he was right. It was a risk. This gang were dangerous and had already killed Seb right on their doorstep. But could she really walk away now?

Jonathan took a sip of his coffee. 'Do you still want to go to Roth Lodge? I could go alone, leave you and Mrs H out of it.'

Nancy shook her head. 'I am nervous but I also don't want to give up. I feel like I can't now I've found out that this has something to do with my family. I have to try to put an end to it all. I can't let anyone else get hurt. If this is personal then it's up to me to find out the truth.'

'Not just you,' he reminded her, firmly. 'You're not alone in this. Like I told you before, together we can do anything. I'll always protect you if I can, Nancy.'

'Me too,' she replied. She trusted their words more than anything in her life right now. They would always be there for one another.

'We'll still go then but we need to be extra careful,' Jonathan said. 'And the fewer people who know we're investigating the better. And we should definitely keep your family connection to Seb between us for now.'

'DCI Brown did say not to trust anyone,' Nancy agreed.

Jonathan reached out to touch her hand on the table. As always when Jonathan touched her, Nancy felt warm and comforted. She looked up from her tea and met his gaze. They smiled at one another.

'Is there tea for me?' Nancy's grandmother walked in then in her dressing gown.

Jonathan pulled his hand away from Nancy. 'I'll make it,' he said, quickly, getting up to go to the kettle.

Jane was surprised. 'Oh, thank you. Are you okay, love, you look tired?' she asked as she sat down.

Nancy was trying to ignore the fluttering in her stomach. She forced on a smile. 'I will be fine. I don't think you should come to Roth Lodge today, Gran. I think you should be at the bookshop with Penelope. I think things are getting dangerous and—'

'Poppycock,' Jane interrupted her, crossly. Jonathan sniggered behind them. 'I mean it. I have let things lie for over twenty years when I should have realised there was much more to Samantha leaving than I thought, but I was blinded by my anger towards her for leaving my George and you. I feel guilty for not supporting my son enough. He must have had so much on his plate and I could have helped. I'm not letting the only family I have left handle this alone,' her grandmother told her, fiercely. 'Yes, it might be dangerous. Yes, there might be someone in this village who wants to stop us getting to the truth but in my book that means we should just try even harder to bring them to justice. We need to find out what really happened, not only when Seb was killed in our church but when your mother ran away. So, no, I'm not going to hide in the bookshop, I'm coming to Roth Lodge with you and I don't want to hear any more arguments about it.'

Jonathan carried over a cup of tea. 'Mrs H, I've never been prouder to know you,' he said, handing it to her.

Nancy admired her gran's spirit, of course she did, but she was worried about her and wanted to protect her. She could see though that Jane's mind was firmly made up and her gran likely felt exactly the same way about her. 'Okay,' she said. 'But if anything feels like it's getting out of hand, we call DCI Brown and we let him handle it. No one else is getting hurt on my watch.'

'I didn't think we'd ever be going back to that house,' Jonathan said as he sipped his coffee.

'Nor me,' Nancy agreed. 'I'm not looking forward to it at all but someone must know something about what happened in the church and we all know that if there's trouble to be found, the Roths are likely to be involved.'

'Don't forget Tricky Dicky,' Jonathan added.

Nancy could never forget her ex-boyfriend unfortunately. 'If any of them know something, we'll find out,' she vowed. 'But first – breakfast.'

## Chapter Twenty-Three

Later that morning, Nancy, Jane and Jonathan drove from the cottage. It was raining again so they were unable to walk. Jonathan drove through the imposing iron gates of Roth Lodge, which sat up on a hill overlooking Dedley End. It was a large, elegant building with ivy covering much of the front of the house. They climbed out of the car and walked up to the front door, glancing at one another apprehensively. After all, the last time they had been inside was after they had caught Lucy Roth's murderer and Marcus Roth had revealed who had caused Nancy's father's car crash. It was definitely not a house full of pleasant memories and Nancy knew none of them wanted to be there.

With a deep breath, Nancy reached out to knock on the door. Before she could, it swung open surprising the three of them.

Frank, the Roth family's ageing butler, was showing DC Pang out.

'What are you doing here?' Pang asked with narrowed eyes as he stepped outside. He was wearing a raincoat and polished black shoes, and reminded Nancy slightly of Inspector Gadget.

'Will invited us for lunch,' Nancy found herself lying. She knew that DCI Brown might be willing to let them help his investigation, but the rest of the police force were unlikely to and DC Pang had made it clear several times that he believed they should leave it to the professionals.

'What about you?' Jonathan asked the policeman pointedly.

'Routine enquiries,' DC Pang replied, giving him a I-really-don't-trust-you look. He nodded once at Frank, then walked off with his head high in the air.

Nancy turned to Frank, who didn't bat an eyelid even though he obviously hadn't heard a word about them being invited to lunch. 'I'll show you to the living room and let Mr Roth know you're here.'

'Thank you so much,' Nancy said, gratefully, and she stepped inside.

The hall was vast with a black-and-white-chessboard floor beneath them. Nancy tried not to look at it as she didn't want to be reminded of the body of Lucy Roth, which had been found lying there at Christmas. She couldn't help glancing up at the ornate ironwork balustrade ringing the first floor, however, which Lucy had been pushed over. Nancy sighed. What a tragedy that had been. Frank directed her to the drawing room so she shook off thoughts of the past and, like the other two, slipped out of her coat and shoes, damp from the rain, and went in there to sit down. Nancy was glad to be dry and warm, although she was unable to relax in the grand house.

'I wonder if Pang is suspicious of anyone in particular here,' Jonathan said in a low voice. He looked at Nancy and Jane. 'And, more to the point, are we?'

Before they could answer, the living room door opened and in walked Will Roth. 'Frank told me you're here for lunch. Did Richard invite you? He just left. He's meeting Mr Peabody who wants some financial advice.'

'That's okay, we're happy to talk to you,' Nancy said, deciding it was a good idea to let Will think Richard had invited them over. 'We're still so perplexed by everything that happened in the church.'

'Ah, you mean you're investigating the murder in the church. I thought you would be.' He sat down in one of the armchairs. He was dressed more casually now he ran his own business with Richard than when he'd worked for the family firm and definitely seemed more comfortable as a result. 'DC Pang was asking me more questions about it all this morning too. The police seem focused on the fact that when I phoned 999 I didn't say Sebastian Holmes had been shot. I was so shocked by it all, I wasn't thinking clearly. I certainly wasn't trying to put anyone in any danger. And I suppose with no sign of a gun or the killer, I didn't think I needed to say... I just said Mr Holmes had been attacked,' Will said, looking worried.

'It all happened so quickly,' Jane reassured him. 'And as you say, it didn't appear that we were in any danger from a gunman.'

Will nodded. 'Exactly. But DC Pang should have had armed back-up they told me. I can't go back though, can I? It wasn't done intentionally. But of course, what with what happened here at Christmas, I think the police are trying to read more into it all. They are wondering if it's too convenient that me and Richard were at the church with you all to find the body.'

'But surely there is nothing to link you both to Seb?' Nancy asked.

'No, I'd never met the man and nor had Richard. But when you're found at more than one crime scene... well, you three know what I mean.'

'Did you or Richard see anything that might help the investigation?' Jonathan asked.

Will shook his head. 'I didn't see anyone around the church, and Richard said you and him looked and didn't either. It's such a mystery. How did someone shoot Sebastian Holmes and get out of the church without anyone of us seeing them? And what did they do with the gun?'

'That's what we're trying to find out,' Nancy said. She had always liked Will and he seemed to be genuine in what he was saying, but she knew what a toxic family he came from and he was in partnership with her manipulative ex-boyfriend so she knew she could never really trust him one hundred per cent. But there was nothing to link him to Seb so at the moment, she wasn't sure what else they could ask him at this point.

The door to the living room opened again then and they all turned to see Marcus Roth walk in. It was the first time they had seen him since the family had fled the village last Christmas. Unlike Will, who seemed to have blossomed since the rest of his family left the village, Marcus seemed markedly older than when Nancy had last seen him. He was in his seventies with salt-and-pepper hair but he had had a handsome face like his grandson before. However, now he looked older, weary and a lot thinner.

'Good morning,' he said, looking at each of them in turn before lingering on Nancy. 'When Frank said you were here, I had to come... I have thought of you a lot since last Christmas and, coming back here, I wanted to see you again but also dreaded it in equal measure. The reason we all left Dedley End was to try to spare you any additional pain. I hope in that small way we did.'

'And because you knew your reputation was in tatters,' Jonathan said.

Jane nodded. 'You did it to spare yourself.'

If Marcus had been used to people simpering around him as the rich and powerful man he was, he had evidently spent the past nine or so months differently, as he didn't even flinch. 'We did what we thought was best for everyone,' he replied, rather like a politician's answer, Nancy felt. He addressed her particularly once again. 'I know I can never make up for what we did but we are trying to do what is right from now on. I assure you of that.'

Nancy didn't know what to say. Marcus hadn't been directly responsible for the deaths of Lucy Roth and her father, but he had tried to protect those who were and prevent the truth from coming out. She couldn't forgive that.

They heard the front door open and Frank greet someone else.

'That must be Richard back so we can all have lunch together,' Will said.

Nancy had her eyes on Marcus as Will spoke and she saw him flinch then. So, the discussion of the past hadn't affected him but the sound of Richard's name had. She wondered why. 'Are you moving back to the village?' she asked Marcus, needing to know so she could prepare herself.

'I'm not sure yet,' he said, vaguely. 'There is much to... sort out first. I'll check on lunch.' He swept out of the room.

'That wasn't much of an apology,' Jonathan said after a moment of awkward silence.

Will lifted his shoulders. 'My grandfather isn't the best at those but I do think he wants to make amends as much as he possibly can. I think he misses his home,' Will said. 'Just so you know, he and my father are in the process of dismantling the family business. They don't want to continue. My father is going to retire early. And I think they would all like to settle back here but I don't think they will if you can't give them your blessing.' He held up a hand when all three of them were about to answer. 'Don't say anything, we all have a lot going on right now. Just think it through, okay? Come on, let's have lunch and see if Richard can help with what happened in the church. He's more observant than I am.'

Nancy stood up. She didn't like the idea of the Roths returning to Dedley End for good but this was their home and, if they were going to abandon the family business and settle peacefully here, could she really stop them? They had done some unforgivable things but she knew the pain of not being with her own family and she could see on Will's face that however he felt about the past, he had missed his family the past few months. She was starting to get a headache with everything that was crowded inside her brain and decided she couldn't think about the Roths right now. She had to focus on finding out who killed Seb and where her mother was first.

## Chapter Twenty-Four

The dining room at Roth Lodge was grand with a huge table. Nancy had once eaten lunch with the whole family and it had been tense. Today, the table was only a quarter full with the three of them, Will and Marcus Roth, and Richard, who walked in after them wearing one of his tailored suits and looking as handsome as ever. Nancy wished she hadn't noticed that.

'Well, this is a pleasure,' Richard said, seeing them. 'We don't get many visitors here outside of the business,' he added, giving Marcus a quick look.

Nancy was sure she wasn't imagining a hostility between the two of them. When they sat down at the table, they were at opposite ends. 'You've been helping Mr Peabody, we gather? He's such a lovely man,' she said when they were all seated.

'Why does he need an accountant now he's retired?' Jonathan asked shortly.

Richard rested his elbows on the table and looked at Jonathan before turning to Nancy who was sat across from him. 'He has come into some money that he wants us to invest for him. So, I assume you're here to talk about the murder in the church? DC Pang warned us you might come by.'

'Warned you?' Nancy asked in surprise.

'He just said it was likely you'd try to look into Holmes's murder yourselves,' Will said. 'As you've done before. He just reminded us that if there was anything important we thought of, we needed to tell him or DCI Brown,' he added.

Nancy wondered if DCI Brown knew his constable had said that. He seemed to be encouraging their help and knew they'd pass anything relevant on to him, but Pang didn't feel the same way, it appeared. 'We're just trying to make sense of that night to see if we can help the investigation. Seeing Seb like that, it was just horrid, and the thought of his killer being here in the village...' She trailed off as the dining-room door opened.

Mrs Harper, the Roths' housekeeper, came in with soup and crusty bread as the first course. She looked at Nancy, Jane and Jonathan, and Nancy knew that, like them, she was thinking back to when they had last seen her at Christmas investigating Lucy's murder. She gave them a nod in acknowledgement, and handed around the bowls of soup and laid the basket of bread in the middle of the table. Nancy knew that the young maid, Natalie, who had been helpful to them, had left months ago, not wanting to work in a house that had seen murder. Only Mrs Harper and Frank worked there now.

When they were alone again, Richard picked up the conversation. 'Surely you don't think Sebastian Holmes's killer is still in the village, Nancy? It was one of his old gang buddies if you ask me.'

'Did you see any of them in or around the church that night?' she asked him.

'Doesn't mean they weren't there, they are experts at killing people,' Richard replied. 'I think we should all stay well out of it. They did what they came to do, end of story.

Of course it was unpleasant but Seb was a criminal, he did terrible things and perhaps he'd been living on borrowed time for years.'

'He did his time in prison for those crimes,' Nancy said, shocked that Richard seemed to have no sympathy for the man. 'That was justice not this cold-blooded murder.'

'I'm sorry, Nancy, but why do you care? You didn't know him. I know you like investigating murders but this is a different league to Lucy Roth or what happened with that author, Thomas Green. These are career criminals. This is organised crime, a gang… It's really not a good idea for you to be involved. It has nothing to do with you.'

Nancy bristled at Richard's superior tone. She remembered all the times he had belittled her when they were a couple. 'Actually, it does. Seb invited me to his cottage the night he was killed. He was going to tell me why he was here, what he knew about his former gang, and how he knew my mother. So, how can I not think it was to stop him from talking to me?' she spat back at her ex, anger bubbling up under her skin at his attitude. He had always acted like he knew better than her. She was tired of it.

Will Roth raised an eyebrow. 'Sebastian Holmes knew your mother?'

'We think so,' Jonathan hedged. He glanced at Nancy anxiously. She was annoyed at herself for telling them that. She knew she should be keeping it quiet but Richard was so infuriating, she couldn't keep her anger in check. 'He mentioned her to Nancy,' Jonathan said, keeping it vague.

Nancy exhaled. She was glad Jonathan had stopped her from spilling more secrets. She knew it was best they didn't know her grandfather had been in *The Club* with Seb. 'So, you can understand why I can't just leave it alone,' she said to Richard. 'Did you see anything in the church that might help the investigation? When you looked around with Jonathan, perhaps?'

Richard sighed but shook his head. 'As I told the police, we didn't see anyone or any sign of a gun. It was just us in that church with Mr Holmes. I don't know who killed him or how they managed it.'

Nancy buttered a bit of crusty bread. She had no idea whether to believe him or not. 'Had you spoken to Seb since he moved here?'

'No. But you said you saw him, didn't you?' Richard asked Marcus. They all looked at him.

'He was hanging around outside the house when I came back. I saw him outside the gates. That was the day he was killed,' Marcus said slowly as if he didn't really want to tell them that. He glared at Richard.

Nancy thought back to her phone call with Seb, the last time she spoke to him, when he invited her to his cottage. He had told her he'd seen Marcus Roth coming back to the village. So, he'd been watching him at the house. Why would Seb have done that? 'Had you ever met Seb before?'

Marcus shook his head. 'Never. I knew of him from the newspapers but he's been in prison for thirty years, hasn't he? It's not like we ran in the same circles.' He gave a hearty laugh although it wasn't at all funny.

'It was strange he moved here,' Will said. 'Out of the whole world, he chose to come to our village after he left prison. I wonder why.'

Nancy glanced at Jonathan. They weren't about to share their thoughts on why Seb had done that.

'It's very different from London,' Richard agreed with some scorn in his tone.

'And yet you're living here, Richard, so it can't be that bad, can it?' Jane said then. Nancy bit back a laugh at her gran's perfect comeback. Richard had always appeared to look down on Nancy's beloved village but he'd moved there anyway.

'It was Will's idea,' Richard said.

'Actually,' Will said, looking at him. 'It was yours. You thought it would make sense to use my house as our office to save on costs. And I agreed.'

Richard looked at his friend and Nancy saw his cheeks turn red. 'Well, it has made sense, hasn't it?'

Nancy watched their exchange with interest. So, Richard had been the one who had wanted to move to Dedley End. Why? To see her again? Did he really think he still had a chance with her romantically?

'I wish I could go back and not have that party,' Marcus said, wistfully then. He gazed out of the dining room window as though he had forgotten they were all in the room with him. 'I should never have let my granddaughter persuade me to celebrate her engagement. Or I should have kept it as family and close friends only, but my friend persuaded me to use it as a business opportunity and invite clients, and then Maria said we should invite all the village too.' His expression turned dark. 'I knew it was a mistake. And I was right. It brought us nothing but trouble.'

'Who was the friend who persuaded you to invite all those people?' Jane asked as she sipped her water.

'I believe you've met him. Hugh Windsor,' Marcus replied, turning back to the table.

'How do you all know him?' Nancy asked. She knew they'd been family friends for a long time but wasn't sure how they had first all met one another.

'Our fathers were friends. They served in the army together before retiring. Hugh joined the army but my father persuaded me not to. We started the family banking business together before he died and I inherited Roth Lodge,' Marcus replied.

'Was Hugh here at the engagement party?' Nancy asked. She wouldn't have known him then, of course.

'Yes, but only for about half an hour as he needed to get back home to prepare for his own annual Christmas party. He missed all the scandal.'

'That's how I didn't meet him then,' Richard said. 'When we met at my leaving do, I wondered why he hadn't been here.'

That was the leaving do where Richard had learned Hugh Windsor had seen Nancy's mother at his party. 'How did you start talking about my mother with Hugh by the way?' Nancy asked.

'Hugh mentioned how awful everything had been with what happened at Maria's party after he left,' Will said. 'He said it had been wonderful to see the house opened up and to have us entertaining after so many years. He said he had loved attending our parties through the years and could still remember all the interesting people he'd met in Dedley End.' The Roths had stopped throwing parties years ago before opening the house up for Maria's engagement, and that night had ended in murder. Nancy sincerely hoped they wouldn't try it again. 'He said he loved the bookshop run by a nice couple – George and Samantha Hunter.'

'I told him I knew their daughter very well,' Richard picked up, looking at Nancy. 'That was when he told us the story of her being at his party and I checked with him that it would be okay to tell you as you hadn't seen or heard from her for many years.'

Nancy thought for a moment. 'That was back when you didn't come into the village. I wonder how he ended up in the bookshop,' Nancy said.

Marcus nodded. 'I never went into the High Street back then. I used to see Hugh, mainly at his house and in London, but he used to keep on about seeing my wife and, as you know, I tried not to let people see her when her drinking became hard to hide – but he did stay a couple of times when I couldn't find an excuse to stop him. We told him she had a migraine and had gone to bed. Maybe he ventured to the bookshop one of those weekends, I'm not sure. He has always been a fan of true-crime books so it makes sense, I suppose.' Marcus thought for a moment. 'I remember we talked about Samantha a little bit when she left the village. Mrs Harper, our housekeeper, told him the rumour was she had gone to London.'

Nancy thought Hugh Windsor had a good memory. She wasn't sure she could place someone who'd served her in a shop years afterwards unless they had really sparked her interest. She remembered him noting her resemblance to her mother in quite a sleazy way, saying he never forgot a pretty face. So maybe Samantha had made a big impression on him. And she supposed her mother leaving the village like she did had meant he had remembered her. And thank goodness he had and had passed that on to Nancy. 'I just wish we knew where she had gone after his Christmas party.'

'Maybe you're better off not knowing,' Richard said.

Nancy looked at him. He had mentioned more than once that she should stop looking for her mother. Suddenly, she wondered if it was because he knew more than he was telling them.

'I need to get back to work,' Richard said before she could respond. He stood up. 'Excuse me.'

Mrs Harper appeared in the doorway then with a tray. 'Oh, but here's another course,' she said as she walked in. 'I've made sandwiches.'

'I'm not hungry anymore,' he replied and walked out quickly.

'That man is always rushing about,' Marcus said with disapproval in his tone.

'Our company is thriving because of that man,' Will reminded his grandfather. He looked at Nancy as Mrs Harper took away their soup and left them with the sandwiches. 'I'm sorry we haven't been of much help about Sebastian Holmes. I do think Richard is right though – you should be careful. He wasn't a good man.'

'I don't know,' Nancy said. 'I think maybe he was, but became friends with the wrong people.'

'Excuse me too. I need a cigarette,' Marcus Roth said. He stood up and pulled out a packet and a book of matches. 'I hope you find what you're looking for,' he said to Nancy, Jane and Jonathan before following Richard out.

'He never used to smoke,' Will said with a sigh.

But Nancy was staring after Marcus Roth because the book of matches in his hand were hot-pink ones. The exact same ones that Seb had made her take from him in the church. 'Will,' she said, urgently. 'Your grandfather's matches – the bright-pink matchbook – do you know where he got them from?'

162

'Oh, those,' Will said with a nod. 'Sure. They're from a private members' club in London. We're all members in the family. And Richard joined a few months ago too.'

'What is it called?' Nancy asked him.

'*Clubhouse13*.'

## Chapter Twenty-Five

It wasn't until closing time in the bookshop that Nancy and Jane could talk about what had happened at Roth Lodge. They'd had to hurry back after lunch there and then, once the schools were let out, Penelope had to pick up Kitty. The shop became busy so they were focused on serving customers. Jonathan had gone to the newspaper office to write up a couple of articles and research the members' club that the Roths and Richard belonged to. Nancy leaned on the counter as Jane turned the shop signed to 'closed'.

'I feel like the day has gone past in a blur. I wasn't really paying much attention; I kept thinking about what happened at lunch,' Nancy admitted to her grandmother.

'I know what you mean. I can't believe the Roths want to come back to live here and seem to think we should be open to it as they stayed away for a few months. Mind you, Marcus Roth didn't look very good on his time away, did he?'

'He definitely looked like things had taken their toll on him,' Nancy agreed. 'I thought things seemed strained between him and Richard too. Maybe he doesn't like someone who's not in the family living here but it felt like he disapproved of him somehow?'

'They're both manipulative liars so you'd think they'd get on,' Jane replied dryly. 'I feel sorry for Will. He's a nice man despite his family and friends, I feel. We didn't do very well on learning anything new about Seb's murder, though, did we?'

'No, but we finally know where his pink matches are from at least. I don't think Seb would be a member of a fancy members' club in London but he had matches from there for a reason.'

'And it was his dying wish to give them to you,' Jane reminded her.

'I suppose you thought the same thing about the name by the way.'

It was testament to all the time they spent together that Nancy's gran didn't have to ask what Nancy meant. '*The Club* and *Clubhouse13*? There could be a link between the gang and this place, couldn't there?'

'And does that mean someone at Roth Lodge is involved in all this? Will, Marcus and Richard are all members. If the gang really have their hooks in some of the most influential people in this country, then owning a private club would make a lot of sense. It would give them access to those people. And a legitimate front for their activities,' Nancy said.

'Does that mean Seb was a member of the members' club or he just knew they were linked to the gang so had the matches to give you that clue?'

'I don't know,' Nancy said. 'Let's see what Jonathan can find about the members' club. And we need to find out if DCI Brown has learned anything about my grandfather and mother.'

'Shall we still talk to Mr Peabody as planned?'

Nancy nodded. 'We should in case he has anything to say about that night in the church that might help. He'll likely be at the White Swan and, after all we learned today, I could do with a drink, I don't know about you.'

'You read my mind.'

–

Mr Peabody was at his usual table in Dedley End's pub. It was a chilly evening and the pub was filling up with villagers having a drink and food after work. Nancy ordered two gin and tonics and a beer, and carried them over to where her gran had settled at Mr Peabody's table with him.

'Evening, Mr Peabody,' Nancy greeted him. 'I bought you another beer,' she said, handing everyone their drinks and sitting down.

'Very kind of you,' Mr Peabody said with a wide smile. 'I was wondering when I'd be seeing you both again. I knew you'd be investigating what happened in the church.' He sipped his beer. 'I do miss my police days when things like this happen. What's this one now – our third murder in less than a year?'

'Fourth,' Nancy said thinking about the death that appeared to be a suicide in the summer. 'Was it ever like this when you were on the force?'

He shook his head. 'I don't think we ever had a murder here. The last suspicious death was your poor father's, Nancy, and it bugged me that I could never solve it until you found out about the Roths being behind it all at Christmas. But no murders here. So, what are you thinking? Why was Sebastian Holmes killed here? You think it has to do with his former gang?'

'They are surely the suspects that make the most sense but we are stuck how they managed to do it. Did you see anything in the church that might help us, Mr Peabody?'

'I didn't, Nancy. Although I don't think you should take my eyesight and hearing as seriously as you once should have done. I'm not as sharp as I used to be.' He sighed and took a gulp of his beer. 'Like you though, I can't see who else would have done it apart from someone from Sebastian's old crime days. Perhaps they'd been waiting the whole time he was in prison for him to be released so they could kill him, you know?'

Nancy leaned in closer, aware that anyone could be listening to their conversation. 'Did you know much about his gang – *The Club*?' Nancy asked him.

'I've heard things. I've had friends at the Met. Read all the newspaper reports. They've always been a tricky organisation. They started out in East London – robbery and gambling were how they made their money. And they put a lot of it back into their community so people there kept quiet about who was involved. It wasn't like the gangs you have nowadays – they were respected locally, and they only hurt you if you hurt them. Then there was the jewellery raid when Sebastian and other members were arrested and one of them died...' Mr Peabody paused to take a sip of his drink. 'Then the gang went under-ground. They couldn't risk someone turning them in again, tipping off the police. They moved to blackmail and corruption. They used letters to threaten influential people to gain them money and power. It's made it hard for the police to track them down. Some of their victims have never even met a member of the gang.'

Nancy nodded. His account tied in with the true-crime memoir about them of her mother's she'd read and what Jonathan had told them about the gang after reading old newspaper reports. 'And they moved out of that community?'

Mr Peabody nodded. 'As I said, they became more secretive, people locally didn't know who they were anymore and things became less focused on that area of London. Other gangs moved in, of course, and things got darker. Drugs, trafficking, things that *The Club* never got involved in, gangs that would kill you as soon as look at you, just for the fun of it. I suppose like most things, it's not how it used to be.'

Nancy and Jane exchanged a look at Mr Peabody speaking wistfully about the change in gang culture. 'But it's not like they're so gentlemanly they wouldn't hurt you or kill you if they wanted to,' Nancy said.

'Of course. As I said, if you hurt them, they hurt you. Sebastian Holmes left them, perhaps he was the one who told the police about their raid, perhaps he just knew too much. Any of those reasons, or all of them, could have made them kill him in the church.'

'It's all so awful. We felt like Seb was trying to turn over a new leaf,' Jane said.

Mr Peabody snorted. 'You don't believe that, do you? A leopard doesn't change his spots, in my experience.'

'He seemed keen to try to bring the gang down. He said he was trying to find out who their leader was,' Nancy said.

Mr Peabody shook his head. 'I'm not sure I believe that there is a leader. Like I said, it's all done anonymously. There could be different offshoots, people claiming to be in the gang but they're not, no way to prove anything… I'd be shocked if there was someone actually in charge. Plus, they would be getting on like I am now. I think Sebastian was clutching at straws wanting to earn forgiveness for his sins. But instead, he ended up dead in the church. Make of that what you will.'

'It really was shocking for him to be killed in a house of God,' Jane said. 'I don't think the vicar will ever get over it. I wonder if there will be a service on Sunday or not.'

'I'll be there if there is,' Mr Peabody said. 'And most of the village I bet. I'm sorry I haven't been much help to you both but I told the police everything about that night, I didn't leave anything out that would help.'

Nancy nodded. She knew he would help if he could. 'We went to see Richard Bank and Will Roth earlier,' Nancy said. 'They were at a loss about who could have done it as well. Richard said he was with you this morning.'

'Ah yes, he's helping me with some investments,' Mr Peabody said. 'He seems like a clever man and I do worry about the future, you know?'

Nancy thought that Richard was also many other things as well as clever though. 'They both said they're part of a private members' club in London, have you heard of it? *Clubhouse13?*'

'Sorry, no. Not the sort of circles I've ever run in I'm afraid.' He finished his beer. 'Any more luck with your mother, Nancy?'

'No. I'm as stuck there as with Seb's murderer,' Nancy said.

'Ah, I hope that changes soon, Nancy, dear. Well, I suppose I'd better call it a night and get myself home.'

'Us too,' Jane agreed. 'We need to get dinner on and Charlie will be wanting a walk.'

'I'll just finish my drink,' Nancy said. 'Thank you for talking to us.'

'Anytime,' Mr Peabody said, standing up stiffly. They said goodbye to him and watched as he shuffled out of the pub.

'You didn't want to tell him about your mother and Seb being connected?' Jane asked her.

'I shouldn't have said anything to Will and Richard. Seb and DCI Brown both told me to be careful who I trust. And although I've known Mr Peabody all my life, better to be safe than sorry. The fewer people we tell the better until we know more, I think,' Nancy said.

'You're right. Well, this didn't give us anything new to go on. I have no idea what we try next to solve either of our two mysteries.'

Nancy sighed. Finding Seb's killer and discovering where her mother was both felt further away than ever. And she still had no idea how the two were linked. She really hoped her mother was far away enough to not be in danger but she knew she could not count on that. 'Let's call DCI Brown when we get home and see if he's found anything else out,' Nancy agreed.

# Chapter Twenty-Six

DCI Brown arranged to meet them at the bookshop the following morning. When he arrived, Nancy and Jane showed him into the back office, joined by Jonathan. As Pen had the day off as her husband was coming home for his leave later, they closed the shop for a few minutes so they could talk in private.

'Would you like tea or coffee? Have a seat please,' Jane said politely to the inspector.

He waved a hand. 'I can't stay long, thank you. I've found out two things that I need to tell you but I have to insist neither go beyond these four walls.' He looked sternly at Jonathan. 'And, of course, no reporting on this.' They all agreed and remained standing like he was. He looked over his shoulder. 'I'm concerned that this runs deeper than we might know. I... I don't know, I feel uneasy.'

'What do you mean?' Nancy asked him.

'There's more to all of this I think.' He shook his head. 'But let's stick with the facts first. I've looked into the gang and Seb's arrest and everything to do with that case. Your grandfather, Nancy, as you now know, was James Marlow and he was a member of *The Club*. He was close friends with Sebastian Holmes. And they worked together.' He looked at them steadily. 'I'm afraid to say he was with Seb on the jewellery raid that got him put away.'

Nancy started. 'He was on that raid? But what happened to him?'

'I'm afraid that he was the man shot during the raid,' DCI Brown replied, heavily.

'Oh.' Nancy couldn't remain standing. She sunk into one of the office chairs.

Her gran laid a hand on her shoulder. 'Are you okay, love?'

'I'm not sure,' Nancy stuttered. She knew her grandfather was long gone and had just got her head around him being in the gang with Seb, but now to find out he was on that same raid and lost his life because of it was a lot to take in. 'Who shot him?'

'It's unsolved. The police suspected at the time that one of the gang killed him, perhaps because they suspected him of tipping off the police, but they could never prove which one shot him. I looked at the interview records and Seb maintained he didn't see what happened. They tried to connect Seb to it but couldn't.'

'Do you think there's a chance he did it?' Jonathan asked DCI Brown. Nancy really hoped not. She wanted Seb's friendship with James Marlow to have been real.

'From reading the notes, I don't think so. There's more...' DCI Brown said, looking at Nancy. She nodded at him to continue, not quite able to speak. He went on. 'As I think you know from reading up on the case, someone tipped off the police before the raid and the gang were caught red-handed during it, but most of them were able to flee. Only three were imprisoned, including Sebastian. The other two died years ago. We assume the gang blamed James Marlow for telling the police, which is why he was killed but the file says it wasn't him,' DCI Brown said. 'I tried to find out who gave the tip-off, but whoever it was was given anonymity in court, presumably because the gang was trying to intimidate them and would likely have killed them to stop the case. They were put into witness protection and it's all classified. I need to go high up for access, giving a good reason for needing the information, but I don't want to tip anyone in the gang, or working for them, off. I have, however, found something important out.'

Nancy prepared herself. 'Okay,' she said, waiting for what the inspector would reveal next.

'I found out your mother's real name. As we suspected, her name wasn't Samantha Smith as she claimed when she moved here.'

'This is all so crazy,' Jane murmured, sitting down then as if she couldn't take this all in either.

'What was it?' Jonathan asked the inspector.

'Your mother was actually called Susan. Susan Marlow, before she came to Dedley End and married your father and became Samantha Hunter.'

'Hang on,' Jane said as Nancy's mouth opened in shook. 'Samantha married George. She had documents for that. Her name was Samantha on them. Her maiden name was Smith. How could she have a different name?'

'Changing her name might mean it was her,' Jonathan said, thinking along the same lines as Nancy was. 'Who tipped the police off about the raid.'

'That's the conclusion I came to,' DCI Brown said. 'I think your mother was put in witness protection.'

'It would explain so much,' Nancy half-whispered. Her mother being on the run, how mysterious she seemed, her connection to Seb. 'But her father was in *The Club*. And was part of that raid,' Nancy said. 'Would she really have grassed on her own father?'

'She might have had no choice,' DCI Brown said.

'What a mess,' Nancy said, shaking her head. 'I can't believe my family were part of *The Club*. That my mother had a fake name. Do you think my father knew?'

'We think he knew she had to leave to protect you all,' Jonathan said. 'Maybe she told him everything.'

'I wonder if Seb knew my mother was the one who told the police about the robbery,' Nancy mused.

'He must have kept in touch with her after the raid either way because he made it seem like she knew he was here,' Jonathan said. 'Can we find out if she visited him in prison?'

'She would have used a fake name,' Nancy said. 'Susan then Samantha then she went by Sally at Hugh's party. She's still trying to hide her identity after all this time. She's still scared of *The Club*.'

'Still trying to stay one step ahead while she tries to dismantle the gang,' Jonathan agreed. 'We found a list in a book in her belongings,' he explained to DCI Brown. 'A list of people the gang could have corrupted. One of them was the MP Sir Basil Walker. It was found he had awarded a government contract to a company that basically didn't exist and went off with a cut of the money. We think Samantha was the one who tipped off the authorities about him. We think she's been trying to do the same thing as Seb for all this time and stop *The Club*.'

'Do you think she was a member too before she tipped off the police?' Jane asked DCI Brown.

'I didn't find that information anywhere,' he replied, which made Nancy feel a tiny bit better. 'And there was nothing to suggest where she might be now. I can't see how this helps us with who killed Holmes. Unless your mother is involved somehow. If Seb found out she was the one who tipped off the police, they could have argued and she killed him?'

'I was with Seb before he died. When I asked him who had done it, he shook his head. He didn't know.'

'Or didn't want to tell you,' DCI Brown suggested.

Nancy really hoped that wasn't the case. 'But we didn't see anyone else in that church.'

DCI Brown nodded. 'We can't find any evidence of anyone else being in that church apart from you three, the vicar and his wife, Will Roth, Richard Bank and Mr Peabody.'

'There is no way the vicar or Gloria could have been involved,' Jane said, firmly. 'And Mr Peabody is older than me, surely he couldn't have...' Jane added, unable to finish her sentence.

'As a former police officer, I can't believe he would be involved but physically, I find it very hard to believe that he was capable of shooting Sebastian Holmes – he has such bad arthritis,' Brown said.

'We don't know who is in the gang's pocket. They could have corrupted anyone. Look at Sir Basil Walker. They seem to have all sorts of influence over powerful people,' Jonathan said. 'This members' club in London that Seb wanted Nancy to know about could be their smokescreen. Which would make Richard Bank and Will and Marcus Roth potential suspects.'

'What club?' the inspector asked. They realised that they hadn't told him about the pink matches, so Jonathan filled him in.

'You can't take evidence from my crime scenes!' DCI Brown cried. 'Honestly, I take one step forward with you three then one step back.'

'Seb wanted me to have it,' Nancy defended herself. 'I was going to tell you, I just wanted to make sure it was important. We couldn't find out anything about the matches until I saw Marcus Roth using them and then we realised they are from this private club.'

'I did some online research into *Clubhouse13*,' Jonathan said. Nancy realised she hadn't had a chance to ask him what he'd found out yet. 'It's a private members' club in Mayfair. As expected, the website is sleek and glossy. You have to know three other members to even be considered and the list is kept secret. High-profile people are reported to be members but it looks like any other members' club – people hang out there to eat and drink, have meetings, network... There's no way Seb would have been a member. He must have had a reason to give Nancy the matches but I have no idea what it was,' Jonathan said, looking perplexed.

'Why does nothing make sense?' Nancy asked, leaning back in her chair, feeling exhausted.

DCI Brown's expression softened. 'I know it's been difficult finding out your connection to all this, Nancy. But all of you, you can't find things out and not tell me, okay?' They all nodded sheepishly. 'Good. I can look into the members' club, see if the police have had any dealings with it.' DCI Brown checked his watch. 'I have to go. I've kept most of what I've found out about your family, Nancy, from my team. Pang knows it all but we're keeping it between us because of the potential witness protection aspect.'

'You think someone found out Nancy's mother was here in Dedley End?' Jonathan asked. 'That's why she had to run?'

'I think it's a strong possibility. If they found out she grassed, they would want to punish her. And she could still be on the run from the gang so we can't let them find her before we do,' DCI Brown said.

Nancy's blood ran cold. She could never forgive herself if her search for her mother put her in danger. Her mother appeared to have left Dedley End to protect her, but now it felt like it was Nancy's turn to protect her mother.

DCI Brown continued. 'You three need to be extra careful. The gang might know you're related to former members, Nancy. And that Sebastian was talking to you. I have asked DC Pang to keep an eye on the shop and your cottage as much as he can, and if you see anything at all suspicious, tell one of us immediately, okay? I'm not letting anyone else get hurt in this village. Leave looking into *Clubhouse13* to me. I'll be in touch.'

They showed him out but Jane kept the bookshop closed after he left so they could digest what he had told them. There wasn't a queue of customers but they couldn't stay shut all day so they spoke hurriedly.

'I can't believe what he told us,' Nancy said. 'This doesn't feel real.'

'I never knew Samantha at all, did I?' Jane said, shaking her head. 'To think she might have been on the run from that gang all these years.'

'Now we know why she might be trying to take them down. I'd want revenge on them after they killed my father, and forced me to leave my husband and daughter,' Jonathan said. 'I think she sent Seb here to look out for you. She hasn't forgotten you, Nancy.'

'It sounds like she's been looking out for you all these years,' Jane agreed.

'Do you really think she's a victim not a villain?' Nancy asked. 'There's still a chance she was in the gang and still is, and is involved in Seb's murder.'

'Well, we should keep open to that possibility,' Jonathan said. 'But do you really think she would kill someone, Nancy?'

The question hung in the air. The problem was Nancy didn't know her mother at all. 'What do we now?' Nancy asked, avoiding his question because it was impossible to answer.

'We need to find out if Richard, Marcus or Will are involved with the gang,' Jonathan said. 'My money is on old Dickie. I've never trusted that man.'

'But also, Marcus Roth is suddenly back in the village,' Nancy reminded him. 'He could be involved somehow. Why don't we watch Roth Lodge, see if one of them gives us a clue as to what is going on?'

'A good old stakeout? I like it,' Jonathan said, his eyes twinkling.

'I could pack us a picnic,' Jane said.

Nancy had to smile. 'And I bought myself binoculars just in case we ever needed them. So, do we start tonight then? Once it's dark, we see what's happening at Roth Lodge.'

'I don't have any other plans,' Jonathan said.

'No hot date?' Nancy couldn't resist asking.

He looked at her. 'This is more important.'

She nodded. It was.

## Chapter Twenty-Seven

She wouldn't have imagined doing this on a Friday night just a year ago but now neither Nancy, her grandmother or Jonathan batted an eyelid at spending the evening on a stakeout.

The three of them piled into Jonathan's car with all their supplies, enough for a weekend away it felt like, and drove away from the cottage, up the hill and parked outside the gates of Roth Lodge. A large oak tree stood on either side of the road that provided a good cover on the dark night. Nancy felt confident that if anyone took a quick glance out of any windows or if someone came out of the gate then they wouldn't immediately be spotted. One gate was left open now that the house was occupied, and they could see that Marcus, Richard and Will's cars were all parked outside, indicating they were inside the grand house.

Nancy pulled out her binoculars and had a look from the passenger seat as Jane poured out tea from her thermos for them and Jonathan opened up a box of mini brownies. 'I can see the kitchen. Mrs Harper the housekeeper is in there but the dining room is at the back, so if they're having dinner I won't be able to see. Oh, hang on, Marcus Roth is in his study. He's pacing back and forth.'

'A lot on his mind, I would imagine,' Jane remarked darkly from the back seat.

'Richard is going into the study,' Nancy said, sitting up straight, which resulted in her banging her head on the roof of the car. 'Ouch!'

'Let me see.' Jonathan took the binoculars while Nancy rubbed her head. 'Richard is going into the study and is sitting the other side of the desk. Marcus has sat down opposite him now,' Jonathan told them.

'Do they look hostile, like they were at lunch?' Jane asked, leaning forward. 'Have a cake, love, it'll help with the pain.'

Nancy didn't really believe it but took one anyway. 'Well?' she nudged Jonathan.

'They look a little bit heated,' he said, straining to see. 'Marcus is definitely gesturing angrily across the desk, pointing at Richard.' He handed the binoculars back to Nancy so she could see.

'They are arguing,' she confirmed, watching the body language. 'I wish we could have bugged their office like someone did to Seb. I want to know what they're arguing about. I mean, until Richard was working with Will, I didn't get the impression he had much to do with Marcus. It's Marcus's son and Will's dad, Peter, who runs the family business, so when Richard was their accountant, they would have dealt with things not Marcus.'

'It wouldn't surprise me if the family business had dodgy accounts,' Jonathan said. 'They probably get away without paying tax. All the rich do.'

'Richard has always seemed legit though,' Nancy said. 'But the Roths could have changed that.' He certainly hadn't been a good boyfriend to her but she had never had the impression that he wasn't all above board when it came to business. 'Maybe that's why they're arguing.

Richard won't fiddle the books like Marcus wants? Maybe his company with Will isn't doing that well.'

'Marcus is selling the family business. Maybe it's something to do with that,' Jonathan suggested.

'Or the businesses are controlled by the gang.' The other two turned to look at Jane. 'Well, they could be working for them, couldn't they?'

'They could,' Nancy said. She thought about something. 'Seb had been watching Roth Lodge and told me Marcus was back, maybe he suspected Marcus is involved with the gang?'

'Someone is coming out,' Jane said, pointing.

'It's old Dickie,' Jonathan said.

They watched as Richard walked out of Roth Lodge and got into his car.

'Has he stormed out because of Marcus?' Nancy wondered.

'Should we follow him, see where he is going?' Jonathan asked her.

Nancy hesitated. 'I was so furious when he had me followed,' she reminded him.

'Totally different. He got that guy to keep tabs on you because he was jealous and wanted to manipulate you into being with him. This is a murder investigation. You're not after him romantically. You're not stalking him or being creepy. He might very well be a murderer.' He looked at her. 'I mean, sorry, I know he's your ex...'

'Stop talking and just drive,' Nancy said, shaking her head.

–

They followed Richard's car for about half an hour. It was a clear night, so the moon and stars lit the way.

The roads were quiet as they twisted and turned through the Cotswold countryside until Richard suddenly turned sharply off the main road.

'This is the way to the river,' Jonathan said quietly as he slowly followed Richard. They stayed close behind as Richard drove for another few minutes then turned into a small car park. Jonathan pulled over to the side of the road. 'I'd better not get any closer, he'll hear the car.' He turned off the engine and they watched as Richard climbed out of his car and slipped into darkness.

It was almost pitch-black, no lampposts to cast any light on him, so Nancy struggled to see what he was doing. 'We'd better get out,' she said. They climbed out of Jonathan's car and walked ahead. The moon cast a pool of silvery light on top of the River Windrush ahead. Nancy lit up the torch on her iPhone and swept around. 'Over there,' she said, softly, seeing a figure walking towards the water.

'What the hell is he doing?' Jonathan wondered as the three of them walked carefully towards the river, Nancy's phone lighting up a narrow path for them to follow.

'I don't like this,' Jane said after a minute. Nancy nodded even though her grandmother couldn't see her in the dim light. This was a very strange thing to do on an autumn night. They walked past willow trees that were swaying from the cool breeze blowing from the river.

They stepped out into a clearing then. Here with the moon and stars up above, it was slightly less dark and they finally could make Richard out. He was standing right by the river now, looking out on to the inky-coloured water.

'He's not going to jump in, is he?' Nancy asked, edging forward.

'He's carrying something,' Jonathan said, straining to see. The three of them stepped a few paces closer cautiously to try to see what he was doing.

Nancy shivered. Something was very wrong, she could feel it in her bones. 'What is he holding?' She frowned. 'It looks like a blanket,' Nancy said. She held her binoculars out again. 'It *is* a blanket. He's unwrapping it. There's something inside.' And then moonlight caught what he was holding and she gasped, dropping the binoculars to the ground. 'I think… he has a gun,' she said in horror.

And then, before the other two could respond, a sudden noise and burst of light startled them. They spun around as three police cars shot out of the silent night in a blaze of blue flashing lights, sirens wailing shattering the peace, as they drove along the bumpy track up to the river's edge. Nancy turned to see Richard look up as the headlights shone on his face, showing his expression of utter shock and terror.

## Chapter Twenty-Eight

Nancy, Jane and Jonathan rushed forward to see DCI Brown climbing out of one of the police cars with uniformed officers and then DC Pang jumped from the car behind. Torches joined the headlights of the cars in lighting up the scene. Now it was no longer dark, Nancy had to believe her eyes – Richard was definitely holding a gun in the unwrapped blanket, frozen in place right by the river as the police swarmed towards him.

DCI Brown held up a hand to stop everyone. 'Is that a gun? Drop it now,' he barked. 'Don't make me call armed response,' he added, his voice fierce and strong in the secluded spot. 'Mr Bank... Richard, drop the gun now!'

Richard seemed to suddenly stir out of his trance and he instantly let the gun and blanket fall to the ground with a thud. Then he raised his arms in the air. 'It's not loaded,' he called out. 'I wasn't going to... I was just going to throw it in the river,' he said, his voice sounding so much smaller than it usually did to Nancy's ears. 'How did you know I was here?'

'We had an anonymous tip-off,' DCI Brown said as he went over, picked up the gun and then gestured to his officers. DC Pang sprang forward and handcuffed Richard's hands behind his back. DCI Brown passed the gun in his gloved hands to one of his officers who bagged it up. Then DCI Brown arrested Richard on suspicion of murdering Sebastian Holmes.

'He killed Seb?' Nancy said, unable to stay silent. She stepped forward out of the shadow of the willow trees that had shielded the three of them from everyone.

DCI Brown, Pang and Richard all turned in shock as Jonathan and Jane stepped out behind Nancy. 'What are you three doing here?' the inspector barked at them.

'Nancy! Thank God!' Richard looked frantically at Nancy, struggling against his handcuffs as DC Pang held on to him. 'You have to help me! I didn't kill Seb, I swear it!'

DCI Brown looked between them. 'Did you send in the anonymous tip, Nancy?' She shook her head. 'Then what are you doing out here?'

Nancy turned from Richard looking at her desperately to DCI Brown. 'We saw Richard leave Roth Lodge so decided to follow him. Did he really kill Seb, inspector?'

'I intend to find out,' he replied, grimly. 'Go home now. I'll talk to you tomorrow.'

'Wait!' Richard called out. 'Nancy, I swear. I didn't kill Sebastian! I was forced to do this, to get rid of the gun. They have been threatening me. Threatening us… they left it on the doorstep and told me I had to get rid of it. I had no choice!'

'Come on,' DC Pang pulled Richard towards the police car.

'Wait!' Nancy cried. 'Who's they? Who has been threatening you?' she called out to her ex-boyfriend.

'Speak to Marcus! Marcus Roth!' Richard yelled desperately as he was taken to the police car. The door was closed on Richard and they saw him sitting in the back, his head bowed in defeat.

'You think Richard is in *The Club*?' Jonathan asked DCI Brown. .

DCI Brown sighed. 'It looks like it. We had a tip-off that the gun used to kill Mr Holmes was being dumped here, and they were right. Either Richard killed him or was part of it, and his job was to hide the murder weapon. We'll get it checked out. See if it was used to kill Sebastian and see if we can get Richard to talk. Tell us who else is in on all this. But there's more...' He looked around and leaned in closer to them. 'I looked into the London members' club. Nothing that suggested anything unto-ward going on there but I found out that not only are the Roths members – they run it.'

'What?' Nancy and Jonathan said in unison.

'*Clubhouse13* records at Companies House list Marcus Roth as its managing director.'

'God, that man!' Jane cried.

Nancy thought about Seb watching the house and telling her over the phone that Marcus was back in the village. That spurred him to want to tell Nancy everything. Because he believed that Marcus was the leader of the gang? 'Do you think that Marcus is who Seb was trying to find? That he's *The Governor*?'

'I don't know. I sent officers to Roth Lodge when I got the call about Richard, but Marcus had gone. Left soon after Richard, his grandson said. Will Roth claims he has no idea where Marcus Roth is. But don't worry, we'll find him.' DCI Brown nodded once at them and then headed back to the car he had been driven in. Nancy, Jane and Jonathan watched as Richard was driven away and the police dispersed, leaving the river as dark and quiet as it had been when they arrived, almost as if nothing had happened.

'Marcus Roth is *The Governor*?' Jonathan said once they were alone. 'Well, on one hand I'm not surprised but I don't know if I believe it. A gang that started in London. All those crimes. All those people in high places corrupted by them. And Marcus was the puppet master behind it all?'

'We never trusted him,' Jane reminded him. 'Look at what he's done to us. And we noticed that Richard seemed to hate him. He told us to speak to Marcus just now. He sounded desperate. Marcus must have been threatening him. Getting Richard to do his dirty work, like this here tonight.'

'Richard said he didn't kill Seb,' Nancy said.

'And you really believe him?' Jonathan asked her. 'He was trying to get rid of a gun. That's not exactly the behaviour of an innocent man, is it?'

'I know but...' Nancy knew her ex-boyfriend hadn't been the man she had once thought he was, but a member of a gang? Tied up in a murder? It was too crazy to believe. 'I need to think. Can we go home?' she asked, shivering.

'Here.' Jonathan took off his coat and draped it over her shoulders. 'Come on.' He led the way back to his car and, once inside, turned the heating on high and drove them back to Dedley End as Nancy tried to understand how Richard could have become embroiled with Seb's former gang without her even noticing.

Nancy sighed. 'How could Richard have killed Seb that night but we didn't see anything?' she asked as their cottage came into view and relief washed over her that she was almost home. 'He arrived with Will looking for us. How would he have known Will would definitely stop to speak to us outside the church? Did he lure Seb there ready? It all seems so far-fetched.'

'And we were all together outside the vicarage when the shots were fired,' Jonathan said. 'I don't know how he did it. But he was there and he had the gun, Nancy. That has to mean he's involved at the very least.'

'Maybe he knows who the killer is and has been helping them?' Jane suggested. 'Thank goodness you're not with him anymore, love, that's all I can say. Come on, you need a brandy after all that. We all do.'

Nancy nodded and followed the other two inside the cottage numbly. The last thing she had expected was to see Richard trying to throw away the gun that killed Seb tonight. 'Also, I wonder who tipped the police off? One of the gang? Or Marcus Roth?'

'The murderer, so all suspicion would be thrown on to Richard and not them,' Jonathan suggested as he greeted Charlie at the door. 'Hey, boy. I just keep coming back to the locked church and how the killer did it. We're missing something, aren't we?'

Nancy nodded. 'We are, but I don't know what yet.' She sighed. 'Richard looked terrified. He begged me for help but I'm not sure what I can do. This feels so much more complicated than the other murders we have investigated.' Nancy trusted her gut though and she didn't think Richard could have faked that shock and panic tonight. He couldn't believe the police had arrived and he was desperate to make her believe he wasn't the killer, that he'd been coerced into abandoning the gun. They went into the living room and Jane went to the drinks trolley to pour them all a brandy. 'Whoever the killer is, we need to stop them. They can't get away with all of this,' Nancy said, determinedly.

'We won't let them,' Jane agreed.

'We need one hell of a plan to stop them,' Jonathan said.

Nancy knew he was right. 'We—' She broke off as furious knocking on the cottage door interrupted her. She turned to look at the front door wearily. 'What now?'

# Chapter Twenty-Nine

Will Roth was on the doorstep when Nancy opened the door. 'Nancy, I need your help,' he said, urgently.

'You might need to join the queue,' she snapped, but then felt bad when she saw how frantic he looked. 'Come in.' She led him into the living room. 'We're having a brandy, it's been a long night.'

'Would you like one?' Jane asked.

'Please.' Once they all had a glass and had sat down, Will leaned forward on the armchair to look at the three of them. 'I can't believe it. The police have been at the house looking for my grandfather. They said they've arrested Richard for murder. And they seem to think I'm part of an organised crime gang!' He finished his brandy in one gulp. The others exchanged looks. He took a breath. 'I haven't even had a parking ticket, for God's sake. I rung my lawyer. He said don't say anything and he'll be in Dedley End first thing in the morning to help Richard at the police station. My grandfather fled the house before I could talk to him and I have no idea where he's gone. I didn't know what to do but then I thought I know there are people who would know what to do. So, here I am.'

'Will,' Nancy said after she'd taken a sip of the brandy and shuddered. It was vile stuff but she told herself it was medicinal. 'Are you really sure you know nothing about *The Club*?'

Will frowned. 'You mean *Clubhouse13*? The members' club in London we belong to?'

'Well, they could be linked. *The Club* is what Seb called his former gang. He made sure I knew the matches he had from your members' club were important. It could be owned by the gang. A place where they can mingle with powerful people. Seb was here in Dedley End to bring the gang down by finding out who the leader was. The person in charge, right at the top. He called them *The Governor*. And he said who that is has been a secret even to top members of the gang,' Nancy said. She leaned forward to look at Will. 'DCI Brown told us that your grandfather is the managing director of *Clubhouse13*. Could he be the leader of the gang too?'

Will let out a bark of laughter. 'A gang? A leader of a gang? My grandfather? Are you serious? He doesn't go anywhere in London that's under five stars.'

'You need a lot of money to fund that life,' Jonathan observed.

'Yes, but I've never seen him do anything untoward.'

'Come on, Will. It's not like your family are saints,' Nancy reminded him.

'No, I know, but it's a big leap from what they've done to protect family members to being part of organised crime,' Will said. 'Look, the reason I came here was to tell you I really can't believe Richard or my grandfather are involved in any of this. Richard has always been legit through and through.' Nancy could see he was sincere. He really appeared bewildered by what the police had told him about the men at Roth Lodge.

'When we were at your house, we thought there was tension between Richard and Marcus,' Jane said. 'How do you explain that?'

Will nodded. 'I'd noticed it too since Grandfather came back to the house. Before that, I hadn't seen anything but mutual respect between them. I haven't seen much of my grandfather since everything that happened at Christmas, since the family left Roth Lodge, so I don't think Richard has either. But I sensed the tension instantly once my grandfather came back. I asked them both about it but they brushed it off. I thought that maybe my grandfather was still angry I'd left the family business to work with Richard and Richard was angry about what he had done to you, Nancy. I thought that made sense. I didn't think there was more behind it but, maybe there was...'

'Maybe Marcus forced Richard to dispose of the gun,' Jonathan suggested. 'We saw them arguing before Richard drove off and we followed him to the river. And when he was arrested, Richard told us to talk to Marcus.'

'I don't understand it,' Will said. 'Neither of them have had a gun before. My grandfather hasn't even tried clay pigeon shooting!'

'What if one of them killed Seb?' Nancy asked.

Will shook his head. 'I just can't believe that, Nancy. Murderers? Surely, none of you really believe they are capable of that?'

'Richard did seem genuine when he told me he didn't do it and begged me for my help at the river,' Nancy said. 'But he is involved somehow because he was trying to get rid of that gun. The gun we assume killed Seb. And he told us to speak to your grandfather who has run off. Neither of them can be completely innocent.' Will sighed and Nancy knew he knew she was right about that.

'But my grandfather can't run the club in London. I would have seen that income in our books. In our bank accounts. I don't see why he would never have told me either. It's a legitimate business despite what you say might be happening behind the scenes. My father would have known too, surely? He runs the family company now. It doesn't make any sense!'

'DCI Brown told us that your grandfather is listed as the managing director. Whatever the truth, we need to find him. We need to talk to Marcus about all of this,' Nancy said.

'I think he's gone to London,' Will said. 'Frank, our butler, said he muttered he would have to hide out there as he fled the house. Shall we see if we can track him down before the police do?'

'Hang on,' Jane said. 'I get that you are finding it hard to believe, Will, but there is a chance that Marcus Roth is the head of a dangerous gang. We need to be careful.'

'He wouldn't hurt me,' Will said. 'I know that.'

'If we go to London then we should go to *Clubhouse13*,' Jonathan said. 'We can snoop around, get a feel for why it was so important Seb made sure Nancy took his matchbook from there before he died.' He turned to Nancy. 'He wanted you to know about that club, there has to be a reason for that and the only way we'll find out is to go there ourselves. And if we can track down Marcus too and see what he has to say about all of this, so much the better.'

Nancy could see her grandmother was nervous but she had to agree. Seb's dying wish had been to give her his matchbook. 'We've hit a dead end when it comes to the murder in the church. But this we can do. We need to go there. It feels like everything is pointing towards *Clubhouse13*. We need to find out why.'

Will shook his head. 'I've been there so many times. I don't get how there could be anything connecting it to this gang, but you need me to get inside and I need to find my grandfather. So, let's go together. Someone there might know where he is as well. Then, hopefully, we can sort this mess out.'

'I don't like this at all, it could be dangerous,' Jane said. 'Are you sure you should do this without seeing what DCI Brown thinks about it?'

'He said himself to be careful who we trust. The fewer people who know we're going to be in London the better,' Nancy said. 'We don't want anyone in the gang finding out and coming after us. Or Marcus, and then he runs somewhere else we can't find him.' She turned to her grandmother knowing she wasn't going to like what Nancy was about to say. 'That's why you need to stay here, Gran.' Before Jane could protest, she carried on. 'We need you to keep the bookshop open, act like everything is okay and, to anyone who asks, say me and Jonathan have gone to see an old friend. Don't let on you know anything about where Marcus or Will are. Or lead anyone to us in London. Will, you should tell your household staff to say you're with your boyfriend if the police need you.'

Will nodded. 'Rupert will cover for me.'

Nancy could see how upset her grandmother was about this plan. 'This is the best way to do it. We don't want the gang to know we're investigating them, Gran, if they don't already, and we need to find Marcus Roth. I'll ask Pen and Ollie to look out for you.'

'I don't need looking after,' Jane said, hotly. She looked at Nancy and sighed as if she knew that her granddaughter wasn't going to budge on this. 'You will be careful, won't you? If anything happens, you'll call DCI Brown straight away? Do not put yourself in further danger, you hear me?'

'I promise,' Nancy said. She turned to Will and Jonathan. 'Let's leave first thing.'

# Chapter Thirty

It was a foggy start to Saturday. Nancy made herself a cup of tea after she had fed Charlie. She'd been up since the early hours and was already showered and dressed ready to head to London but she needed a few quiet moments in the kitchen before they left Dedley End. She looked out at the garden, but she could hardly see it with the grey mist circling over the trees that were changing from greens to yellows and oranges, creating what looked like a patch-work blanket draped over the small space. She reached down to ruffle Charlie's fur as he pressed into her, seeming to sense that she needed comfort from him this morning. 'It'll all be okay, won't it, Charlie?' she murmured to her beagle, feeling a mixture of anticipation and anxiety about her trip.

Nancy had been to London many times but this visit felt different. She had discovered her family had ties to the city that she hadn't known about. She still couldn't believe that her family had been mixed up in organised crime, that her grandfather had been in a gang. She wanted to hide from such a past, but she knew she couldn't.

Nancy had always finished a mystery once she started one, in books and in real life, and she knew she had to see this one through. She had to know what had happened to her family. And to find out who had killed Seb. And how it was all linked.

Nancy was nervous though. Not just about the potential danger from the gang – she'd seen what they had done to Seb right in front of her eyes, after all – but also because of what she might find out about her own past while she was in London. She looked at the hot-pink book of matches on the kitchen table. Seb had been determined she should have them and she knew the only way to really find out why was to go to the members' club they were from, but that didn't stop her from feeling uneasy about it. She was grateful she wasn't going alone though. She knew with Jonathan she could handle anything. Will, she was less sure of, but he could get them into the club so they needed him. And she was relieved that her grandmother had agreed to stay home. It would be one less thing to worry about today at least.

'Morning, love.' Jane seemed to materialise out of Nancy's thoughts as she entered the kitchen in her dressing gown, looking as tired as Nancy felt after her own restless night's sleep. 'Gosh, it's so misty today. Will you be okay getting to London?' she asked, looking out of the kitchen door with a frown.

'It's not far to the station. Here, I've made tea.' Nancy brought over two cups to the table and sat down with her gran. Charlie followed and sat by her. 'At least you'll have Charlie with you.'

'I don't think he makes a particularly good guard dog,' Jane said with a laugh.

Charlie let out one bark and Nancy chuckled. 'You've upset him now.' Nancy didn't really think the loyal dog could put up much of a fight if required, but she supposed people didn't know that. It made her feel slightly better anyway that her grandmother wouldn't be completely alone in the cottage.

'I know that finding out about your heritage and your family links to the gang has been hard, Nancy, love, but I wanted to say that no matter what happens in London, don't forget what kind of person you are. Someone who looks out for others, who fights for justice, who seeks the truth and who is always there to help people who need it. That's what matters. Not what kind of man your grandfather was or what kind of woman your mother is,' Jane said.

Nancy smiled. 'Thank you, Gran.' She reached across the kitchen table to squeeze Jane's hand. 'You made me the person I am today, you know that, don't you?'

They looked at one another with misty eyes. 'Goodness me, we are a sentimental pair,' Jane said, shaking her head.

There was a knock at the door. 'That must be Jonathan.' She shouted out to come in and was surprised when not only Jonathan but Will Roth, followed by Penelope, her husband Ollie and their little girl Kitty, all traipsed into their small kitchen. 'What's all this?' Nancy asked as Charlie ran off eagerly to greet everyone and Jane touched her undone hair in horror.

'We thought we'd come to see you off, and take Mrs H out to breakfast,' Pen said. 'We met Jonathan and Will coming in at the same time.'

Nancy was grateful her friends were there to look after her gran even though Jane would never think of herself as needing looking after. 'Great, I'll get my things.'

'Well, there really is no need for that, but I'll get dressed,' Jane said, hurrying out behind Nancy. 'Goodness, everyone seeing me in my dressing gown. Take care, love.' She hugged her granddaughter fiercely. 'And you find out the truth, love.'

'I'll do my best.'

—

They got to Dedley End train station and bought tickets from Old Bill to take them to London. The platform was misty and cold, and the sun hadn't fully risen yet. Nancy looked down the platform. A minute after they arrived, a man stepped on to the platform to wait for the train too. He wore a long dark coat and a thick scarf that hid part of his face from view. He glanced their way and then turned to watch the train as it rolled in to the platform. Nancy knew most of the people in her village, at least by sight, but he was unfamiliar to her.

As they climbed on to the train, Nancy glanced at him and saw he climbed into the next carriage to theirs, which was a relief as theirs was empty, so they could talk.

The train drew away from Dedley End parting through the mist with the sound of a whistle. Nancy took a window seat but she could barely see the Cotswold countryside as the train set off towards London. Beside her, Jonathan sipped his takeaway coffee they had picked up on the way and, opposite them, Will Roth was checking his phone.

Will looked up after a minute. 'I heard from our lawyer this morning, he's at the police station and Richard is about to be interviewed,' Will said. 'He said he'll update me later. And he told me to try to get my grandfather to contact the police. A warrant is out for his arrest now. They are looking for him and it would be much better if he came forward of his own free will.' He sighed. 'Why do problems follow my family around?'

'I feel the same way,' Nancy said.

He raised an eyebrow. 'What do you mean?'

Nancy looked at Jonathan unsure whether she should tell Will or not.

Will saw their look. 'I am your friend, Nancy. I know you don't feel the same after everything my family's done but I trusted you at Christmas. I told you about my boyfriend and I'd never told anyone about him. I hope you know you can tell me anything and it goes no further. And if it's important to what we're going to London for then I need to know. I need to find out the truth too.'

Nancy nodded. For better or worse, they were on this trip together and both were looking for answers from their family. And Will had indeed trusted her with his secret. They needed to work together in London if they were going to make all of this right, so she looked around to make sure they were still alone in the carriage before telling Will about her connection to Seb. 'I found out that my grandfather was part of *The Club*. He was friends with Seb and during the jewellery raid that put Seb in prison, my grandfather was killed by a member of the gang.'

Will's eyes widened. 'Wow. Maybe that explains your love of crime. You know what I mean,' he said, seeing her expression.

'I know,' she said. It was in her blood.

'So, what about your mother? Do you think she's connected to it all as well?'

'She must be,' Nancy said. She took a breath. 'She changed her name after that raid. DCI Brown says there's a possibility she called the police on the gang and ended up in witness protection.'

'She could have been working with Seb to try to bring the gang down,' Jonathan said. 'That's our current theory.

But Samantha Hunter is still an enigma in all of this. Seb was going to tell us more about her but then he was shot.'

'You think he was killed so he wouldn't tell you about your mother?' Will asked, shocked.

'It has to have been to stop him telling us something,' Nancy replied. 'It might have been about my mother or the gang or who their leader is. Or all of it. Maybe he was going to be killed all along for leaving the gang, but I think it's too much of a coincidence that he said he'd tell me everything and then he was shot on the same night. DCI Brown said his cottage had been bugged, so someone knew he was meeting me that night. And Seb had already told me his mission after leaving prison was to bring the gang down. To find out the leader of it all.'

'It can't be my grandfather. It can't be,' Will insisted.

Jonathan shrugged. 'He's involved in some way, Will, you must accept that. He's fled Dedley End and Richard told us to speak to him when he was arrested. They're both involved in this somehow.'

'Then they need our help,' he replied, stubbornly. Nancy did admire his loyalty. Will looked at them. 'I know you think I'm stupid to trust my family after everything they've done. I know they've made mistakes, they've not treated people well and they made me feel like I couldn't be myself, but they're my blood and, when they're in trouble, I need to help. I'm the first to tell them when they've done wrong but this doesn't feel like that. I think something else is going on. My grandfather and Richard could be being framed, right?'

'Could be,' Jonathan said. 'But often there's no smoke without fire.'

'Well, look, at least we can find out the truth one way or another,' Will said, seeming to sense they weren't going to agree with him just yet. 'That's all I'm asking.'

Nancy turned to look at the fog outside the train window again, hoping it would lift soon. It was hard to see things clearly through it, just like this case was hard to make sense of. 'The problem with the truth is, once we find it, there's no going back,' she said, half to herself.

# Chapter Thirty-One

They couldn't talk for the rest of the journey as their carriage filled up with people the closer they got to London. When they arrived, they joined the throngs climbing off the train and Nancy recognised the man who'd been waiting on the platform at Dedley End with them. He followed them through the barrier and on to the station.

Nancy felt a bit overwhelmed as she looked around. She hadn't been to London since Christmas when she half thought she would reconcile with Richard, so she felt as if she had dodged a bullet – pun intended – given the circumstances. Nancy had never been the biggest fan of the bustling city, she had long known that Dedley End was her forever home, and her nerves about what awaited them, coupled with the misty weather, filled her with unease as they walked through the station. Then she had that horrible prickly feeling on the back of her neck. A feeling that someone was watching her.

She looked over her shoulder as they walked through the busy train station packed with people looking forward to enjoying the sights and sounds of the city, and she caught sight of the same man from the train again. He was a few feet behind them and seemed to have his eyes on her back. But they were walking towards the exit and he'd been on the same train so it made perfect sense for him to be following them, didn't it? Nancy told herself to stop being paranoid.

They walked outside then. The fog hadn't fully lifted so only the tallest buildings were poking through the sky as if someone had laid a carpet across the city. They found a taxi waiting outside the station to take them to Mayfair and to *Clubhouse13*. Nancy glanced behind one last time as she climbed into the taxi but there were so many people outside the station, she couldn't see the man from the train anymore.

'Do you think your grandfather will be at *Clubhouse13*?' Jonathan asked Will once they were seated in the black cab and weaving their way through the heavy traffic.

'Maybe or someone there might have seen him. When the police came for him, I rang my father and mother, they are visiting my brother in Paris and hadn't heard from him. But they've alerted their housekeeper at the London house to let me know if my grandfather turns up. He hasn't yet.'

'Let's hope someone at your club has seen him,' Jonathan said.

'I'm allowed two guests at the club so we're fine on that front,' Will said. 'But if anyone asks, and they likely will as it's a chatty club, who should we say we are to one another?' He looked nervous now they were close.

'Just say we're cousins,' Jonathan said with a shrug. 'Rich people have hundreds of cousins, right?'

Will looked at him despairingly. 'That's rather stereo-typical, but I suppose I do have a fair few.' He bit his lip. 'Will anyone know that Richard has been arrested or that my grandfather is wanted by the police?'

'DCI Brown has just said a man has been arrested; they are keeping it vague while they investigate. It's such a high-profile case, the police have to get it right.

I agreed not to post about the arrest if they give me the exclusive when Brown is ready to release the news,' Jonathan replied.

'Okay, so I keep it under wraps as to why I want to find my grandfather?' Will checked.

'Exactly. We want one of his friends to tell us if they've seen him,' Nancy said. 'I'd definitely not mention that Marcus is in trouble. Just that you've made an impromptu trip to the city and thought your grandfather would be at the club today, see what people say to that?' Nancy suggested.

'Good idea. What do you two need to do there?'

'I want to look around, see if we can find the office, and find something to either confirm or deny the fact that your grandfather runs the place. And if there are any connections to *The Club*,' Nancy said. 'And why Seb thought it was so important he made sure I knew about the place as he was dying.' A cold shiver ran down her spine that had nothing to do with the chilly weather. Nancy tried not to relive the look in Seb's eyes as the life faded out of him, but it came to her when she least expected it and she knew she'd be haunted by it for a long time. She'd seen dead bodies but no one had died in her arms before. The only thing keeping her in one piece was the determination to bring whoever had done that to him to justice.

The taxi drove alongside Hyde Park before turning into a small side street and pulling up outside a beautiful eighteen century townhouse made of distinctive cream stone with a black front door. They climbed out and watched the taxi drive off.

'Well?' Will looked at them. Nancy and Jonathan turned, followed Will up to the door, and watched as he used a key card to open it. They stepped into an opulent hallway, which had a marble floor and an ornate carved fireplace. Will went over to the discreet reception desk, where he signed them both in, and then they trailed after him into the lounge area.

Nancy marvelled at the hidden world she had stepped into. The room was long, narrow and traditionally decorated, with panelling and wallpaper, heavy drapes, leather chairs and a rich red carpet. Small tables were dotted around and some people were sipping coffee and tea, reading newspapers or chatting. She glanced up and saw the ceiling was gold tipped; at one end was a huge painting in a gold frame that was likely worth a fortune.

'Tea?' Will suggested, finding a table in the corner that had a good view of the room. They sat down and he nodded to a waiter, who seemed to appear out of nowhere wearing all black, and requested tea for three, pastries and a newspaper. Once they were alone again, he leaned forward and spoke in a soft voice. 'This is the lounge. Through there is the formal dining room,' he said, gesturing to one end. 'And I believe the kitchen is behind it. Back through the lobby where we came from is the library, a games room and then the bar, which has stairs leading up to the second floor where there are private meeting rooms and the offices. This is a good location to see who's here today.'

Nancy was glad she had dressed smartly in her wool dress and beret as she glanced round. All the men wore suits and the women were in dresses or skirts, and she could see the average income was at least double hers by the jewellery and designer handbags on display. Tea was bought in delicate china and she made a note to describe it to Jane – her grandmother would have really enjoyed this. She couldn't really though as she felt like she was only seeing what this place wanted her to see. She leaned in to speak in a low voice to Jonathan and Will. 'Now I'm here, it's even stranger that Seb had a book of matches from here. I mean, he's not the typical clientele, is he? So, was he bought here as a guest? Before or after prison? Is it a front for his gang or is there another reason he wanted me to know about this place?' Nancy was frustrated by how many questions were running through her mind.

'If there are links to that gang, they are kept completely hidden,' Will replied as he put sugar in his tea. 'I've never seen anyone here whose family didn't go back generations or were filthy rich or famous for something. That's why it's so crazy to imagine anything untoward could be going on here. If it is a smokescreen, it's the most impressive one.'

'But you didn't know your grandfather was the MD, so what else has been kept from you all this time?' Nancy asked him.

Will shook his head. 'I just don't see how he could have hidden that from me.'

Nancy wasn't sure if Will was just too stubborn for his own good or if there was something more going on here.

'We'll find out the truth,' Jonathan said, firmly. He glanced around as he bit into one of the pastries. 'But at least we can enjoy these first. Delicious.' Nancy rolled her eyes at him.

'William,' someone said, and they turned to see a man and woman walking over to their table with bright smiles on their faces. 'I thought you were still in the Cotswolds?'

'I've just come down for a couple of days to show my cousins around,' Will said. 'This is Mr and Mrs Castle, they are old family friends,' Will introduced them to Nancy and Jonathan, and everyone shook hands. 'We thought my grandfather would be here for breakfast but there's no sign of him,' Will said then.

'I didn't know he was in London, I thought he was still in Paris?' Mr Castle said. Marcus Roth had an apartment there as did Will's older brother Harry, both of them having moved there after the scandal at Roth Lodge at Christmas. Marcus's son and his wife lived in London at the family home and Nancy knew that Will's sister had made a home in Woodley with her husband.

'He came back last week to see me in Dedley End and then said he was coming to London for a bit so I assumed he'd be here. Perhaps I got it wrong though,' Will said, his face falling when he realised they didn't know where his grandfather was.

'I'm rather jealous he lives there now and young Harry too,' Mr Castle said, referencing Will's older brother.

'They do love it there,' Will replied.

'And Maria is enjoying married life?' Mrs Castle asked about his sister. 'My Annie…' She chatted about her own family for a minute.

'Well, we'd better head into the dining room for something to eat,' Mr Castle said after a couple of minutes of catching up. 'Enjoy London, you two!'

Nancy and Jonathan thanked them and watched them walk into the dining room. 'So, Marcus didn't tell people he was coming to stay in Dedley End with you?' Nancy asked Will once they were alone again.

'He's very good friends with Mr Castle, so if he thinks my grandfather's still in Paris we might not have a lot of luck tracking him down through his friends. It looks like he didn't tell anyone he was coming to stay in Dedley End.'

Their server came back to ask if they wanted anything else. 'Sam, has my grandfather been in today?'

'No, Sir. I haven't seen him here in several months. Actually, someone else was asking about him yesterday, asked me to let him know if he came in.'

'Oh, who?'

'Hugh Windsor.' The waiter nodded and left them to it.

Will turned to Nancy and Jonathan. 'Hugh knows my grandfather is back in England then. So, he told some of his friends? Perhaps Hugh called at the house and they told him he had left, so he assumed he'd come here. Like me.'

'He's a member too here then?' Nancy asked. Will nodded. 'Well, if your grandfather hasn't told his closest friends maybe it's because he has things to hide?'

'Or he doesn't know who to trust,' Will argued. 'Okay, if he's not been here and his friends don't know where he is… My parents asked their housekeeper to tell me if he came to their house, but maybe we should check there anyway? And he does have a key to my flat too so it's worth a try going there as well. I'm guessing though he'd avoid anywhere obvious to the police.'

'That would be what I would do,' Jonathan said.

'Okay, let's look around here now. See if we can find out anything about him being the managing director,' Nancy said.

'We need to go upstairs to the meeting rooms and offices,' Jonathan agreed. 'Stay here, Will. Ring my phone if we need to make a hasty exit, okay?'

'Be careful,' Will said, pulling his phone out of his pocket and laying it on the table.

## Chapter Thirty-Two

Nancy and Jonathan walked through the reception area and the library into the bar – it was empty as it was still morning. 'Let's go upstairs,' she murmured. She paused though and saw a glass bowl on the bar filled with the hot-pink matchbooks like Seb had had. 'Do you really think Marcus Roth is *The Governor*? I can't picture it even though he has done some unforgivable things. And would Will really not have any idea about what his grandfather was up to? For all these years?' She found it hard to believe that such nefarious activities could be hidden from one's own family for so long.

'I'm not sure about him either, but Seb was watching Roth Lodge and phoned you to say Marcus was back, and then wanted to tell you everything. And everything we've found out so far does suggest Seb came to Dedley End as part of his mission to find the gang leader. Someone in our village must be linked to the gang – if not Marcus, then who?'

'I know,' Nancy said with a sigh as they walked to the spiral suitcase. 'If only Seb hadn't been so secretive, we could have helped him. But at least he gave us this clue. Now we just need to work out why he wanted us to come here. Let's see if we can find any more evidence linking Marcus to this place or anything that suggests the gang are involved here.'

They climbed the stairs carpeted in red up to the second floor, which was silent and still. They peeked into meeting rooms that were empty and then walked down a corridor that had closed doors off it. 'Shall we try one?' Nancy whispered. Now that she was up here it suddenly seemed unlikely there would be an office for the leader of the gang or any documents relating to *The Club*. Why would anyone keep such things in plain sight?

'Can I help you?' a voice asked. They turned to see a woman standing in the doorway of one of the rooms, eyebrows raised.

'We're here with Will Roth. We were interested in what we need to do to become a member,' Nancy said, quickly, trying to not look as flustered as she felt.

'Ah, of course, well, our membership process is all online now so if you go to our website you can fill in the application form,' she said. 'I'm the manager, Ruby Davis, and if you are friends with the Roth family then you'd be very welcome.'

Nancy looked at the young woman wearing a pencil skirt and blouse, her hair black and sharp like her expression as she eyed them. There was something familiar about her name to Nancy, but she couldn't place it. 'The manager, how wonderful, it looks like such a lovely place,' Nancy said, smiling and hoping Ruby would not find them suspicious.

'We just found out Marcus Roth is the managing director, but he seems to have wanted that to be kept a secret,' Jonathan said, watching Ruby carefully to see her reaction.

'We don't discuss members or our board of directors as part of our tradition,' Ruby said, not giving anything away. '*Clubhouse13* was set up in the 1880s by a member of the royal family who opened it behind his family's back. Since then it's been passed from owner to owner as privately as possible.'

'Oh,' Nancy said. So, they still didn't know if Marcus Roth ran the place or not and Ruby seemed like she would remain tight-lipped. 'How… interesting.'

'Now as you two are not currently members, I will need to ask you to head back downstairs,' Ruby said, gesturing towards the staircase. She smiled politely but it didn't meet her eyes. Nancy was certain she was suspicious of them.

'Of course, we know the way. Come on, Nancy,' Jonathan said.

'Lovely meeting you,' Nancy lied as she followed Jonathan. She glanced back to see Ruby watching them with a hard stare as they hurried down the stairs. 'Do you believe the tradition of keeping who runs this place a secret?' she asked him once they were out of Ruby's earshot.

'It's a very convenient one,' he said dryly. 'It means the gang could easily be running this place and no one knows. And *The Governor* has never needed to reveal to anyone who they are.'

'But listing his name at Companies House seems point-less if he's meant to be kept secret? Why not put Ruby's name on there? If Marcus really does run things here but kept it from his family, it doesn't make sense to be open about it officially.'

Jonathan nodded. 'You're right. So, has someone put his name there to cover up the true owner? And was it with or without Marcus's knowledge?'

'We need to find him and make him tell us what he knows,' Nancy said, not understanding what was going on.

'Let's hope he can tell us something because right now I don't know why Seb gave you those matches as the very last thing he did before dying. They really haven't helped us at all,' Jonathan said.

Nancy had a worrying thought. 'Do you think if *The Club* does run this place, Ruby knows about it? She could be part of it all.'

'In that case, she could be tipping the gang off that we're here,' Jonathan said as he led the way back downstairs into the reception area.

Nancy looked at him in horror. 'You're right! We need to leave right now and—' Nancy broke off with a panicked gasp as someone grabbed her from behind. She tried to reach for Jonathan who spun around, his eyes wide, as someone pulled Nancy by her dress into a dark alcove behind the stairs.

# Chapter Thirty-Three

'What the hell?' Nancy cried as she spun around and came face-to-face with a blonde woman wearing a white apron over her clothes.

'Nancy!' Jonathan charged in. 'Let her go!'

'Who are you?' Nancy demanded.

'For God's sake, shh,' the woman hissed at them. She beckoned with her hand and opened up a cupboard, walking inside and waving for them to follow her.

Nancy looked at Jonathan before cautiously following the woman inside. Jonathan crept in too and the woman closed the cupboard door behind them. It was tiny and filled with members' coats. There was a dusty dim light-bulb so they could barely see one another. 'What's going on?' Nancy asked.

The blonde woman stepped under the light. She pulled at her hair, which came away in her hands revealing her natural hair underneath the wig – hair the same shade as Nancy's albeit in a cropped style with streaks of grey running through it. Then she took off her glasses and faced Nancy.

Nancy looked at her in shock. Her heartbeat was thumping so hard in her chest she was certain the other two could hear it in the cramped cupboard. Her mouth fell open in a perfect 'O' shape. She stared at the women, who looked back almost defiantly, waiting for Nancy to say something. Nancy wondered if she was dreaming. After more than twenty years, she was standing in front of... She was about to call her 'mother' but she couldn't bring herself to say that word. 'Samantha?'

'Oh my God,' Jonathan said, looking between the two of them, back and forth as if he were watching a tennis match at Wimbledon.

'It is you, isn't it?' Nancy demanded when her mother didn't respond, just stared at her as if she'd seen a ghost.

Finally, Samantha nodded. 'Hi, Nancy,' she replied.

'Hi, Nancy,' Nancy repeated in disbelief. 'You... after all these years! You just say hi!' She shook her head incredulously.

'I wasn't expecting to see you here. Why are you here? To find me? Did Seb tell you I was working here?' Samantha Hunter asked, urgently, almost impatiently as if their reunion meant nothing.

Nancy swallowed her emotions down as best she could. 'Seb gave me his book of matches – it's from here so I knew this place was important. We thought it was because he'd found out that Marcus Roth runs this place and that he also is the leader of *The Club*.' She looked at Jonathan who reached out in the cupboard and squeezed her hand. She appreciated the comfort. She saw her mother look at their hands. Nancy strengthened her voice. 'But I guess Seb gave it to me so I would find you here.'

'He gave it to Nancy just before he died. We found him in the church after he was shot,' Jonathan added. He sounded angry on her behalf.

Samantha winced. 'I wondered if Seb had managed to tell you anything before... I heard about his death on the news, of course.' She looked away, distracted for a moment. Nancy couldn't see her mother's eyes clearly to see how she was feeling. Was she upset Seb died? Finally, Samantha turned back to them. 'I've been working here since I realised a lot of the people who *The Club* were blackmailing were members. I saw Marcus Roth was listed as the managing director so I thought if I got a job here I could find out if *The Club* really does run this place and if he is *The Governor*. I found out Marcus had moved to Paris. When Seb got out of prison, we agreed he'd move to Dedley End to do more digging on the Roths and to be there in case Marcus came back and caused trouble…' She trailed off. 'Seb phoned me to tell me Marcus was back and that he'd arranged to meet you, Nancy. He thought you needed to know everything, that he should warn you about him,' she said, her voice cracking a little bit at the end.

'And have you found a link – do *The Club* run this place, is Marcus in charge of it all?' Nancy asked, wondering if it had just been Seb worried about Nancy being harmed by Marcus, or if her mother had been too.

'I haven't got proof to go to the police with, no. When I saw Seb had been killed, it seemed to confirm it must be Marcus, but then the police arrested someone else and said Marcus was missing. I've had no idea what to do. Whether to come to Dedley End, stay here… I didn't know if Seb had had a chance to warn you either,' she said, her calm mask slipping a bit.

In a way Nancy was relieved that her mother had dived straight in to talk about Seb, the gang and everything. It helped to control her emotions at seeing her for the first time since she was six. She had expected they wouldn't have an emotional embrace upon seeing one another again, but she hadn't expected quite such a business-like manner. She decided the only thing to do to get through this was to mimic how Samantha was acting. 'Hasn't anyone realised who you are here?' Nancy asked.

'I admit my disguise isn't great but working in the kitchen, it's enough. The members here don't pay attention to staff. And I got the job with a fake identity. I thought no one would expect me to just walk in and I was right. Hiding in plain sight, I suppose. But now you're here, Nancy. It's too dangerous,' she said, narrowing her eyes. 'They might be watching you, seeing if you'll lead them to me. You need to go.'

Nancy swallowed another burst of anger down. She'd only just seen her again but already Samantha wanted her to leave? To protect her or because she didn't really want to see her? Nancy tried not to show she was upset.

'We can't go. We're here to find Marcus Roth. Richard Bank is the one who's been arrested and he says he's being framed. He said that Marcus knows something even if he isn't behind all of this. Will, his son, is with us too.'

Samantha looked impressed. 'I didn't think the Roths would speak to you after you had one of them arrested for murder.'

'You know about that?' Nancy asked, surprised.

'Everyone knows about the amateur bookshop detective,' she replied dismissively. Nancy felt herself sag. So, her mother hadn't been keeping a particular eye on her then? 'I suppose I should have known it would run in your blood.'

'And what is that exactly?' Nancy asked. 'I know my grandfather was part of this gang. Are you? Why are you even trying to find *The Governor*?'

'I want to destroy them all as they've destroyed everything I've ever held dear,' Samantha said, fiercely, her eyes flashing with sudden fire, her matter-of-factness fading as her emotions finally came to the surface. 'You can't be part of this. I haven't spent the past twenty years—'

'I am already part of this,' Nancy snapped, cutting her off. 'You made me part of this. Seb made me part of this. The Roths made me part of this. We're going to find Marcus with Will now, I don't care what you do.' She yanked open the door behind her and hurried out of the cupboard.

Jonathan rushed after her and she heard Samantha call her name but she kept on walking.

Nancy pushed open the black door and stepped out on to the London street breathing in air as fast as her lungs would allow.

A moment later, Jonathan appeared behind her. 'Nancy,' Jonathan said, hurrying after her. 'Are you okay?'

She looked down at her hands and saw they were trembling. 'No, not even a little bit,' she admitted.

'Nancy!' Samantha burst out after them. Nancy and Jonathan turned to look as she stepped through the *Clubhouse13* front door to stand on the pavement with them. 'Seb wasn't only in Dedley End to investigate Marcus. I asked him to move to the village to keep an eye on you. To make sure you were okay. That the gang wouldn't hurt you. To protect you. We were getting close to *The Governor* and I didn't want you there alone,' she said, desperately. She glanced around as if she suddenly realised they were out in public. 'I can't be out here like this. And I need to finish my shift. Give me your number,' she said, holding out her phone. Nancy was too stunned to speak so Jonathan punched in her number and Samantha hurried down the alley to the side of the front door, pulling her blonde wig back on as she went.

Jonathan and Nancy stared after her as she disappeared as quickly as she had appeared.

'What happened?' Will appeared behind them then. 'I saw you run out from the window. And who were you talking to?'

Nancy shook her head. 'Let's go. I'll explain on the way. Let's find Marcus, and sort this mess out once and for all.' Then she felt that prickle on the back of her neck again. She turned and saw a familiar-looking man watching them from across the road. She frowned as he climbed into a black cab before she could see who it was. Jonathan called her name then, so she followed him and Will into the taxi they had just hailed, but the moment left her even more unsettled than she had been before.

# Chapter Thirty-Four

'That was your mother?!' Will cried as they sat in the back of the black cab and drove to his parents' home. 'She's working at *Clubhouse13*?' He whistled.

'Now I know why Seb was desperate to give me the matches from there. He was trying to tell me that's where my mother was,' Nancy said.

'So, he was killed so he couldn't tell you?' Will asked.

Nancy shook her head. 'No. My mother said he was going to warn me about Marcus Roth – that they suspected he was *The Governor*,' Nancy said. 'No one has found out she's working here. She's been trying to find proof connecting Marcus and the gang to the members' club but hasn't yet.'

'My grandfather isn't their leader,' Will said again. 'That's why she hasn't found any proof.'

'She said the gang had destroyed everything for her so she's trying to bring them down. Seb was working with her. He wanted to make amends for what he had done by stopping them. They must have teamed up because they both wanted revenge on the gang. To destroy *The Club*. But all it's done is get Seb killed.'

'Does she know who killed Sebastian?' Will asked.

'She seemed more focused on proving Marcus is *The Governor* than who had killed Seb. Unless she assumes the leader of the gang murdered Seb, so finding who that is would kill two birds with one stone?' Nancy knew she could have thought of a less disturbing way of saying it under the current circumstances.

'Well, my grandfather wasn't in the church with us,' Will pointed out.

'But someone there could have been working for him,' Jonathan countered. 'Look, we're going around in circles. We need to speak to Marcus.' He glanced at Nancy. 'How did it feel seeing your mother again?'

'I feel kind of numb, I'm not sure how it felt,' Nancy admitted.

'She wanted Seb in Dedley End to protect you. She's been trying to look out for you,' he said gently.

'I know. But to not contact me for all these years...' Nancy trailed off. She wanted to believe her mother had done it all to protect her but it was hard. She felt abandoned by the woman. 'It was so strange to finally see her again,' Nancy said. She really had no idea quite how to feel about their reunion. There had been no tears, no clinging to one another, no embrace, but the way her mother had run out after them to tell her that Seb had been trying to protect her showed she must care a little bit. Now Nancy had no idea what would happen next. Would her mother just disappear again? She glanced at her handbag where her phone was and wondered if she would hear from Samantha again or not. She couldn't help but hope she would. 'The whole point of everything since Richard told us Samantha had been at Hugh Windsor's party was to find my mother. Where she was, why she left Dedley End, why I never heard from her but I didn't even ask half the questions I had.'

'You'll get a chance to ask them,' Jonathan said. 'That wasn't the last time we'll see her, I feel sure about that.

Right now, we need to find Marcus and find out what he and Richard have to do with all this, and get justice for Seb. If your mother wants to help us then great, and if she doesn't, we'll do it without her. Like we've done before.'

Nancy nodded. She knew he was right. She had so many questions for Samantha, but she did feel some sense of relief. She had finally found her mother. She was alive and despite what she might or might not have done in the past, was focused on bringing *The Club* down. Nancy understood that determination to get justice. She had had it herself twice before and now she wanted to do it again for Seb. Maybe that was what they were both meant to be doing right now. They could talk about the past another time. She bit her lip. Unless her mother ran from her again. But if she did then Nancy would have to accept it. She knew you couldn't stop people leaving you. It was their choice. You had to let them go if they wanted to. She just had to hope that her mother would want to see her again.

The taxi took them first to Will's parents' house just to make sure Marcus wasn't there. Jonathan and Nancy waited outside in the taxi as Will went in. Fifteen minutes later and, just as Jonathan and Nancy were ready to storm in and find out what was going on, Will emerged shaking his head. Getting back into the taxi, he sighed. 'He's not there. I called my parents again but they haven't heard from him. He's not answering any of our calls. So, we can try my flat and see if he's there?'

They agreed and the taxi set off again, this time crossing London towards Islington. It was lunchtime now and Nancy was getting jittery wondering if they would be able to find Marcus. Then, her phone vibrated with a text.

Even Samantha's text messages were business-like and matter-of-fact. Nancy messaged back Will's address and hoped this time they were heading to the right place. 'Samantha is coming,' she said after she had sent the message. Jonathan gave her an anxious look and Will just nodded. Both of them thankfully sensed she didn't want to say anything more about it.

It was slow progress through the traffic but, finally, they passed Angel tube station and reached a block of flats around the corner. 'We're here,' Will said as the taxi parked outside his building. They hopped out of the taxi and stood outside.

A moment later, another taxi pulled up and out stepped Samantha. She had shed her uniform, wig and glasses, her natural hair framing her face, and was now in black ankle-grazing trousers, a black jumper and ballet pumps. Nancy noted her mother had a tall, slim frame like her and looked chic, almost Parisian. There were lines on her face and the dark circles under her eyes though that showed her years on the run had been tough.

'Why do you think Marcus is up there?' Samantha asked briskly without greeting them, looking up at the building they were outside.

'This is my flat. My grandfather hasn't been to *Clubhouse13*, my parents and most of his friends think he's still in Paris. He has a spare key to mine so it's worth a try,' Will said.

'If he's trying to run from the police, it seems unlikely he'd go to known addresses. It's the first place they would look,' Samantha said.

'Our lawyer said they were sending the Met police to look for him,' Will agreed. 'Let's check anyway and then we can decide where else we can try.' He started to walk up to the main doors of his building.

Nancy turned to follow but then she realised who the man outside *Clubhouse13* had been. She froze and felt goosebumps travel up her body.

'Nancy, something wrong?' Jonathan asked when he saw her still standing there. Will and Samantha paused too.

'I think we're being followed,' she said, slowly. 'I think we've been followed all the way from Dedley End.' Nancy scanned the area and there he was across the road, leaning against the wall casually in his dark coat and thick scarf. It was the man she had seen on the platform at Dedley End. She hadn't been paranoid after all; he'd trailed them across London and there he was again. She turned back to the others. 'The man across the road. He was on our train this morning and he was outside *Clubhouse13*. There he is again.'

'That's not good,' Will said, stating the obvious.

Samantha looked over her shoulder. 'By the alleyway?' Nancy nodded. 'I recognise him,' Samantha said. 'He has to be part of *The Club*.' Then her mouth dropped and she looked at them in horror. 'I didn't have my wig on when I left *Clubhouse13*. They'll know I was there. I won't be able to go back,' she said with a sigh.

Nancy stared at her. 'Not just that… What if he sends the gang here for you?' Nancy asked her.

'Let's stop him,' Jonathan said, setting off before anyone could react. The other three took off after him but traffic was heavy and it took a few seconds to get across the road. The man spotted them and, in a flash, turned and ran down the alleyway he was standing by, his scarf flying out behind him. They rushed after him and ran down the alley but at the other end was a busy road. Cars and people moved back and forth, and they stood there looking around but he had slipped into the hustle and bustle.

'He's disappeared,' Jonathan said with a frustrated sigh. 'Maybe he had a car waiting.'

'It's easy to hide in London. Why do you think I'm here?' Samantha said, bitterly. 'Let's hurry up to your flat, Will. He could be calling in all sorts of people now he knows where we are.'

'Hurry,' Nancy agreed. They walked back to Will's building.

–

'What do we do if the gang come here?' Will asked as he unlocked the main door and led them inside.

'What do we do if your grandfather really is *The Governor*?' Jonathan countered. The four of them stood in the lobby area looking at one another. 'This could be a trap,' he said, saying what they were all thinking Nancy knew.

Nancy turned to her mother. 'Maybe you should go home, let us go up there. Marcus won't hurt Will but you…' She trailed off meaningfully.

'If Marcus really is *The Governor* then I need to look him in the eye,' Samantha Hunter said, breathlessly. 'I need to face him after all this time. I've been hiding and running for a long time. I've been searching for him ever since he had my father killed. And now I have found him, I can't hide or run anymore. I need to face him.' She pulled out a gun from behind her back drawing shocked gasps from them. 'And I have this. Just in case.'

# Chapter Thirty-Five

Will shook his head. 'Are you crazy?! You can't bring a gun into my flat. My grandfather won't hurt any of us,' Will said, his eyes wide as he stared at Samantha's weapon.

'If you knew half the things *The Club* have done, you wouldn't hesitate either,' Samantha told him, her voice harsh. Nancy wished she had known what her mother had been like before she'd gone on the run. The years must have changed her, given her this coldness. 'I need to protect us.'

Nancy turned to Will. 'They know we're here. We don't know who might be behind that door,' she said. 'I don't like it either but maybe it's better to be safe than sorry.' She didn't like the idea of her mother brandishing a gun but there was a real possibility Marcus Roth was a far more dangerous man than any of them knew. And if the man watching them was in the gang, he would have been warned they were there. He could have half *The Club* in there with him for all they knew. They had no idea what they were walking into. 'Just in case,' Nancy said, firmly to her mother.

'I agree with Nancy,' Jonathan said. 'Just in case.'

Will looked at her gun again and visibly swallowed but, finally, he nodded once. 'Okay. Just in case.'

'Come on then,' Samantha said, impatiently.

With shaking hands, he put his key in the lock, turned it and with a click, the door opened. They stood there for a moment, listening.

'Grandad?' Will called out as he stepped through the doorway cautiously. 'Are you here?'

Nancy was behind him followed by Jonathan. A few paces behind them was Samantha with her gun still out, ready for whatever they might find inside.

'Nothing,' Will said with a sigh as he looked around his open-plan living area. 'I'll double check.' He walked through the rest of the flat.

'It was too obvious a place for him to come, I suppose,' Jonathan said.

'What now though?' Nancy asked. It felt as if they had been on a wild goose chase around London.

'My company credit card has gone,' Will said, returning from his bedroom. 'I left it here by mistake last time I came down, so I've been using Richard's if we needed anything for the business. Shall I check the account to see if it's been used?'

'Yes! He might have booked into a hotel,' Nancy said. She perched on the sofa, Jonathan sitting next to her as Will pulled out his phone to check the app. Samantha paced back and forth, her gun visible in her handbag. Jonathan looked at Nancy who looked back at him. It felt so surreal to be with her mother and not discuss their years apart. She opened her mouth but Samantha stopped pacing and turned to them.

'I know we have so much to talk about, you must have so many questions for me. I've thought about seeing you again so many times and what I'd say, what you would say…' Samantha let some emotion into her voice as she looked at her daughter. She smiled slightly. 'You look like George. So much.'

Nancy felt a lump rise up in her throat. 'I know,' she managed to say. 'Did you…'

'He has used it,' Will said, interrupting their moment. 'My grandfather can't even deign to stay somewhere under five stars while hiding from the police. Mind you, he knows they will be discreet. He's at The Ritz. Shall I call the hotel and get them to ring his room?'

'He might run, we should just go there,' Jonathan said.

Nancy looked at her mother. The conversation they needed to have would need to wait. They had to find Marcus Roth, and *The Club* knew they were in London – that left no time for a heart-to-heart. 'Let's go,' she said, jumping up. Samantha nodded once and Nancy knew her and her mother were on the same page. Jonathan followed as they walked back out of Will's flat and into another taxi outside. There was no sign of the gang member who had been tailing them, but that almost made Nancy worry even more. What would *The Club* do now they knew Samantha was in London with them? And if Marcus was really their leader, what awaited them at The Ritz?

As their taxi took them back across London, Nancy was forced to remember her first and only experience at the fancy hotel. Richard had taken her for dinner there at Christmas and it had been so fabulous but it had almost been like a dream, not something that she wanted or needed in a relationship – she liked the simple things in life. She would have preferred him to have been an honest man instead. Nancy wondered what was happening at the police station and if her ex would really be charged with murder.

The Ritz came into view finally and they all hurried out of the taxi. A uniformed doorman opened the door for them and they walked through the lobby. 'I know which suite he'll be in,' Will murmured. 'Just look like we belong,' he added, giving the three of them a doubtful look. He led the way to the staircase, avoiding the lift and a bell man, and they walked up in tense silence. At some point, Samantha pulled her gun out of her handbag again, which made Nancy even more nervous.

'Here.' Will checked no one was in the corridor and then he led them to a door. 'We've all stayed here,' he explained as he knocked. Predictably, there was no answer. 'Granddad, I know you're in there. Just let me in.' Will crossed his fingers. 'I'm alone.'

Seconds ticked by but, finally, the hotel door clicked and opened to reveal Marcus Roth.

'Grandfather,' Will said, exhaling with what sounded like relief as he stood in front of them alone and unharmed. 'Why did you run from Dedley End like that? We've been looking for you!'

'Because I knew the police would come for me after they arrested Richard. You said you were alone,' he replied, shaking his head. 'I suppose you'd better come in.' He stood back and watched them. 'Of course, you're here, Nancy and Jonathan and...' He trailed off with a frown.

'Samantha Hunter,' Will supplied.

Marcus shook his head. 'Well, I never.' He led them into the room, then closed the door. It was an exquisite suite decorated in gold and cream. He turned around as they joined him and then saw what was in Samantha's hand. His eyes grew wide. 'Why do you have a gun?'

'Because we know the truth. We know who you are. We know you're the leader of *The Club*,' Samantha said, stepping around the others to face Marcus. 'It's taken me a long time to find out who you are. To finally look you in the eyes.' She trained her gun onto him.

Marcus raised his hands quickly while shaking his head. 'No. Please. You have to listen to me! It's not me. That lot have tried to ruin my family for too long. Now they have framed Richard and are trying to pin God knows what on to me! I might have had to give them money, but I have never been part of them. And I'm certainly not their leader.' He let out a hollow laugh. 'You might as well shoot me if that's what they are pinning on me. I'd rather die than spend the rest of my life in prison. But not before clearing my name.'

'Why are you listed as managing director of *Clubhouse13* then?' Nancy asked him.

'I only found that out yesterday. Richard told me. He thought that meant I was the leader like you do and he wouldn't believe me when I said I wasn't. We argued,' he said. Nancy now understood what they'd seen when they had staked out Roth Lodge. Richard had thought Marcus was behind the gang and they had been arguing about it. 'He thought I was the one making him ditch the gun used to kill Sebastian Holmes but I told him I wasn't. It had been left on the doorstep with a note telling Richard to dump it. A threatening, anonymous note like usual. Richard didn't believe me that I wasn't behind it all. He stormed out with the gun and then Will came to find me and told me Richard phoned from the police station and he'd been arrested. I guessed the gang had framed him and maybe they were going to do the same thing to me so I left and came straight here.'

Nancy tried to make sense of it all. 'But why would Richard dump the gun because the gang told him to? Why was he involved in the gang in the first place? I don't get it.'

Marcus looked away from Samantha's gun for a second to glance at Nancy. 'Because of you, Nancy. Once they found out he'd dated you, Samantha's daughter, they wanted him to get you to lead them to Samantha. They are experts at manipulation, blackmail... There is nothing they won't stoop to to get what they want. The note they left telling him to ditch the gun – they said they'd hurt you if he didn't. That's what they've been using to get him to do their dirty work. Threatening your life. And holding him prisoner over your company,' he added, looking at Will. 'If he did what they asked, you got lots of business, but if not, they would have shut you down. They can do it too. They can do anything.'

'What? Richard has been working for the gang?' Will asked in shock.

'We both have had to do what they asked of us,' Marcus replied, bitterly. He looked at Samantha. 'They want you, Samantha. More than anything it seems.'

'They've wanted that for a long time. Ever since I tipped off the police about that jewellery raid. They even found me in witness protection in Dedley End. I still don't know how,' she said, not moving her gun away from Marcus.

Nancy looked at her mother. They had been right then. About her mother calling the police and having to go into witness protection. 'But your father was there...' She trailed off, knowing he'd been killed on that raid.

'Dad knew I was tipping the police off. He was ready to do his time to stop the gang. But someone got wind of it, guessed he was behind it and they shot him,' Samantha said. She shook her head. 'I was given protection and put a few of them away but the leader, *The Governor* as they call him, the police couldn't get to him. I thought he'd go underground and the gang was over. Finished. I was sent to Dedley End and, for a while, I could be normal again. I stopped looking over my shoulder, I built a life for myself but then…' Samantha turned to Nancy. 'That's why I had to leave – Seb tipped me off from prison. He knew it had been me and my dad who had told the police but he hadn't been angry with us. He'd wanted to get out of the life for a long time. He felt he deserved his time. He heard people talking in prison. *The Club* hadn't disappeared at all and they'd found out where I was so he called to warn me. So, I knew the gang were on their way and I couldn't risk anything happening to George or you. I thought I led them away from Dedley End back here to London but I was wrong. There was always someone there. Watching. Waiting. And it was you,' she added, turning back to Marcus.

'No. I swear it! They have blackmailed me for years. Ever since my wife's hit-and-run accident. She was drunk… Nancy knows… I protected her. And the gang knew. Somehow. They've been blackmailing me ever since.' Nancy winced at the mention of that accident, the one that had killed her father. Marcus sighed. 'You're right. They are always watching. When my daughter-in-law was murdered, they helped us. Made sure only her killer went to prison, the rest of us were safe. So, they wouldn't lose out on our money that I give them every month. They have people in all sorts of high places. I shouldn't have been surprised that included the police.'

'The police?' Nancy cried.

'Someone made sure we were safe,' Marcus said. 'Please. We're all in this together. We have all been ruined by *The Club*. My wife ended up killing herself. I don't want anyone else to get hurt.'

'You really aren't their leader?' Will asked.

'I promise, I'm not.'

'Then who is?' Samantha half growled.

'Put the gun down,' Nancy said, turning to Samantha. 'It isn't helping. We need to work together. We can't let them make us turn on each other.'

'He won't be going anywhere,' Jonathan added. 'Let's all sit down.' He sat down on the chaise longue, Will perched on the hotel bed and Nancy leaned against the wardrobe.

Samantha shook her head but she lowered her gun. 'Fine, but it stays in my hands.' Marcus let out a long exhale in relief then sat down next to Will on the bed. Samantha remained standing near to the door.

'I promise that I don't know who their leader is,' Marcus said, his voice quivering a little bit. He kept a nervous eye on Samantha. 'I can't even tell you who's in the gang. Or if there is someone in Dedley End, who it is. Every contact from them has been anonymous. I received a letter threatening me and my wife just two days after the car accident. Typed so you don't even know their handwriting. They also make sure we know that they know our secrets and can bring us down. Or they threaten loved ones. And I tried once to walk away but my son Peter was mugged. They made it clear it was them and, next time, he wouldn't get bruises, he would be killed. After that, I just accepted I needed to stay on their good side.'

Nancy stared at him. He sounded serious. Genuine. That he really didn't know. He seemed to have been beaten down by the gang. But she wasn't sure they could trust him. She turned to Jonathan who looked as unsure as she did. 'What about the money you've given them? Is there a way to trace it?'

Marcus shook his head. 'It's always cash left somewhere they can pick it up. They're old school.'

Samantha exhaled loudly. 'It's almost impossible to find out who's part of it all. I've been able to target the figures they've been blackmailing or corrupting through the years, because they always slip up or make a mistake or the gang throws them to the wolves to protect themselves. But ever since that raid they have tried hard to hide who they are. And I am sick of it.'

Nancy let that sink in. There was only one person she could think of to help them. 'We need to speak to DCI Brown—'

'No!' Marcus interrupted her. 'He'll just arrest me. He's made up his mind about me. He hates rich people.'

'Can you blame him?' Jonathan asked with a raised eyebrow. Marcus glared at him.

'Shall we get some food and drink up while we decide what to do?' Will suggested.

Samantha let out a hiss of frustration. 'I should go.'

'No, we should stick together,' Nancy said, quickly. 'We have no idea what the gang know, what they'll do next, we're safer together and we'll make a plan about what to do. Will's right. Let's get our energy back and then we can...' Nancy's phone rang, interrupting her. She glanced at her phone screen. 'It's Penelope, I'd better...' She stepped towards the door. 'Pen, this isn't a great time...'

'Nancy,' Penelope said, urgently. 'I'm so sorry. I don't know how this has happened. I don't know what to do,' she said, her voice breaking.

Nancy felt a shiver run down her spine at her friend's desperation. 'Pen what's going on? What's happened?'

'It's Mrs H… your gran… Jane… She's missing. We think she's been kidnapped.'

# Chapter Thirty-Six

'Nancy?'

Nancy wasn't sure how much time had passed since she dropped her phone with a thud onto the carpet in the hotel room, until Jonathan's voice broke through the roaring in her ears. 'Gran's missing,' she said, her voice sounding like just a squeak to her. She squeezed her eyes shut for a couple of seconds. Her beloved grandmother. What would she do without Jane? 'No,' she whispered, opening her eyes again. She turned to her mother. '*The Club* have taken her, haven't they?' she asked, her voice sounding small.

'Oh, God, Nancy,' Samantha said, her eyes wide with shock.

'Hello? Nancy?'

Jonathan bent down to retrieve Nancy's phone as Penelope's voice cut through the thick silence in the room. He scooped it up and turned on the speakerphone while keeping his eyes on Nancy. 'Pen, tell me exactly what happened.'

'Okay,' Penelope said, sucking in an audible breath. 'We were going to pop in to the bookshop to see Mrs H, me and Ollie, but it was open and empty. We called out, looked around but she wasn't there. We thought maybe she'd popped into another shop to help someone but then...' Pen sniffed. 'We saw someone had ripped out the CCTV cameras. Then Ruth Stoke came in. She said she'd seen a black car with two men outside. When I said she should have checked on Mrs H, she was so upset she hadn't thought to raise the alarm. She assumed they were delivery drivers bringing books. Ollie has called the police and they've been to the cottage. But it's all locked up. And her mobile phone is off. The men in the black car must have taken her from the bookshop…' Pen trailed off upset. 'She's gone.'

'And no one else saw anything?' Jonathan asked her.

'It's raining really hard here, no one is about and I don't know… maybe it looked like Mrs H was going with them willingly?'

'She definitely wouldn't have been,' Jonathan said. 'Thanks, Pen. Let us know if you hear anything else. We need to make a plan.' He hung up. 'Nancy?'

'I can't believe this. I should never have left her there alone but I wanted to protect her. I thought she'd be safe in the bookshop,' Nancy said, her eyes filling up with tears.

Samantha stood up and moved towards Nancy but Jonathan put his arm around her and she leaned into him so Samantha stopped. 'I don't understand why they've taken her. I left Dedley End to protect you all,' she said.

'It's the man who's been following us. It has to be. He alerted the gang,' Jonathan said. 'Told them we are all here so maybe they've taken Mrs H to…' He trailed off, unable to finish.

Nancy looked up at her mother. 'They've taken Gran so we will give you up,' she finished Jonathan's sentence for him. If only she had taken seriously the feeling that they were being followed at the train station. She could have warned her gran. Panic rose up in her at the thought of anyone hurting her grandmother.

'I never wanted anything like this to happen,' Samantha said. She turned to Marcus. 'Do you know where they could have taken her?'

He shook his head. 'I swear I don't. What about Richard? He might know.'

'Can you contact the gang, tell them to come and get me?' Samantha asked him.

'Wait,' Nancy said. 'Let me call DCI Brown.' She saw their faces. 'We have to trust him. We can't let *The Club* get away with this again.' She was desperate to find her grandmother but handing over her mother would mean everything that had happened had been for nothing. There had to be a way to save her grandmother but bring the gang down. She held out her hand and Jonathan passed her phone back. She walked out into the hotel corridor and tried to breathe, to calm down, but it was pointless. She couldn't calm down knowing that her gran had been kidnapped. She called the police station in Woodley and asked to speak to DCI Brown urgently. '*The Club* have my grandmother,' she said when he'd come on to the phone. 'I found my mother here in London but someone from *The Club* followed us and saw her. Penelope said Gran has disappeared from the bookshop, there were two men in a car outside, we think they've taken her...' Nancy said in a rush. 'It has to be the gang, doesn't it?'

'It looks like it,' he said, grimly. 'As soon as DC Pang told me Mrs Hunter had been reported missing, we thought it must be related. I was just going to call you to find out where you were. You should have told me you were going to London.'

'We came with Will to try to find Marcus Roth but we also found my mother.' She paced up and down, unable to stand still.

'What? You found Marcus Roth?'

'He swears he's not the leader. That the gang have been blackmailing him. Richard too. I think I believe him. They have been caught up in it all but they're not in charge.' She quickly told him everything Marcus had told them.

DCI Brown sighed. 'Nancy, I don't know where to even start with all of that. Whoever took Mrs Hunter took out your shop CCTV, but I have officers looking through the High Street cameras to see if we can find where the car that was parked outside the bookshop went, where they may have taken your grandmother. And we're talking to all the other shopkeepers to see if anyone saw anything that might help us.'

'Where could the gang have her?' Nancy asked, panicked.

'I don't know. We'll do all we can to find out.'

'We think they're doing this so we hand over my mother to them. That means they will get in contact soon, right?'

'I think so but we can't just wait for that. You need to come back to Dedley End. Would your mother be willing to come back with you? This could be our chance to trap the gang. To finish this.'

Nancy really hoped that was possible but she was worried. 'I'll ask her. Listen, Marcus thinks police are involved, that some might have been corrupted by the gang. I don't know who we can trust.'

DCI Brown sighed. 'I was afraid of that. Okay, when you come back I'll meet you just with DC Pang. Richard's prints aren't on the gun. We have no evidence to charge him with Seb's murder. But he and Marcus must know more than they are saying. They must be able to help work out who is pulling the strings. I'll bring Richard with us too.'

'I'll get everyone to Dedley End and meet you. Where?'

They made arrangements. 'Be careful, Nancy. Marcus Roth could still be lying. And let me know if the gang make contact about your grandmother. I'll get in touch if we find out anything our end.'

She nodded even though he couldn't see her. 'I know. Just please help me get my gran back safe and sound.'

'I promise,' he replied.

Nancy hung up and shook her head. Her gran had been worried for her safety in going to London but they should have realised that Dedley End was no longer safe. They had let their guard down and now Jane was missing. They had no idea if she was okay or not. Nancy would never forgive herself if they hurt her grandmother. She had to make sure that didn't happen. She hoped DCI Brown was right that someone would be in touch from the gang and that they could finally stop them, but she knew they couldn't underestimate these people. They had killed many times before and wouldn't hesitate to do so again. She steeled herself and returned to the hotel room.

'Well?' Jonathan asked as she walked in, looking relieved to see her back.

'DCI Brown wants us all in Dedley End. He says it's the only way to stop this and I think he's right. If none of you are really part of this gang then you need to do the right thing and help us stop them. We need to find my grandmother and bring her home. We need to get justice for Seb and everyone else who these people have hurt or ruined. And we need to do it together,' Nancy said, addressing each of them in turn. Finally, she looked at her mother. 'If you really did all of this to protect us then this is your chance to make it all worthwhile. You need to come back with us. Please.'

'You really trust this DCI Brown?' Samantha asked.

'I do, but I have a plan I didn't tell him about.'

Jonathan grinned. 'Of course you do. Come on, Mrs H needs us. Marcus, Will, surely you have a fancy car that can get us back to Dedley End quickly?'

'I'm on it,' Will said looking pleased to have something to do. He pulled out his phone.

'I'll get my things,' Marcus said, walking towards the wardrobe.

'Samantha?' Nancy asked.

Her mother looked at her for a moment and then for a second her mask slipped. 'Not Mum?' she said, softly.

'I think it's a word that needs to be earned,' Nancy replied.

Samantha winced but nodded. 'I deserved that. I'll come, but I'm bringing my gun.'

Under the circumstances, Nancy wasn't going to argue with that. She nodded her head at Jonathan and they stepped out of the room into the corridor. She explained her idea quickly and quietly to him, and they made a plan together that she really hoped would work. When they returned, Samantha looked a little hurt to have been left out of what she and Jonathan had been discussing but Nancy couldn't worry about hurt feelings right now. She had to save her grandmother.

Will got off the phone as his grandfather packed his bag. 'A car is picking us up in ten minutes. Did DCI Brown say what was happening to Richard?'

'They can't prove he killed Seb,' Nancy replied. 'DCI Brown is bringing him along. He thinks Richard and you,

Marcus, can tell us more than you have, and I think he's right. The gang have been blackmailing you both. They put *Clubhouse13* in Marcus's name. They got Richard to ditch the gun then called the police to try to frame him. They want the police to be looking at you two. Why? Are you just random scapegoats or is this personal?'

'What do you mean?' Marcus asked.

'I think you know the leader or *The Governor*,' Nancy said.

'I told you, I don't…' Marcus began, indignantly.

Nancy held up her hand to stop him. 'I'm not saying you're lying about knowing who it is, what I'm saying is the leader knows you personally. They aren't just framing anyone for this, they're doing it to you. So, you need to think about who in your life might want you to take the fall for this and why.'

Marcus stared at her in shock but he nodded once and she knew he realised she was right.

# Chapter Thirty-Seven

Will had ordered a minivan to drive them back to the Cotswolds and he sat in the first row of seats with his grandfather, leaving Jonathan and Nancy to sit with Samantha in the back. The fog had completely lifted now it was lunchtime but it remained a grey and gloomy day fitting their mood perfectly. Marcus passed around sandwiches and cakes The Ritz had given them to take, but Nancy couldn't face eating much. She knew the only way to stop herself from going crazy worrying about her grandmother was to try to get as much information out of her mother as possible on the drive to Dedley End. 'How did it all start? How did your father end up being part of *The Club*?' Nancy asked as the car weaved through the London traffic.

'He drifted to London when he was eighteen. He'd fallen out with his family and had no idea what to do. Homeless, unemployed, broke – he hoped that London would be the place to make his fortune. He ended up working in a pub and sleeping in a tiny room out back and, one day, this group of men came in. He said they were all dressed immaculately, bought the best booze on offer, and had flashy watches, talked about their cars, their women... They seemed to have the best of everything, you know?' Samantha said, staring out of the window as if she were lost in the past. 'My father was entranced by them. He started to follow them around hoping that whatever it was that made them successful would rub off on him. He idolised them. And they let him tag along. They started asking him for little favours, got him to do things for them, you know? Then they said they'd pay him more than he made in the pub if he wanted to be their assistant. And one of them gave him a room in their flat. My father wanted their lifestyle so badly. Once he'd moved in, he began to realise just how they made their money. Suddenly, picking up their dry cleaning or getting their shopping turned into collecting money from people who owed them, organising gambling in the local pub or sitting outside in a car waiting to drive them away from a robbery. He was in the middle of it before he knew what "it" actually was.'

'And once he realised, he didn't want to give up the lifestyle?' Jonathan asked.

Samantha nodded. 'Exactly. He rose up the ranks and then Sebastian Holmes took him under his wing, became his friend and mentor almost. They were given more control, they headed up a group in East London and they started making some real money. My father met my mum about this time. She was seduced by exactly what had hooked him when he was younger and by the time she worked out that he made his money from criminal activity, she was pregnant with me. She begged him to run away with her but he wouldn't. Couldn't. I don't know. We lived in a house together when I was growing up in East London and my mum protected me as much as she could but, as I grew up, they grew further apart and my dad started disappearing for days at a time,' Samantha continued. She sighed. 'I lost contact with him a bit. Then I started working in a pub and I heard rumours about what my dad really did and I realised that I didn't know him at all. One night out of the blue, he turned up bruised and battered. He'd been involved in a fight with another gang and came close to losing his life. That night, I begged him to get out of it all but he said he was trapped, he couldn't leave, they wouldn't let him. They'd hurt not just him but my mother, me… he was terrified and stuck.'

'And then the jewellery raid happened?' Nancy prompted when her mother fell quiet.

'Yes. My dad came to me and asked for my help. He said he and Seb had been ordered to raid a jewellery store in Hatton Garden. An armed raid that would net the gang thousands, even a million maybe, and they'd been told to shoot anyone who got in their way. He was scared. He had never had to do anything that might hurt members of the public. It was a step too far for him. Seb had misgivings too but *The Governor* had directly asked for them. My dad and Seb were annoyed that they'd never met the leader. They were high up but still they only communicated with him through others. Only a handful of people knew who they were and they were ready to die to protect their name. Seb wanted out but he was stuck too, like my dad. They didn't know what to do.'

'What did you say?' Nancy said.

'I told him I would sort it out. I think he knew what I was going to do but asked me not to tell him anything, just in case he let on somehow. So, I went to the police and told them everything. They said they'd protect me and my father but I don't know if someone warned the gang because when the police showed up, my dad had been shot and most of them had fled, leaving Seb and a few others to take the rap for the robbery. My dad died a couple of days later in hospital. They arrested Seb and the others but no one was able to tell them who the leader was. The gang went underground and we had no idea what happened to them. I was taken to a safe house by the police and kept there until the trial. Then, I was put into witness protection.'

'How did you and Seb start communicating?' Nancy asked.

'He wrote me a letter passed on by the police. Said he realised my dad had come to me and that he forgave me and that he and my dad had been right to try to stop it. That he wished he'd done something but he'd been too weak. And he'd never forgive himself for my dad's death. He told me that he'd always be there for me if I needed him,' Samantha said. 'So, I moved to Dedley End. I didn't tell anyone where I'd gone in London, not even my mother. I cut off all contact with her to protect her. None of my friends knew, no one. And I started a new life.'

'But how did they find out where you were?' Jonathan asked, as transfixed as Nancy was by her mother's story.

'I wish I knew. Seb heard about it in prison. He realised the gang was very much still operating and that they wanted to find me and set an example that grassing on them gets you killed. They had found out I was in Dedley End somehow and that I ran the bookshop there. Seb phoned me at the bookshop to tell me they were coming. At first, I thought I could handle it. I put in extra security, I told George everything. I had a handler for my witness protection and he said he'd contact the local police and get them to watch the house. I spoke to Seb in prison once more and told him I wasn't going to run or hide anymore. I was protected. But Seb told me that he believed it was someone in the police who had tipped the gang off and that I shouldn't trust them, that I should run. I knew that my job was to protect you, Nancy, and George. And Jane too. I loved her like she was my own mother. George didn't want to let me go but he knew that you were our priority so I left, knowing they'd follow me to London.' Samantha's eyes filled with tears. 'It was the hardest thing I've ever done in my life, Nancy. You have to believe that. I vowed on that train that I'd spend the rest of my life trying to bring the gang down once and for all so no one else would have their life ruined by them. And I've spent twenty years trying to get to the top. And I'm close. So close. Taking Jane, risking exposure, they haven't done something like this for a long time. They are scared, Nancy. I can feel it.'

'I hope so,' Nancy said, quietly. She understood her mother's desire to get justice. Revenge even. But… 'What about when my dad died?' she asked her mother. 'Why didn't you come back then?'

'I looked into it. Made sure George's death was an accident. And it was. The gang didn't do it. I knew if I came back, all we'd both done to protect you would have been for nothing. They would be watching at the funeral. What if they were waiting for me to come to you? It would have been the worst time to come home. You see that, don't you? I asked the vicar to keep an eye out for you and Jane. I trusted him. I kept an eye on the bookshop and when the press caught on to you solving crimes… I know I don't deserve to be but I was proud of you. But it scared me too. I thought that you might come into contact with the gang. And then I started to follow a trail that led me to Marcus Roth. So, when Seb was released, we agreed he'd move to Dedley End to watch the Roths and to protect you, Nancy, in case we were right and the gang were in the village. And you know what happened next.' Samantha leaned back, exhausted by her story.

Nancy wiped her eyes. A tear had squeezed out without her knowing it. Jonathan touched her hand with his. She nodded at him. Samantha watched their exchange. 'Why did you both think it was Marcus Roth in charge?' Nancy saw Marcus and Will were blatantly listening to their conversation now but she couldn't blame them. She had waited for so long to hear Samantha's story. She was relieved, in a way, that her mother had done what she had done to protect her, but she couldn't help but think that she had let the gang win by leaving her family and spending years focused on destroying them. She had left their village to stop them from ruining her life but hadn't she let them do it anyway?

'I saw how a murder was committed in Roth Lodge and the truth about who caused your father's crash came out, but the Roths seemed to come out of it all unscathed. Yes, they fled Dedley End, but that was it. I thought they must have influence over the police. I already suspected corrupted police helped the gang. And then we found out he was the managing director of *Clubhouse13*. I'd seen a lot of the people who had been corrupted by the gang were members there so I thought that it could be owned by them, so then Marcus had to be involved.'

'I found your book with a list of names in,' Nancy said.

'I thought George would have destroyed that. Maybe he wanted you to have a clue,' she said, smiling a little. 'I have spent years going through that list and making more, trying to stop everyone who was helping the gang and I think I got a couple of members of the gang too, but they've always hidden who they are so well.'

'What happened at Hugh Windsor's party?' Samantha looked surprised by Nancy's question. 'We found out you'd been there and we wondered if you'd had something to do with Sir Basil Walker getting caught for corruption.'

Samantha nodded. 'Sir Basil Walker had long been touted as someone involved with *The Club* as you know from that memoir I left at home, so I began watching him. I saw the company he'd given a government contract to had backed out of the project, taking the money with them. It looked like it was a shell company so I wondered: did he know that when he gave them the contract or had he been in the dark like he was claiming? I followed him to a bar with his wife and he talked about going to a friend's fancy Christmas party, but she couldn't come as he would be there to network. I thought maybe I could get him to tell me what had really happened with that contract.'

'You weren't nervous about going to the party?'

'I had my disguise, my fake name and I knew there would be a lot of people there. I thought I could fly under the radar to talk to Walker then get out. Obviously, I was wrong,' Samantha replied with a grimace. 'I went to the town where Hugh's estate is and found out from locals that they were always invited, so I got dressed up, went to the pub and got this guy called Pete to take me along. He thought he had a chance with me... I kept an eye on Sir Basil and when he went to the loo, I followed and intercepted him on the way out, pulling him into the library. I had to flirt with him, tell him how much I admired politicians doing all this noble work for not much money when they could be doing something else,' she continued.

Nancy had to smile. 'I bet he had no idea what you were doing.'

'No. He thought I was a dumb blonde he could bed for the night, let's be frank. Told me how there were ways to make extra money while you were an MP and he'd made a lot. I acted like I was so impressed but I couldn't quite understand what he meant and could he please explain it to me? He told me how he'd got this company a contract but they didn't exist. The Government never tried to get the money back and he got a big cut of the whole thing. He never mentioned *The Club* – even he wasn't that stupid – but he told me enough to shoot himself in the foot. I told him I needed a drink, he went to get me one and I slipped out. Unfortunately, I walked right into Hugh Windsor, who recognised me, so I had to run out of there, but I got Walker's confession on my phone and I sent it into Parliament. I heard he had to flee the country due to the scandal, but probably also because *The Club* wouldn't have been happy he'd been found out.'

Nancy was impressed. She couldn't help it. 'I'm glad you stopped him but it was a big risk going to that party knowing Hugh Windsor might recognise you there.'

'I still don't know how he knew me,' Samantha said.

Nancy raised an eyebrow. 'You didn't know Hugh Windsor knew you?'

'No, as soon as he said my name, I got out of there as fast as I could in case other people connected to *The Club* were there, not just Walker, and they heard him say my name.'

'He met you in the bookshop he said,' Nancy told her.

'I didn't remember,' Samantha said. 'He has a great memory then as I usually don't forget a face.' She turned to Marcus. 'Before I had to leave, I heard a few people talking about you, Marcus. That you weren't there and it was a shame. Walker joined in so he knew you too. It got me wondering if there was a connection to you and the gang. I knew when I moved to Dedley End that you shut up Roth Lodge thirty years ago. Jane told me your housekeeper had stolen from you and you'd hid away after the scandal. To me that seemed a perfect smokescreen for you to hide behind. Who would suspect a reclusive millionaire in the countryside of running a London organised criminal gang? So, I kept an eye for news of you and your family. And at Christmas, you opened the house up again and threw a party and someone was murdered at it. I couldn't believe it, especially when my daughter helped track down the killer.' Samantha gave Nancy a quick admiring glance. 'It made me even more suspicious about you,' she continued to Marcus. 'I kept an eye on your London office, you and your son and your grandsons, and I soon gathered you were all members of *Clubhouse13*. Sir Basil Walker had been too. I hadn't thought much about it but, seeing you were too, I started to find that a lot of the people I'd investigated through the years were members. I wondered if it was a front for the gang so I got a job there. When Seb got released, we met up and he said he'd move to Dedley End to see if he could find more evidence to link you to *The Club*. And he found something. He got a few locals to talk over drinks in the pub about you, Marcus, and found out that your wife caused my George's car crash.' Samantha's mouth set in a hard line. 'You'd managed to cover that up, I thought, so what else were you covering up?'

Nancy could see why Samantha and Seb had trained their gaze on to Marcus Roth. He ticked all the boxes. Nancy looked at Marcus. 'The car crash that killed my father. Was it really an accident? Did your wife really drink-drive that night? Or was Dad killed by *The Club*?'

Marcus looked steadily back at her over his shoulder. 'Nancy, I promise you that if I thought for one minute they were behind it, I'd tell you. But I think you're right about someone in Dedley End being involved. I was definitely being watched because someone saw my wife that night and they've been blackmailing me over it ever since. Every month, I pay them cash to keep them quiet. When my wife took her life, I thought about just telling everyone to get them away from me but they threatened to hurt my family then.'

'And once I found out the truth about my father's crash?' Nancy asked.

'They stepped in to make sure we weren't arrested. My family were frightened, worried… I went along with it to protect them.' Marcus sighed. '*The Club* makes you think you can't survive without them.'

'And if you think you can, they destroy or kill you or hurt the people you love as punishment,' Samantha agreed, bitterness tinging her voice.

'Not for much longer,' Nancy vowed.

'You remind me of me back then,' Samantha said with a wry smile. 'I thought I could tear it all down with my bare hands. And look at me, still trying, still failing.'

'We can do this,' Jonathan said. 'No one knows Dedley End or the people in it more than us. If someone there has been watching us all this time, we must know who they are. We just need them to make a mistake. To show themselves.'

Nancy nodded. 'Hopefully the lure of my mother will do just yet.'

Samantha muttered something about bait.

# Chapter Thirty-Eight

The phone call came just as Dedley End appeared ahead of them. 'Hello?' Nancy, with shaking hands, answered and put it on speaker so the others could hear what the unknown caller had to say.

'We have your grandmother,' said the distorted voice on the other end of the phone.

'I swear if you've hurt her—'

'She's fine,' the caller cut her off sharply.

'I need to speak to her, make sure she's okay,' Nancy said, quickly. She didn't trust them at all.

There was a shuffling sound. 'Nancy, I'm okay, don't worry about me!'

Nancy breathed a sigh of relief at the sound of her grandmother's voice. 'Gran, where are you?'

There was a shuffling sound again then the distorted voice came back on the phone. 'Now you know she's fine. We know you're in London. We know you've found your mother. Bring her to meet us and you'll get your grandmother back unharmed. If not, then you know what will happen.'

Nancy squeezed the phone so tightly she wondered if it might shatter. 'What do you want me to do?'

'Meet us with your mother tonight at nine p.m. We'll text you the address thirty minutes before. Come alone with your mother. If we see anyone else nearby, the deal is off.' And then whoever it was hung up.

Nancy took a breath. 'They want Samantha in exchange for my grandmother and for us to meet them tonight. They're texting the address. They let me hear Gran's voice. She sounds okay,' Nancy said, really hoping that was true. 'They think we're still in London so once we tried to find the man watching us, they must have lost track of where we were. That gives us a chance to do something before we have to meet them.'

The minivan drove into the village. She bit her lip. 'I want to go and see the bookshop but I also don't,' she admitted in a low voice to Jonathan beside her.

'I know. But it will feel safe soon,' he promised. 'We'll make sure they can't touch you or any of us ever again.'

She nodded. She couldn't speak but she felt much better that Jonathan believed they could stop the gang. She hated to think how scared her grandmother must have felt when people entered the bookshop and took her away. Nancy was terrified of losing the most important person in her life. She couldn't lose her. She wouldn't, she promised silently. She turned away. The bookshop and going home to her beloved cottage would both have to wait. She had to find her gran and make the gang pay first.

The minivan stopped then, parking under the cover of a large oak tree.

'What's happening?' Samantha asked.

'Jonathan has something to do, he'll meet us in a bit,' Nancy said as she looked at Jonathan. It was time to put the plan they had agreed on, back at the hotel out of earshot of the others, into action. She wanted to trust the people in the car with them but it was better this way.

They didn't have to worry about anyone tipping anyone off. 'Good luck,' she said, her throat tight.

Jonathan nodded. 'Be safe, okay?' He met her gaze and held it for a couple of seconds. She gave him a small smile. Part of her wanted to grab his hand and tell him to stay with her, but she knew this was their chance to find out who in Dedley End was on the wrong side. He nodded back and climbed out of the car.

'What are you two up to?' Marcus asked her, eyes narrowed.

'You'll find out soon,' Nancy replied. 'Let's go,' she added to the driver.

They continued on to meet DCI Brown while Jonathan went into the White Swan. Now that they were sure someone in Dedley End was either working with the gang or could even be behind the whole thing, Nancy had thought they should make use of the gossip network in the village and Jonathan had agreed to head to the pub and see if that might work. Nancy just hoped that DCI Brown wouldn't be too cross she had done something without telling him. Again.

The minivan dropped them off outside DCI Brown's house. He had thought it was the safest place to meet. Nancy eyed it curiously. She had never been there before. The inspector lived at the edge of Dedley End in a small cottage and opened the door before they could even knock. It looked remarkably neat as they filed into the space. DCI Brown gave them a nod in greeting, his eyes moving to Samantha as she walked in. He closed the door behind them and showed them into the living room where Richard sat on the sofa with DC Pang in the armchair. Richard looked like he'd been through hell. 'Nancy,' he said with relief as she walked in. 'Oh my...' he added, trailing off, eyes wide when he saw who she was with.

'Is that?' DC Pang spluttered. Nancy supposed he'd been looking at the old files with DCI Brown and recognised her mother, although she was now fifty.

'This is Samantha Hunter, my, uh, mother,' Nancy confirmed. Both DC Pang and Richard stared at Samantha as if they had seen a ghost. Nancy supposed in some ways she had been for a long time.

'I see my reputation proceeds me,' Samantha said filling the stunned silence with sass. Nancy admired her bravado. She had to be nervous. This was the first time she'd been in Dedley End since she'd run away. Nancy glanced nervously at the handbag, which she knew concealed her mother's gun. She had no idea how DCI Brown would react if he found out her mother had a gun. It definitely was not legally obtained.

'I've seen pictures,' Richard said. '*The Club* made sure everyone knew what you looked like...' He trailed off, looking guiltily at Nancy.

'Welcome back to Dedley End,' DCI Brown said.

Samantha snorted and sat down in a free chair. She looked at Richard. 'So, are you still claiming that you didn't kill Seb?'

'I didn't, I swear it. The gun turned up at Roth Lodge with a note telling me to ditch it or suffer the consequences. I thought Marcus was behind it,' Richard said, throwing him an angry look. 'He told me he wasn't, so I said we should go to the police, things were going too far now, but he told me to ditch it – that he wouldn't back me up if I went to the station. I knew it was a bad idea. Look where I am now.'

Marcus sighed. 'You know what they would have done if you didn't do what they asked. They would have hurt someone we care about.'

'They? Or you?' Richard threw back at him. 'You could still be behind all of this.'

'Well, I'm not,' Marcus replied shortly. He threw his hands up. 'We can't keep going around in circles on this.'

'No, we can't,' Nancy had to agree with him even if she didn't like agreeing with him on anything. 'My grandmother is in trouble. I want to know how you're involved, Richard.' Nancy eyed him. 'How did you end up part of all of this? Did you come back in my life because *The Club* told you to?' she asked, sharply. She might not have been in love with Richard anymore, but it hurt that he had been so ready and willing to lie to her.

He winced at her tone. 'No, I swear. I didn't even know of *The Club* until Marcus told me,' he said, giving the older man standing behind her a hard stare. 'After I set up the company with Will, and we decided to make Roth Lodge our office, Marcus met me in London on the gang's request. He said I'd have to give a monthly payment to them if I wanted the business to succeed. They told him they'd put business our way if I did, or they'd stop anyone working with us if I didn't. I refused at first so Marcus told me everything. That they'd been blackmailing and threatening him for years. That he paid them in cash every month to keep them sweet. That not only could they ruin our business but they could hurt people in our lives. That they weren't people I should double-cross.'

'They didn't believe me that I had nothing to do with your company,' Marcus said. 'They said my family were part of it as much as me. I'd tried so hard to protect you all from them, but I knew this was the only way to keep them at a distance.'

'Why did you never tell me about all of this?' Will asked then. He looked hurt. Both his grandfather and business partner had kept him out of it.

'To protect you,' they replied in unison.

'It didn't really work, did it?' Will said, bitterly.

'Then what?' Nancy asked Richard, trying to get the conversation back on track.

'At my leaving do, I met Hugh Windsor, who told me he'd seen Samantha at his party. I…' Richard hung his head. 'Marcus had already told me that *The Club* were looking for her. That they knew I knew you, Nancy, and had told Marcus to make sure I kept them informed if you ever got in contact with one another,' he added, looking at Nancy and Samantha. 'As I said, they showed me a picture of what Samantha looked like.'

'Then what?' Nancy said, forcing him back on track.

'I told Marcus that Hugh had seen Samantha and he left it in a note with his money cash payment. It's the only way we've communicated with them,' Richard said. 'They told me to tell you about your mother being seen and to encourage you to find her. I tried to warn you not to—'

'Not very hard,' Nancy said. 'You could have told me what was going on!'

'But they would have hurt you,' Richard said, looking at her. 'They hurt Peter when Marcus tried to get out. They wouldn't have thought twice. I know you don't think I care about you but you're the person I care about most.'

'You could have warned me,' she insisted. 'And don't make out it was all selfless to protect me, they helped your business and you enjoyed that.'

Richard sighed. 'Okay, yes, I wanted us to be successful.'

'At any cost?' Nancy asked, shaking her head. She turned to Marcus. 'Why did you tell them that Hugh Windsor had seen my mother at his party? I thought you were tired of them blackmailing you. Why help them find her?'

Marcus looked as abashed as Richard. 'I thought they might leave me alone if I was the one to help them find Samantha.'

'Selfish cowards both of you,' Nancy said, turning away from them in disgust.

'Pathetic,' Samantha agreed. 'And now even though you helped them, they're trying to pin everything on you. I kind of wish they had succeeded.' Nancy didn't blame her for that feeling at all.

DCI Brown stepped in then, giving Nancy and Samantha a sympathetic look. 'If we accept that they are trying to frame you and neither of you are behind this gang, then you need to help us find out who is and stop them. We need to find Jane Hunter.'

'They just phoned us,' Nancy explained, remembering the inspector didn't know they had got in touch on the way to his cottage. 'They want us to exchange my mother for my grandmother at nine o'clock tonight. They think we're in London so we have some time.' Nancy wasn't quite sure what they could do with that time though.

There was a knock at the door. DCI Brown looked startled but Nancy told him it should be Jonathan and, when he went to look, she heard with relief Jonathan's voice along with Pen and Ollie. When they walked in, it took all Nancy had not to crumple to the floor in a heap.

Pen rushed at her and she tried to hug her without falling over.

'Are you okay?' Pen whispered.

'I think so. You? How's Charlie?'

'He's fine. We checked on him. He's happy at the cottage,' Pen promised. 'And the bookshop is all locked up securely.'

'Thank you.' Nancy met Jonathan's eyes over Pen's blonde hair and he nodded. He'd done what they had agreed he would then. Now they just needed to hope it worked.

'I know you, don't I?' Marcus said then, looking at Oliver, Penelope's husband, as he walked in behind her and Jonathan.

Ollie nodded. 'Yes, Sir. You came to my barracks once.'

'That's right.' Marcus saw their curious looks. 'Hugh Windsor served. He rose up to colonel before he retired. They invited him to see the new barracks in Surrey and I tagged along.' He turned back to Ollie. 'You're on leave?'

'Yes, for a week with my family, Sir,' Ollie said. 'How is Hugh Windsor?'

'Oh, he's fine, I think.'

'He's thought of with great respect by everyone,' Ollie said.

'So I gather,' Marcus said, drily, as if he'd heard that a million times before.

'That reminds me,' Will said. 'They said at *Clubhouse13* that Hugh was trying to find you.'

Marcus nodded. 'I'll call him after all this is over. If it ever is.'

'He doesn't know about *The Club*?' Nancy asked.

Marcus shook his head. 'He would never have got himself tied up with those low lives. I suppose I never wanted to admit to him that I had. Hugh met my wife first. But when we met, it was love at first sight. Hugh always said I was the luckiest man alive. And I thought I was too. How could I tell him what she had done? That I was being blackmailed over it all to boot? I suppose I wanted him to keep on believing that I was lucky.' Marcus sighed.

That didn't sound much like friendship to Nancy.

Jonathan elbowed her then. He'd been looking out of the window ever since they arrived. She followed his gaze and saw who was out there. A shiver ran down her spine when she saw who it was.

'He was in the pub?' Nancy guessed in a low voice but everyone listened anyway.

'He heard every word,' Jonathan confirmed.

Nancy shook her head. 'He could just be curious...' She couldn't quite believe this person was involved but then again, did anything surprise her anymore? She had asked Jonathan to go to the White Swan and call Penelope and tell her that they'd found Samantha and that they needed her to come to DCI Brown's house with him. Nancy had felt sure that whoever it was in Dedley End who had been watching them wouldn't be able to resist seeing for themselves that Samantha was back. She had assumed gossip would fly around the village and would draw them out but it looked like the man outside had overheard in the pub and had come straight there. 'Okay,' she said, deciding something. 'I have an idea. I think we need to do a reconstruction of Seb's murder.'

'Shouldn't we be looking for Mrs H?' Penelope asked her in surprise.

'There's no point,' Nancy said. Penelope gasped. 'We have no idea who is behind this,' Nancy said, quickly explaining. 'We have no clues. Nothing to lead us to her. Except the fact that a murder happened in our village. Whoever killed Seb is involved in trying to find my mother and kidnapping Gran. It could be one person or a group. It could be *The Governor* themselves. We don't know. But I think if we can find Seb's killer, we can find out where Gran might be.'

'You want us to reconstruct the murder in the church?' DCI Brown asked.

'But we've been over the statements...' DC Pang protested.

'But acting it out, putting everyone exactly where they were that night is so much better. It's the only way to make sense of how Seb was killed in a locked church and how the killer escaped without being seen. We find the killer, we find the gang, I'm sure of it.'

Samantha stood up. 'Nancy is right. Seb was killed to stop him getting to *The Governor*. We have no idea where Jane is but if we can find Seb's killer, we might be able to get them to tell us where she is. And if not, we'll meet them at nine tonight. And I'll hand myself over.' She looked at her daughter. 'I will always protect you.'

'It won't come to that,' Nancy said, hoping that she wasn't lying to them both.

# Chapter Thirty-Nine

Nancy phoned the vicarage and asked the vicar and Gloria to come to the church. Then she called Mr Peabody on his mobile and asked him the same thing. Penelope and Ollie needed to collect their daughter from school and Nancy preferred they weren't involved in any of this so she encouraged them to go, promising to keep them updated with what was happening.

Then Nancy, Jonathan, Samantha, DCI Brown, Richard, DC Pang and Marcus Roth walked over to the church in tense silence. The person who had come from the pub had disappeared, although Nancy knew they could be watching them leave DCI Brown's cottage.

Samantha looked around with wide eyes. She gave nothing away by her expression as to how she felt being back in Dedley End, but Nancy knew she was taking it all in. The church soon rose up into view, its steeple reaching up into the cloudy sky. It had always been a sanctuary to the village but Nancy felt uneasy walking back inside it after what had happened there and what might happen there now.

Rev. Williams and Gloria walked out of the vicarage when they saw them coming up the road. 'Samantha! My goodness,' Gloria cried when she saw her.

Samantha smiled properly for the first time since Nancy had seen her again. It made her look so much younger. 'Lloyd. Gloria.' And then Nancy watched in disbelief as Samantha hugged them both tightly.

'Blimey,' Jonathan said, close to her ear.

Nancy nodded. Suddenly, she could picture her mother in the village with friends and a family. She tried not to wish her mother would hug her. She looked away. Her gran was her family now and she had to focus on helping her right now. 'Let's go,' she said and led the way inside the church.

It was a chilly day and inside the church the air was icy. She was glad she'd worn her coat. She stopped just inside the door. 'Okay. The door was locked and we were all outside when we heard the gunshots. We rushed over and unlocked the door and came in. And we saw... Seb.' She turned around. 'Marcus, can you please take on the role of Seb for us? No need to lie on the floor but if you can stand in the aisle where he was...' She pointed to the spot and Marcus, sensing he had to go along with everything they asked of him, went right over.

'I'm here,' Mr Peabody said, coming inside the church. 'I came as quickly as these old legs would allow. Is that...?'

'Mr Peabody,' Samantha said, with a nod in greeting.

'I didn't think I'd ever see you again,' he replied in wonder. He looked around the church and frowned. 'Where's Mrs Hunter?'

'That's what we're trying to find out,' Nancy said, trying not to meet his gaze in case she gave anything away. 'Okay. Let's all stand where we were when we came inside. Jonathan, you unlocked the door and I followed you then came Gran – DCI Brown, can you please be her in her... absence? Then Rev. Williams and Gloria and Richard, Will and Mr Peabody. DC Pang, can you please wait outside as you weren't here when we came in?' He looked at DCI Brown as if he wanted to argue but the inspector nodded, so he slunk out with a sigh, standing just through the open church door so he could still see and hear them.

Nancy watched everyone all line up in the aisle. She moved to stand by Marcus playing Seb as she had done that night. She checked. 'This is where we were. I looked around quickly when I came in but then Mr Peabody said Seb was still alive so I crouched down beside him. Okay, Samantha, can you please play the killer?'

'I thought we didn't know where the killer was,' Mr Peabody said with a frown.

'Yes. Isn't that the whole point?' Richard agreed, looking at Nancy.

'This is where we think they were when we came in,' Nancy said, telling her mother to crouch behind the statue at the side of the church. They watched Samantha go over there. 'Can anyone see her?' she asked once Samantha was behind the statue.

'I can a little bit,' Jonathan said. 'But I wasn't looking that way, I was looking at Seb.' Everyone agreed they were too.

Nancy nodded. 'Okay, so the killer could have been there when we came in. We were so focused on Seb, we didn't look over that way so we didn't see them.'

'But how did they get out?' Samantha called from behind the stone.

'Hang on, let's do the next bit,' Nancy called out as she wasn't sure yet. She walked forward to stand in front of Marcus. 'I went to Seb while you phoned the police and ambulance, Will.'

Will nodded and moved to where he had called them.

'Mrs H was there,' Jonathan said, gesturing to DCI Brown who moved to that position.

'We stood here,' Rev. Williams said, gesturing to his wife, behind Nancy.

'Then I suggested we look outside in case there was any sign of the killer,' Jonathan said, stepping closer to Nancy, Marcus as Seb and DCI Brown as Jane.

'And I said I'd go with you,' Richard said.

'Can you see Samantha?' Nancy asked as Jonathan and Richard walked back down the aisle to the church door.

'I was looking ahead,' Jonathan said. He turned. 'I can only see her if I look like this, which I didn't.' Richard agreed he hadn't either.

'Okay, so that's why you didn't spot the killer. When they went outside then, did anyone else move? Would you have seen the killer if they had been behind the statue still?'

The vicar and Gloria who had remained behind Nancy and Seb in the aisle that night said they had kept their eyes on the two of them so hadn't looked in the direction of the statue. Mr Peabody who was slightly behind them, the last person in the aisle, closest to the church door, said the same. 'And my grandmother didn't turn that way either,' Nancy said. 'Will?'

He shook his head. 'I went to talk to Mr Peabody,' Will said, moving to stand by him. 'So, I had my back to the statue.'

'Okay, so we can assume the killer was still behind the statue at this point. Then you two came back,' Nancy called to Jonathan and Richard by the door.

'We hadn't found anything. Nancy, you called out that maybe the killer was still here,' Jonathan said as he and Richard stepped forward. 'I think it was you, Mr Peabody, who suggested we check past Seb and Nancy towards the altar, so we did.'

'You told us all to stay where we were,' Gloria reminded Jonathan.

'I was focused on the altar,' Richard said as they walked past the others towards the front of the church.

'I was looking at Nancy and Seb,' Jonathan said. 'Why didn't I sense someone was there though?'

'If I duck this way,' Samantha called out. 'Would you have seen me?'

Richard and Jonathan looked over as they walked up to the altar. 'Only if we had turned around once we were up here and seen you from this way,' Jonathan said. He whistled. 'Wow, the killer really found the perfect spot to stay hidden. We were all so focused on Seb that none of us looked over that way.'

'Does that mean they had been in the church before?' Gloria asked her husband.

'They knew the layout well it seems,' he replied.

'We then searched over here,' Richard said and he and Jonathan turned away once again from the statue.

'So, then the worst happened,' Nancy said with a shiver as she remembered watching the life draining out from Seb. 'I called out that Seb had died and everyone rushed forward to be with us.' She gestured for DCI Brown to come closer as her gran had done and then Will, the vicar and Gloria stepped forward with Mr Peabody behind them. 'So, again we were all facing this way. That must have been when the killer snuck out from behind the statue. Samantha, come out now!' she called. 'Everyone keep looking down at Marcus,' she said to the others as they had done that night with Seb. 'Are you moving, Samantha?'

'Yes. I'm out from the statue and there is a row of pews here. If I duck behind them and move softly so you can't hear my footsteps...' She trailed off as she moved. 'Then what?' she called out.

'Can you get behind Mr Peabody in the aisle?' Nancy called without turning to look at her mother.

'I'm here,' Samantha said a couple of seconds later. They all turned around to see her standing behind Mr Peabody.

'Did anyone notice Samantha walk from the statue, behind the pews, to stand by Mr Peabody?' Nancy asked.

Everyone said no, just as she had thought they would. She hadn't seen the killer do it that night either. They had all been too focused on poor Seb.

'Not even you?' Will asked Mr Peabody. 'You were the closest to the church door, they would have been right behind you.'

'I didn't notice anyone,' Mr Peabody insisted. 'Like you, I was watching Nancy with Seb. I didn't turn around until DC Pang came in.'

'But then where did they go?' Samantha asked, confused.

'Let's do the next bit,' Nancy suggested. 'Okay, DC Pang, you're up.'

They watched as DC Pang ran in and hurried up the aisle. He stopped by Mr Peabody at the end of the aisle, his footsteps echoing around the church. 'I rushed in from the High Street after hearing on the radio that Will Roth had called in to say Sebastian Holmes had been attacked in the church.'

'And did you see anyone on your way here?' Nancy asked.

'No, but I was rushing and it was dark,' Pang replied.

'You asked Mr Peabody to step aside,' Nancy recounted. 'Then you came to check Seb's pulse. Then Richard and Jonathan came back from searching the front of the church and realised Seb was dead.'

Jonathan and Richard re-joined the group as they had done that night.

'And then, just after that, DCI Brown and the rest of the police arrived,' Nancy finished.

'We checked everywhere. No murderer. No weapon, no prints,' DCI Brown said.

'Well, no, because the killer and the gun never left this church,' Nancy said, everything having clicked into place for her. 'Everyone stay where you are.'

'I've had enough of this. DCI Brown, we can't let—'

'I think I know what happened,' Nancy interrupted DC Pang impatiently. She turned to her mother. 'Can you sit out the way? I'll be the killer now. DC Pang, please sit with her. Everyone else stay where you are.' She saw DC Pang about to protest. 'It'll take two minutes. You want to find out who did this, don't you?'

He sighed but DCI Brown told her to go ahead.

Nancy walked to the back row of pews. 'So, as we've just seen, the killer had been behind the statue waiting for the perfect moment to slip out. Once Richard and Jonathan came back in and walked up the aisle passing us all, they were facing the altar and we were all looking at Seb. We were all facing forward so the killer was able to slip out from the statue, duck down behind the back row of pews and then appear in the aisle behind us as if they had just walked into the church and not been there the whole time. But what to do then? They had the gun in their hands and if they ran they could be seen by the police on their way or picked up on CCTV. As you said, Gloria, the killer knew this church. They were prepared. They had taken the vicar's keys, copied them, and led Seb here. They locked the door so he couldn't escape and to slow down the vicar, who they knew would come in when they heard the gunshots. The killer knew that the best way to escape was simply to be here after it happened and not try to run. But they had the murder weapon and that's not easy to explain. So, they had to plan for that too. They had an accomplice. Here waiting to take the gun from them and then hide it. They were confident no one would search their accomplice. Because they were someone the police would never suspect.' Nancy walked into the aisle and to the person who was the closest to her. 'Isn't that right, Mr Peabody?'

# Chapter Forty

Everyone gasped in shock.

'What are you talking about, Nancy?' Mr Peabody asked, turning slowly to look at her. His face was shocked and there was hurt in his eyes. 'I've known you all my life.'

'You can't really believe that Mr Peabody would do such a thing,' Gloria said, her hand on her chest.

'He was one of us,' DC Pang said from behind them, shaking his head.

Nancy looked at DCI Brown, who was frowning as if trying to put the puzzle pieces together. Her mother was glaring at Mr Peabody. Jonathan's eyes were wide. The vicar wobbled on his legs unsteadily. Richard and Marcus looked at one another. Nancy knew none of them could believe it. And nor could she but the evidence was overwhelming.

Nancy took a breath and continued. 'Hold out your hand behind your back,' she said, firmly to Mr Peabody.

'This is preposterous,' he burst out. 'You can't expect me to partake in this crazy endeavour anymore,' he said, turning to go.

'Hold on,' DCI Brown called out. Mr Peabody stopped, his eyes flashing with anger then fading so fast Nancy wasn't sure if anyone else had noticed but her. 'Just hear Nancy out. Let her finish. Please,' he said, calmly.

'Fine,' Mr Peabody muttered. 'But I've never been so insulted in all my life. From someone I thought of as a dear friend, all these years...' he muttered as he stepped back in front of Nancy.

'Hold out your hand,' Nancy repeated to Mr Peabody. 'Obviously, none of us were likely to point to Mr Peabody as being involved in all of this.'

'I should think not! My record as a police officer is spotless,' Mr Peabody spat out.

'And we knew there was no way, with his arthritis, that Mr Peabody could fire the gun that killed Seb. And he didn't. But as we've just acted out, we know the killer slipped out behind the statue but couldn't get out of the church and not be caught, so they walked behind Mr Peabody – who can't tell me he didn't notice someone suddenly behind them! The killer couldn't leave with the gun, it would be noticed, but Mr Peabody always wears that raincoat in autumn with its big pockets. Mr Peabody took the gun from the killer like this...' She pulled her mother's gun out and laid it in his hands behind his back.

'What the...' he spluttered as everyone gasped again. DCI Brown stepped forward in shock.

'It isn't loaded,' Nancy assured everyone. She'd got it from her mother as they walked to the church and Samantha had taken out the bullets, reluctantly. 'But now, do you see? The killer passed the gun behind Mr Peabody's back. Mr Peabody put it in the pocket of that raincoat he always wears. He and the killer knew that no one would search him. That none of us would dream for a moment that he was hiding the gun. Until it was dropped off at Roth Lodge,' Nancy said.

'Where's your proof?' Mr Peabody asked her, not hiding his hard expression this time. That steel in his eyes

273

was so very different to the gentle twinkling ones Nancy usually looked into. She had seriously misjudged this man. He had been wearing a mask for all these years.

'You were in the pub,' Jonathan called out. 'I rung Penelope to tell her we had Samantha and were going to DCI Brown's cottage. You followed me and we saw you outside his cottage. You couldn't resist coming to see her here so you could then tell *The Club* that she was here.'

Mr Peabody glanced behind him in panic. 'But why? Why would I have done it?'

Richard moved then. 'For money. I told you,' he said, turning to Nancy. 'I was helping him with investments as he'd come into money. That's why, wasn't it?' He turned back to Peabody. 'Seb's killer paid you to protect them.'

'Do it,' Nancy said grimly to Mr Peabody, who had turned pale as if he was realising that none of them believed him now. 'Put the gun in your pocket. Like you did that night.'

'Show us what you did,' DCI Brown added.

Mr Peabody closed his eyes and sighed as if he realised he was defeated. When he opened them, he took the gun in his hands and put it in the inside pocket of his coat.

'Mr Peabody,' Rev. Williams said, stunned. 'You really took the gun?'

'Nancy was right?' Gloria asked in horror.

'We knew no one would search a retired police officer and old man to boot,' Mr Peabody said. 'There was someone waiting when I got home to take it.'

'And try to frame me with it!' Richard said, angrily.

'I didn't know about that,' Mr Peabody said. 'I just did what I was asked.'

'Hmmm,' Nancy said. 'I wonder how long you've been doing what you've been asked to by *The Club*.'

'How could you? You were supposed to catch criminals, not help them,' DCI Brown said.

Mr Peabody spun around to look at him. 'I worked for years not getting anywhere, never appreciated, for a piddling salary. While all the time I watched criminals coming in and making millions! Why shouldn't I have a piece of that pie? Can you really blame me? Can you really tell me you wouldn't have done the same if it was offered to you on a plate?'

'Never,' DCI Brown said. 'Why join the police in the first place unless you want to fight crime?'

'I didn't realise you were so naïve,' Mr Peabody replied coldly.

'You stood idly by while someone was shot in here! You helped the murderer get away. What else have you done for their dirty money?' Nancy cried, furious with his complete lack of caring about anyone but himself. Poor Seb was dead just so Peabody could make some more retirement money.

'You turned me in,' Samantha said, suddenly stepping forward. 'It was you, wasn't it? You told the gang I was here. I always wondered who in Dedley End even knew who I was,' she said, her eyes flashing dangerously.

'No,' Nancy gasped, she hadn't thought of that.

'Tell us the truth. Was it you?' DCI Brown barked at Mr Peabody.

Mr Peabody sighed heavily. 'I went to London to do some training with the Met. Some scheme they came up with back then to supposedly make us sharper. I saw a couple of officers turning a blind eye to a crime and when I confronted them, they admitted they were on the payroll of *The Club*, and would give me an in if I wanted. I thought why not? I'd worked so hard and had been overlooked time and again for promotion, I was tired of it all. And they offered a lot of money. Money I could enjoy and which would keep me in real comfort once I retired. So, they brought me in to it all. They told their contact about me and that I came from Dedley End. That got me on the payroll straight away.' His eyes slid to Marcus and Will Roth. 'They told me you needed watching. And it would be useful to have someone in our neck of the woods, so to speak. So, when I came back that's what I did. I would pass on anything I noticed and every month my pay from the police was almost doubled by the gang. I was in the pub one night after I came back from London and I saw you, Samantha, with George. Nancy was at home with Ms Hunter I think, and it hit me like a bolt. My police officer friends in London had shown me a list of people *The Club* wanted to find. Including a picture of you, Samantha. Top of their wish list. I realised it was you that night. You looked different – you'd changed your hair, your makeup and style, and you had a new identity, but I knew you were Susan Marlow. Can you imagine the feeling when I realised the woman they'd been looking for was living in my village?'

'Didn't you think about my family?' Samantha cried.

'Honestly, I just thought about the money. I knew they'd pay a lot for the information. And they did. I waited a bit so it didn't look suspicious but I took early retirement thanks to giving them your address,' he replied with a shrug. 'The gang weren't happy that you managed to run before they got to you but now they knew you were back in London, they thought it was only a matter of time before they'd find you.'

'And yet here I am.'

'I'm impressed,' Mr Peabody said. 'But you made a mistake being seen at that party and Richard finding out.'

'I thought maybe I had.' Samantha looked at Nancy. 'But it wasn't a mistake because it brought me back here.'

DCI Brown came over, reached into Mr Peabody's pocket and removed Samantha's gun. 'I'll be taking this. Peabody, you're under arrest.' He read him his rights. 'And I'm sure we'll find a hell of a lot more to charge you with once we start digging,' he added.

'You think they'll let me go to prison?' Mr Peabody taunted him. 'This goes far higher up than you could even imagine.'

'Hang on,' Jonathan said. 'Mr Peabody took the gun but from who? Who actually shot Sebastian?' he asked, frowning.

Nancy had known this question was coming. The whole time she had been talking to Mr Peabody her mind had been whirring. Because if the killer gave the gun to Mr Peabody, there was only one person who could have shot Seb. And it was unthinkable but she had seen Mr Peabody glance their way when he realised the game was up. After they nodded at him, maybe letting Mr Peabody know to tell the truth, and Nancy had sensed them stand up from beside Samantha and then carefully edge inch-by-inch towards the door. She felt in her bones she was right. But still she had to take a deep breath before telling everyone else. She looked at Jonathan. 'We were stuck on how someone could have got *out* of the church without us seeing them but we should have thought about who came *in*.'

'I'm lost,' Jonathan admitted. 'What do you mean?'

'It's like Mr Peabody says – it goes higher than we could even imagine. Isn't that right, DC Pang?' she asked, whirling around to the police officer whose eyes had been glued to her back. He was almost at the door. She caught a flicker of a smile on his face.

Before anyone could react, DC Pang spun around, flew through the door and ran.

'No!' Nancy cried as DCI Brown and Jonathan started out of the church after him. But it was no good. The police officer tore out of the church and on to the road where a car pulled up, and he dived into it leaving DCI Brown and Jonathan standing at the side of the road watching them drive away.

Mr Peabody chuckled. 'Always have an exit plan, Nancy.'

'This isn't funny!' she told him, but she could see he thought they were all untouchable. And she was really worried that maybe he was right.

DCI Brown returned, calling in to the station to get everyone looking for DC Pang. His shocked voice stunned the operator by telling them Pang was a murderer. He looked at Nancy. 'How did you work that out?'

'I knew it was impossible for anyone in the church to have gotten out without being seen by you and your team when you arrived or on CCTV, so I guessed the killer had hidden behind the statue but I still was stuck on what they did after that. Acting it out now, I could see there was no one else it could have been,' Nancy replied. 'DC Pang was first on the scene. He acted like he'd hurried inside and I didn't question it until I realised Mr Peabody was involved. He would have sensed DC Pang walking up behind him in the aisle; he would have known he hadn't just run in from outside. They both acted like Pang had just arrived when he'd been here all along. And none of us questioned it because Will had called the police and you arrived not long after. Pang had known that all he had to do was wait for the perfect moment to slip out from behind the statue once the police were called and Mr Peabody was here to cover it up and hide the gun for him.'

'An ingenious plan, you have to admit,' Mr Peabody said. 'I wondered if you'd ever work it out, Nancy, you really do have a detective's mind.'

'I just remembered you were shocked to see us that night. You didn't want us to go into the church and, when we did, you tried to stop Jonathan and Richard looking outside but, then when they came back in, you encouraged them to search the church at the front because you knew it was Pang's opportunity to get out from behind the statue,' Nancy said.

Peabody nodded. 'Pang lured Holmes to the church pretending to be the vicar scared someone was following him. Holmes thought the gang were here and rushed here. Pang paid me to turn up and draw the vicar outside so we'd hear the shot and go into the church and call the police so Pang could pretend to have just arrived, and I'd take the gun from him. We didn't bank on all you lot turning up and I wasn't sure we'd pull it off but, like you say, when you were searching, Pang saw his chance and got out from behind the statue. It was rather fun actually.'

'You're sick,' Nancy said to him, disgusted.

'So, he locked the church door to give himself time to hide?' Jonathan asked.

'And for your benefit,' Peabody said with a smile. 'He thought it would be a mystery even you couldn't solve and I think he would have gotten away with it if you hadn't turned up.'

'I can't believe Pang is corrupt. He was the only one I told things to, I thought I could trust him,' DCI Brown said. 'I've been a blind fool it seems.'

'You need to be more suspicious of people. I learned a long time ago you can't trust anyone but yourself,' Mr Peabody said.

'God, what a sad way of thinking,' Nancy said, shaking her head. He just shrugged.

'Do you know where Mrs Hunter is?' DCI Brown asked him then.

'Honestly, no. None of us know who's in charge. I hear they have Jane though. She's with *The Governor*.' He looked at Samantha. 'You're too important to them. Their power has been diminishing a little bit these past few years, there have been murmurings of other people trying to take over. Pang tells me the gossip sometimes,' he continued as if he wasn't talking about a dangerous criminal gang but something in the playground. 'But finding Samantha would cement their position again.'

Nancy shivered. She had to stop them hurting her grandmother and mother.

'No wonder Pang hated us looking into the murders in the village,' Jonathan said to Nancy. 'He wanted to be the one to decide who got justice and who didn't. Not us.'

'I should have seen it,' DCI Brown said with a groan. 'I should have realised he was working for someone else all this time.'

'He fooled everyone,' Nancy said. Her phone beeped. 'It's a message from them,' she said as she saw an unknown number appear. She read it aloud to everyone. 'We know you're not in London. We'll come to you. We'll be in Dedley End at nine p.m. We'll message you again then.'

She looked up from her phone. 'Pang must have told them we're here. What are we going to do?'

## Chapter Forty-One

Everyone split up. DCI Brown took Mr Peabody to the police station. The inspector looked as stressed as Nancy felt. He had to deal with arresting a former police officer, trying to track down a current corrupt officer after DC Pang had fled, and work with his team to see if they could get any leads that might help them find her grandmother before this meeting with the kidnappers that night. Nancy just didn't know how that meeting wouldn't risk the lives of the people she loved. She knew that if they could find Jane before then they had a far better chance of bringing her home safe and sound. With that in mind, she knew she couldn't just go home to the cottage, and sit and wait for news. She needed to try to do something that might help.

'I need to look in the bookshop, I know the police searched it but...' She looked at Jonathan knowing he'd understand.

'We'll take a look,' he said, instantly.

'We're coming too. We can't just go home while Jane is in trouble,' Gloria said, her husband nodding along in agreement.

'Let's go,' Samantha said.

Will, Marcus and Richard returned to Roth Lodge but promised they'd help if Nancy needed them. She preferred not to have to deal with seeing them again for a while, but she couldn't shake the feeling that they either knew more than they had said or were connected to it all in other ways than they hadn't worked out just yet.

Nancy and the others walked back to the High Street and the bookshop. Nancy called Penelope, who said she'd dropped her daughter Kitty at her grandparents because she and her husband Ollie wanted to help. She said she would bring Charlie along to the bookshop. Nancy had never been more grateful for the support of her friends.

As Nancy, Jonathan, Samantha, the vicar and his wife walked to the bookshop, Nancy was nervous to walk inside for the first time in her whole life. It was the happiest place in the world for her but now it had been tarnished. They approached the door, which had been locked by Penelope once the police had finished looking it over. Nancy used her keys to let them in.

They stepped inside and glanced around. It was strange. It looked exactly as Nancy had left it the day before. Then she looked up and saw the camera pulled out from the wall. 'They were clever to do that,' she said, pointing. 'Other than that, there's no sign of anything untoward having happened here. Not even a book out of place.'

'I guess that's why the police didn't find anything to help. So what, the kidnappers just walked in like they were customers, grabbed Mrs H and put her in their car? It happened so quickly, no one knew anything was wrong?' Jonathan said.

'I can't believe something like that can happen in broad daylight,' Gloria said with a shiver. Rev. Williams put a hand on her shoulder. 'Jane must have been terrified. And no one helped her.'

Nancy let out a shaky breath. She knew she'd been running on adrenaline since Penelope called her to say her grandmother had been taken and now it seemed to hit her like a sledgehammer. She felt herself drop to her knees right there on the bookshop carpet. 'Oh, Gran, where have they taken you?' she said in despair. She felt a tear roll down her cheek and she brushed it away angrily. She couldn't just sit there crying. How would that help Jane?

Jonathan crouched down beside her. 'She's going to be okay.'

Nancy looked at him. 'She must be so scared. I tried to shut it out to focus on the case so we could get her back but, being back here, I keep thinking what if she isn't going to be okay? What will we do?'

Jonathan wrapped an arm around her. 'No,' he said, firmly. 'We don't even think like that. Mrs H will be back here tonight. Whatever it takes. Okay? She'll be giving them hell, I bet, won't she?'

'I hope so.'

'Oh, Nancy!' They turned as Penelope and Ollie walked in and then Charlie pushed past them to run over to Nancy and Jonathan on the floor.

'Charlie, it's good to see you, boy,' Nancy said, instantly feeling better as her beagle pushed against her and she wrapped her arms around him. He wagged his tail and licked her face as Jonathan patted him. 'You'll help us get Gran back, won't you?' Charlie let out a bark and pressed himself harder against her. Nancy looked at everyone. 'What would Gran do right now if she was here?' she asked them.

Jonathan grinned. 'Make everyone a cup of tea.'

'She always says people think better with a cup of tea in their hands,' Pen agreed.

'Okay then.' Nancy climbed up and Jonathan got up too. Charlie sat down on Nancy's feet, looking up at her.

She patted him as she looked around the bookshop. 'Okay. Let's channel Gran and make tea, and then decide what we can do to help her.'

'Good plan, I'll make them,' Jonathan said, going out the back into the office.

Nancy glanced at her mother. She'd stepped over to look at the picture that hung on the wall of Nancy's father. Nancy went over to her. 'I keep it up so it feels like he's still running the shop with me,' she explained.

'I took this photo,' Samantha said, smiling at it. 'Not long after we opened the shop. It was George's pride and joy. Second only to you.' She looked at Nancy. 'I'm sorry they have Jane. She was always so good to me. Treated me like her own. Always.'

Nancy nodded. 'That's Gran.' She lowered her voice so the others wouldn't hear her. 'What if they've hurt her?' she asked her mother, fearfully. She had no idea what she'd do without her grandmother. She could feel that she was close to breaking point and could quite easily start crying and never stop but what good would that do? He grandmother needed her to be strong to help her. She just wished she knew how.

'They won't,' Samantha said firmly. 'They want to exchange her for me. It's in their interest to keep her safe. They've been after me for years, Nancy. And now they are so close. I can only say how sorry I am that Jane has been caught up in it all.'

Jonathan came out of the office then with hot drinks on a tray. 'I think I made everyone's how you like it.' He put the tray on the till. 'Come and get them.'

'I hate thinking about how scared Gran must be,' Nancy said as everyone took a tea, even if they didn't want it – it was something to do.

'I doubt it. They're probably more scared of her,' Jonathan said with a grin.

Despite the situation, she smiled slightly. She knew her gran would be doing all she could to make them regret taking her.

They sipped their teas in silence for a minute.

'You said someone saw a car outside but they didn't see them take Mrs H?' Jonathan said after a moment, looking over at Penelope.

Pen shook her head. 'Ruth Stoke. She was walking past the bookshop, and saw a large black car and two men sitting in it watching it. She says she feels awful that she didn't go in and see Mrs H, but she just thought they were delivering something, you know? When we passed her, walking to see Mrs H, she told us. When we arrived, though, the car was gone. And then we went inside and realised so had Mrs H,' Pen said. 'I phoned her but her phone was off. I tried to call the cottage too but nothing. I knew Mrs H would never leave the shop open and unlocked like that. And then we saw the CCTV cameras had been destroyed... Ollie called the police and I called you straightaway,' she added to Nancy. 'If only we'd come earlier!'

'If only I hadn't gone to London,' Nancy said. 'It's my fault.' She looked at Samantha. 'I should have known you had a good reason to stay away. If the gang hadn't followed me to London, they would never have found you,' Nancy said. 'And they wouldn't have taken Gran to blackmail us with.'

'No, it's my fault for never telling you the truth. I should have found a way—' Samantha began.

'You can't do that,' Gloria interrupted them. 'You will drive yourself crazy thinking "what if" scenarios like this.

Jane wouldn't want that. None of you are responsible. The people in this horrible gang are. They are the ones we need to blame,' she said, passionately.

Rev. Williams nodded. 'My wife is right. We're not responsible for what terrible things these people have done. All we are responsible for is trying to ensure our village becomes a safe place to be again.'

'You're both right,' Samantha said. 'We can't waste time blaming ourselves. At the end of the day, this is on them. *The Club* are the ones who are guilty. They need stopping and we will do it. I swear we will.'

Nancy recognised the fierce look in her mother's eyes. She felt the same way. 'How do we do that though?'

'Well, I can't stand around here talking,' Samantha said, pacing back and forth. 'We have to do something otherwise it'll be nine o'clock before we know it. I don't believe the gang will let either of us go when it comes to do this so-called exchange. It's like you say, Lloyd, no one is safe. I tried to stop them coming to Dedley End but I should have known they were already here. Mr Peabody and his love of money forced me to leave my family and I'm not doing it again. We need to stop this once and for all today,' she said, firmly.

'Hear hear,' Rev. Williams said.

'If only we knew who had taken Mrs H or where they're keeping her,' Pen said. She looked at Ollie, who rubbed her arm reassuringly.

'I wish Mrs H could tell us,' Ollie agreed with his wife.

Nancy had been absentmindedly patting Charlie. Something clicked when Ollie said that though. 'You're all right. Jonathan, what you said just now about the kidnappers probably being more scared of Gran than she was of them. She wouldn't have just let them take her without putting up a fight.'

'Well, no, but they did take her,' Jonathan said, gently.

'I know but if she knew that it was impossible to get away, then what would she have done?'

He looked at her. 'You mean, would she have tried to leave us a clue?'

'I doubt she would have been thinking that clearly,' Samantha scoffed.

Nancy looked at her. 'I think that's exactly what my gran would have done. It's what I would have done if I had been in the same situation. I would have tried to give us a clue, a sign, a message about who was there or where they were taking her,' she said, feeling more certain by the moment that her grandmother would have tried everything to make sure Nancy could find her.

Jonathan nodded slowly. 'It would be just like Mrs H to do that.'

'If she could, she would have,' Nancy said.

Penelope looked at them. 'You guys might be right,' she said, slowly. 'She would have tried to do something. Not me, I would have just panicked but Mrs H is remarkable, right?'

Gloria's eyes lit up. 'You're right. Jane wouldn't ever go down without a fight. But what could she have left us to help? And where would she put it?'

'Let's look around,' Jonathan said.

'What could she have left?' Samantha asked, doubtfully. 'She was probably just overpowered and…' She trailed off seeing Nancy's face. 'Okay, okay, let's look.'

'You look out here, I'll take the office,' Nancy said. She called Charlie to come with her not wanting to be parted from him.

Samantha followed Nancy and the beagle out into the back. 'I know this isn't really the time but I might not get another chance to ask you. The bookshop looks great, Nancy, and I've seen in the press how successful it's been. Have you...' she cleared her throat as they walked into the office, 'been happy working here, and living here?'

Nancy glanced over her shoulder at her mother. It was so strange to be in the bookshop with her. A place they had both worked in, but never together. 'Yes. I love the bookshop and Dedley End. I have never wanted to leave. It's mostly because of the people here... we have such good friends, which you've seen today.'

'I have. Jane was always the life and soul of this village.'

'My grandmother is a very special person. She has been everything to me. I can't rest until we find her.' She looked around the office. It looked the same as it always did. But she clung to the faith that her grandmother would have tried to send her a message somehow.

Samantha looked at the picture of Jane and Nancy that stood at the tea-making station. 'I thought only about protecting you all. I didn't think about... leaving my family behind. I filled the hole as best as I could focusing on bringing down *The Club*, but it never really worked. Half my mind and heart were always back here in Dedley End. And when I heard George had died...'

'How did you find out?' Nancy asked her.

'I got all the local papers to check for any mention of you all. I only phoned George once here at the shop to let him know I was safe in London. I didn't dare ever do it again in case someone was listening.' She sighed. 'When I found out George had been killed, I didn't know what to do. I almost came back. You have no idea. I ended up booking into a hotel half an hour away. I wanted to come and hold you, but I was too scared of them finding us and hurting you. Maybe I didn't do the right thing. I'll never know. But you're here, alive, safe and you've been happy here. It's all I ever wanted,' Samantha said, sinking down into one of the office chairs with a sigh. She looked at her daughter. 'Can you ever understand?'

'I have been happy but I always had part of myself missing. First, because I didn't know where you were and then my father dying... I had two mysteries that plagued me all my life. If it wasn't for my grandmother, Jonathan and our friends here, I don't know what would have happened to me. And the bookshop. It gave me a purpose.' She patted Charlie who sniffed the carpet. She wondered if he could smell the kidnappers. Her blood boiled at the thought of them invading their scared space. 'I have a full life. I still wished you had been in it too, though.'

'Maybe I can now, if you would let me. I can in no way make up for our lost years. But maybe we can start over. Be friends?' Samantha asked tentatively.

'Friends?' Nancy wasn't sure what to say. She was her mother. But she had never mothered her. She nodded. 'We can try. Now let's see if Gran did leave us anything to go by... Charlie, what are you smelling there? Help us find Gran,' she said, watching him following this scent around the room. Nancy turned and looked in the book cupboard. Samantha got up and looked in the desk drawers. For a couple of minutes, they searched in silence.

'Can I ask?' Samantha broke the quiet then. 'You and Jonathan, how long have you been together?'

Nancy turned around in surprise. 'Together? We're just friends. Best friends.'

Samantha raised an eyebrow. 'Come on! I see how you look at one another. And you're always touching. When anything happens, he's the first person you turn to.'

'Oh,' Nancy said, standing still.

Samantha looked at her. 'Nothing's ever happened between you?'

'No. Not really. A couple of moments in the past few months, I guess.' Nancy thought about the times when she had felt something in the air between them. 'You really think…?' She broke off when Charlie barked by the desk.

Nancy rushed over. 'What are you thinking, boy?' she asked, looking at the desk. They always kept it pretty clear so it was just the computer and phone on there. She looked up at the shelf above it but it was empty. She checked the drawers again but nothing. Charlie barked again. Nancy realised he wasn't looking at the desk after all. He was looking at the coat rack. 'Gran's coat is gone but my trench coat is here.' She only used it on rainy days and once it got colder, changed to her tweed one, which she had worn today.

'What's that?' Samantha asked, from behind her. She pointed to Nancy's coat pocket.

Nancy looked. 'There's something inside it…' She reached for her pocket and pulled out a piece of paper.

# Chapter Forty-Two

Nancy unfolded the piece of paper she pulled out of her coat pocket. 'Gran must have asked them to let her bring her coat. When she took hers, she slipped this into mine,' Nancy said, excitedly as she looked at it. 'Oh, it's a page from a book,' she said, reading it. 'It's from the book she's reading at the moment. It's a murder-mystery, of course, from the shop. I haven't read it though.'

'Does the page have a clue on it?' Samantha asked, bending her head over the page to look as well.

'No, it's just about a meal the characters have...' Nancy frowned. Was that a clue?

'What's the book?' Samantha asked.

'It's called *The Butler Did It*,' Nancy said. Charlie whimpered at her. She patted him. 'Well done for finding the page from the book, Charlie. I'm not sure what it means but I'm glad we found it. Come on.' She led Samantha and her dog back out into the shop and over to the till counter. 'I knew I'd seen it when we came in.' She held up the book that her gran had left by the till. 'She must have brought it to work to read in quiet times. So, she ripped a page from it and hid it here so I would find it. It must be a clue then.'

'What's this?' Jonathan asked, coming over. The others stopped their search to join them.

'We found this,' Nancy said, holding up the torn page that had been in her coat pocket. She flicked through the book by the till. 'There. Gran ripped it out from the book she's reading. *The Butler Did It.*' She showed them the page that was missing.

'This is the clue Mrs H left us?' Jonathan asked with a frown. 'What does it mean?'

'What's the book about?' Penelope asked Nancy. 'That might help us work it out.'

'Gran said it's a funny murder-mystery, which uses detective story tropes in it for comic effect. That's why it's called *The Butler Did It* – everyone thinks it's a really clichéd plot in mystery books that the murderer ends up being the butler. But actually, it's hardly ever used. It comes from an old detective novel…' Nancy mused, looking up from the book. 'So, she's telling me she was kidnapped by a butler? Or the butler is the leader of the gang? I don't get it.'

'Do you know any butlers?' Samantha asked. 'They don't still exist nowadays, surely?'

'Well, the royal family have them. But no, not really. Wait,' Nancy said. 'We do know a butler. The Roths have one! Frank!'

'Mrs H gave us a clue about the Roths' butler? So, Marcus Roth is *The Governor* after all?' Jonathan said. He held out his hand and Nancy passed him the torn page. He read it then passed it around so the others could read it.

'But Frank is such a sweet man and, let's face it, he wouldn't be up to much at his age. I can't see him coming in here and kidnapping Gran,' Nancy said, shaking her head. 'Gran could have easily taken him.'

'I definitely would put my money on Mrs H in a fight between those two,' Jonathan agreed.

'Maybe because it's a cliché, she's saying the butler didn't do it?' Penelope asked as she read the page. 'It's a red herring?'

'I don't think she'd go to all this trouble to leave us a red herring,' Nancy said. 'Unless it made it obvious who it was instead, which it doesn't.'

'Let's go to Roth Lodge and speak to their butler,' Samantha said. 'See if he knows anything.'

'We don't have anything else to go on,' Nancy agreed. 'I'll ring DCI Brown though and tell him where we are. Maybe he'll meet us.' It was getting close to teatime and the light was starting to fade outside. 'There are only a few hours until we're supposed to meet them. Time is running out for us to find Gran.' Jane had gone out of her way to help them with this clue and it was frustrating that Nancy couldn't see how it helped. But at least going to see Frank would be doing something, she really couldn't bear to sit around and wait for tonight. Nancy told the others if they wanted to go home, she understood but everyone wanted to come with her and she was happy to let them. She was so worried, she needed all the help she could get.

They all walked down the High Street and paused first at the road where Nancy and Jane lived. Nancy dropped Charlie off at their cottage and he gave her a mournful look as she left him there alone, but she preferred that he was safe at home. Then they walked to Roth Lodge together. Autumn was sweeping in. Usually, she would have noticed all the pretty colours of the leaves on the trees overhead but, today, she couldn't enjoy the kaleidoscope of shades around the village. The village seemed grey to her while it was missing her grandmother.

Nancy wondered what the group of them looked like to anyone catching sight of them inside the houses they walked past in determined silence – a motley crew of people united today in one mission. She wondered if anyone would recognise her mother and wonder what kind of reunion she and her mum had had. She hardly knew what to make of it herself. It had been a very long and strange day.

The gates of Roth Lodge came into view then as they climbed the hill at the edge of the village where the grand house stood. They were open apparently in welcome but Nancy doubted that anyone inside would be particularly pleased to see them. She wished she could turn back time and never have anything to do with this family. Them and their mansion had caused nothing but headaches for the past nine months.

Samantha fell into step with her. 'Look,' she whispered and showed Nancy she had her gun again in her bag.

'How?' Nancy asked.

'DCI Brown dropped it when he chased after Pang and I slipped it back in here. He didn't ask about it. With everything that happened, maybe he forgot we had a gun. I've loaded it. Just in case.'

'Where did you get it in the first place?' Nancy hissed back, not liking the thought of that at all.

'After I left Dedley End, I thought I needed one. An old contact of my father's got it for me. Taught me how to shoot it.' She looked at Nancy. 'When I saw you'd solved a murder there,' she said, gesturing to Roth Lodge as they walked through the gates, 'I knew you were just like me. Unable to leave a mystery unsolved. I think I knew in that moment I'd be seeing you soon. Maybe I should have tried harder to keep us apart – to keep you out of this, to keep you safe – but maybe deep down I wanted you to find me.'

Nancy looked at her in surprise. It was the most emotional she'd seen her mother so far. 'I didn't want to find you. Years ago, I decided that someone who didn't want me didn't deserve me to look for them, but when Richard told me you'd been seen at that party, I knew I'd been lying to myself and I did want to see you again. If only to know once and for all why you left and never came back. You're right. I hated not knowing. I'd finally found out what happened to my father,' she said, her voice shaking a little bit. 'And I wanted to know what had happened to you. Nothing you could have done would have stopped me.'

'I'm beginning to see that. I don't deserve to, I know, but I can't help feeling proud of that... and, of you.'

Was Nancy mistaken or were there tears in her mother's eyes? Before she could ascertain quite how she felt, they reached the Roths' front door and she reached out to ring the bell.

'Hello, Miss Hunter... oh, and everyone,' Frank, the Roths' butler, said as he opened the door, his eyes widening to see Nancy on the doorstep with her mother, Jonathan, the vicar and his wife, and Penelope and Ollie too. 'To what do we owe the pleasure?'

'We need to talk to you. All of you,' Nancy said, walking inside without invitation as this really was no time for manners. 'Can you call a house meeting? The family and Mrs Harper?'

'Of course,' Frank said, his professionalism overtaking. 'Please wait in the drawing room.'

They went into the grand room until Frank returned with Marcus and Will Roth, Richard and housekeeper,

Ms Harper, who looked uncomfortable at being there. 'Shall I do teas?' Frank asked, stepping back towards the door.

'No, stay,' Nancy said. 'We need to talk to you.'

The butler looked surprised. Nancy supposed he was used to leaving the family to talk, to being almost invisible in this house.

'What's happened now?' Marcus asked Nancy with a heavy sigh.

Nancy ignored him. 'Where were you today?' Nancy asked Frank. 'Can anyone vouch for your movements?'

Frank was so taken aback he couldn't speak for a moment but Mrs Harper stepped forward. 'Whatever can you mean? What could Frank have done?'

'Please answer the question. It's important,' Nancy said.

'I've been here all day,' Frank replied.

'I can vouch for that. I've been here too. We've been changing all the beds, which is no small task let me tell you,' Mrs Harper added.

'I'm sorry, it's just I'm trying to find my grandmother and she left us a page torn from the book she's reading. About a butler.' Nancy had known in her gut Frank couldn't be involved, but why then had her gran pointed to a butler?

'She left you a page from a book?' Richard repeated after a moment of silence. 'Why would she do that?'

'It's a clue,' Jonathan replied, shortly. Those two would never agree on anything, Nancy knew. 'Mrs H would never have left it if it wasn't important. We came here because you have a butler.' Nancy racked her brain. Why would her gran tell her the butler did it? If it wasn't Frank?

'We're not the only people in the world to have a butler,' Marcus said, haughtily.

'It's not exactly common place,' Jonathan said. 'I mean, I've only met two in my life.'

Nancy stared at him. The puzzle pieces started to fall into place. 'That's it! We have met another butler. That's why Gran tore that page out!' She shook her head, feeling annoyed at herself for not realising it as soon as she saw it. 'We met him just a few weeks ago! You know him too,' she said, pointing at Will and Marcus. 'Hugh Windsor has a butler.'

'Oh, of course,' Jonathan said, slowly. 'He showed us into his house. Gary, wasn't it?'

'That's it. He didn't look much like a butler, I remember thinking. Nothing like Frank.' Nancy turned to him. 'I'm sorry for even considering you could do something to hurt my grandmother.' He gave her a little bow. Nancy looked at the others. 'So, is Gran pointing us towards Hugh Windsor's butler and if so, why?'

'But Hugh can't be involved in all of this,' Marcus said. 'He's never said *The Club* were blackmailing him as well.'

'Sir Basil Walker was at his party,' Samantha said. 'So, he knows people corrupted by the gang. It's not a great stretch to say he might have been as well.'

'His guest list read like a who's who of powerful people,' Jonathan agreed.

Nancy pulled out her phone. 'I took a screenshot of the guest list for his Christmas party.' She turned to Ollie. 'You said that Hugh came to your barracks with Marcus, that everyone respects him…'

Ollie looked at her curiously as if wondering where this was going. 'That's right. He was shown all the new recruits. In fact, I think it happens every year. He's great friends with my colonel.'

'Is that him?' Nancy showed him the list. Ollie nodded. 'How does Hugh know so many influential people?' Nancy asked them.

'He's rich,' Richard said with a shrug. 'And he was important in the army and he gets involved in local politics. Gives a lot of money to charity, I believe.'

'I told you, Hugh is perfect,' Marcus said with bitterness.

'Look at the names though — Sir Basil Walker, the local mayor, the Met police commissioner even was there, and...' Nancy trailed off as she stopped at another familiar name. 'I knew her name was familiar! I should have made the link to this list after we met her,' she said. With everything that had happened, she had pushed meeting her to the back of her mind. But she really shouldn't have done that.

'Met who?' Jonathan asked, leaning over her phone.

'Ruby Davies,' Nancy said, showing him her name on Hugh's guest list. 'The manager of *Clubhouse13*.'

'I keep telling you I have nothing to do with that place,' Marcus snapped at them.

'What are you thinking, Nancy?' Samantha asked, ignoring Marcus.

Nancy looked up at them all. 'I think Ruby lied to us. I think she knew full well that the real owner of *Clubhouse13* wouldn't name themselves on official documents and that your name was filed at Companies House, Marcus, to frame you in case anyone found the connection to the gang. We know the names of the members' club and the gang are too similar and, Samantha, you told us that people you know to have been working for the gang are members at the club. It has to be part of the gang's portfolio. Ruby is running it for them,' Nancy said. 'She must be part of the inner circle as the manager of their biggest asset. I presume the place where they meet and manipulate influential people. She could hear and see so much in the club. All the staff could. And pass on things that could help the gang with their crimes. It's the perfect place to trap people.' Nancy turned to Will, Marcus and Richard. 'I bet they were keeping tabs on you all.'

'Ruby has always seemed so nice,' Will said. 'Are you really sure she would be involved with the gang?'

'No one is what they seem,' Samantha told him, darkly.

'Why would Hugh invite Ruby to the party otherwise?' Nancy asked.

'He likes lots of people to be there?' Richard asked.

'It wasn't just a party though,' Samantha said. 'Sir Basil Walker told his wife he was going to network. And he was corrupt so it makes sense that I found other people there might have been as well.' She looked at Nancy and Nancy could tell her mother was on her wavelength about it all.

'Like Ruby,' Nancy agreed. 'Did you ever invite her to a party here?' Nancy asked Marcus.

'Of course not, she's practically staff,' Marcus said in snobbish horror.

'So, why then would Hugh want her at his party? She would have had to leave the members' club at the busiest time of the year too. It's all been right under our noses this whole time.' She looked at her mother again.

Samantha nodded. 'It's all adding up, isn't it?'

'What is?' Richard demanded.

Nancy had another thought and turned to her mother. 'And we didn't really think much about it, but the fact that Hugh recognised you at his party is suspicious in itself,' Nancy said. 'He supposedly met you in the bookshop once – or twice maybe at a stretch – although he never mentioned it to Marcus at the time but, over twenty years later, you're at his party in a wig and using a fake name and he recognised you anyway?'

Samantha nodded. 'I am great with people and I didn't know him, I didn't know his name or face. I'm sure I would have felt some recognition if he'd been in the bookshop enough for him to know me still. I told you I never would have gone to the party if I thought he would know me as Samantha Hunter. I was so shocked he knew me, I ran.'

Nancy's pulse sped up. 'Oh my God. That's it then. He didn't recognise you from the bookshop. He never went to the bookshop,' she said slowly.

'Nancy, what are you saying?' Jonathan asked, watching her think it all through.

Everything made sense to Nancy now. She remembered her repulsion when Hugh Windsor looked at her and noted the resemblance between her and her mother. But he didn't have an amazing memory, recognising someone after only meeting them briefly in a bookshop. No, he had clocked Samantha at his party over twenty years later because he'd been looking for her all that time. And when he met Richard at his leaving party, Hugh had already known Richard had dated Nancy. He had targeted Richard so he would tell Nancy he'd seen her mother and draw Nancy into the search. 'Acting like the pillar of the community, well, it's the perfect cover, isn't it? And just in case your cover slips, you have a back-up... a plan B. You have enough to frame your old friend for everything instead. I know who *The Governor* is,' Nancy said. 'It's Hugh Windsor.'

## Chapter Forty-Three

'You can't possibly mean that Hugh is behind all this?' Marcus said after a stunned couple of minutes of silence as everyone digested what Nancy was saying.

'But why?' Richard asked. 'Why would he try to frame Marcus?'

'It can't be him – I used to call him Uncle,' Will said, shaking his head.

Samantha nodded. 'Nancy is right. I can't believe I missed it. The look on his face when he realised who I was. It wasn't a case of seeing someone you knew years ago – he was shocked and… elated. Like he'd just won a really big, really important game.'

'He thought he had,' Nancy said.

'He's my friend,' Marcus said, shaking his head.

'With everything you know about the gang, is it really that hard to believe that the leader of it all could target his friends? They are ruthless. The leader has to be the most ruthless of them all,' Samantha said.

'I knew he had always been competitive with me,' Marcus said, still looking like he was trying to understand why his friend would have blackmailed him. Then he looked at Will as if he had just thought of something. He stumbled backwards and Will reached out to steady him. 'My God. Could he really be that petty and jealous, that bitter, that vindictive?'

'If he is *The Governor* then he is capable of anything,' Samantha said with conviction. Nancy felt a cold shiver run down her spine. What did that mean for her poor grandmother? Jonathan noticed and placed a hand on the small of her back. She saw Richard look over at them and frown.

'What happened, Grandad?' Will asked him as his grandfather gazed out at the garden at Roth Lodge, a faraway look in his eyes.

'Remember I told you that Hugh met Louisa first,' he said, finally. 'My wife,' he added for everyone's benefit. He looked back at the room. 'At one of his parents' lavish parties. And, of course, he was attracted to her. She was beautiful but she also had this sparkling, magnetic personality. Everyone was drawn to her, everyone liked her. Hugh was smitten. He invited her on a cruise that a big group of us was going on. She came with her friend. There were, gosh, about twenty of us on this cruise around the Med. When I saw Louisa, I just knew. She was special. And, I was a lucky man, she felt the same way. I talked to Hugh and he was his usual self – laughed and thumped me on the back, told me I caught myself a real catch, and so on, and only six months later, he met his wife. We have been friends ever since. I don't know if he realised how much Louisa's demons consumed her as we grew older. Her party personality became an addiction and alcohol blotted out her sparkle. And when Louisa…' Marcus trailed off unable to finish that sentence. He had only admitted a few months ago that she had killed herself. 'Died,' he managed to say. 'Hugh was one of the first to come by and support me. But now you're saying he was the one blackmailing me after Louisa drove into your

303

father's car?' Marcus said, looking at Nancy. 'Why would he have done that if he had loved her?'

'Because he loved her but hated you,' Nancy suggested. 'Perhaps he thought you were the reason she drank, that you deserved to be punished. So, when she died, he decided you'd take the fall for his crimes if it ever came to that. He never forgot that you took her from him all those years ago, in his eyes.'

'It feels unbelievable and yet… there was always something about him. I never felt like I really knew him. That he was really there for me. And you said the leader would be ruthless?' Marcus nodded. 'Hugh has always been ruthless. I've always known that. God, has he really lied to me all these years?'

'And our party,' Will said. 'Maria's engagement party. He encouraged us to have that party and to invite all those people. Was he there to check up on us?'

Marcus stared at him. 'I bet *The Club* were the ones your aunt owed money to.'

'So, Lucy's murder can indirectly be blamed on him,' Will said.

'And he probably came to see if I would show my face too,' Samantha added. 'The first Roth party in so long, my daughter invited, the whole village there… I hadn't been fully on Marcus's tail until I heard about the murder so I hadn't been tempted to go. Hugh must have wondered if I might show though.'

'But I thought *The Club* started in East London?' Jonathan asked then. 'How does that link to upper-class Hugh?'

'That's where he came from,' Marcus said. 'He shed the accent a long time ago but he was born and bred there. His father rose up in the army and they moved in different circles then, but I remember he told me that people looked down on them and it took a long time for them to be accepted. He worked hard in the army wanting to go further than his father, better himself even more. When he bought his estate in Norfolk, he told me he'd finally got the country mansion his father dreamed of. I was born into this,' Marcus said, gesturing around them. 'Perhaps in hindsight that was another mark against my name.'

'He has that painting in London. He said it was to remind him where he came from,' Nancy suddenly thought, thinking back to her trip to his Norfolk estate. It hadn't meant anything to her at the time. 'Hugh has been behind it all,' she said, anger rising up inside her at the thought of him sitting pretty in his mansion not caring that he had ruined so any lives. She couldn't believe that *The Club* had been in the background of all her life – starting when they chased her mother from Dedley End and then in the shadows of her father's death, stopping them getting justice for him. They were behind the murder at the house and made sure the Roths got off lightly for what happened that night.

'I can't believe I was right there at his house. I could have...' Samantha trailed off, unable to finish.

'We all missed it,' Nancy reassured her.

'Not only that but I worked at *Clubhouse13* and all I could find were things that led me to Marcus and Dedley End,' Samantha said. 'I should have realised that the clues were there as red herrings, to throw anyone looking into things off the scent, to stop anyone realising who was really behind all of it. My God. Thank goodness Ruby left the running of kitchen to the assistant manager. If she'd have seen me working there...' She trailed off.

'Now that we know it's Hugh Windsor, what do we do?' Penelope asked.

'If he really is friends with that many influential people, it won't be easy to pin anything on him,' her husband said.

'We already know he corrupted DC Pang and Mr Peabody. It's likely more police are on his payroll too,' Jonathan said with a sigh.

'Right now, I just want to find Gran,' Nancy said. 'Could she be there – at Hugh's house? Well, mansion. I mean, Gran pointed us towards his butler. If Gary the butler was her kidnapper, maybe he took her there. Mr Peabody said that he and DC Pang thought the leader had my gran; that my mother was too important, *The Governor* wanted to deal with it himself.'

'You can't be thinking about going there,' Richard said then. 'Nancy, if Hugh is the one behind everything then we know he's dangerous, and has a lot of people and resources at his disposal. There's no way you can just walk in there and demand to have your grandmother back. And who knows if the police are involved or…'

Nancy didn't want to hear what Richard had to say. There was no way she was going to just stay in Dedley End while her gran could be at Hugh Windsor's house. 'I trust DCI Brown. I'll ring him,' Nancy said. 'He'll help us.'

A new voice spoke up then from behind Nancy. A voice that sent shockwaves through the room. 'It's too late for that, I'm afraid.'

## Chapter Forty-Four

They all turned to see DC Pang in the doorway. And he had a gun pointed at them. 'Nope,' he said as Samantha moved for her handbag. 'Don't even think about reaching for your gun, Samantha,' he told her, his voice harsh in the stunned silence. 'I can react faster than you, I promise you that.'

'There's no need for this,' Rev. Williams said, holding up his hands. 'No one needs to get hurt.'

'You're right, vicar, no one needs to get hurt if you all do exactly as I say.'

'We thought you'd run away,' Richard said to Pang. 'Now that everyone knows you killed Seb.'

'Don't speak to me in that high-and-mighty tone of yours. You didn't mind helping when it suited you,' Pang snapped back at him. 'And don't worry, I'm going to disappear but not before I do one more thing. I was about to leave but then I thought why would I do that when I have the opportunity to make a fortune? Enough money that I don't need to be a police officer or work for *The Club* or anyone else ever again?' His eyes glittered dangerously.

Nancy could see how desperate Pang was and knew that meant only trouble for them. Desperate people were capable of desperate things. She glanced at the gun nervously then back at him. 'They made you kill Seb and now they've let you get caught for it,' she said.

He looked at her. 'Ah, our little amateur detective. You think you're so smart Nancy, figuring out all the crimes in the village because you have nothing else in your sad little life. It's pathetic. But I have to say well done on finding your mother. You made it easy for us and now I'm going to finish this. I'm going to get in touch with *The Governor*. Let them know I have you and can bring you to them – they don't need to come here.' He turned, training his gun on Samantha. 'And I'm going to be rewarded extremely well for it.'

'We know *The Governor* is Hugh Windsor,' Nancy blurted out. Pang's eyebrows flickered as he looked at her. She saw his expression. 'You didn't know, did you? You weren't important enough to know.'

'No one knows,' he snapped. 'We communicate electronically. Like everyone in *The Club*. Only a handful of people know. That's how he's stayed one step ahead for a long time.' He glanced at Richard. 'Is it really Hugh Windsor?'

'We think so,' Richard said, looking annoyed to have to speak to him.

Nancy stared at DC Pang. She still couldn't understand how you could join the police and pledge to serve but go back on it all and help the very people you were supposed to protect the public from. To get everything you could for yourself instead of justice for others. Pang had made her feel bad for getting involved in the police's murder investigations and, all the time, he was working against the police, against them all. 'I know you think you'll be rewarded for this but now you know the truth, you'll be a liability to him. Once he has Samantha, he has no need of you. You can be the fall guy for not just Seb but anything else Hugh Windsor decides to pin on you. You know he's capable of it. Why wouldn't he double-cross you like he's done to so many others?' Nancy said, hoping she could get through to him.

'That won't happen, she's too important,' Pang said, glancing across at Samantha who was reaching for her bag again. Nancy saw what she was doing at the same time as Pang and she cried out in panic but, instead of firing his gun, Pang leapt forward and encircled Nancy with his arm. He pressed his cold gun against her neck as she gasped.

'Let her go!' Samantha and Jonathan cried at the same time.

'Stay back,' Pang ordered, gripping Nancy against him, holding the gun against her skin. 'I don't want to shoot anyone but I will. I've got nothing to lose. You,' he said, pointing the gun away for a second at Samantha then back at Nancy. 'Take your gun out and throw it over there. Now,' he said, his fingers moving to the trigger of his gun. 'I'll shoot if you try anything with it.'

Samantha glanced at Nancy and nodded. She pulled her gun out and laid it carefully down, kicking it with her foot away from them. 'I did it, okay? Now let Nancy go,' she said, straightening and looking at him with as much hatred as Nancy felt for him.

'Stand by the door,' Pang said. 'And don't try to run.' His voice was so cold, Nancy felt like someone had dropped ice cubes down her neck. She tried not to look at the gun but across at Jonathan, the only thing that was capable of calming her rapid heartbeat right now. 'You're coming with me.'

Nancy knew that if Samantha walked out of here right now with Pang, she'd never see her again. She didn't think they'd keep her grandmother alive either. Why would they? They didn't need her as a hostage once they had Samantha. It would be tidier to dispose of them both. Nancy's knees trembled and she wondered if she might collapse onto the floor, but she held on to the hope of seeing her gran again. She straightened as much as she could and took a deep breath to try to make her voice come out stronger than it felt right now. 'Take me too,' she said.

'No,' Jonathan said, instantly. 'Nancy, don't even...'

She pleaded with him with her eyes. 'It'll be even better for you, won't it, if you bring in the meddling amateur sleuth as well?' she asked Pang, who was frowning as if trying to work out what she was playing at.

'This is ridiculous,' Richard said, stepping forward.

'No further,' Pang barked out.

'Nancy, you can't... your mother abandoned you, just let him take her and then all this will be over,' Richard said.

'Charming,' Samantha muttered but she looked at Nancy. 'Don't do this. I'll be fine, you know I will be.'

'I need to see my grandmother, one last time,' Nancy choked out.

Pang sighed. 'So melodramatic.' He shrugged. 'But fine with me. You're right, if I bring in all the Hunter women, I'll be set for life. Let's go then.' He nudged Nancy's back and she started walking towards her mother at the door.

'You can't do this!' Richard sprang at them then just as Jonathan yelled at him and tried to grab his shirt but Richard connected with Pang, pulling his arm away from

Nancy. Nancy managed to slip out of Pang's grip as he turned around to shake Richard off. 'Let them go!'

'Get off me!' Pang cried as Richard tried to grab the gun and they struggled. Nancy went to her mother and watched in horror as they tussled. She saw Jonathan moving towards them but she shook her head. She couldn't bear for him to get hurt in all this. It was bad enough—

A shot reverberated through the room.

## Chapter Forty-Five

Silence followed the gunshot.

Think, heavy, tense silence.

Everyone was frozen in fear.

Nancy couldn't bear to look for a moment. Then slowly, she turned and first of all she looked at Jonathan. He met her gaze anxiously as they checked one another was okay silently, relief washing over Nancy when she sure Jonathan wasn't hurt. Then Nancy heard a groan. She winced, recognising who it was and watched in horror as Richard clutched his chest, blood pooling across his crisp white shirt. 'Richard—'

'Oh my,' Gloria cried, her hands covering her face. Rev. Williams pulled her close to him.

Penelope leaned on her husband. 'He's been shot,' she gasped.

Marcus Roth's face looked almost grey as he shakily grabbed a table for support.

Nancy saw her expression of horror duplicated around the room as what had happened sunk in.

DC Pang had actually shot Richard. Right in front of them.

Richard reached out to the nearest person for support. Unfortunately, that was Pang, whose face twisted in horror and he stepped away. Richard fell to his knees.

'No,' Pang cried when Nancy moved forward to help. 'You two out now,' he barked at her and Samantha, pointing his gun back at them.

'You shot him,' Nancy said, still in disbelief that he'd been capable of that. She was relieved to see Will rush over and crouch down to offer Richard support.

'We need to stem the bleeding,' Ollie said, also jumping into action. He crouched down next to Will and took off his jacket.

'Richard, hang on,' Will said, as he helped Ollie use the jacket to hold over the gunshot wound.

Nancy couldn't take her eyes off of Richard. She could see it was just like Seb. The colour and the life were draining out of him. She felt sick and helpless. But Pang was moving towards her. She looked at her mother who gently took her arm and pulled her out with her. She glanced over her shoulder as everyone moved towards Richard and Jonathan got out his phone. She didn't want to go. Had she been utterly stupid to let Pang take her as well? But her poor grandmother…

And poor Richard. Even though he'd hurt her, there had been a time when she had really loved him. His groans were terrible to listen to. There was so much blood. Too much blood, surely?

She and Samantha stumbled out of Roth Lodge. Pang was right behind them, gun still out, marching them towards his waiting car.

'Phones,' Pang barked then. Reluctantly, Nancy and Samantha handed them over and he tossed them onto the Roths' driveway. Then, he went to the boot of his car. Nancy thought for an awful moment they'd have to climb in but he produced cable ties instead.

Wordlessly, he tied each of their hands together. Nancy pleaded with the universe to not let this be the last drive of her life as he opened the back door of his car and waited for them to climb in. Then he locked both back doors before getting into the front. He was so calm and measured, Nancy noted with fear taking root in her bones. He had just shot someone, perhaps killed them, but he looked so unruffled it was unhuman.

'Nancy,' Samantha whispered. 'We'll get through this.'

Nancy nodded even though she didn't really believe it. She watched as Jonathan came out of Roth Lodge and stood in the doorway as Pang drove out through the gates at top speed looking as terrified as she felt.

Please don't let this be the last time I see him, Nancy thought to herself, looking back at Jonathan. Her best friend. The one man in her life who had been constant and loved her for exactly who she was. She knew in that moment that he was so much more than her best friend. He was everything to her. And she really hoped she'd get a chance to tell him that.

Nancy kept her eyes on Jonathan until she couldn't see him anymore, then she turned around and watched as Pang drove them to Hugh Windsor's house. She had no idea what awaited them in Norfolk but she definitely knew it wasn't going to be anything good.

–

It was late by the time they arrived in Norfolk. Pang opened the car door and held his gun as Nancy and Samantha struggled to get out, their hands still tied. The car ride had been silent and unbearable. Pang had driven like a maniac, which would have been terrifying enough but Nancy's thoughts flitted: wondering how Richard was... the panic on Jonathan's face as they drove away... the thought of seeing her grandmother again and hoping she was okay... how they could make it out of all this alive.

Nancy wished she could go back in time. It had been almost fun solving murders – she had been able to distance herself from it and focus on securing justice. There had been scary moments but nothing compared to this. This was not fun. She should never have thought she was meant to solve mysteries. All she had done was put everyone she loved in danger. She glanced at Samantha, who was looking at Hugh's estate with her mouth set in a grim line. Her mother had thought she was protecting her but Nancy had ruined it by digging everything up. Now *The Club* had got exactly what they had wanted for years. Not only Samantha, but Jane and Nancy to boot. All Nancy could do now was try to save as many of her loved ones as possible. Even if it took her last breath, she would make things as right as she could.

She followed her mother up to the door of Hugh Windsor's house. She had had no idea when she first came there that she was walking into the home of the leader of a gang. She had dismissed Windsor as a rich old fool. She'd made the crucial mistake of underestimating him. She could have saved everyone if only she'd opened her eyes and really seen him when she had first come here. Now, she told herself not to miss anything again. She had to find a way to save her grandmother and mother. Even if that meant sacrificing herself. Because this was all her fault.

'I don't know what you're planning,' Samantha hissed under her breath, so Pang couldn't hear as he walked behind them, his gun forcing them forward to the house. 'But let me take the lead on this. I'm not going to let you get hurt.'

'This is my fault,' Nancy whispered back, shaking her head.

'No, this is all my fault.'

They looked at one another.

'Maybe we're both right,' Nancy hissed.

'Maybe we're both wrong,' her mother countered.

The front door opened revealing Gary, the butler, who had greeted Nancy last time and had in all likelihood taken her grandmother from the bookshop. His eyes grew wide when he saw the three of them. 'What the hell are you doing here?' he asked Pang. Nancy was sure there was fear in his eyes.

'I know now that Hugh Windsor is *The Governor* and I have Samantha Hunter. And her daughter,' Pang said, his gun still trained on them. 'I brought them to him.'

The butler looked at the two of them, his eyes widening further as he recognised Samantha. 'Hang on.' He disappeared and then returned a moment later. 'Give me your gun,' he barked at Pang who rather reluctantly, it appeared to Nancy, handed it to the butler who trained it again on Nancy and Samantha. 'Come in,' he said, stepping back to let them walk inside and then, rather ominously, bolted the door behind them.

## Chapter Forty-Six

'Well, well, well, we meet again, Nancy.' Hugh Windsor got up from his armchair as they walked into his grand lounge, opening his arms in apparent welcome. He wore green tweed trousers and a jumper as if he was about to play golf. His smile was wide and sickening to Nancy. He had the nerve to look pleased to see them. But she supposed he was. He'd been trying to find her mother and now she had come to him. Somehow, he'd managed to catch them all in his web. And he knew it. 'And Samantha. I was losing hope that we would be in the same room together again. And now all the Hunter women are under my roof. How delightful,' he added.

'Not the word I would use,' Samantha replied, dryly.

'Is my grandmother okay?' Nancy demanded, relieved that he said she was here too.

'Why wouldn't she be?' Hugh asked, his tone still affable, as if they were old friends. He turned to DC Pang. 'We meet at last, Pang,' he said, giving him the once over. 'When Gary said you were at my door, I was quite shocked that you out of anyone figured out who I was, if I'm honest. How did you know?'

'He didn't,' Samantha said, scornfully. 'Nancy worked it out,' she added. Nancy wasn't sure if they should shout about that fact.

Hugh's eyebrows lifted. 'Of course, I should have known. Pang, you were always a second-rate detective but Nancy Hunter… what gave me away?'

He was being chatty, almost friendly but Nancy didn't trust him for a moment. 'A few things… you recognising my mother at your party after twenty years despite only claiming to have seen her in the bookshop.'

Hugh sighed. 'I didn't know you worked there until Peabody raised the alarm that you'd moved to Dedley End and owned a bookshop. I sent my best men as I knew he wouldn't have the stomach to actually get his hands dirty and bring you in. He was upset enough at having to turn in a neighbour, the fool. It took me a long time to get over the fact you had been living in the same village as an old friend. Marcus Roth had been in spitting distance of you for six years and I had no idea. All because he lived like a hermit and refused to go into the village after all that business with his housekeeper stealing and, of course, his wife had a lot of problems.' Hugh's expression went dark. 'But by the time I found out you were there, it was too late. You ran back to London and my men lost you. I wasn't happy, as I'm sure you can imagine. I kept Peabody then Pang watching in case you ever came back, but you were clever and you stayed away,' Hugh looked annoyed at Samantha. 'Even your own daughter couldn't draw you out. So, what else, Nancy?'

Nancy continued. 'You told Richard she was there and made sure *The Club* encouraged him to tell me and try to get me to find my mother. Then there was your Christmas party guest list. All those powerful people in your house. Some of them known to be corrupt, like Sir Basil Walker. The manager of *Clubhouse13* was invited and I know you're a member there. And we all thought it had to be linked to *The Club*. Then there was the fact it was in Marcus's name but he denied all knowledge. And when we realised why you were trying to frame Marcus, we knew for sure you were *The Governor*.' Nancy thought it was best not to mention the clue her gran had left about the butler. She didn't want to make him angry with Jane.

'Marcus told us how you loved his wife once,' Samantha said.

'Marcus's wife took her own life. Marcus had taken her from you and ruined her, in your eyes. You wanted revenge on Marcus Roth for her sake and yours,' Nancy said.

Hugh looked impressed. 'Marcus Roth thought he could have whatever and whoever he wanted and then he killed the woman I loved. We grew up together in London, did he mention that?' Nancy shook her head. 'I knew her years before he did. My empire was all to try to impress her, to show her I was a better man than my father, I was going places, she'd have money and be set for life. But she never would commit to me and when she met Marcus, she went and fell in love. It didn't bring her happiness though, did it? She took to drink and became a shadow of her former self. They thought they had hidden it from her friends but we all knew that's why she never left that house of theirs, why they kept away from society. I managed to see her a couple of times and I was shocked by how broken she was. I told her to leave him but she wouldn't. I watched him destroy her piece by piece until there was nothing left.' He shook his head. 'He deserves everything he gets.' He turned to Pang then. 'Wait in my office. We'll need to talk,' he said, coldly. Nancy wondered if Pang really would be praised for bringing her mother to Hugh. It was undoubtedly what he'd wanted for twenty years but he'd tried hard to hide who he was and Pang had turned up at his home. She was sure that can't have been what Hugh wanted. She glanced at Pang and she could see that he felt the same as he sagged and backed up, looking like he wished he could run away. She was unable to muster any sympathy for the man.

'Let's sit, ladies,' Hugh said when they were alone.

'We'd appreciate the use of our hands,' Samantha said to Hugh.

'Please, take a seat,' he said again, ignoring her. Samantha and Nancy glanced at one another and, seeing no choice, they went to sit side-by-side on the deep cream sofa. Nancy looked to see the 'butler', if that was even what he was, and another man take up position just outside the door as Pang finally left them. She exhaled. Yes, they had guns but, with the door closed, she couldn't see them and it hadn't been easy to breathe with a weapon trained on her back. Not that she could relax much with Hugh seating himself back in his armchair across from them, but it allowed her to think a tiny bit clearer.

'So, now you have me here, what are you going to do with me?' Samantha spoke up beside her. Nancy flinched at the almost flirtatious tone of her mother. But she saw Hugh lean forward and smile, his eyes twinkling. Perhaps it was the only language he would really respond to from them. She wondered how on earth he'd found a wife. Could she really love this foul man? Perhaps it was the money and power that had attracted her. Nancy knew she'd never be swayed by such things. They meant nothing if you had to align yourself with someone who had no care for anyone but himself. She tried not to think about Jonathan because if she let herself do that, she might break in two.

Hugh leaned back in his chair and looked at them. 'You signed your own death warrant when you ratted us to the police all those years ago. Your father too when he went along with it. And Seb when he told you we were coming for you,' Hugh said.

'Is that why you had him killed?' Nancy asked.

'We knew he'd warned Samantha to leave Dedley End so his card was marked. A prison guard on our payroll overheard him on the phone to you,' Hugh said as if they were chatting about the weather. 'But I wanted to let him rot in prison, biding my time until he got out, it seemed more poetic that way. And I wanted to see where he went in case he led us to Samantha,' Hugh explained matter-of-factly. 'He went to Dedley End. I assumed he was still in contact with you, Samantha, but he was careful. We bugged his cottage but he didn't contact you once in Dedley End. But he did ask Nancy to meet him, indicating he knew who *The Governor* was.' Hugh sighed. 'I keep things on a need-to-know basis as I'm sure you can appreciate. Not everyone has the intelligence or flair for these kinds of things.' Nancy and her mother exchanged an incredulous look. 'Only my inner circle knew I had scattered breadcrumbs to lead anyone looking to Marcus Roth as being the leader. Pang was listening in on Seb's bug and was supposed to report anything important back to us but when he heard your phone call, he panicked and thought Seb knew who I was, so he lured him to the church and killed him.' Hugh sighed as if that had been irritating. 'I wasn't impressed that Pang had done so before Seb could lead me to you, Samantha, but I admired his loyalty.' He looked at Nancy. 'I've been watching you for years, Nancy. In case your mother ever made contact. I was delighted when you solved the murder at Roth

Lodge. And then when we nudged Richard to draw you into searching for Samantha yourself, I knew you'd beat me to it. I've even thought about recruiting you myself.'

'I would never have worked for you,' Nancy said, her voice as cold as ice.

Hugh raised an eyebrow. 'Interesting. What if I said you still could? No one has ever realised I was *The Governor* without me telling them. I'm very impressed you worked it out. I could use someone like you, Nancy. What if I said if you joined me then your grandmother and mother would be safe?'

'Nancy…' Samantha again.

Nancy ignored her. 'I'd need to see my gran first.'

'Of course. Let's bring her in to join us, shall we?' Hugh got up and went out barking to his butler to get Jane.

'We need to keep him talking,' Nancy hissed to her mother. 'Jonathan and DCI Brown—'

'We need to find a gun,' Samantha hissed back.

'Where were we?' Hugh returned. 'Oh yes, Nancy, you were going to mull over my offer.'

'But now everyone knows you're *The Governor*,' Nancy said. 'How can you carry on?'

A momentary shadow passed across his face but then he shook his head. 'The Roths won't be believed because all the evidence I've left points to Marcus being the leader. And either I let you go because you're going to work for me or unfortunately you won't leave here at all, so I don't need to worry about you spilling the beans, do I?' Hugh asked her, his voice no longer as calm and friendly as it had been, there was an edge to it now. Nancy could tell he was no longer as confident as he once had been and she wasn't sure if that was to their advantage or not.

'And DC Pang?'

'He will be the perfect scapegoat if I do need to kill you all. He hasn't been my best recruit, if I'm honest. Killing Seb before I gave a direct order to do so. And then you worked out that he did it so he had to run. And now he's here, all excited that he knows I'm *The Governor*. I don't think we can trust that he'd keep that a secret, can we? But at least him being here means I can pin more murders on to him. Depending on your decision, Nancy. If I say he took us all hostage, who is going to argue with me? The Met commissioner plays golf with me every week. I think he's more likely to believe me over a murdering corrupt young police officer, don't you think?'

She stared at him. Was he bluffing or did he really believe that he could wriggle out of all this somehow? She knew he'd kill them all if he thought he could keep his position and that thought was terrifying.

'Nancy!'

Nancy's heart lifted at the sound of her grandmother's voice. She watched angrily as Hugh's butler pulled Jane into the room roughly. Her hands were tied behind her back like theirs, and she looked pale and shaken but Nancy was relieved that she didn't look like they had hurt her. 'Gran, are you okay?' It was a stupid question and she knew it.

'I'm fine, I'm fine! Are you? Oh my...' Jane trailed off in shock. 'Samantha? What are you both doing here?'

'We worked out who had you,' Nancy said, giving her gran a significant look so she would know that they had found the clue she had left them. 'But DC Pang showed up and heard us... He's been working for Hugh all along, he killed Seb and he made us come here and...' Nancy trailed off, swallowing hard. She had been supposed to save her grandmother and now she was trapped here along with her.

'DC Pang?' Jane repeated, as stunned as they had been when they realised what he had done.

'As much as I want to enjoy this reunion, I need to have a little chat with my staff and make arrangements,' Hugh said. 'Nancy, what do you think? Will you come and work for me?'

'Nancy, don't even consider it,' her grandmother said, fearfully.

'Well, of course I will. I'm not going to let him hurt you,' Nancy said, fiercely. 'Either of you,' she added to Samantha. She turned to Hugh. 'I'll do whatever you want.' She was clinging to the hope that he would stick to his word and let them go.

He looked delighted. 'Excellent. Your first job is to kill Pang. We can't have him trying to tell a different story to us now, can we?'

'What?' Nancy's stomach plummeted. She should have realised it was a trap.

'You didn't think I'd just take your word that you'd work for me? You need to prove your loyalty is now mine,' Hugh said, standing up. 'And to do that you need to kill DC Pang.'

# Chapter Forty-Seven

Nancy sat there stunned. She felt all their eyes on her. Could she really kill someone? To protect her grandmother and mother? To save her own life? She knew Pang wasn't a good man. He was a murderer and a corrupt police officer. He'd helped *The Club* do God only knew what. But to actually take someone's life? Nancy had no idea if she'd even be capable of that.

'I'll do it,' Samantha said quickly. 'I'll kill him.'

Hugh shook his head. 'No. Nancy has to do it if you want me to let the three of you walk out of here.' He was smiling, enjoying himself. He knew Nancy couldn't win here. Either she let her loved ones die or she became Hugh's for the rest of her life.

'Nancy,' her grandmother said then, stepping closer to where she and Samantha sat. Gary put a hand on her arm stopping her from moving any closer to them. 'Remember what I told you about that book,' she hissed. 'Who the main character is and what he does.' She struggled against the butler.

'What are you talking about?' Hugh asked, sounding bored.

Nancy stared at her gran, thinking the same thing. She looked from her gran to the butler who was holding her. The page from the book *The Butler Did It*. Her gran had ripped the page from it as a clue. But surely that had been to remind Nancy of Hugh's butler and tell her that her gran was at Hugh's house? To show Nancy he was *The Governor*? What else? Then it came to her. 'Okay,' she said, pulling her eyes away from her gran to Hugh, hoping she was right about the other part of Jane's clue. 'I'll do it.'

Samantha gasped but Jane nodded with satisfaction. Samantha looked between Nancy and her grandmother bewildered at the turn of events. Nancy hoped she was willing her mother with her eyes to trust them. Samantha didn't speak but Nancy thought that was because she was too taken aback for words.

'Because of a book?' Hugh asked. He sniggered. 'You Hunter women are a mystery to me but I like you. Excellent. Come with me, Nancy. Gary, hold the fort here.'

Nancy got up, which wasn't easy with her hands still tied. She glanced at her mother then her gran then at the butler as she followed Hugh out of the room, hoping she was doing the right thing. She stumbled a little as she left the room.

'Allow me,' Hugh said, stopping to untie her hands. 'After you.'

Slowly, reluctantly, she walked towards where he pointed to, moving her wrists to ease the pain from them being tied for so long.

She found herself outside the closed door of his office. She felt Hugh's eyes boring into her back as she walked. Could she really do this?

Nancy played through the people she loved the most in life in her mind as if she were watching a slideshow, hoping that they would give her courage. Finally, she thought about her father as she reached Hugh's office door. She hoped he was with her somehow and would help her to have the strength to do this. She took a shaky breath as she reached for the door handle.

'What's going on?' Pang asked when they walked into the office, looking between Hugh and Nancy. He had obviously become more nervous while waiting alone. Nancy thought he must now be regretting turning up here.

A man came in behind them. Nancy glanced at him and she wasn't sure who was now more nervous – Pang or her. The man was huge. He seemed to fill all the space up in the room. And he was holding a gun.

'Tiny will show you what to do,' Hugh said to Nancy. He stepped back but stayed in the room. Nancy understood then that he intended to watch. 'Assuming you've never fired a gun before?'

'What the…' Pang spluttered and looked at Nancy in horror. Then he laughed. Actually laughed. The sound echoed around the silent room. 'She won't shoot me. She'd never shoot anyone.'

Nancy felt annoyed at his mocking. He had underestimated her since the day they had met.

'I think we should let Nancy decide whether you're right about that or not,' Hugh said.

Nancy watched Pang turn to look at her. It was so strange to look into the eyes of someone she was meant to kill. He hadn't had the guts to do that. He had shot Seb in his back. She felt like she should look him in the eyes for Seb.

Nancy looked away then as Tiny showed her how to use the gun. It felt like she was in a weird play or something. This couldn't be her real life. Although perhaps her life had been leading up to this point all along. Her grandfather, her mother and then her… all three had been given a choice about what to do – choose good or bad. It was nowhere near that simple in reality but it came down to that at the end of the day, Nancy knew. She just had to decide which path she was going to take now.

'I think I've got it,' she said, finally, as Hugh let out an impatient sigh. When she looked up, Pang eyes widened as if he suddenly realised the gravity of the situation.

'Nancy, please,' Pang pleaded with her, his face turning deathly white. 'You can't do this.' He stumbled backwards into the desk chair behind him. 'You're not a killer!'

'But you are,' she told him.

Pang looked at the gun then darted forward towards the door but Tiny grabbed him. He pulled desperately but he had no hope of breaking Tiny's hold on him.

'You either let Nancy here shoot you,' Hugh said lazily then, 'or Tiny takes his time with killing you, Pang.'

Tiny grinned showing off a set of gold teeth. 'Stop struggling.'

Pang stopped and his terrified eyes found Nancy again. Tiny let go and went to stand by Hugh. 'Nancy…' he whispered, his chest rising and falling with rapid breaths.

Nancy grabbed the gun, shakily. The gun was cold against her fingers. It felt like it should weigh more than it did. How could something so small be able to take away someone's life?

'Come on, Nancy, we need to get this show on the road,' Hugh said with impatience. 'Do it or give the gun to Tiny.'

But she knew what he'd do with it. He wouldn't only kill Pang but her grandmother, mother and her too.

She pointed the gun at Pang and flicked the safety off. He flinched. She thought about what her gran had said. About the book she'd left as a clue. And hoped she was remembering the story correctly. Who the butler really is in the book. And what he does to get himself out of a very similar situation to this one…

'Okay,' she said, loudly, hoping those outside the room would be able to hear her. Hoping someone was outside the room! 'I'm sorry Pang, but I have to do this.'

'Nancy, no!' Pang cried as she squeezed the trigger, and prayed that all the years she'd won at the Dedley End summer fete shooting game meant her aim would be good enough.

As the gun went off, the office door burst open and a man barrelled into Tiny, sending him flying against the wall. Nancy saw the blur of Gary as he wrestled with Tiny. He was followed by Samantha and Jane grabbing Hugh between them and holding an arm each as he roared with indignation.

Nancy lifted her head to look and breathed a sigh of relief. She'd managed to do what she had aimed for – she'd shot the bullet off to the side, narrowly missing Pang's ear, sending it into the painting on the wall. She realised then the painting was of Hugh standing with his horse. The bullet was in his head. A happy accident.

'Oh my God,' Pang said, slumping in the chair when he realised he hadn't been shot.

'What is going on?' Hugh demanded as he struggled against Samantha and Jane. 'Gary, what are you doing?'

'Actually, my name's not Gary,' his butler replied as he looked away from Tiny crumpled on the floor. 'It's Ben. Ben Clarke. MI5.' He smiled. 'Pleased to make your acquaintance.'

The colour drained from Hugh's face. 'You can't be,' he spluttered. 'You can't be.'

'I assure you, I can,' Ben replied. He looked at Nancy and nodded at her. She nodded back.

They heard the front door open then and footsteps thundered through the house.

'In here!' Ben called out.

'Nancy, are you all right?'

Nancy had never been happier to hear that voice in her life. 'Jonathan?'

Jonathan rushed into the room followed by DCI Brown. 'Thank God,' he said, his eyes finding Nancy.

Hugh yanked his arm free and made a lunge, grabbing the gun from Nancy as she was looking at Jonathan. 'No!' she cried, trying to stop him but he took hold of it. Samantha was there though. She stood hard on his foot and, as he yelled, he dropped the gun on to the carpet.

'Oh no, you don't,' DCI Brown cried as Hugh tried to get past him and escape the room. He yanked his arms around his back and slipped a pair of handcuffs on him.

Pang stood up then, about to try to make a run for it in the chaos. Ben grabbed the gun off the floor and turned it on him. 'Hold it right there,' he said. 'It's over. It's over.'

'You'll never get anything to stick on me,' Hugh snarled. 'I have friends in every high place you can think of.'

'Oh, we know,' Ben said. 'The Met commissioner, for one, but what you don't know is he turned against you. He came to see my boss at MI5 and told us all about your little operation six months ago. You thought you could corrupt him by blackmailing him about his affair? But what you didn't know was, his wife already knew. They have an open marriage,' he said, raising an eyebrow.

Hugh stared at him. 'Lies,' he said, angrily.

'I was put in here to gather evidence,' Ben continued. 'And when DCI Brown phoned me to say that Nancy and Samantha were being brought here by Pang, I got the okay from my superiors to stop you hurting anyone at any cost.' He turned to the inspector. 'Thank God you called me and not your boss.'

Nancy turned to DCI Brown questionably. He sighed. 'When the murder at Roth Lodge happened, I saw how the Roth family were protected. By my superiors. I was confused. Then I started to dig as quietly as I could and found that there were a few cases when they stepped in and stopped convictions from happening. I went to see MI5 in secret and they confirmed they believed my boss had been corrupted and told me to report to them on anything related to the gang and they'd keep me informed. Six months ago, they gave me the heads-up that they'd gone undercover with *The Governor* but couldn't tell me who that was in case I was compromised,' DCI Brown explained. 'When Ben was told to kidnap Mrs Hunter, he phoned me to tell me who he worked for and what was going on, and we both thought we might be able to draw out the person in Dedley End who was the go-between for the police and *The Club*. I'm sorry I couldn't tell you that Mrs Hunter was in safe hands, Nancy,' DCI Brown said. 'But we couldn't risk tipping Windsor off. And then you solved the murder in the village church and I realised first Peabody, then Pang were the gang contacts, so I told MI5 and they came to the station to make sure my boss couldn't cover anything up this time. They are pretending it's a joint police and MI5 operation now,' DCI Brown said, shaking his head. 'When Jonathan called me to tell me Pang had taken Nancy and Samantha here, we alerted Ben to make sure he was prepared.'

'We've gathered enough evidence to make sure we can pin a lot on you,' Ben added looking at his former employer. 'Including kidnapping Mrs Hunter here. I recorded you telling me to take her by force and that you were going to kill all the Hunter women.'

'How did you know who Ben really was?' Nancy asked her gran.

'When he came to the bookshop, Hugh's other man tore down the CCTV while Ben ushered me into the office to get my coat and told me who he really was. It was really a case of art imitating life. The book I was reading was about a butler being accused of murder, but it turns out he's a spy and he pretended to kill someone to get them out of a bad situation. So, the butler did it, but not in the way the reader thinks. So, I left you a page from that book as a clue before they took me away from the bookshop so you'd know where to find us. I knew you'd work it out, Nancy.'

'The book pointed me towards the butler and Hugh but until I was here and you told me to remember who the main character really is and what he does, I didn't put it all together. I just hoped if I pretended to kill Pang, you'd all come in and save the day,' Nancy said, looking fondly at her grandmother. Their love of books had served them well.

'You'll never put me away,' Hugh said to DCI Brown. 'You know that, don't you? It'll be covered up again. No one will give evidence against me.'

'Actually...'

They all turned as a woman walked into the room. Nancy recognised her from her pictures. She smiled at her husband. 'They will now that they have my evidence and testimony. I was so terrified of you for so many years,'

Mrs Windsor said. 'But I believed somehow you loved me. When Marcus phoned me to tell me you were trying to frame him because he married Louisa and not you, I knew I'd been a blind fool. I had mistaken control for love. I had told myself that half the things I thought were happening couldn't have been, that the money we had was worth me turning a blind eye to how you got it, and you deserved my loyalty... but you know what? I was wrong about it all. As soon as Marcus told me, I knew it was true. I remembered how you used to look at Louisa Roth. How you were when you found out she had died.' She turned to Ben and DCI Brown. 'I'll tell you whatever you need to know.'

'You bitch!' Hugh spat, trying to get at her.

'Hell hath no fury...' Samantha murmured. She turned to Hugh. 'I always knew a woman would bring you down. Looks like it was four women in the end.'

'Ruby Davis is on board too,' Hugh's wife told him. 'Hugh nearly destroyed her and her family. She hates him as much as I do. And she has a lot of evidence at *Clubhouse13*.'

'Five women then,' Samantha said.

'They will still protect me,' Hugh Windsor said, but he sounded far less confident now. 'I can bring a lot of people down. Fear will make them see sense. They'll hush it up.'

'It's too late for that,' Jonathan said as he looked up from his phone. He held it up so they could all see. Nancy leaned forward to read it. It was a news alert from the *Cotswold Star* newspaper. She saw the picture Jonathan had taken of Hugh Windsor in handcuffs with the headline '*The Governor is nicked!*' 'Not my best headline but I didn't have much time. I've alerted all the nationals too. The police won't be able to hide the truth now the news is out.'

'I'll kill you!' Hugh roared. DCI Brown pulled him back. Nancy and Jonathan looked at one another and smiled.

# Chapter Forty-Eight

Hugh Windsor's home was soon swarming with police and MI5, and other agencies Nancy had never even heard of. The press had gathered too and she knew Jonathan would be itching to write the story from their first-hand experience. Once again, he would have the inside scoop. Now that the mighty had fallen, everyone Windsor had trampled on, corrupted, manipulated, coerced and controlled, was coming together to make sure both he and his criminal gang were dismantled piece by piece.

In Hugh's grand living room, Nancy sat with her mother, grandmother and Jonathan with a cup of tea in front of each of them. A blanket was draped over her gran's shoulders. She had been checked out by paramedics and was given the all-clear but she was still rather shaken. They all were. Nancy and Jonathan kept looking at one another as if they couldn't believe the other one was really there. And Samantha was smiling. Which was a little bit disconcerting if Nancy was honest.

Finally, DCI Brown found them and shut the door and the noise of everyone in the house out as he walked in. 'Well,' he said, sinking down into a chair.

'Tea, inspector?' Jane asked him.

'I might need something stronger.'

'I was hoping someone would say that.' Samantha jumped up and went over to the drinks trolley in the corner. 'Anyone else?'

'Well, I suppose a brandy wouldn't go amiss after today,' Jane said.

'Is it really the same day?' Nancy asked. She looked outside at the dark evening. She had got up early to get the train to London and chaos had reigned ever since. She was exhausted down to her very bones. 'When can we go home?' she asked DCI Brown. That's all she wanted right now. To go back to Dedley End and curl up in her cosy cottage with her dog. And everyone she loved. She leaned against Jonathan's shoulder, strong and steady beside her as always.

'Soon. I thought you'd want to see what's about to happen first though,' DCI Brown said. Samantha delivered a glass of brandy to each of them. 'With the testimony of Hugh's wife, the evidence Ben found here and Ruby Davies showing us everything incriminating at *Clubhouse13*, plus Hugh kidnapping you Mrs Hunter and taking you all hostage, and confessing to you that he's *The Governor*, we can now finally take down one of the most notorious, dangerous, and organised gangs in the country.'

'That deserves a toast,' Jane said, raising her glass.

'To the end of *The Club*,' Nancy said. She looked at her mother as the others echoed the toast. Samantha raised her glass and drunk it all in one gulp. Nancy wondered what would happen next between them. She hoped her mother wouldn't run again, but she knew it was a strong possibility now that Samantha's years-long mission had been accomplished. What would Samantha do next? What would Nancy do next? She swallowed her brandy and hoped the answers would come soon.

'Come on then,' DCI Brown said. 'Then we can go back to Dedley End.'

The others followed him out of the room, but Jonathan put a hand on Nancy's arm as they stood up. 'Nancy, I thought...' He looked at her and she understood the pain on his face.

'I know, me too.'

'I have so many things I want to say to you.'

'Me too. At home,' she said. Then she bit her lip. 'Is Richard...?'

'He's in hospital. He was alive when the ambulance came. Just.'

She exhaled. 'Okay.' She turned to go but then paused again and looked at him. 'And Jonathan?'

'Yes.'

'Thank you for coming after me.'

'It looked like you didn't need me at all but I always will, you know that,' he replied with a grin. 'Always.'

She threaded her hand with his and squeezed. 'Always,' she agreed.

They walked out of the room and stood at the front door out of the mansion and saw a crowd had gathered in the driveway. Not only the authorities and the press but locals too wondering what was going on. Police officers were trying to keep everyone back behind the cordon they had set up. Cameras flashed as Nancy and the others stepped outside Hugh's home. Nancy blinked from the glare and turned to see her mother and grandmother exchange a smile when they saw her and Jonathan's entwined hands.

DCI Brown gestured for them to move to the side as officers came out with Tiny and Hugh's other household staff who were being taken in for questioning. They were led to one of the waiting police vans and driven out through the gates.

Then, Hugh Windsor and DC Pang were led out by two police officers, hands handcuffed behind their backs. The crowd watched as Hugh tried to hide his head and Pang struggled against the officer with him. Flashes and shouts from the press were accompanied by jeers from locals as the officers led them to the other waiting police van.

'They will get justice, we'll make sure of it,' DCI Brown said, looking on with satisfaction as the two police officers placed the criminals into the back of the van and locked the door.

Ben joined them. 'It's about time,' he said with a satisfied smile.

Everyone watched as the officers walked to the front of the van to get in. It was so sudden that no one even had a hint that it would happen. As the officers walked around the van, an almighty bang sounded and the van burst into flames instantly. The two police officers were thrown backwards from the vehicle as everyone cried out, pushed back by the flames. Heat engulfed them.

Nancy watched as Jonathan let go of her hand and as if in slow motion, fell backwards right next to her onto the ground.

She felt her mouth open but her ears were ringing so much from the explosion, she couldn't hear herself scream.

–

'In here!' Samantha called to Nancy in the hospital.

Accident and Emergency was packed.

The explosion at Hugh Windsor's mansion had resulted in two deaths, two police officers left in a critical condition and twenty people injured from the fallout of the explosion.

DCI Brown had driven Nancy, Jane and Samantha to the hospital after the ambulances and, in the chaos, Nancy had been panicked about where they'd taken Jonathan. Her mother had disappeared but was now calling them from down the corridor. She and Jane hurried on to the ward and to where Samantha was pulling back a curtain.

Nancy reached him first and she stopped, her hands going to her face. In bed Jonathan was asleep, his arm in a sling, bandage at the back of his head and a cut on his lip. 'Jonathan,' she said, walking over and sinking down into the chair by his bed. She took his hand in hers. He looked so pale. Her heart thumped in panic.

Jonathan's eyelashes fluttered and he opened his eyes. 'Nancy,' he croaked.

'He'll be fine,' a nurse said, appearing at the end of his bed. 'A broken arm, bruised ribs and a gash on the head from the fall, slight concussion, so we need to keep an eye on him, and his lip was cut from some glass, but that'll heal nicely,' she said, kindly to them.

'Thank you,' Jane said. 'Jonathan, I've called your parents, they're on the first flight from Spain to come to see you.'

'I'm fine, they didn't need to,' Jonathan said, weakly.

'You're their only son. Honestly Jonathan, of course they're coming,' Jane snapped at him, then she walked over and tucked the bedding in round him. 'Are you drinking enough water? Do you want some food?'

Nancy smiled. She knew her grandmother had been as worried about him as she had. 'You gave us all a scare back there.'

'Not quite as steady on my feet as I thought I was,' Jonathan said, trying to sit up.

'Rest,' Nancy said, sternly. 'We need you back safe and sound in Dedley End.' She brushed her hand with his. She had so much she wanted to say but now she was here, she was lost for words. Jonathan squeezed her hand as if he could guess her thoughts. Which, after all they had been through, he probably could. She turned around. Samantha had gone. 'I'll be right back,' Nancy said to Jonathan, getting up and going out of the corridor, relaxing a little when she saw Samantha by the coffee machine. 'I thought...' She trailed off, embarrassed.

Samantha picked up her coffee and turned to smile at her. 'I know. I suppose I haven't given too much reason for you to think that I won't run again.'

'How do you feel about what happened?' Nancy asked her. In the panic after the explosion, no one had had much time to take it all in.

Samantha sipped her coffee and grimaced at the bad taste of it. 'I don't know,' she admitted. 'Hugh Windsor and Pang are dead so they can't ruin anyone else's life but also, I wanted to see them rot in prison. Who do you think planted that bomb?'

'It could have been anyone. Someone in the gang, someone he had hurt or...' Nancy didn't like to think or say it aloud, but she whispered it to her mother anyway. 'The authorities.'

Samantha nodded. 'Either someone wanting to make sure they were stopped for good or that they wouldn't spill any important people's secrets,' she said. 'Go and see Jonathan. I'm not going anywhere.'

Nancy smiled. 'Good.'

## Chapter Forty-Nine

Nancy slept at the hospital in the really uncomfortable chair beside Jonathan's bed. They didn't talk very much – Jonathan was on strong painkillers and he slept most of the time – but she hadn't wanted to leave him. She knew he wouldn't have left her if the roles had been reversed. She remembered the panic she had felt when he'd fallen to the ground beside her, and knew he had felt he same way when Pang had dragged her and Samantha out of Roth Lodge. They would need to talk about what it all meant but, for now, he had to focus on getting better and coming home.

In the morning, she told him she'd be back soon. She got up and found coffee and a pastry to eat, and then walked to the ward that Will had texted her the number of. She wasn't sure if she really wanted to see him but she knew she needed closure – it was her nature. She had solved so many mysteries and, finally, she had solved the biggest one of all – her heart.

She found Richard attached to machines, his eyes closed. He was still unconscious, but Will had told her they thought he would pull through. The bullet had missed his vital organs. Just. She would never wish anyone to lose their life but she certainly couldn't wish him well after all he'd put her through. She stood by his bed and sighed. She had once loved this man and seen a future with him. Even just at Christmas, she'd wondered if they did belong together. But he had proven himself to be someone she could never trust.

Richard let out a heavy breath then and Nancy couldn't believe it when he opened his eyes. 'Nancy?'

She turned around and called out, then remembered the call button by the side of the bed so she pressed it. 'I'm getting help,' she said. 'You were shot, Richard, but you're going to pull through.'

He looked at her and maybe it was for the first time. 'I'm sorry for everything,' he said, croakily.

'I know,' she said, softly. 'Goodbye, Richard.'

He closed his eyes then opened them again. 'Goodbye, Nancy,' he replied.

Nurses and doctors rushed in and Nancy stepped back as they checked him over. Richard kept his eyes on her as they fussed around him, checking everything. She looked back at him and mourned for the past, the couple they had once been at university and would never be again, for the man she had thought he was, not the man he had turned out to be, and for the regret she knew he would be now living with.

'He's going to be fine,' a doctor said to her.

Nancy nodded. 'Okay.' She looked at Richard for one last time and then she turned and walked away, knowing she'd never see him again. On her way back to Jonathan, she texted Will to tell him Richard had woken up. Will seemed to care about his friend even after all the lies, but whether they'd ever be the same and able to run the business together, she doubted it.

I'll come and see him later.

A second later, he sent another message.

> My grandfather has been arrested.

Nancy had expected that. Everyone who had been under the thumb of *The Club*, who had done whatever bidding they had wanted, would now be open to investigation, and would likely finally be held to account for their crimes. Slowly but surely, Nancy hoped, *The Club* would become a thing of the past. She cared about Will though. She knew he couldn't be put in the same box as his family.

> I'm sorry, Will. I hope you'll be okay. I'm here if you need me.

She returned to Jonathan then and was relieved to see him sitting up in his hospital bed with a cup of tea, the colour definitely returning to his cheeks. He smiled to see her and she wondered if he'd remember the moment they had had yesterday or not.

'Nancy,' he said, his eyes lighting up.

'How are you feeling?' she asked, perching on the edge of the bed. 'You look much better, thank goodness.'

'I feel a lot better. The nurse said she thinks the doctor will discharge me later today, hopefully.'

Nancy exhaled with relief. 'Oh, good. I didn't want to go home without you.' She reached out tentatively and touched her hand with his. Jonathan held it tightly. They both looked at their entwined hands, then at each other. 'I thought I'd missed my chance,' Jonathan said then.

'When I saw you fall like that...' She trailed off, her voice catching.

'When I watched Pang taking you away...' he said, with just as much emotion. He squeezed her hand. 'We almost lost each other and I don't want that to ever happen again. I should have told you ages ago.' His hair fell across his forehead as he sighed.

Nancy shook her head. 'I wasn't ready to hear it,' she admitted. 'I don't think you were ready to tell me either. This is the right time.'

'I suppose you're right,' he agreed. 'I think I've always known it deep down, but we met when we were so young and we've grown up together. I never wanted to ruin our friendship. And I don't think I would have been a good boyfriend back then.'

Nancy smiled wryly, remembering Jonathan as a teenager. 'You would have broken my heart,' she said. 'We'd never have managed to stay friends. You almost asked me to the school dance, didn't you?'

'Yeah, I chickened out. You went with Pen and I went with Ollie, and the four of us were together all night anyway. When the two of them became a couple, I thought then should I say something, try to kiss you. But I was too scared. And then you met Richard at university, and I accepted that you loved him and not me. I tried so many times to fall in love with someone else but it never happened.'

Nancy exhaled. 'I thought I loved Richard but it was never the right relationship. When we met again, I wondered if I'd made a mistake breaking up with him before. But look at the man he turned out to be.'

He sighed. 'I have never wanted to hit someone before but there were so many times I imagined knocking Dickie flat out.'

Nancy chuckled. 'I knew that.'

'But I knew you had to figure it out. You had to know for sure if he was The One or not.'

'Every time you met someone, every time you went on a date, I was scared you'd fall in love and that we'd never be together. And your job... I kept worrying you'd leave for a newspaper in London. I didn't know what I'd do if you left Dedley End.'

'I stayed for you, you had to know that.'

'But you never said anything and nor did I, so I accepted we'd always just be best friends, I think.'

'Me too. But it's not what I really want. I want to be with you, I always have,' he said. He let go of her and reached out to touch her cheek. 'I love you, Nancy. I would love us to be together, but if you only want to be friends then you'll never lose me, I promise I would understand.' He looked so vulnerable then.

'Jonathan, shut up and kiss me please.'

Jonathan grinned, leaned forward and kissed her. After all this time, Nancy hadn't been sure if it would feel like she had imagined it or if she'd be disappointed. She needn't have worried.

Despite the fact they were in hospital, it was the best kiss of her life.

# Chapter Fifty

It felt like everything had changed as they returned to Dedley End. Nancy, her grandmother and mother, and Jonathan got a taxi home to the cottage. It was a quiet journey back, each of them lost in their own thoughts it seemed. Samantha was up-front with the driver and Jonathan was by the window. When their beloved village came into view, Nancy and Jane looked at one another in the back of the taxi and they both nodded.

They were home.

The door of the cottage flew open as the taxi parked outside and out sprung Penelope, waving happily, with Charlie who was barking excitedly. They climbed out, Jonathan easing himself with a wince as he did so.

'Thank God you're all okay,' Pen said, holding out her hands. Nancy tumbled into her friend's arms and breathed in the scent of her floral perfume, so familiar to her. 'I was so worried. We all were.'

'It was crazy,' Nancy said into her hair. 'We're so happy to be home.'

Penelope pulled back to smile at the others. 'Come on. Everyone is here. I told them you'd all be shattered but they all needed to make sure you're okay. We have so much food and drink, it's ridiculous.'

Nancy leaned down to pat her beagle, who was pushing against her legs eagerly. 'Good to see you, boy.

347

Lead the way, Pen.' She paused and turned to Jonathan. 'You could go back to your flat if you're not up to it?'

'This is home,' he replied, simply. She beamed at him.

'Come on, you lot,' Jane said, following Penelope inside. Charlie barked and hurried after her. Jonathan followed, walking slowly behind them.

Nancy was about to follow, but she realised her mother was still frozen on the pavement. 'Are you okay?'

Samantha turned from the cottage to her. Her mother suddenly looked so much older to Nancy. She looked tired, like they all did, but perhaps it was because her twenty-plus-year quest was over; it was as if it had all finally caught up with her.

'Nancy, are you sure you want me to come in?' She stepped forward and took Nancy's hands in hers. 'I wouldn't blame you if you told me to leave. We've been so focused on everything, we haven't really had a chance to talk about us. I know I said that maybe we could try being friends... I lied. I want to be your mother. I know I don't deserve it. I don't deserve to have you in my life. And I know you won't be able to forgive me, so maybe it's best for everyone if I don't come in. If I just leave Dedley End and let you live your life without me,' she said in a rush, the words falling over themselves as she spoke, looking urgently at Nancy, her eyes wide and worried.

Nancy looked back at the woman she had spent her whole life wondering about and knew that there were so many things she wanted to ask her, that she wanted to get to know her, that she wanted her to come inside. But only if Samantha wanted it too. She took a breath, preparing herself for heartbreak. 'What do you want to do?'

'I want to get to know my daughter in whatever way you'll let me. But I understand if that's not what you want.'

Nancy exhaled shakily. 'I told myself growing up that I didn't want to find someone who could walk away from me, that if you didn't want me in your life then I didn't want you either, but it was all just a way to protect myself. I always knew if you came back, I would want to see you. And now I know everything. Why you left, why you stayed away… I don't know if there were things you could have done differently so that we could have still been a family, but what I do know is life is short. I lost my father and I'd give anything for another moment with him. I don't want to look back on this conversation and regret what I said. I think we should start again. Try, if we can, to put the past behind us and get to know one another as who we are now, here, today. Yes, we'll never get back those lost years but what's the point of losing any more time?'

Samantha's eyes swam with unshed tears. 'Oh, Nancy, I knew you were a hundred times the better woman. I have no right to be as proud of you as I am, but I could never have wished for a more magnificent daughter.' She hesitated for a second then pulled Nancy to her and hung on tightly. 'I am so, so sorry. I thought I was protecting you, but I should have stayed and fought for you and George. I think I lost myself when I left you both. I focused on getting revenge instead of finding a way back to you. I'll never forgive myself for leaving you, even if at the time I thought it was the only way. To give me a second chance like you are…' She pulled back and looked at Nancy. They were both crying now. 'I will do everything I can to make things right. To earn your forgiveness and your trust. To be your mother again. I promise, Nancy. No, I swear it,' she said, fiercely.

Nancy smiled through her tears. 'You were always my mother and you always will be.'

'Are you coming in?' Jane appeared back in the doorway of the cottage to see Samantha and Nancy hugging again. She smiled. 'Oh, you two...'

'We're coming,' Nancy said. She looked at Samantha and knew what she wanted to call her. 'Come on, Mum.'

Samantha's smile lit up her whole face. They walked inside together and headed for the living room. Nancy gasped to see everyone she loved packed into the tiny space. Charlie made his way to her again and she patted him as she looked at everyone. Jonathan had sat down on the sofa and was being fussed over by Gloria; Rev. Williams was pouring brandy while Ollie was talking to Jonathan's mum and dad, who had arrived from Spain to check on their son; Jonathan's editor was also there; Pen and Ollie's daughter Kitty was on the floor eating a cupcake; Pen was adding more food to the table in the corner, already piled up high; Will Roth was by the window looking a little bit awkward but pleased to be there; and Nancy's grandmother went to sit in her armchair. Nancy was stunned to see DCI Brown coming out of the kitchen with a plateful of food.

'I didn't leave you alone, did I?' Samantha said in a low voice. She looked like she might cry again.

'No, Mum,' Nancy said. 'You really didn't.'

DCI Brown came over to them. 'I can't stay long, there's so much to do at the station but I got away for a bit.' He looked at Nancy then Samantha. 'You're all right?'

'We will be,' Nancy said. She thought she saw DCI Brown looking for a little longer than necessary at her mother and she smiled to herself. 'Excuse me.' She went over to sit down next to Jonathan. 'This isn't too much for you?'

'Nowhere else I'd rather be,' he replied. 'Will everyone have kittens if I kiss you because, I'll be honest, kissing you is all I want to do right now.'

Nancy nodded. 'Oh, they definitely will, but we might as well get it over with,' she said with a laugh. Jonathan pulled her to him and gave her a long, lingering kiss. When they parted, the whole room was silent and still. Nancy turned to everyone and chuckled. 'I didn't know there was a way to quiet you all down like this, I would have tried it before otherwise.'

'Are you two...?' Penelope squeaked, the first to recover.

'Nancy is the love of my life,' Jonathan said, simply.

'Well, duh, took you long enough to realise!' Penelope cried.

Nancy looked over at her grandmother, a little worried about what she was thinking.

'About bloody time,' Jane said, making everyone laugh.

'Okay, we need a toast,' Jonathan said, struggling to stand up. Ollie stepped forward to help him to his feet. He raised his glass and looked around the room. 'The past few weeks have been crazy. We used to all talk about how quiet, safe and peaceful our village was once. Unfortunately, we didn't know there were people here who weren't who we thought they were,' he said. Nancy thought of Mr Peabody and Pang. The Roths. Richard. Hugh Windsor. Everyone who had allowed *The Club* to reign supreme for far too many years. She wasn't sure she'd ever trust anyone who wasn't in the room right now. But that was okay. She had more people she could count on than others ever found in their whole life. 'I hope that things can go back to how they were before. I enjoyed the excitement, but I enjoyed knowing that all of you are safe and sound much more.' A few people said 'hear hear' to that. Jonathan's eyes fell on Nancy. 'Nancy has forgiven me for being an idiot and not telling her how much I loved her before now. I'm going to make sure I do all I can to measure up to this incredible woman. It's not going to be easy but I'll spend the rest of my life trying. I think we need a toast to Nancy. We wouldn't all be here now without her. The mystery bookseller who solved the biggest mystery of all.' Everyone toasted Nancy, who blushed and felt like running out of the room, but Jonathan took her hand and she knew she never wanted to leave his side.

'What do we do now? Can things really go back to normal around here?' Pen asked when they'd all taken a sip of their drinks. 'What if there's another murder or a mystery to solve?'

'Then we move,' Jane replied, making everyone laugh again. 'I need at least a year to recover from what's happened, I don't know about you.'

'Me too,' Gloria agreed with her friend.

Nancy turned to Jonathan and asked, in a low voice so no one else could hear: 'What if you get bored if things do go back to normal here?'

'What if you get bored?' he replied, raising his eyebrow.

Samantha walked over to them. 'DCI Brown just asked me if I'd consider joining the police. But I told him I'd never trust anyone there. But he has got me thinking. What if I became a private detective instead?' Her eyes twinkled with the idea. 'Maybe there's room in the book-shop for another business?'

Jonathan looked at Nancy, who chuckled. 'I don't think we need to worry about being bored after all,' she said.

# Epilogue

It was December in Dedley End and the Dedley Endings Bookshop was packed to the brim as evening fell. The Christmas tree in the corner twinkled with fairy lights while snow drifted down outside. The shop was warm though, and rang with laughter and merriment.

Jane handed around mulled wine while Penelope was dishing out mince pies. At the table in the centre sat Jonathan with a pile of books and a waiting line of people wanting him to sign a copy. Beside him, Nancy was adding her signature with Charlie, the beagle, laying on her feet.

'I can't wait to read this,' Ruth Stoke said as she reached the front of the signing queue. 'I hope I get a mention in the chapter on the summer fete. I still can't read a Thomas Green book without shivering over what a cold man he was. I bet your memoir will be much better than this. He kept saying what a clever man he was the whole way through, which didn't really work after he got caught by you two,' she said to Jonathan and Nancy, shaking her head.

Nancy smiled. 'We've already sold more copies than his book, which, I can't lie, has been a bonus. He sent a congratulations card from prison last week. I threw it straight into the bin.' The disgraced bestselling crime author was still trying to claw back success with a memoir about his murderous past, which thankfully wasn't really working. Nancy and Jonathan's true-crime book about the mysteries they had solved together along with Jane, however, had caught the imagination of the public and was climbing up the bestseller list as everyone bought it as a Christmas gift.

'Jane, you should have co-written it with them,' Gloria said to her friend as they watched Nancy and Jonathan sign Ruth's book.

'We did ask her,' Nancy called over.

Jane shook her head. 'I'm no writer. And I had to keep the shop running while they were writing, along with dear Penelope. Kept an eye on that one too,' she added, nodding over at Samantha, who was chatting away with DCI Brown.

'How's that all going?' Gloria asked. Everyone in Dedley End was intrigued by Samantha Hunter opening up a private detective agency in the village.

'She's found one adulterous husband and a missing dog so far,' Jane said. 'I think she's hoping for a bigger case soon although I, for one, hope she doesn't get one that's too big – I suspect we'd all get dragged into it.'

Nancy glanced at Jonathan, who grinned. They both knew that Jane would relish another mystery to solve one day. Despite being kidnapped, she looked back almost fondly on their adventures last year and had been the first reader of their book, telling them when they'd made a mistake or not got her 'character' quite right. She was outraged that they'd included the time she'd broken in to someone's flat with them but, when their publisher had told her it was the best bit, had changed her mind about making them delete it.

'I didn't think it would be this busy,' Nancy said, giving Pen a grateful smile when she replenished her drink during a short lull. 'The whole village has come in tonight, it feels like.'

Penelope smiled. 'Everyone wants to support you both – and see if they get a mention in the book,' she said. She looked at the time. 'Oh, Ollie will be home soon for Christmas. Well, for good,' she added, still shocked that her husband wouldn't have to keep going abroad soon – he was leaving the army now that she was pregnant with their second child. 'He's excited for his first best-man duty,' she said, grinning at Jonathan.

'I really hope he doesn't want to do anything crazy for the stag night,' Jonathan said, looking worried.

'We're going to a murder-mystery dinner for the hen do,' Penelope said. 'I knew as soon as I saw it, it was right up our street. We're not really spa ladies, are we?'

'We'd better win or our reputation will forever be tarnished,' Nancy said. She glanced down at the sparkling diamond ring on her finger. It was her mother's engagement ring. Samantha had given it to Jonathan and he had proposed to Nancy when they were on holiday in the summer. She had always wanted a Christmas wedding and couldn't believe that her best friend (and co-author, of course) was about to become her husband. 'Only a couple of weeks to go until the big day. I can't believe it.'

'I can't wait,' Jonathan said. 'Oh, here's Will,' he added, waving as Will Roth walked in. Roth Lodge had been sold by the family, none of them wanting to return to the house after everything that had happened. Will had moved back to London and was living with his boyfriend, Rupert. He had dissolved his company with Richard and was deciding what to do next.

Richard, Marcus and Mr Peabody were serving prison time for their crimes, as were a lot of people involved in Hugh Windsor's criminal activities. No one had been held to account for his and Pang's death, and Nancy didn't think they ever would be. But *The Club* was over. And *Clubhouse13* in London had been shut down for good. The country was a much safer place now the gang had been dissolved, that was certain.

'My hand is starting to cramp,' Jonathan moaned as Will joined the signing queue.

'Man up, Jonathan,' Pen said as she went back to the till.

Nancy chuckled. 'Only an hour left then we can go back to the cottage and curl up with a Christmas film,' she said to him, leaning in for a kiss. Jonathan had moved in with Nancy and Jane. The cottage was small for three but it was home. And it just made sense to all be together. She was happier than she ever thought was possible. She glanced at her mother, still chatting to DCI Brown. They had grown closer than she could have hoped and it was lovely to see her mother so settled in Dedley End. Where she belonged. Where they all belonged.

'I'm having the last slice of Mrs H's Christmas cake as my reward,' Jonathan said, his eyes lighting up.

'What do I get?' Nancy pouted.

'Another kiss? No, hmm, how about this then?' He handed her a wrapped present. 'A book-launch present for my co-author and soon-to-be lovely wife.'

Nancy opened it up eagerly, the gold paper floating away to reveal a book. She ran her fingertips over it. 'Is it...?'

'A first edition,' he confirmed.

She gasped as she clutched the copy of *Murder on the Orient Express* to her chest. 'Oh, Jonathan, I love it so much, thank you!'

Nancy glanced up at the picture of her father hanging on the bookshop wall and wondered, if he walked in now, what he would think to see her: about to marry her childhood best friend, surrounded by the people who meant the world to her; living in her beloved village and running his beloved bookshop; her mother back with them after so long apart; having written a book after loving books like he had for all her life.

Then she remembered something Dad had said to her when she was young. 'Home, Nancy, is where the heart is. Not everyone is lucky enough to have a home like we do. We should always treasure it.'

She looked away from his picture, and turned to look at the bookshop and all the people she loved in it.

'I will treasure it forever,' she whispered.

# Acknowledgments

A huge thank you to my editor, Keshini Naidoo, for all your support on this book and the Dedley End series, it's been so much fun discussing how to commit murders with you! As always, my agent Hannah Ferguson has been by my side while I wrote this book – thank you for everything you do. Thank you so much to everyone at my publisher Hera and Canelo, and all at Hardman and Swainson for your hard work and support. I am so grateful to have such a fabulous team supporting me and my books!

Thank you so much to my copy editor, Andrew Brass-leay, and proofreader, Vicki Vrint, for being so meticulous. And my amazing cover designer, Cherie Chapman, for such a gorgeous cover. I love it so much.

I am so grateful to everyone who has supported the Dedley End Mysteries – retailers, reviewers, bloggers and amazing readers who message me to ask just when Nancy and Jonathan will get together – I hope the ending made you happy, haha!

I love murder mysteries and a lot of the characters in Dedley End are named after literary or TV detectives, and I have always enjoyed a locked-room story so I knew for Nancy's biggest case of all, I wanted to create one of my own. So, thank you so much to the creators of my favourite books and TV series for the inspiration.

But most of all, if you picked up this book, I really hope you enjoy reading it...

Just as the Bolshevik revolution defined the early politics of the twentieth century, the transition from communist rule is the landmark event of its final years. In this important new textbook, based on a wealth of references including interview and survey material, Stephen White offers a full, discriminating account of the dramatic process of change in what is still the world's largest country. After an early chapter examining the Gorbachev legacy, the book analyses the electoral process, the powerful presidency, and the intractable problem of economic reform. Later chapters cover social divisions, public opinion, and foreign policy, and a final chapter places the Russian experience within the wider context of democratisation. Clearly written, with numerous figures and illustrations, this book takes up Russia's story from the author's best-selling *After Gorbachev* to provide an unrivalled analysis of the politics of change in what is now the world's largest postcommunist society.

STEPHEN WHITE is Professor of Politics and a member of the Institute of Central and East European Studies at the University of Glasgow. He was President of the British Association for Slavonic and East European Studies between 1994 and 1997. His many books include *The Bolshevik Poster, Russia Goes Dry, The Origins of Detente, After Gorbachev,* and (with others) *How Russia Votes, Values and Political Change in Postcommunist Europe,* and *The Soviet Elite*.